Price of Innocence

She runs a foundation dedicated to forgiveness. He's a cop running down the guilty to make them pay. If they don't work together, people will die.

All cases are important to Fairlington County Police Detective Ford Belichek. But some are personal. Especially when he realizes this murder scene is the home of Jamison Chancellor, the cousin of Assistant Commonwealth's Attorney Maggie Frye, his close friend.

The family tragedy that forever scarred Maggie and her cousins, Jamie and Ally, reaches into the present, threatening to claim more lives if Belichek can't find this murderer. And to do that he has to shut down emotions he'd thought were gone for good.

The Innocence Trilogy

Proof of Innocence

Price of Innocence

Premise of Innocence

PRICE OF INNOCENCE

Book 2, The Innocence Trilogy

Patricia McLinn

PROLOGUE

Labor Day Weekend

SHE NEEDED THIS.

A chance to get away from everything and everyone.

She didn't mind the rain pouring down outside. Not at all. It made it a great day to finish up, then be on her way.

Things had … piled up lately.

Not the first time in her life. She'd learned that sometimes the only way to get out from under the pile was to leave.

Step out of her life, let the curtain close behind her, take a break to do something else, then restart fresh.

The front doorbell rang.

Odd.

The only person who knew where she was had been here last night … to their mutual satisfaction.

As far as anyone else was concerned, she wasn't here. Nobody was. That was the whole point.

Must be something random. A kid selling candy, magazines. Miserable weather for it, but she wouldn't mind some candy.

She opened the door.

CHAPTER ONE

LIGHT, GLARE-WHITE, GLAZED the lower two-thirds of a townhouse, reflected blindingly off its windows, and darted shadows behind an early drift of leaves pooled at the bottom of its steps. Across narrow Red Hill Street, police tape ribboned the sidewalk.

Walking between two television vans toward the light, Detective Ford Belichek stopped and looked behind him.

It wasn't only light that changed at this border. Dark did, too.

In the distance, night softly blurred into misty midnight. A quiet place, where people relaxed into peaceful rest.

That's where he was supposed to be, starting *vacation*. Though *leave* was more accurate. As in, he was ordered to leave.

But when he heard this call, something deeper than habit and a hell of a lot more insistent than obeying the human resources department impelled him.

He half-turned, focusing on the close-range darkness.

On porches, spectators became wraiths topped by pale, shocked ovals of faces. At street level, those behind the light had no form. Only movement betrayed them.

Murder did this, Belichek knew, dividing its universe into light and dark, truth and doubts.

Inside the glare, a slender young woman in a vibrant blue dress stepped before a man with a camera perched on the shoulder of his Washington Capitals t-shirt.

The camera carried the logo of a network-affiliated station from across the Potomac River in Washington, D.C.

Homicide among the neat brick houses and tidy lawns of Fairlington, Virginia, still had a shock value lost in too many places. Put that homicide in Fairlington's historic Old Town and media interest ratcheted up.

A camera light came on, focused on the woman in the blue dress. Holding a microphone near her mouth, she spoke.

He couldn't hear words, yet he knew they would recite facts without sharing the truth.

Because the truth had not yet been excavated. That was his job.

"Belichek! Over here."

Detective Tanner Landis shouted from where he stood, fully in the light. It shaved the clear-carved lines of his face, glossed his dark hair, and starched the white shirt under his sports jacket.

Some dismissed the guy for how he looked and dressed.

Lousy policework in Belichek's view. Reserve judgment until the facts are in.

The facts of their partnership proved Landis was a good cop.

Landis called again, impatient. "Told them you'd be listening and wouldn't go off on vacation like a normal person. The brass will have something to say when they find out, but in the meantime, I can use you."

"Coming." Belichek didn't say the word loud enough for Landis to hear above the hum of machinery and chatter of humans. Landis hadn't waited for it anyway, moving with characteristic ease toward the house. Sure of Belichek's response.

He caught up with his partner at the base of the steps leading to a front door that looked as old as the house and those surrounding it in Old Town Fairlington, Virginia, which—considering George Washington actually had slept here, along with a number of his contemporaries—had it pushing three centuries.

"What've we got?" he asked Landis.

"*We?* As of twenty-seven minutes ago, *I've* got primary on a body, likely homicide. Lucky me, with the department developing a leak some scumbag podcaster's spreading to the world. What—"

"Gossip."

"—*you've* got is a sickness that brings you here when you're on vacation as of tomorrow. A sickness I fully intend to take advantage of. You know who they've proposed giving me as second in place of you? Terrington. Can you believe it? Terrington. You'd think it was a conspiracy to make me appreciate you. As for the leak, yeah, gossip so far. Doesn't make me feel warm and fuzzy about the prospects of something about my case not slipping through."

Landis jerked his head to the uniform coming down the townhouse's steps toward them. Ford recognized him. Smith? Was that his name? He'd done a decent job on a domestic murder-suicide earlier in the year.

"What've you got for us, Schmidt?"

Schmidt, not Smith. Figured Landis remembered.

✧　✧　✧　✧

OLIVER ZEEDYK WAITED until the guy, surely a cop, quit looking around like a murderer was about to drop out of the sky in front of him.

He took the camera out of his jacket, smoothly to not attract attention, turned it on, and caught that cop talking to the others by the steps.

With luck—But when was he lucky?

It probably wouldn't be usable on the show. Maybe, just maybe, he could use it to help ID the cops. Put faces with names.

Three cops—two in plainclothes, one in uniform—went up the steps and inside. There were still a lot of cops around, but low level. If he didn't make a big deal of it, he had a chance to get atmosphere footage for the next show.

Damn. The light was crap, washing out even the garish police tape.

Didn't matter, he reminded himself. People subscribed to the show to hear him, not for glossy video. Maybe the bit with the cops would do for a moody background to sound bites and banner quotes to make an audience salivate. A big audience.

And there *would* be sound bites. Killer sound bites.

He clamped his mouth into a straight line to keep from grinning.

He'd known this would happen—known *something* would happen—and he had all the pieces in place to make his mark.

Screw those jackasses who'd pushed him out. Sanctimonious prigs. Saying he hadn't lived up to their standards.

Screw their standards.

He knew what he was after and he was going to get it.

Everything was in place.

This was exactly what he'd planned for.

"Hey, aren't you, uh…?"

He wouldn't mind mainstream media recognizing him, but if the cops… He turned.

Not a cop. Not media, either. Had to be a hanger-on. A crime junkie. There was lots of talk about groupies drawn to true crime podcasts, especially women who got their jollies following serial killers, but plenty of guys listened to him, too.

This guy was young, skinny, pale.

"Yeah. Oz Zeedyk. I have the DMV podcast."

That was aw-shucks modest. He *was* the DMV podcast.

"Right, right. Great name. Taking the DMV for the District, Maryland, Virginia, and using it for Death—"

"Murder and Violence."

"Right, right. Suppose I shouldn't be surprised you're here, huh?"

"I go where there's death, murder, and—"

"Violence. Right, right."

"—violence," he completed himself. Didn't like this guy rushing the end of the name. Never knew who could overhear. He repeated the podcast name as many times as he could. "Especially a murder in this sort of neighborhood."

"Right, right. That's the big interest in this situation, huh?"

"Of course. Rich neighborhood, rich people." Bitterness eased under a flow of warmth through Oz at knowing more than ordinary people. "This is going to be a big case. Really big." He tapped the guy lightly on the chest. "Be sure to listen to Death, Murder, Violence. Going to be lots of surprises on DMV during this investigation."

CHAPTER TWO

"A REEKER, THAT'S what we've got for you. From what the neighbors report, the owner was supposed to have left Labor Day weekend. It must've been in the house these past three weeks," Officer Schmidt said.

Three weeks with a string of heat records for September dates in the Washington, D.C., area—which produced more than its share of hot air at the best of times—and kept air conditioners running on high.

Everywhere except in this house, where life had fled, leaving its disintegrating shell. The disintegration hurried along by no AC.

"Actually, body doesn't reek much now, but the house—"

"ID?" Landis interrupted.

"Tentative. No ID on the body, which makes sense, being at home. No sign of a purse or wallet on cursory look when we made entry. Backed out when we saw the body. Neighbors say a woman lives here alone. Late twenties. Body looks to be the right size, hair color to match the descriptions. The woman who found her is pretty shaken, but she says the clothes—what she saw of them—look like the resident's."

Belichek looked up, frowned.

The uniform added, "Since she was supposed to be away. Nobody was surprised there wasn't activity."

"Have you lined up somebody to officially ID her? Why not?" Landis asked as Schmidt shook his head. "There's gotta be family, friends, co-workers, neighbors."

"There's plenty of those," Schmidt said, starting acid dripping into

Belichek's stomach. "What there isn't is a face to recognize."

"Shit." Landis snapped the word.

"With the heat and the time... Not much in the way of hands, either."

"Cut off?" Landis' tone didn't change, yet Belichek knew the possibilities shifting through his partner's brain acquired an additional stream.

"No. Bones are there. More like, maybe she put her hands up in front of her face. Didn't do any good."

Schmidt looked like he wanted to spit. The kind of body he'd described could do that... when it didn't suck your mouth and guts dry. He glanced toward the TV cameras, refrained from spitting, then continued reporting.

"Shotgun, from what I saw. Close range. ME's investigator isn't committing, but sure looks like both barrels."

Landis muttered another curse. "Fingerprints?"

Eyes on the leaves at his feet and hands propped on his hips, Schmidt shook his head again. "Scientists aren't optimistic. As I said, best guess is she put her hands up to try to protect herself. Add on three weeks being shut up in a house with no AC in this heat. There's not much there."

In the silence, Belichek guessed the others were thinking, as he was, that instinct could be damned futile against a double-barreled shotgun.

"*Shee-it.*" This time Landis drew the word out to multiple syllables of resignation. "That means dental records, we'll have to—Now what?"

Schmidt's head-shaking didn't cease at Landis' sharp tone. "Told you there's not much there. ME's investigator said she's not optimistic about putting the jaw back together any time soon. Or getting enough useful teeth. They're mostly shattered."

"*Shee-it,*" Landis repeated in disgust. "At least with bones we can check medical records. Let's go."

Landis started up the stairs, and Belichek followed, reporting their identities and getting outfitted.

Inside, Belichek skirted the mass that had once been human, and now was the province of the medical examiner's office. Landis stopped, considering the disposition of the body, judging angles and distances.

Belichek would do that, too, but not until the lull when the ME team was packing up, after this beehive of activity and before they took the body.

Landis looked over his shoulder at him. "Suppose you're going to do your open house tour?"

"Yeah."

He usually started by looking around the crime scene—especially if it was someplace personal. Victim's or suspect's, a home gave color and depth to the crime the dead body so seldom could.

It worked for them—him and Landis—coming at the crime from slightly different angles right from the start. They saw different things.

He left his partner with the body and the ME's people. Schmidt stayed there, too, attaching himself to the primary.

Smart if he had his eye on making detective.

A break for Belichek, who preferred to observe alone. Except for the crime scene investigators, of course. They had true possession of the house for now. Everyone else was here on sufferance, as long as they didn't get in the way.

From the entryway to the living room, he nodded at the woman in protective gear over by a knot of dead plants at the front window as she methodically processed the room.

"Stay behind the coffee table," she ordered.

He nodded again.

They'd done this before. Her setting the limits, him sticking to them.

There'd be plenty to process. From here, he could see the living room and, partly visible through connecting archways, a smaller room past it with an antique desk, with more dead plants. Then, beyond that, lit up like the inside of a snow globe, a tiny glass-enclosed porch extending into a patio, where the plants were not dead. Yet. Winter would be gunning for them soon enough.

A privacy fence separated the brick patio from the neighbor next door and the alley behind. The side of a garage formed the third wall. Flower beds lined the entire area, with breaks only for the lockable gate to the alley and the doors to the garage and back door.

Drawing his gaze to close range, he considered a layer of debris littering the living room. Contents of drawers and shelves spilled across each other, mixing richly colored paisley napkins with a broken ivory candle, two playing cards, a book with a brick mansion on its cover and another with a plain red leather binding, resting on the edges of fanned pages.

Gaps showed.

Gaps where a TV, other electronics might have been expected to sit. And smaller gaps. He wondered if this victim had boasted the sort of silver and antique collections he'd seen in houses in this part of Fairlington.

Not wanton destruction. All tied to searching for or removing items. Saleable items.

Beneath the debris, the room presented the kind of place anybody could like. Nothing fussy. Straight-lined beige sofa with plenty of cushions. An ottoman for your feet and a coffee table for a drink. Bookshelves filled with books, not doodads. An oil painting over the brick fireplace, where most people might put a portrait. Instead, this edged toward abstract, though even he could tell it showed trees arching over a river without it looking like a photograph. It gave him the impression of a breeze moving through the trees. Pretty good for a painting.

He stepped over an upside-down tray that appeared to have been displaced from the ottoman.

Without going any deeper into the room, a framed photograph, askew on an eye-level shelf, drew his attention.

A group photo. By a river, with trees arching over it—

His gaze snapped back to above the fireplace mantel.

—like the painting. Close enough to be the same place.

A place important to the owner of photograph and painting.

The painting bought because of the resemblance or because it was the same place?

Possibly the other way around—the photo taken at that spot because it was so close to the painting.

He focused on the photograph. Squinting a bit to bring it into sharper focus, both because of the distance and the angle.

A hard *thwump* in his chest felt as if someone punched him.

On the right side of the group in the photo, a little apart, yet still looking more relaxed and at ease than usual, stood Maggie Frye.

Assistant Commonwealth's Attorney Margaret Frye.

Mags.

The most tenacious prosecutor in Fairlington County. The one he and Landis worked with most. The one he respected most. One of the rare people he'd call a friend.

The fiercely private person who'd guarded her past.

And the last person on this earth who needed any more tragedy and grief in her life.

Staring at the photo that included Maggie Frye, memories surfaced. Ones he thought were long settled. He swore.

A litany of curses. Long and vehement. He was aware of heads turning toward him, the woman by the window, more techs in the hallway, the group around the body, but he didn't stop. And he didn't move.

"What is it?" Landis asked, now beside him.

Belichek pointed.

"The photo? What about—? Is that…? Maggie?" Landis leaned toward the photo, also without going farther into the room. "It is. It's Mags. What the—?"

Belichek swung around on Schmidt, still trailing Landis. "Who lives here? The name."

"Chandler—No. Chancellor. Sorry. It's Chancellor."

"Jamison Chancellor." Belichek heard the heaviness in his own voice, failure the anchor dragging it down. Felt the stillness as everyone watched him. "Founder of the Sunshine Foundation. The one everybody said was creating something good out of the murder of her aunt years back. Vivian Frye—her aunt, and Maggie's."

A murmur rose now. *Maggie? Maggie Frye? From the CA's office?*

No sense holding on to that secret any longer. Maggie's past was going to be out there for everybody to paw over now.

But he said the words only to Landis.

"Our victim is Maggie's cousin."

CHAPTER THREE

Ford Belichek hung up from the worst phone call he'd ever made.

And there was tough competition. A lot of tough competition.

He stared out the windshield of his vehicle, back in the dark, where he'd retreated for privacy for the call.

He'd made sure the uniform he'd sent to pick up Maggie was already outside her townhouse before he called.

He figured they had twenty, maybe thirty minutes before Maggie got here, but only because the uniform would be driving. Maggie behind the wheel, and it would be fifteen, tops.

He needed every second to start trying to get answers to the tough questions she would ask.

Instead, he found a phone number he'd tracked down a while back but hadn't had cause to use before.

"Hello." The voice sounded a damned sight more alert than most people when they were called in the middle of the night. Made sense, since the guy had been some hot shot Army special ops type.

"Carson? J.D. Carson?"

"Yes."

Not *who's calling?* Or any of that stuff. Another sign he had more than a passing familiarity with being called for business in the middle of the night.

"This is Detective Ford Belichek of the Fairlington County Police Department. You know Maggie Frye.

This "Yes" came just as strong, but still triggered *So, the guy's human after all* in Belichek's head.

"She's okay," he said, because he wasn't a sadist. Then, because he was a realist, he added, "Physically."

"What the—?"

"Listen. I don't usually—I know some of what happened up there in the mountains, in Bedhurst. You and Maggie. And I'm saying you should get down here to Fairlington. Fast. Her cousin's been found dead. Looks like murder." *Looks like?* Hell. Hard to make this anything other than murder. "She knows. She's on the way to the scene. Maggie needs ... a friend. Support."

And he wasn't going to be able to be either.

Not and investigate her cousin's murder at the same time.

His own reactions? ... Those would come later.

CHAPTER FOUR

THE SMELL IN the house might have been what bothered him the most when Maggie arrived, not twenty minutes after he'd called her.

Not the smell itself. He'd encountered that enough. So had she. Not enough to ignore it, if you ever could, but enough to work through it. What bothered him was Maggie smelling that smell. And knowing it had come from the remains of her cousin reaching the state they were in now.

She'd given no sign of noticing it.

She'd given no sign of anything.

Unless you knew her really well. And then you saw that under the tough, intelligent, dogged Maggie Frye everyone knew, she was crumbling. Shreds of heart and bone disintegrating before his eyes.

She certainly hadn't stepped on their toes—his and Landis'—or on the toes of any of the crime scene techs.

That had some of the old hands exchanging glances. It was totally unlike her.

She had not given a single order to add one more shot, pick up one more piece of evidence. Maybe because, watching her from the corners of their eyes, everyone had already gotten every shot, every piece of evidence.

But other than a few gruff, *Sorry, Maggies*, no one said anything about her connection to this crime.

"Maggie," Belichek said to her, hands in his pockets, head down as if contemplating the tall baseboard that ran around every room, even in this small office where they stood. "What's with this?"

"With ... this?" She sounded groggy.

"Your cousin. Living here."

"Oh. Owning this house." Her face seemed to crack, but not into a recognizable smile or a sob, and the pieces remained out of sync, not sure which direction to go. "Jamie inherited it from a great-aunt on her mother's side. Along with the money to run it."

"That's how she funded starting the Sunshine Foundation?" Landis asked.

The foundation was renowned for practical aid to families, admirable finances, and its youthful founder.

The cracks in her face deepened. "No. She hadn't inherited when she founded Sunshine. She wasn't even in high school when she started it. Earned money with all kinds of fund-raisers, including damned bake sales, if you can believe it. Also marching into businesses, soliciting funds. Didn't know what hit them. By the time she was out of college and had this place, she'd put the Sunshine Foundation on the map."

"Why was she found here like this? Why didn't somebody notice? Had to be weeks."

Landis cut him a look, surely remembering the uniforms reporting neighbors said she was supposed to be on some trip. Belichek wanted to hear from Maggie—if she knew, what she knew.

She loved her cousin. He didn't doubt that. But best to know from the start how tuned in she'd been to her cousin's life.

He suspected not very, considering how much Mags worked and how good she was at stiff-arming people from getting close.

At least she had been that way.

She'd been different since she came back from a case in Bedhurst in the western part of Virginia. Not cuddly—hell, she was still Mags. But different.

"She left—she was supposed to leave Labor Day weekend to spend a month at a cabin in Pennsylvania, somewhere along the border with western Maryland. Final push to finish another book. She'd done this before with three previous books. You know about her books?"

He nodded, Landis grunted acknowledgment of the books acclaimed for a straightforward, unpretentious approach to becoming a better person, making a better world.

People loved reading her books. As far as Belichek could tell, none of those people actually changed.

Jamison Chancellor didn't ask for much—just to have everyone be happy, just to change human beings.

Had she died for that goal? Or something a lot less esoteric?

Maggie continued. "Said she needed to shake free of the daily running of the foundation to finish."

"When was she supposed to leave, get back?"

"I don't know precisely. She might have told me. I don't know. Her parents, our other cousin, the foundation, they'll all know."

The words came flat, but Belichek knew. He thought Landis did, too.

She blamed herself for not knowing those details.

Then, she said something more. "They wouldn't be surprised not hearing from her. Any of them, all of them. When she does these stints, she cuts herself off. No phone, no Internet, nothing. I don't believe anyone even knows where this cabin is precisely. I don't. But we need to find out. Check it. Be sure she hadn't been there and come back. Pin down the timeline."

So there was still their Maggie inside.

"We will."

Except the body wouldn't be in this state if Jamie Chancellor had come back recently.

Nobody could blame Maggie for not incorporating that bit of detail into her thinking, even as they all noted how different it was from her usual every-detail-sharp focus.

One question from Landis and she spelled out the basics they needed.

Names, addresses, relationships, work and romantic history. She acknowledged gaps in the romantic history. What she told them was accurate, but there might be guys she hadn't known about. Everything presented logically, organized—perfect for their purposes, except it took the guts right out of her.

Then she stood, silent and still, watching the techs some, but mostly staring.

Nobody suggested she get out of there.

Not until one of the uniforms assigned to the door came up to Belichek apologetically and said in a low voice, "There's a guy insisting we let you know he's here. Won't take no for an answer. Name of Carson."

"Check him in as far as the front steps."

Then Belichek went to Maggie.

"Time for you to go, Mags."

She blinked. It didn't change the dullness in her eyes. "I'm not getting in anybody's way."

"No, you're not. Still, time for you to go."

"If I leave…"

"It's going to be just as real if you stay. C'mon."

He gestured her to go ahead of him. The fact that she did with no more protest confirmed what he'd thought.

Landis fell in behind him. "She can't drive."

"She won't," he told his partner.

Outside, Maggie slipped off the coverings and checked out automatically.

"I'll leave you all to it. I know you'll do everything you can to find out who did this, and I'll tell her—" She swallowed. "—family exactly that."

She went down the stairs.

They remained at the top.

She half turned back toward them, to say something more, Belichek thought. Then a figure stepped from the shadow cast by a police vehicle and moved toward her. She stilled.

The man looked better than in photos a few years old Belichek looked up. More settled. Solid.

Getting out from under a murder charge could do that for a man.

J.D. Carson didn't put his arms around her, which would have been the absolute wrong thing to do for Maggie. He didn't touch her at all.

He said, "C'mon, Maggie. I'm driving."

"I have to tell her parents. They're down in Fredericksburg."

Landis had already dispatched a pair of officers to the parents' house an hour away with orders to wait for Maggie, but to go in with her, to catch those first, uncensored reactions. Just in case.

"Then that's where I'm driving."

After a long moment of staring at Carson, Maggie said, "Okay."

As he turned to head back into the darkness with her, Carson met Belichek's look and gave a single, short nod of acknowledgment.

Landis elbowed his back. "Your doing?"

"Yeah."

"The guy from Bedhurst?"

"Yeah."

"Good."

They stood there for another fifteen seconds.

"C'mon," Landis said.

✧　✧　✧　✧

BEFORE THEY ENTERED the house, a male voice called, "Are you the officer in charge?"

It didn't come from the scattering of spectators in front of them, but from their left. They both turned.

A man stood on the steps of the house next door.

"Sir?" Belichek stepped half in front of Landis.

His partner didn't need a second invitation. He went into the house.

"It's a tragedy. Young woman like that." The man didn't sound particularly broken up. But some people didn't.

"It is."

He shifted his head, as if trying to see into the house, though it was impossible from his angle. "When will the house be released?"

"That decision's well above my pay grade."

"Going to be caught up in bureaucracy, is it?"

"Less bureaucracy, more a murder investigation."

The man expelled a sharp breath out his nose. Impatient, scoffing. "Shame. As I said, a real shame a young woman like that."

The right words, even the tone was right. But that breath…

Incongruity always caught Belichek. When words said one thing, actions another, lies often caught in the cracks. Lies that revealed truth.

"You knew the household, then?"

"Household?" he repeated sharply. "You make it sound like there were others. It was only her on the deed."

"Is that so? Have you given your statement, sir?"

"I don't have anything to say for a statement. Don't know a thing. Wasn't here. Don't know—"

"With your familiarity with the *household*—" He emphasized it. "—we want to be sure to get your statement. Officer Schmidt?"

The young uniform had been about to follow Landis inside, but came immediately to Belichek's side. "If you'll get this gentleman's statement with as much information about the neighborhood as possible?"

"Yes, sir."

"I just wanted to know—"

"If you'll come down here, sir," Schmidt told the neighbor. "Or we can go inside your house and—"

"No, no. I'm coming down."

Belichek went inside, feeling good about Schmidt's career prospects.

Landis came up to him. "Interesting?"

"Odd."

He nodded, knowing Belichek's distinctions. "Now? Or later?"

"Later."

Then they got back to work.

Examining the proof of the worst failure of Ford Belichek's life.

CHAPTER FIVE

THE ACCUMULATION OF information and observation was a talisman of sorts.

Protecting Belichek against horror, against smell, against pity, against guilt, against the burn chewing on his stomach and spitting bile into his throat. His mind and motor skills followed a familiar path over the next hours, collecting views of unique scenery.

Finally, with the crime scene crew working toward wrap-up, the neighbors questioned, the body mercifully dispatched, the TV lights and cameras long departed, the sky in the direction of the Potomac River pearled gray, Belichek and Landis sat on stairs to the second floor to drink tepid coffee.

"First question," Landis said, beginning a routine they'd developed at the start of their partnership to help shift mental gears from the first gathering of information—any information, all information—to the beginning of sorting and assessing. "Why wasn't she found until now?"

It was a good first question. And a much more specific one than the global ones Belichek started with in his own mind. Like how could anyone see murder as the solution?

There were no satisfactory answers he'd ever found for that.

Or, the ones it would take the entire investigation to answer, like why had Jamison Chancellor been murdered and who had done it?

Landis' question had an answer. One both he and Landis knew. Didn't matter. It was the posing and answering of the question that got them started.

Belichek played his role. "Like Maggie said, Jamison Chancellor was supposed to leave for a month."

"Left and came back? Or never left?"

"Never left, pending more information. Or she came back almost immediately, based on the decomp." Even with no AC, that didn't happen in a couple days. "Car's in the garage."

The building off the back patio was so small it looked as if it had been built around the compact. A spill of potting soil churned the floor near the driver's door, probably from somebody trying to get in.

"She could have gone train, plane, hitched, got a ride—"

"Not to the mountains. But we'll have to cross it off. Find out where she was supposed to be and get with authorities there, too."

Crossing off possibilities, even improbabilities, was a substantial part of their job.

Landis nodded. "Everybody thought she was away. Nothing looked wrong. Mail, newspaper, all stopped. Lights scheduled and a neighborhood kid taking care of the back garden. It wasn't until the neighbor with a spare key came by this evening—yesterday evening—" he corrected in acknowledgment of the arrival of another day, "to borrow a book that they found the body. Looks like she never got out of here."

Belichek looked between the uprights of the open railing. Some painter had a picture of kids sitting like this on steps, peeking out at the grownups' party. Norman Rockwell maybe.

No party here. The pro cleaners who came in after crimes would have plenty to do, even though the forensic team had taken the grossly stained rug from the front hall off to the lab, along with cartons of other carefully transported evidence.

"Then where's her purse and phone?" His turn to ask a question.

"Killer took the purse with the phone in it."

"What's the fourth key to?" In a pocket, the victim had four keys on a ring. One checked to the garage, a second to the car, a third to the front door. The fourth didn't fit anywhere, including the Sunshine Foundation, which they'd checked in the past hour. "And why take the purse? He took the time to check out the rest of the house, take what he wanted. He had time to go through the purse and take only what he wanted."

"First question's no good. No use speculating without more intel. As for the purse, he might have gotten interrupted," suggested Landis. "He didn't touch the third-floor office—computer, printer. So, he grabbed the purse on the way out."

"They usually start with the purse. Cash, credit cards—and why not take the car? Not a luxury vehicle, but not junk."

"A specialist. Computer stuff not on his list, couldn't be bothered with the car. Pressed for time. Or rattled after killing the homeowner."

"You think the mess was from being rattled? Feels dismissive. Going after specific things by the most direct route possible."

"Okay. This burglar wasn't as organized as most and he forgot to start with the purse, had to grab it on his way out. Maybe interrupted by Jamison Chancellor."

"That's a big one—killed first? Or surprised the burglary in progress?"

"Trick question," Landis objected.

Murderers trying to look like a burglar rarely looked like burglars panicked into murder. Landis knew the signs as well as he did. Not to mention the body's position right where it would be if someone fired from just inside the doorway. As if the victim opened the door to someone with a gun and backed up or heard someone at the door, headed that way, only to be met by the intruder who'd let themselves in.

Landis kept going. "Maybe the killer wanted something in the purse and it was easier to grab the whole thing."

"Something that gave away the identity of the killer? Or something the killer needed and killed her to get?" Belichek expected no answers, so he asked another question. "Something to do with her work?"

"Doesn't seem likely." Landis' view of partnership was full-time devil's advocate. He did the job damn well. "What could she have done at the Sunshine Foundation to get herself killed? Not smile enough?"

The organization gave funding, training, and support to struggling low-income families, with its definition of family open-minded.

"Have proof of embezzling, misuse of funds, sexual misconduct, illegal political contributions, drug smuggling, laundering money for the mob—"

"Whoa, Belichek. Remember, these are the people who're determined to make lemonade out of the lemons the world dishes up. Help the unfortunate."

"Can you think of people more vulnerable to being exposed doing something nasty or a group that'd be a better front for bad guys?"

"Okay, okay, Mr. Optimism. But before we get too deep down that road, it's my turn. Why didn't anybody hear the shot—or shots?"

"Corner lot, so no neighbor on one side. According to Schmidt, next door says he had acoustic insulation put in during recent renovations and nothing from outside is heard inside. Something to check. The old lady behind is across the alley and… well, old lady. Also, possibly shot during the day when most people are at work and kids at school."

"She was supposed to have left Labor Day weekend when people were home, so more likely to have heard."

"People away for the weekend. Or she was shot during the Fairlington Labor Day fireworks."

Landis groaned. "Perfectly timed? If it's one of those, I'm handing the whole thing over to Terrington."

"No, you're not."

"No, I'm not. We need to work this timeline. We'll get her phone records. Talk to people at her work. Confirm the timeline by more than the old lady neighbor who found her and said she talked to her the Friday evening of Labor Day weekend. It's still going to be a bitch to pin down this long after.

"You know what the homicide detective's gold mine is?" Landis didn't expect an answer. "Twenty-four hours before the victim dies and twenty-four hours after. And it looks like we don't have a single second of those forty-eight hours. Not a nugget, not a trace of dust. Nobody saw anything, heard anything, suspected anything. Jamison Chancellor had no enemies, never did a bad thing in her life, those who benefit financially from her death don't want it, and the ME says no sexual assault.

"On top of which, Jamison Chancellor apparently spends the twenty-four hours before getting dead alone, packing for a trip, talking to nobody, seeing nobody. And we don't come on the scene until three weeks after she dies. That trail isn't cold, it's Duluth in January."

"We build it slowly—"

"Not the pebble and mountain stuff again. We've got nothing there, either."

"Knowing what's not part of the mountain is also important."

"Well, we've got one hell of a discard pile, but nothing else."

Landis drained the last of his coffee and levered himself off the step. His shirt still looked white, unwrinkled. Belichek's shirts never looked that good, even when he first put them on, that's why he'd taken to wearing dark shirts.

Landis said, "Starting phone records tomorrow—actually, later today. Right now, I'm going to the office, check with the team that made notification, get a couple hours' sleep, then get started. How about you?"

"Think I'll stick around a while, look through papers in the upstairs office."

They'd seen neat, undisturbed files in the third-floor office on their first survey.

Unlike the small room on the first floor with the antique desk, the upstairs office was clearly where she worked. The computer setup. A broad expanse of built-in desktop in front of a large window facing the back. An upholstered chair with a knit throw on it, bracketed by bookcases.

And oddly, almost eerily, untouched.

"Okay. Let me know if there's anything hot. When you come in to the office, we'll go to the Sunshine Foundation."

CHAPTER SIX

FROM WHERE HE sat, Ford Belichek could see through the office's entryway to the living room and the back of the photograph still angled on the bookcase.

He'd asked for it to be fingerprinted. The tech returned it to the same position.

That photograph bothered him.

The cousins were adults or nearly so—too old for it to have been taken before their aunt's murder.

He also wondered about the way it was turned. As if someone meant to pivot it—so they didn't have to look at it or so it didn't look at them?—but didn't finish the job.

He chewed on that a minute before he rose from the step and headed upstairs.

Another, narrower set of stairs came up from the back door, through a back hall off the kitchen. Probably originally servants' stairs, from a time when lots of people had servants or were servants.

He didn't pause at the second floor, with its two bedrooms and 1950s bathroom, but went directly to the third floor, where the slanted roof and bump-out window created an office, with a bathroom beside it, decades younger but smaller than the one below.

First, he prowled the office, looking at book titles and studying photographs of smiling faces, blooming flowers, and blazing Christmas trees.

He took the desk chair, drew on gloves and pulled open the drawer with files marked "bills" and "financial statements." These files were too thin to have everything. Most likely backups. The tech guys had the computer, which likely had the up-to-date information. He might get to these files eventually, but first he'd check material that didn't duplicate.

He let the drawer's own weight slide it closed.

He got up and returned to the bookcase. Crouching before it, he pulled out several photo albums and six bound books filled with writing. He selected the most current and went to the end. It ended in August. The handwriting was slanted, with dots trailing the i's and crossbars displaced from the t's. But it was surprisingly readable.

He dropped into the cushioned chair with a matching ottoman, flipped back to the start of that journal and started reading the soul of Jamison Chancellor.

DAY ONE

CHAPTER SEVEN

SHOCK DIDN'T LAST forever.

It couldn't. Humans adjusted. Accepted. Moved on.

Hendrickson York had seen it many times.

He'd done it himself once before with Vivian.

He'd do it again.

He just had to control the situation.

He stood at the side of Jamie's desk in the modest offices of the Sunshine Foundation. The top of her desk was cleared of its usual neat but ever-proliferating piles because of her hiatus to write another book.

There'd be no sense moving to this office to mark his ascendence in the Sunshine Foundation, because it had been one of Jamie's conceits to have all the offices the same size. The ones on this side of the hallway each had the same low half-circle window.

It all looked a little strange at this early hour.

But he hadn't been able to return to sleep after the police came to his door with the news, so he'd come here.

Maybe he'd move the foundation headquarters. Somewhere polished, where donors could visit.

He stooped slightly to look out the window from this angle. He'd seen the view from the numerous guest chairs, of course, but not from the chair behind the desk.

If anything, he believed the view from his desk was better.

That would have been typical of Jamie.

Who was dead now.

He needed to remember that.

To continue thinking things through, so he said the right things.

Shock wouldn't last. He'd adjust, accept, move on.

Especially with what he'd learned from Jamie.

And he *had* learned from her, as young, as inexperienced, even naïve as she'd been, especially at the start.

Ah, the start. So unlike the more recent years.

Those early days of the Sunshine Foundation, when Jamie's youth and inexperience had been the charm, the key to unlock donations, when each dollar had seemed a miracle, rather than a pittance. And she had so looked up to him. That couldn't last forever, either.

Nothing did.

Not even shock.

He'd already gone a long way toward adjusting.

Fairlington County Police Department News Conference

Good afternoon. I'm Public Affairs Officer Elliott Kepler. That's E-L-L-I-O-T-T. K-E-P-L-E-R. This will be a brief update at this time, with further updates as circumstances call for them. First, we will have a statement from Chief of Detectives Wilson Palery. That's W-I-L-S-O-N P-A-L-E-R-Y. Then I will take a limited number of questions. All inquiries will come through my office. You all have my contact information. Now, Fairlington County Police Chief of Detectives Palery. Chief Palery.

Chief Palery: Thank you, Officer Kepler.

Ladies and gentlemen, the Fairlington County Police Department was called to a residence on Red Hill Street in the Old Town area of Fairlington at eleven thirty-seven last night. A person was found deceased within that residence.

The call originated from a neighbor who obtained entrance to the residence with a key known to have been shared by the homeowner.

We are not releasing the identity of the deceased or other matters pertaining to the investigation, pending official identification of the victim and notification of next of kin.

We ask the media's cooperation and professionalism in not speculating on the identity of the deceased to avoid potentially causing distress to family members. We will share the identity when it is confirmed.

Public Information Officer (PIO) Kepler: Thank you, Chief.

Chief of Detectives Palery leaves the room.

PIO Kepler: Now, I'll take a few questions.

Washington Post: That residence, the one where there was police activity last night, is the home of—is listed as the property of Jamison Chancellor, founder of the Sunshine Foundation. Do you have any reason to think the victim is *not* Jamison Chancellor?

PIO Kepler: We are not speculating on who the deceased is or who it is not. When we have ascertained the identity of the deceased and in accordance with the pursuit of our investigation, we will release that information.

WTOP Radio: Why has the identity not been established?

PIO Kepler: That is an aspect of the investigation which we will not go into at this time.

Washington Post: Will you confirm Jamison Chancellor owns and has been known to live at that property.

PIO Kepler: We are not speculating on the identity of the owner of that property.

WTOP Radio: It's not speculation. It's on the tax records and—

PIO Kepler: We are not speculating. If you have no other questions…

Unidentified Media: (shouting)

PIO Kepler: ABC.

ABC: Has the family been notified of the identity of the deceased?

PIO Kepler: We are not commenting on identity or family connections of the deceased. Ted, your question.

Fairlington Leader: What about the connection to Assistant Commonwealth's Attorney Margaret Frye? Why was she at the scene?

PIO Kepler: Members of the Commonwealth's Attorney frequently go to crime scenes. Ms. Frye, in particular, works closely with our department—

Death, Murder, Violence Podcast: Yeah, real closely.

Unidentified Media: Shut up, Zeedyk.

PIO Kepler:—in making sure our investigation leads to the conviction of the perpetrator.

Fairlington Leader: What was the cause of death?

PIO Kepler: That will be determined by the medical examiner.

NBC: When will the cause of death be released?

PIO Kepler: You'll have to ask the ME's office its likely timeline for making that determination.

Washington Post: How is the investigation proceeding without the victim's identity?

PIO Kepler: There are many avenues to pursue.

Washington Post: Including the official identity?

PIO Kepler: Of course.

Death, Murder, Violence Podcast: What about the detectives on this case? Why aren't they here?

PIO Kepler: They are pursuing the investigation.

Death, Murder, Violence Podcast: That's Tanner Landis as lead and Ford Belichek as second? Why isn't Detective Terrington the secondary? He was originally, wasn't he? And Belichek was supposed to be on vacation.

Fairlington Leader to *Death, Murder, Violence Podcast:* Hey, you had that on your podcast this morning. How do you know—?

Death, Murder, Violence Podcast: Found sources. Try it, you might like it. Does the department not have confidence in Detective Terrington? Is that why he was pulled off? Was Belichek called back from vacation?

PIO Kepler: The Fairlington County Police Department does not discuss personnel matters publicly. The entire department is working as a team to investigate this situation. All—

Death, Murder, Violence Podcast: Yeah, yeah, but it's clear the higher ups didn't have confidence in Terrington or why stop Belichek from going on vacation? Or is it Landis they don't—?

PIO Kepler: The Fairlington County Police Department has confidence in all its detectives or they would not be detectives. That's it for now, everyone. I'll let you know when we have more information to share.

~~ End news conference transcript ~~

CHAPTER EIGHT

LANDIS PUT AWAY the earbuds he'd used to listen to the in-house stream of the news conference.

He left the privacy of the back stairwell and spotted Roy Isaacson the instant he walked into the detectives' area.

The detectives had the dubious pleasure of being housed in a bullpen of pods in an area left open when a line of glass offices along the outside wall met an oddly angled interior wall. That interior wall held a bank of elevators at the far end, a break room, two conference rooms, and the back stairwell.

The glass offices—a design feature used throughout the building and that served as shorthand for those of higher rank—let more daylight into the area than it otherwise would have had. That was the pleasure.

The dubiousness came from those offices—with the exception of the one belonging to their Chief of Detectives—housing free-floating bureaucrats. Too senior to fob off with a regular pod, not yet persuaded to retire or move on, they dotted these glass cubes that diminished in size like nesting dolls the closer they got to the corner. Several of their occupants enjoyed poking into the business of the working-stiff detectives in the bullpen.

Talk around the department made them the most likely source for the leaks to this podcaster who'd appeared out of nowhere.

Reasonable.

Landis, though, wondered if the leaks also involved Roy Isaacson.

Isaacson was pleasant enough on the surface. But that's what you got with Isaacson—surface. Maggie learned that before breaking up with the jerk last spring. The only thing that kept the breakup from happening faster was Maggie hadn't been around him much, because she worked constantly.

Unlike Isaacson. Who found enough free time in his shifts to hang out where he didn't belong—like here—picking up tidbits he traded and leveraged like a peddler in a bazaar.

Isaacson also spotted Landis.

He finished what he was saying to Danolin, a long-time detective who gave nothing away, then sauntered out as if he hadn't been rousted by Landis' arrival. If everyone in the detectives' room was like Danolin, Landis wouldn't mind Isaacson's forays here. Not as much, anyway.

Before Landis could reach his desk, Terrington's head popped up over the top of his cubicle. "Landis, have you heard what this shithead podcaster said?"

"How do you have time to hear what some shithead podcaster said, much less care? Did you put together the paperwork for phone records?"

"I wasn't listening to it." If he didn't have a deep voice, he'd sound like a whining kid. "Isaacson told me about it. I was checking the transcript. And it wasn't only the podcast. It came up at the department's news conference just now. Kepler should've stuck up for me, made it clear—"

"I don't care what—"

"You should."

Landis pivoted to the voice behind him.

Roy Isaacson himself.

He'd circled back through the back stairwell to see what he might have stirred up to the surface of the bullpen.

"Nice of you to take time out of your busy day to visit again, but we've got this case—"

"You should care what this Oz guy is saying on his Death, Violence, Murder Podcast," Isaacson repeated. "Not as much as Terrington does about being called second-rate, but, still, you should care that his latest podcast said Detective Tanner Landis, the lead on this very high-profile case, is famed for spending more of his time in bed—not his own bed—than on the job."

"The little slime," Terrington muttered, solely in his own defense.

"Don't pay attention to him—or any of them," Landis advised. If Isaacson took *any of them* to include himself, he wouldn't mind. "Clearly doesn't know what he's talking about. Everybody knows I give equal time to the job."

Even Isaacson allowed a slight smile, though he didn't join in the general guffaws.

Neither did Terrington.

Truth be told, Terrington wasn't first rate. If he put the energy into the job he wasted on being touchy about his rep and whining about other detectives getting bigger assignments, he'd be a hell of a lot closer.

"Yeah, funny for you, being half of the department's hotshot duo. Even when this podcaster delivers what sounds like a slam, it's still praising you for being a sword master. Me—"

"*Sword master?* What kind of bullshit is *that?*" Eddy Knarr asked.

"I like it," Landis said. "That's how I'm answering the phone from now on. *Sword Master Landis.* Can somebody get me a nameplate?"

"Meantime," Terrington said with sufficient loud vehemence to compete with more guffaws, "this Oz-something podcaster's making me look bad. But he's right about one thing—I *should* be secondary. How can Belichek be secondary? He's supposed to be gone. In fact, he *is* gone. Maybe he did leave on vacation, otherwise why isn't he here doing his jo—?"

No longer amused, Landis said, "He is doing his job. Same way everyone should be. Get on that records request and, Knarr, where is the report on the neighborhood canvass?"

Everyone snapped back to business. Except Terrington, still pouting. And Isaacson, who waited another half a minute, smirking at them all before turning to leave again.

CHAPTER NINE

CELESTE RENFRO ARRIVED at the Sunshine Foundation even earlier than usual. Hendrickson's car was already parked there. First time he'd ever beaten her in.

Why?

No, don't get distracted. Prioritize. On a day like this, that was vital. Prioritize.

The first matter was when would the police get here? Even more important, how much did they know?

If they knew some, there was no sense in trying to hide anything except the vital issue. Maybe that was a better approach, anyway. Be as open as possible, which made it seem more likely she was being entirely open.

Jamie would say to be completely honest.

Jamie...

Celeste forced herself forward when she wanted to stop. Just stop. Stand still and do nothing.

Jamie wasn't here anymore.

Jamie had no say in this.

Celeste had to decide on her approach. And once she decided, it couldn't be changed.

Tell them as little as possible?

Or go as close to the truth as she could?

$\diamond \quad \diamond \quad \diamond \quad \diamond$

"**YOU SPENT ALL** night there, didn't you?" Landis asked as he drove them from the neighborhood of mid-rises where the Fairlington County Police Department resided to the offices of the Sunshine Foundation in a section of Old Town.

Belichek, who had met him in the parking garage, didn't bother to make Landis define *there*. They both knew he meant Jamison Chancellor's house. He grunted confirmation.

Landis hadn't guessed from his clothes, because he'd changed from the kit in his trunk, the one all smart detectives kept for the unexpected.

"Anything?"

"Background. Victimology."

"Tell."

"The sunshine's not an act for her."

Landis considered that for half a block. "Could've made her more vulnerable. A saint?"

"No. Not entirely blind to the dark, either. But she fights—fought it."

"Anyone specific lurking in that dark?"

Belichek drew in a long breath and sighed out. "Not that I've cracked yet. Either she was worried about someone else reading it or she knew so clearly what she was writing about she didn't need to make it clear. Think there were a couple guys who made her uneasy. No names."

"Statement from the neighbor—the one who found her—says she'd been dating a guy named Carl Arbendroth, but broke it off. First half of August, somewhere in there. That matches what Mags said last night." Though she hadn't known the name.

"Any idea of the identity of the second guy?"

"No. Someone she sees regularly. One entry she wonders about the guy, the next she dismisses her concerns."

"Could be somebody at the foundation, a neighbor, another boyfriend. Or somebody she encounters on a regular basis in her daily life, a coffee guy, a restaurant worker, or anybody. We'll check."

Concerns... Jamie Chancellor had deep concern for the two cousins she'd spent a big chunk of her childhood with and—even more defining—shared a tragedy with. Knowing Maggie as he did, Belichek had no trouble separating her thread from Ally's in the journal, despite Jamie's elliptical references.

But neither Maggie Frye nor Ally Northcutt was a hot suspect for showing up on Jamie's doorstep and putting a shotgun blast into her face.

"Where'd you go to, Belichek? Not like you to go all unfocused when we're talking a case, like you're worried about Jamison Chancellor." His grin disappeared when he looked at his passenger. "Oh, God, you are. She's dead, Bel. *Dead.* Too late to worry about her. You can only do what we're doing for her—trying to find who made her dead. You are *not* falling for a *victim.* You talk about *me* getting involved with the wrong women? How much wronger can it get than dead?"

"You're full of it, Landis."

"I see your face. Looks exactly like that obsessed detective in that old movie."

Belichek shot his partner a look. "Do not start again on that. Never should have told you."

"That's what partners do. Tell their deepest, darkest secrets. You're challenged in that area because you're boring as hell. That's why you resorted to telling me about your grandfather and how obsessed he got with an old movie."

Not exactly what his grandfather had been obsessed with, but Belichek had veered off from telling Landis that complete truth. Looked like a real smart move now.

"And you have driven it into the ground ever since, going on and on about—who is that actor? Dana Andrews?—and—"

"Gene Tierney. Now there's a woman." Predictable that Landis knew the name of a good-looking woman. Even one old enough to be his grandmother. "But this time I got a better one to tell you about. Carol Burnett."

That got Belichek to look at him. "I follow most of your loop-da-loop non sequiturs, but what are you talking about Carol Burnett for?"

"Saw her show on one of the cable stations that specializes in old

TV shows. Love those. Old westerns. *Perry Mason. Twilight Zone.*"

"That's the one I'm living in right now."

Partner ignored that. "So, on *Carol Burnett,* they were doing a skit based on an old movie, like their classic on *Gone With the Wind,* where she wears the curtains. Only this one was on—"

"Don't tell me, let me guess. *Laura.* Will you ever let that go?"

"No. Not after I watched it. The scene with the spotlight in her eyes—those were the days, huh, when men were men and detectives were detectives."

"I told you that wasn't the part—"

"Side issue. The core was the detective falling in love with the dead victim."

"Landis—"

"Not that your grandfather did, since it was always your grand-mother for him. But you? Spending a lot of time inside the journals of Jamison Chancellor…? Dangerous. Real dangerous."

"Victimology. Like always."

Landis' voice sharpened. "Not like always." He smoothed it out as he continued, "Anyway, this *Carol Burnett* skit was *Flora* instead of *Laura,* and it fits you even better. The detective's falling for the portrait of the woman killed. The live one shows up, like in the real movie. And she and the detective get it on. But it turns out the detective prefers the portrait to the woman. Makes his life a whole lot simpler. And I can see, with your personality, that a woman who's dead might be perfect."

"I'm working the case, Landis. Reading to know the victim's life. I'll see if I can pin down who the guys are. It would help to confirm one is this Carl Arbendroth. In the meantime, what's happening on your end?"

Belichek's phone rang. "Mags," he informed his partner.

"Hi, Maggie—"

"You're with Landis? Put me on speaker. We're on our way to the cabin where Jamie was supposed to go to. Just… Just in case there's any evidence here."

The knowledge that her real *just in case* was that her cousin was at some cabin this moment, alive, writing away, banded around Belichek's heart.

"How do you know where?" Landis asked.

"Ally—my cousin Ally—came to Jamie's parents' house first thing and she knew where Jamie had gone before. She got us close enough on the map and—"

"You need to call law enforcement."

"I did, Landis. I haven't turned into an idiot. They're meeting us there. They're the ones who knew the precise location. Should be there in under three hours. I'll call back."

After she ended the call, they remained silent a moment. As if that could stop Maggie's hopes from being crushed.

After a sigh, Landis ticked off what was happening, as the medical examiner, trace scientists, computer forensics, and the rest processed evidence. Routine unwound at a pace dictated by the facts of the case, the necessity of covering bases, the demands of workload and staffing, and the vagaries of luck.

Never fast enough for the media. Never dramatic enough for the public.

"No such thing as an eyewitness on this thing. The closest thing— that neighbor who found the body—hasn't provided exactly case-breaking details."

"We haven't talked to her yet."

"Yeah. You want to bet if she comes up with something when we do?" Landis was deep into his grumble. "Worse, no official identity. How is that even possible in this day and age? Fine, DNA takes a couple decades because the lab's backed up and we can't even try to wheedle lab help from the FBI with them up to their gonads with that serial killer, but no medical records? How does that happen?"

Obligingly, Belichek told his partner what he already knew. "Fire at her doctor's office consumed the records and the server that was supposed to be the backup."

"That's exactly what I mean—what sort of idiot stores his backup onsite? That's the whole fucking idea behind backup. The asshole never heard of the cloud?"

"Guess not. How about the neighborhood canvass?"

Landis snorted. "Two-thirds of those people were off to the Eastern Shore or the Outer Banks or Bora Bora over Labor Day weekend. And that doesn't count the ones who were gone all of August and don't rush back."

"Their security cameras don't leave."

"Yeah, but a lot of them record over, the cheap bastards. The tech guys are still gathering, cleaning up, cross-checking, but so far all they've got of interest is someone going up to Jamison Chancellor's front door the week before Labor Day. *Possibly* ringing the doorbell. No way to tell for sure because it's a blurry image of a figure in a big rain poncho with a hood—couldn't even determine male or female. Pretty sure nobody answered the door. How's that for case-breaking?"

"Week before?"

"I know. Jamison Chancellor was still alive. The figure goes to her front door, lingers a moment. Does the same thing next door, though. Could've been selling something. Useless. In fact, the only item added to my store of non-knowledge this morning is that the house's AC wasn't turned off using the app. I was hoping that would give us a time to build around. The killer—or whoever—turned it off manually. No fingerprints, of course."

Belichek watched his partner's hands tighten on the steering wheel.

Landis felt the weight of Maggie's connection to this, too. But, beyond that, he had a sharply honed sense of when a case was going to be a bitch, with a strong tendency to go sideways from the start.

"Anything from the ME's office?" Belichek asked, though Landis would have said if there was something important. Trying to distract his partner? Himself?

"Dragged a prelim out of them. Pretty much what we expected. Shotgun, two barrels, compounded by the AC being turned off and decomp."

"AC turned off by someone who was there, since it wasn't done remotely, unless—power cut off at any point?" Belichek asked.

"Danolin's covering that ground with the power company."

"So, for now, we say the AC's turned off deliberately. The killer—"

"No guarantee it was the killer. If she was about to leave—"

"Even if the murderer showed up at that precise instant, who turns off their AC when they leave? It was hot the last week she was alive and forecasted to be hot most of the time she was supposed to be gone."

"It's not like winter when pipes can freeze. Turning it off wouldn't do damage."

"It's not normal."

"Any sign in her diaries she's a cheapskate?"

"They aren't diaries. But, no. Still… Something to check with Mags."

"How is she related to Maggie? Cousins, I know. But cousins how?"

"Maggie's father and Jamie's father were brothers. The other cousin they talk about—Ally—her mother's their sister."

"Shouldn't Jamie be a Frye, then?"

"Jamie's father died when she was a baby. Cancer. Her mother remarried Wade Chancellor. He adopted her. But they didn't want to cut Jamie off from her Frye relations. All three girls spent time with the fourth Frye sibling, Vivian."

"Maggie's aunt who was murdered."

"Yeah."

"Okay, I admit it. Your reading the journals hasn't been a complete waste of time."

"Glad to hear it."

Except none of that came from Jamison Chancellor's journals. Not from Maggie, either.

Navigation software announced their imminent arrival at the Sunshine Foundation.

Without interrupting a string of red-brick buildings, it stood out—discreetly. Like the wealthiest matron among a bevy of peers, displaying her impeccable pearls, this building presented its pediments with assurance. A large pointed one over the main door on the first floor, rectangular ones above the tall windows on the first and second floors, then smaller fan windows under the largest of all the pediments forming the roof's profile.

Landis drove past. "I've been here. Better parking in back. They renovated an old bank, put a restaurant in about two years ago. Guess there are offices above."

Figured Landis knew about the restaurant.

Belichek visualized the personalized map of Fairlington he carried in his head—one pockmarked by crimes he'd investigated. This area wasn't as well known to him as others. "What is this? A little over a mile from the Chancellor house?"

"Yeah. Still Old Town, but not as ritzy a neighborhood."

"She didn't inherit office space."

The back of the building was a hodgepodge of centuries, with practical additions for modern amenities of varying eras added with varying amounts of discretion. Also parking, as promised.

The kitchen's rear door was on one side. An unobtrusive door on the opposite side opened to a small entry that mostly provided a landing for a set of stairs. Four plaques stacked on the wall across from the door.

Belichek tipped his head toward the Sunshine Foundation plaque. "Suite 301. Third floor."

"No elevator? They make people climb the stairs to give away their money?"

"More likely, they go to the donors. And the people they help don't mind a climb."

Landis grunted, starting up with no more complaint.

What awaited them at the top of the stairs and through a doorway on the left wouldn't impress donors. Unless they were the kind who preferred their money go to the cause.

The space was neat and clean. The aging furniture didn't match, though it had the same general look and similar wood tones. Furnished by someone who cared how things looked but not more than sticking to a tight budget.

The small space was crowded.

A middle-aged woman sat behind a desk, with an air of belonging.

A young man with wild hair showing from under a ubiquitous dark hoodie looked as if he'd been crying, from his red eyes and pale face. Two other women, each around forty, and standing across the desk from the guy, were actively crying.

Add in two detectives and the small space was like a crowded elevator with a desk in the middle.

"May I help you?" The woman behind the desk wasn't crying.

Force of will? Lack of emotion?

"I'm Detective Landis from the Fairlington County Police Department." His pause let Belichek identify himself, without looking away from the people of the Sunshine Foundation, before he continued. "We're investigating a homicide."

"Oh, my God, it *is* Jamie," wailed the taller of the two women standing. "I knew it was her address, but kept hoping and hoping—"

"Keep still, Kimby," ordered the woman behind the desk. "How can we help you, Detective Landis?"

"We're here to talk to each member of the staff," Landis said. "And you are…?"

"Celeste Renfro, office manager." Jamie had written about Celeste's calm in a crisis. Was that why the woman seemed oddly familiar to Belichek? "You should start with Hendrickson York."

He recognized the name—he'd been with the foundation since Jamie started it.

Landis looked toward the young guy. He shook his head and pointed toward the hallway behind him. "First door on the left."

"And you are?"

"Delattre. Uh, Adam Delattre. IT."

Landis nodded, started turning to the two women on the right.

Released from Landis' attention, Delattre scooted down the same hallway he'd indicated, but he went past the first door and entered one on the right.

"They're volunteers," Celeste said.

Landis made a mistake then, bypassing her to continue to the two other women. He was more than good with most women, but he had a blind spot with women like Celeste Renfro, who prided themselves on not being won over by men like Tanner Landis.

"Your names, ladies?"

"I'm Kimby Curtis and this is Denise—"

"Denise Gutierrez." The other woman claimed her right to identify herself.

"Thank you. Will you be here awhile?"

"Oh, yes," Kimby said. "All day. We'll—"

Celeste Renfro said, "There's no need for either of you to stay. I won't have jobs for you today."

"Oh, but, Celeste—"

Again, Denise Gutierrez cut across Kimby. "We'll work on organizing the clips Jamie—" Her voice fluttered, then steadied. "—asked us to do when we could. With no one using the conference room, this is the perfect time. C'mon, Kimby, let's get started."

If Celeste Renfro weren't already irked, that would have done it.

Landis appeared unaware, though Belichek knew otherwise. His partner nodded at all three women and started down the hall.

Belichek looked directly at Celeste. "Thank you for your help on this extremely difficult day."

In the couple strides before they reached the closed door marked "Hendrickson York," Landis muttered, "Keep mending that fence when we talk to her."

"Yeah, after you broke it," he muttered back.

Landis knocked.

CHAPTER TEN

"**WASN'T SURE YOU'D** be open today," Landis said mildly after performing introductions.

Hendrickson York was in his mid to late sixties. He wore his thick gray hair combed back to one side from a sharp widow's peak. Gray also salted his dark brows. A gray mustache was trimmed precisely above his top lip and not allowed to extend beyond the corners of his mouth, where it would have met a sharp line on each side cutting from nose to chin.

"We at the Sunshine Foundation are, of course, devastated by the tragic death of our founder, Jamison Chancellor. At the same time, we understand not only what the foundation is meant to do and what many rely on us to do, but what Jamie herself would *want* and *expect* us to do. After all, she created this foundation to find meaning and value from the murder of her aunt, Vivian Frye."

That sounded like a drafted, edited, and polished news release to Belichek.

That might explain the stilted delivery.

The office furnishings were a cut above that in the entry area, perhaps the pick of the litter. The desk chair significantly more impressive than the two guest chairs on the opposite side of a desk outfitted with old-fashioned blotter, pen holder, leather portfolio. The computer was consigned to a side table. The star of the room was the half-moon window that started close to the floor and gave a view across rooftops. Some grimy, but looking their best under a bright blue sky.

"Interesting that both the aunt and the niece were murdered," Landis said mildly.

"I can't imagine any connection between these two tragedies, especially with the separation of time and place. Not to mention that Vivian's murder was solved almost immediately and her murderer himself was killed. I can only say that we, those who most loved Jamison Chancellor, count on you to bring the same resolution to her death."

Did he not recognize that *he* was at least one more connection between the two cases? Or was he excellent at masking that recognition?

"That's why we're here." Landis' flat tone told Belichek he was irked, but would tell Hendrickson York nothing. "You knew Vivian Frye, too?"

"I did. Very well. *Very* well. She was a marvelous woman. Incandescent. She could dazzle you with one look. No one else like her. No one."

Belichek noted the repetition and the choppiness of his words. Strong emotion behind them.

"What about Jamison Chancellor?"

"Jamie is a great deal like Vivian. Not in looks. Of the girls, Ally looks the most like Vivian. But personality—yes, Jamie is very like Vivian. The spirit. The energy. The innate ability to draw people to her. But also the drawbacks. Impulsiveness, failure to see beneath a glossy surface, failure to sort through the many drawn to her to focus on those of value. Vivian never learned."

Interesting that Landis' broad invitation to talk about Jamie took Hendrickson York back to Vivian.

His priorities? Or a deliberate detour from the recent murder victim?

"What did those traits in Jamison Chancellor lead to?" Landis asked.

York spread his hands, indicating a topic too broad to encompass.

"Here at the foundation," Landis added as if that's what he'd always meant.

Belichek appreciated that, especially since disappointment crossed Hendrickson York's face. He'd been building toward telling them something. He'd invited them to inveigle it out of him.

Good move by Landis to delay his gratification.

"Ah, here at the foundation. You've met our staff." York smiled thinly. "Some hired for inexplicable reasons of Jamie's, not for their professional experience."

"The foundation reputation for being well-run is not accurate?"

York didn't like that blunt question exposing his intimations to the naked eye. "Even the most well-run organization can and should look for ways to improve."

"Uh-huh," Landis agreed, then turned the steering wheel. "When did you last communicate with Jamison Chancellor?"

"I told all that to the officer who came to my home to inform me of Jamie's death."

"We like to go over material again with witnesses after we've laid some of the groundwork," Landis said.

Something flickered in Hendrickson York's eyes that indicated he recognized that this time counted more than his first comments. "It strikes me as most inefficient. However, I will cooperate with your unwieldy process to the best of my ability to bring Jamie's murderer to justice."

"That's all we ask. What do you do here, sir?"

"Senior adviser and donor liaison."

"You were aware Jamison Chancellor was leaving to complete her book?"

"Of course. We planned for the time she would be away."

"Did you know where she was going?"

"No."

"Did you have a way to contact her?"

"No one did. As well as geographic distance, she said she needed to sever communication on these occasions. We needed to plan for no communication regardless, because the work of the foundation could not stand still while she was in the mountains."

"How was she going to get there?"

York looked at him as if he'd said something obscene. "Drive, of course."

"Drive herself?"

York wouldn't hear it, but Belichek did. A delicate thread of hope that maybe Maggie was right. That maybe the car in the garage and all the other circumstances were wrong.

"Of course. She does not—did not indulge herself by hiring a car and driver."

"When was she leaving Fairlington?"

"I do not know. Jamie did not know. She said she preferred to leave it *loose*."

"When did you last have contact with her?" Landis asked again.

"I last saw her the Friday evening before Labor Day. When we were all leaving these offices at the conclusion of that work day."

"You say *all*. Who was that, specifically?"

"Myself. Jamie. Celeste Renfro. Bethany Usher, a recent hire to assist Celeste in her duties as office manager. Adam Delattre, who does social media and other promotional efforts of the foundation. And two volunteers."

"Which two volunteers."

He raised one hand, opening his palm in a gesture of not knowing, and not concerned about that lack of knowledge.

"Did all or some of you go somewhere? Have a drink? Toast Jamison's time off?"

"No. We dispersed to our various weekends."

"What did you do that weekend?"

He squinted slightly. "I dispatched personal errands, attended a concert Saturday night with three major donors, and another alone on Sunday. In between, I read." He flipped one hand over. "Perhaps a bit of television."

"That Friday or the days before, was there anything out of the ordinary here or in conjunction with Jamison Chancellor? Something that happened or was said or how anyone acted?"

"Not at all."

"Not even with Jamison preparing to be away for an extended

period?"

"The foundation *can* run without Jamie. As it has these past weeks. Not to say that she could not be an inspiring and uplifting presence in the office, but her planned absence was not a major disruption. Even with her permanent absence, the foundation is well-positioned to thrive."

"What kind of leader was she?"

"She was quite adept at being a public face for the Sunshine Foundation."

A public face. Not *the* public face.

Did York fancy himself as a public face for the foundation? Did he see himself at the same level as—or higher than—Jamie?

Landis clearly heard the same thing, because he played into it.

"Someone so young must not yet know all the ins and outs a more experienced manager or leader like you has learned."

"Jamie was exceptionally quick in some areas, however there is much that only experience can provide."

"Can you give me an example?"

"One example would be that she allowed herself to accrue *stress*, as they call it now. Unnecessarily, as a more mature and experienced person would recognize."

"How did she do that?"

"Take this book. She felt a great deal of pressure about it because there had been a gap between books. Yet, she and no one else created the gap that put pressure on her. She created it by putting off the writing, I'm afraid. More generally she caused herself stress—" His tone dismissed it as an indulgence. "—by failing to handle matters in a decisive, forceful matter as they arose. Now, if there's no more… I have a great deal to do today, important donors to contact."

Landis had several ways of playing this. He went for head-on.

"There is more. Earlier, you must have misunderstood something I asked, because you said the last time you saw Jamison was the Friday before Labor Day, but I asked when was the last time you communicated with her? Of course, phone records will reveal that, but it helps us to know earlier in the investigation."

Under the precise mustache, Hendrickson York's mouth tightened. "Jamison and I spoke that Saturday morning. We spoke nearly every day."

Good catch, Landis. Even if York's switch had been inadvertent, it was a good move to call him on it. Having it pay off was icing. Lots of icing.

"Even when she went on these writing retreats?"

"No, not then." Was there a flicker in his eyes?

"On the Saturday morning before Labor Day, when you talked on the phone, did you call her or did she call you?"

"I don't…" Possibly recalling the comment about checking phone records, he amended whatever he'd been about to say to, "I believe I called her."

"What did you talk about?"

"I merely wished her a good trip and successful writing."

"What was her mood?"

"Entirely normal. Upbeat. Looking forward to her break."

"Did she say anything at that time about exactly when she planned to leave for the cabin?"

"She had previously told me she planned to leave Sunday, midafternoon. She gave no indication of changing that plan."

"Any other details of her departure?"

"Nothing."

"Any indication she had any concerns or worries, whether about the trip or anything else?"

"Not at all."

"More generally, were you aware of or suspect any concerns or worries she might have had."

"Ah." The older man sat back and templed his fingers. "There were—are—issues here at the foundation, though Jamie was not aware of them. Some might say deliberately so. Her thoughts…" He gestured, open-handed above his head, hinting at air headedness without saying it. "One forgives the young for being blinded by a physique and a certain cast of features."

"Was that directly connected to the foundation?"

"Perhaps not directly, but it did indicate a lack of... mature judgment that showed in other areas. I'm not blaming Jamie. After all, one must remember how the foundation started. She was a little girl who started something that outgrew her. It's been difficult to watch her struggling with that.

"I finally persuaded her to get the help the foundation needs. Professional management. To ensure that no longer could her amateur efforts—well-intentioned as they certainly were, but not what an organization needs to attain the next level—possibly hold back the foundation. She eventually saw the wisdom of that. Because at the core she truly did care about the Sunshine Foundation."

"You were behind a plan to bring in outside management?"

"Jamie was a lovely girl. With a great deal of generosity. Alas, generosity is not the best rudder for steering through the real world."

Landis nodded noncommittally at York's failure to answer his question.

Belichek slipped in, "Seemed to work for Mother Teresa." A poke from another side might prevent this guy from getting too settled and comfortable.

"Ah, yes. Though Mother Theresa was not an attractive young woman. Jamie Chancellor was. And that added so many complications."

"What complications?" Landis asked.

CHAPTER ELEVEN

Hendrickson York touched his mustache. "For starters, in aspects of her personal life. She let it bother her greatly that she has not had support from cousins one would expect to share this cause. One *seems* supportive, but rarely musters the time to actually contribute—"

Presumably Ally Northcutt, who happened to have a husband in a coma, a cop shot by an unknown assailant.

"—and the other a hard-driving woman without the nuanced intellect to understand Jamie's advanced thinking for a girl her age."

Landis clicked his pen.

Yeah, Belichek got the message—both parts of it. The guy was dissing Mags, and Belichek was not to lose his cool. But, c'mon, how often did he?

"A woman who refused to associate her name with the Sunshine Foundation when it might have been of benefit at the beginning. We've gone along without her dubious name recognition and her knee-jerk support for law enforcement."

Landis clicked his pen. Louder. The point and the thin plastic reservoir of ink protruded from the pen's tip, then took a left. It would write no more.

Belichek's irritation deflated when he saw Landis' rigid jaw—he hadn't been warning Belichek, but reminding himself.

"Jamie had far more advanced thinking on such matters. That's why she had the imagination to start the foundation to help the underserved. Although advanced thinking did not save her from more predictable foibles of her age."

The guy kept angling for an opening to tell them something to do with Jamie's personal life. *Let him get it off his chest.*

Landis did. "What kind of foibles?"

"Ones with impressive physiques and unimpressive intellects."

"Any names?" Belichek allowed no expression into his voice or face.

"I am reasonably certain each of them possessed a name, although I either did not know or did not retain such information, consigning it to the region of my memory tasked with ephemeral matters."

"Hard to track down ephemeral," Landis said with an edge.

Hendrickson York raised his hands and shoulders in a man-of-the-world shrug. "I cannot help you with that, uh, gentlemen."

"If you do remember them, please let us know." In addition to Carl Arbendroth, they had a couple other names from neighbors, one from Maggie. And they'd likely pick up more once they talked to more foundation staff members. "What about—?"

"Although the most recent one… The name… It's on the tip of my tongue. Charles? Or was it Claude…? Ah. Carl Arbendroth, that was the name."

Landis began to reach in his jacket for another pen to make a show of writing down the name. Belichek handed over his.

"He and Jamison Chancellor were seeing each other when she was preparing to go away to write?"

Belichek liked that question. They knew Jamie hadn't been dating immediately before her death—from the neighbor and Maggie. But asking York could show what he knew or what he would share of what he knew.

"I don't believe so, though it was hard to keep track when they came and went so quickly. Quite—"

"Ephemeral. Yes, sir. What else, if anything, do you know about their relationship?"

"I know he was unwilling to relinquish his claim to her when she ended the affair." The snap of those words said Landis' implication that York didn't really know anything got under his skin.

Having pricked the guy's ego, Landis paved the way for the interviewee to apply balm to that prick with a gush of words.

"How did he demonstrate his unwillingness, sir?"

"Incessant phone calls and other communications. Deliveries of flowers that started cloying, then turned, well, I can only say macabre. Black roses—not at all original—followed by dark purple blooms with a skeleton hand among them. Faux, I hardly need say, though sufficiently startling to set off a number of the volunteers, especially since it was early September, not the time of Halloween jokes. In addition, he tried numerous times to get in to see her—trying to force his way into this office."

"What about other places?"

"I cannot attest to what extremes he employed elsewhere, though it seems highly improbable that he limited his distasteful behavior to this office. There was an incident at the restaurant downstairs with our staff and volunteers gathered for a lunch meeting. He had to be escorted out, still insisting he talk to Jamie. It is the sort of drama one is not surprised to find surrounding a very young woman."

"Why didn't you tell the police officer who came to your home about Carl Arbendroth when you were questioned immediately after her body was found?"

"The uniformed officer—" That rankled. "—who first came to my house did not ask me about that aspect of Jamie's life. Nor did you or your nearly silent companion until a moment ago. As soon as you asked, I revealed what I knew."

"This is a murder investigation of someone you have known for a couple decades, someone you work for, someone you presumably—" Landis tapped the accelerator on that word. "—liked. This is not a game show. You need to reveal what you know without waiting for the precise question. For your own sake, because you certainly wouldn't want us to spend unnecessary time investigating you as a suspect."

York huffed in outrage.

Landis kept going. "And for the sake of the investigation into this homicide. So, let's get this clear. If there is any information you know or suspect that pertains to Jamison Chancellor, this foundation, or otherwise, that might help with our investigation, you will volunteer it. From now on."

Silence.

"Is that understood, sir?"

"Yes, yes."

"Were you aware of anyone who had a quarrel with Jamison Chancellor?"

"There were always families who became impatient with not receiving as much help or as soon as they wanted it, though you would need to talk to Celeste about that. She handles that aspect of the foundation."

"Anyone you know of specifically?"

"No."

"Anyone else who had a quarrel with Jamison Chancellor."

"Not that I'm aware of."

Landis paused before slowly standing. "All right. I'll leave you my card. If you think of anything about Jamison Chancellor, the people who surround her, the fortunes of the Sunshine Foundation—anything—we will expect a phone call from you."

CHAPTER TWELVE

THAT WAS THE best.

The. Best.

Oz Zeedyk closed his eyes to relive the moments.

The look on their faces—the cops and those full-of-themselves assholes who liked to call themselves the legitimate media. If they were legitimate, he'd be a bastard every time when it meant he got a scoop and the chance to shove it up their asses.

Not to mention the other podcasters who sat silently and lamely.

That so-called Public Information Officer looked like an idiot, woodenly defending the detectives when politics and rivalries were tearing apart his precious detective section. And he had no idea what else was to come. No. Idea.

Zeedyk checked his phone. Nothing.

Yet, he reminded himself. Nothing yet.

The turd he hired to video the news conference so he wouldn't be bogged down with that crap better have gotten good footage.

DMV's numbers were going to jump like crazy with him breaking the news on the Jamison Chancellor case.

Video would bring in even more. The advertisers would be begging him to take their money any second now. He'd get the turd to do posts all over social media, too, keep the juice flowing.

No story was so big it couldn't get bigger.

Especially the stories that never got told. The ones too small for the cops to care about.

So, yeah, it was the best ... but only for now. There was more to come and it was going to get better and better.

And he was going to love every second of it.

About damned time.

✦ ✦ ✦ ✦

WITH YORK'S OFFICE door closed behind them, Belichek and Landis exchanged a look.

If caught on a camera, it would appear to be two stoic law enforcement officers glancing at each other.

They knew better.

Landis said, *Smug bastard. Setting all his poison darts out in a row. Doesn't mean some of them aren't true.*

Doesn't mean all of them aren't lies. Who next?

After the silent, deadpan communion, Landis tipped his head toward the far end of the hallway, where they could see an open door.

Only the top of a messy head of hair showed above one of five computer monitors arrayed around a desk.

The name plate on the door read Adam Delattre. The guy who'd been by the front desk.

"Adam Delattre, hi. Detective Landis from the Fairlington Police Department." Belichek identified himself, before Landis continued. "We said we wanted to talk to you, gathering information to help us investigate Jamison Chancellor's murder."

A head with more messy hair nearly reaching narrow shoulders popped up over the top of the monitors. "I'll help you any way I can."

Delattre shoveled loose cables off a couple chairs. Landis' lip lifted slightly as he sat amid the dust on the seat.

"Jamie was the best," the younger man said, not waiting to be asked a question. "It doesn't seem possible. Have you made any progress?"

"It's early."

"Yeah? Huh."

"What do you do for the foundation?"

"Just about anything that has to do with a computer. I started as a volunteer as a kid, fixing their old computers, then getting the new set-up. They were going to buy a package, until I showed Jamie how I could get them a lot more power for less money by putting together components myself. After that, Jamie would come to me about lots of stuff. Repairs, but also deciding which apps to use, figuring out financial software that meshed with the accountant's, all sorts of things."

Considerably more than York's description.

"Social media?"

"Yeah. Jamie was good at it—just being herself—but I put together a lot of the posts and videos and stuff to save her time, then do all the scheduling and tracking. The rest of them… They couldn't upload to save their lives. And if they did, they were all over the place on message. Now, it all comes through me. For quality control, consistency, scheduling."

"Do you like that? A true IT guy like you?"

"It's not my favorite, but it's what the foundation needs."

"Tell us about the last time you saw Jamie."

Sorrow shadowed his face. "You mean when we were all leaving that Friday after work?"

Landis made a noncommittal sound, letting him decide the direction of his answer.

"She was like always. A little excited, I think, to get back into her book, get it done. A little sad, too, to leave us for the month."

"Tell us about when she left."

"We all walked out together. She was shooing us out, saying we shouldn't work on a holiday weekend. I should have stayed, but she worried about me working too much, so I left then and came back Saturday."

"Who walked out together?"

"Me and Celeste, with Jamie." He looked toward the ceiling, recalling the moment. "Bethany—she's a new hire to help Celeste, although… And then Denise. She's one of our most reliable volunteers. And a new volunteer. Then Hendrickson at the back, making a big deal of locking up, as if Celeste and I don't have keys, too."

"What happened next?"

He looked a bit mystified. "We all went downstairs and out the door to the parking lot, is that what you mean?"

"Yeah. And then what?"

"Uh, everybody sort of scattered. Jamie walks most days and she did that day. Celeste went the other direction toward the Metro. I got on my bike to go to my apartment. The others got in their cars and…" His thin shoulders lifted. "I don't know. Went home, I guess."

"When did you next see them?"

"The next Tuesday. Hendrickson and Celeste, anyway. Don't remember about the others. Sometime that week, I'm sure. Denise is in at least once a week, usually more."

"What about the other employee, Bethany Usher?"

"Oh. That's right. She was on vacation that week. I didn't have much to do with her so it doesn't have any effect on me, honestly."

"What did you do Labor Day weekend?"

"Besides working here Saturday? I was mostly on my computer at my apartment."

"Playing video games?"

He hunched one shoulder. "Nah. Waste of time. I did stuff for the foundation. I have an idea for a new program to look for perfect donors. Not waste a lot of time on people who won't stick with us, not guessing who's a long-term prospect and who's not."

Probably not going to concerts with them, either. York and Delattre did not sound as if they were in sync.

"When you came in here that Saturday of Labor Day weekend, was anybody else here while you were?"

Head shake.

"Hear from anybody? See anything? A message, maybe, a phone call?"

A head shake for each.

"I'm sure nobody was here when I arrived. I was working on the program, but I think I'd have known if someone came in. Hey, when am I going to get my equipment back? Your people took key components and these replacements are not equal to my set up. It takes a lot of time to configure them to do what I need, not to mention there are things like that donation program I can't work on."

"Sorry. That happens in murder investigations. How long it takes depends on a lot of factors. But you're helping to make it as fast as possible by answering our questions. What did you know about Jamie's plans?"

"For going to the mountains to write her book, you mean? She'd done it before, you know. Couple times since I got hired. What I knew about it?" He lifted thin shoulders. "Left from work to start getting ready to leave Sunday. She'd been working late all week, getting a house lined up for a new family in Silver Springs. That came together Thursday. She used Friday to catch up. The family got into the house the next Wednesday. Jamie would have liked that."

"What time Sunday did she plan to leave?"

Another lift of his shoulders. "No idea. And it wasn't for sure. She said she might go Monday instead."

"Did you have any contact with her after she left here that Friday after work?"

He shook his head.

"Phone, text, anything?"

Continued head-shaking.

"Did she tell you where she planned to stay in the mountains? Or how she planned to get there?"

Still more head-shaking.

Nor did he appear interested in these logistics.

"Did Jamie talk to you about things around here at the foundation?"

"Yeah. Jamie liked to get lots of input. She'd ask everyone's opinion and then consider what they said seriously."

Behind the young man's wistfulness, Belichek suspected, lurked the shadow of Hendrickson York.

"She talked to you about things beyond your specialty in IT?"

"Yeah. Right from the start. She was like that with everybody, including the volunteers."

"What about Bethany Usher?"

"I guess. Course I know a lot more about the foundation and what it needs and what's good for it than I did when I started." He grimaced. "Or than Bethany does after a few months here."

"She was hired to help the office manager?"

"Celeste, yeah. Though Celeste does a whole lot more than run the office. She does that all right, but also a lot of the financial stuff, and contact with the client families—prospective and the ongoing clients. She keeps up with them, makes sure they have what they need to get over rough patches. Jamie calls Celeste her eyes and ears with the clients. Plus, she coordinates the volunteers."

"What about Hendrickson York?"

"He deals only with donors."

"And Jamie?"

"She deals—dealt—with donors, too. A lot of the big ones wanted to meet her in person and Hendrickson was always on her to spend more time on outreach. She'd also work with the client families—that's what she liked best—and volunteers."

"What about the financial aspects? Did she stay up-to-date on those?"

"Sure. She kept on top of everything. Knew the donor figures and trend reports I put together as well as every listing on the roster of potential client families."

"What do you think of having management coming in from outside."

"I didn't like that at first. Changing things. But Jamie showed me how it was the best thing for the foundation and that has to be the top priority. Always. That's what she said, that's what she lived. She showed all of us that our sacrifices made the foundation a better place. And now, the management company's really important."

"Because of Jamie's death."

"Yeah. I was just looking at what's coming in from the website and already donations are through the roof. The good we'll be able to do— Jamie would be the first one to be thrilled by that." Tears stood along his lower eyelids.

He turned toward the far monitor, as if something had called his attention there. He wiped the tears with his back turned.

"Are you aware of Jamie having issues with anyone?"

"You mean that jackass she'd dated?"

CHAPTER THIRTEEN

"**Tell us about** him," Landis invited.

"He wouldn't leave her alone after she broke up with him."

"Did you see that first-hand?"

"Yeah. We were having a lunch meeting downstairs, and he came in, insisting he had to talk to her. Tried to drag her out. I, uh, I grabbed his arm so she could get away."

"Did you see other instances? With him or anyone else? Anything that indicated someone might want to cause her harm?"

"Is this like that did she have any enemies question? No way. Everybody loved Jamie. Too much. That was the problem with that jerk. Called her all the time. Texts—could always tell when they were from him. She'd look at her phone and her face would sort of go stiff. Not like Jamie at all."

"What about a client family? Any disgruntled?"

He looked stunned. "No. They all loved her."

"What was Jamie like?"

"Jamie's like no one else. She's… she was magic for the foundation. With donors, with the clients—that's what she called the people we help."

"So she was the public face, but you do all the work getting the word out on social media and—"

"No, no what I do is nothing. Anybody could do this. Jamie brought so much attention to the foundation. Her story *is* the story of the foundation."

"Like celebrities do with their foundations, huh?"

"*Celebrities.*" He dismissed them with one word. "They have it easy. They slap their names on a charity and half the work's done for them. They're not slogging in the office the way Jamie did."

"She wasn't going to do that anymore, was she?"

"You mean the management company? Like I said before, she got that so she could spend more time representing the foundation. That's what came first with her always. Whatever she could do, however she could do it.

"It's like what people talk about back when Princess Diana died and everybody was mourning and seeing all the good she did. Now people are realizing how wonderful and special Jamie was. They're seeing what she was working for."

"And you're working for?"

"Sure. But not like Jamie. No one was like Jamie."

"What kind of place is this to work?"

"The best. We're doing important things here. Changing lives. I know first-hand what it means. My family was one the Sunshine Foundation helped. I remember when Jamie and Celeste came to talk to my family. And then the day we moved into the new place." He looked around. "Got me my first computer that day."

And changed his life. Words unspoken, but clear in the room.

THE SUNSHINE FOUNDATION'S office manager, Celeste Renfro, was the woman who'd greeted them when they arrived. The one who would not let herself cry. She still sat at the desk. No one else was in sight.

Belichek realized the sense of familiarity was because she reminded him of his grandmother.

They were both women to be reckoned with and blessed with formidable bosoms, as Gran used to say.

He flashed back to watching an old movie with his grandparents. Something with Cary Grant—his grandmother's favorite. In a Paris nightclub, Grant tried to maneuver an orange over a matron's front without using his hands. Grant looked uncomfortable. The matron looked pained.

"He should be enjoying himself," Grandpa protested.

"Rutherford, behave yourself," his wife scolded. Her tone changed when she added, "Though she certainly should be enjoying herself with Cary Grant."

"Talk about behaving yourself," Grandpa scolded back.

Then they looked at each other and laughed.

He was old enough to pick up at least some of the subtext and be mortified that they could possibly think—much less do—such things.

Law enforcement certainly broadened your horizons on what people could think and do.

Now, he hoped his grandparents had enjoyed themselves to the max.

Before Landis could ask her anything, Celeste Renfro called out, "Denise, please come sit at the desk. I need to talk to these detectives."

She stood and led them back down the hall to the door past Hendrickson York's.

"Wait. This is Jamison Chancellor's office. Please take us to your office."

"I don't have one. We can stay at the desk in the middle of everything or go in what we laughingly call the conference room with those two big-eared volunteers. I thought you'd want to see Jamie's office."

She'd unlocked the door by that point.

"This has been locked since she left before Labor Day?"

"No. Told you. We don't have the room to spare to leave an office closed up. It's been used most days since she left, as it was used most days for something or other beyond her individual work when she was here. She would go in the supply closet if she needed to. By herself. It wouldn't hold the three of us."

They'd need to search the office, but forensics, with people in and out over the past three weeks? Small hope.

She swung the door open.

The room had the same window as York's. A smaller and older desk with packed bookshelves behind it. More visitors' chairs.

Photographs, drawings, and charts all over the walls.

"I locked the door when I came in this morning."

"Why?" Belichek asked her.

She paused several beats. "Barn door after the horse is gone, I suppose. Especially with all of us in and out these past weeks, still…"

"Had someone been in here to your knowledge—since you heard of Jamison's murder, I mean," Landis said.

Another pause. "Hendrickson was in here when I arrived this morning. To my knowledge he had not touched a thing. He was standing by the desk. Just standing." A tinge of shared grief came through. As if she heard it, she briskly added, "Might as well sit down. Don't use the green chair. It's going to break the next time someone sits in it."

She also took a visitor's chair, so they sat in a triangle.

"How long have you worked for the foundation?"

"More than twelve years. As Jamie got her degree and took it full-time."

"You must have seen a lot of changes."

"No and yes. The cause didn't change. Jamie didn't change, not who she was. But the Sunshine Foundation certainly grew. Especially once she started writing the books. The first one did fine, but that second one lit a fuse and the foundation exploded. Donors coming in from far and wide instead of the tight little circle who supported us from the start. And they all wanted access to Jamie. That meant she hardly had time to breathe, much less think about the follow-up book. She needed to get away, to be by herself—"

She broke off and swallowed hard.

Was she thinking that Jamison Chancellor had been by herself when she died? Except for her killer.

If so, it didn't color her voice as she continued. "That's why the transition to professional management was so important. It would free Jamie up to be Jamie, to let go of so much of the day-to-day running of the foundation and, instead, take being its public face to another level."

"That's sort of what Hendrickson York said in explaining why he led Jamie to the decision to bring in that outside management company."

She snorted. "You don't believe that for a second."

She was good. Belichek thought Landis had done a great job of delivering that statement.

CHAPTER FOURTEEN

"OR, IF YOU do believe it," Celeste Renfro continued, "you're a lot stupider than you look and I don't believe that. Hendrickson loves the idea of Jamie backing off, but hates the idea of the nonprofit management coming in. He wants to be in charge. He's always wanted to be in charge. The fool. Lying about it now when everybody here knows how he felt. That man couldn't conspire over a surprise birthday party."

Landis chuckled lightly. Celeste appeared to take it as genuine without being overtly relieved.

"Then give us," he said, "the real rundown about how the Sunshine Foundation operates and the decision to bring in this management company."

She went into the operations.

Not with enough detail to be blatant she welcomed that topic, but plenty to put off talking about the management company.

Landis caught her taking a breath and said, "Did you feel the management company would fill in Jamison Chancellor's weaknesses?"

"No." A near-snap. "She didn't need any weaknesses filled in. She did fine running the Sunshine Foundation. More than fine and better than anybody else could have done. She's—she was—the heart and soul of this place. On top of that, she could do every aspect of it better than any of the rest of us. Problem is, she couldn't do all aspects all the time. Had to make choices. So, she worked with Hendrickson on donors, with me on most of the rest, and a bit with Adam on the tech stuff. Suppose she gave him his head the most of any of us because of what he did. But to do all that she did, she was working all the time.

Working and working and working. Can't go on like that without getting burned out."

"You sound worried about her."

"I was worried about her."

"Others here at the foundation, too?"

"I did not chatter with them about her."

"But you could have drawn an impression of whether they were concerned about her. Adam Delattre?"

"Not that I ever noticed."

"Bethany Usher?"

"No."

"Any of the volunteers?"

She paused half a beat. "I heard Denise say to Jamie that last week that she looked tired. Jamie was working extra to get things cleared out before she left, stayed late each night until Friday."

"What about Hendrickson York?"

"I have no idea."

"Would you be surprised to know he called her at home Saturday morning?"

"I would not be surprised to hear that he called her at home that Saturday or anywhere else any other day. He fussed at her constantly. Calling her every day like she was a schoolgirl who needed to check in with him."

"Including while she was on her writing retreats?"

"No. Not then. Probably why she made them so remote—no signal."

"When did she plan to leave?"

"Sunday." No equivocating from Celeste.

"Do you know how she intended to get to the cabin this time?"

Her eyes sharpened. "Why? Is something wrong with her car?"

"Do you have reason to think there was?"

"Okay, I see. You're not going to answer my questions. This is a one-way street. Fine. I assumed she'd drive herself. That's what she'd done the other times."

"If she weren't going to drive, how would you think she might get there?"

She looked at each of them for a long moment. "She might ask someone else to drive her. When she's done these retreats to finish books before, she gets all her provisions in ahead of time and never leaves the cabin. That's part of her routine, part of focusing only on the book. So maybe she decided she didn't need a car while she was up there. Especially if she felt there was a reason to leave her car here."

"What kind of reason?"

"Someone else needed it," she said immediately.

"Do you have reason to think that happened?"

"Beyond logic? No."

"If she let someone borrow her car, who might that be?"

Celeste breathed out shortly through her nose. "Anybody. Everybody. A neighbor, the girl who cuts her hair, one of the waiters down in the restaurant, anybody. But, no, I have no reason to think a specific person wanted to borrow her car."

"So, leaving her car here, who might she ask for a ride to the mountains?"

"Not me. I can drive, but prefer not to. Adam doesn't have a license. Or a car. Perhaps Hendrickson. Or one of the volunteers. A neighbor, maybe. There's a woman who lives behind her she likes a lot. She was close to a couple next door, but they moved last year and she hasn't connected with the new people."

"One of her cousins?" Belichek asked.

Her gaze slid to him. "No." No elaboration on that.

Landis said, "You didn't mention the other foundation employee. We need to talk to her, too. Bethany Usher."

"She's not here. Don't know where she is. She hasn't returned from vacation."

Landis let surprise show. "Why?"

"I have no idea."

And then Celeste didn't say more. Forcing Landis to push with another question. "Have you heard from her?"

"No."

He went super polite, which few people recognized as his most dangerous mode. "Ms. Renfro, please explain, in detail."

"Bethany Usher was given leave to take off the rest of the week after Labor Day. She was scheduled to return to work the next Monday, a week after Labor Day. She did not."

"Neither Hendrickson York nor Adam Delattre mentioned this."

"Don't imagine either of them cared. They don't like her. I cared because it's meant about twenty percent more work for me." In other words, Bethany had done some, but not much work.

"Do you like her?" Belichek asked.

Celeste Renfro turned her head to him. For half a second he expected his grandmother's voice to come out. "No."

"You haven't heard from her?"

"No. We tried calling, leaving messages, texts, Adam checked out her social media, and said she has not been active."

Landis took in a lot of air. "It didn't occur to any of you to report this, a woman overdue to return to work for more than two weeks?"

She clicked her tongue. "When? The day she didn't return to work? Is that a job for the police? A week later, when she's most likely extended her time at the beach because the weather's good or she met a guy? Or this morning, in the eight minutes between stopping the wailing of shock when those two volunteers found out about Jamie and your arrival? Okay, you think it's suspicious she didn't come back on time. But we don't. She never came to work on time, never came back from a break on time, and never worked until quitting time. The woman is a flake. Do you know how many days she didn't show up without calling in? Six—*six*—in three and a half months. And Jamie knew what she was getting when she hired her. Bethany Usher's work history is like Morse code—dashes and dots. Nothing longer. Only thing surprising about her disappearing act is it took this long. I told Jamie that I didn't expect her to last more than a month or two."

"Was there anyone here she's spent time with?"

"No. You don't think I asked around in the past couple weeks?"

"But you didn't report her missing to the police."

Celeste half growled at Landis. "If every employer she's stiffed reported Bethany Usher missing you'd need a separate department for her."

"We'll need a copy of all the information you have on her. We're also going to ask your cooperation in locking the door to Jamison Chancellor's office and giving us any keys to it."

"Search warrant?"

"We'll get one if necessary, but you can help our investigation into this matter by not making that necessary."

"Fine." She started to rise.

"We're not done yet, Celeste. What did you do over the Labor Day weekend?"

"I painted my living room."

"Anything else?"

"Have you ever tried to cover up dark red? Primer and two coats."

"Did you have any communication with Jamison Chancellor after leaving here the Friday before Labor Day weekend?"

"No, I did not."

"Did you know, specifically, where she was going?"

"No, I did not."

"What about Carl Arbendroth?"

"What about him?"

"What was his relationship with Jamison Chancellor?"

"*Over* was what it was."

"He never came here after it ended?"

"He tried. Didn't get past me."

Landis stared at her a moment, then cast a wide net. "Do you know or suspect anything that might benefit our investigation?"

"No."

CHAPTER FIFTEEN

DIDN'T TAKE LONG with the two volunteers to realize Denise Gutierrez knew more and talked less than Kimby Curtis.

But without sending one into Jamie's now-locked office, they were stuck with both in a conference room barely bigger than the oval table with eight chairs around it.

After easing in with the basics of names, home addressees, how long they'd volunteered here and what they did for the Sunshine Foundation, Landis asked when they'd last seen Jamison Chancellor.

"It must have been the Wednesday before—" Kimby hiccupped a sob. "Oh, God, poor Jamie. Poor, poor Jamie."

"What were you doing that day?"

"Helping Celeste update the profiles of prospective families. They'd piled up because Celeste has so many other duties and that was the whole reason for hiring Bethany, but she honestly doesn't help much, and with her not coming back from vacation—after Jamie was super generous in giving her any, considering what a short time she'd worked here and *not* reliable. We've had to go back over everything she did and—Well. I tried not to complain to Jamie about Bethany's work—so-called work—but I'm afraid some of it came out the Wednesday before Labor Day. And I feel so bad about it, bothering her about that when she only had a few days to live and her last days should not have been bothered by such things and she already looked so worn down. Not to mention I'm sure it was a text from that guy who would not leave her alone she got while we were talking that made her look so *strained*. I mean, truly, not like herself at all. The only other time I'd seen her look like that was when that guy—Carl something—broke into the restaurant. I mean, literally broke in and grabbed her, yanking her out of her chair and dragging her after him and we were all *frozen*. Absolutely frozen until it was almost too late, then Adam jumped up and pushed the Carl guy at the same time Jamie hit him in the face with her purse—Carl she hit in the face, not Adam. But who would have predicted little Adam Delattre would be the hero, making that Carl scuttle right out of there? But that didn't stop him from bothering her and bothering her."

"Did he ever come here to see her?" Belichek asked.

"He tried. Celeste *rousted* him," Kimby said with satisfaction.

"And you, Denise?" Landis slid in when Kimby took a deep breath.

Turning toward the other volunteer, Belichek noticed a particular photo among the montage on the wall—a duplicate of the one from Jamie's house.

"The Friday before Labor Day. We all wrapped up about the same time and left together. I had been working on the profiles, in between training a new volunteer on sending donation thank yous."

"She's a wonderful trainer. Absolutely wonderful," Kimby inserted. "She trained me three—no, four years ago. It will be four years in November."

"How new a volunteer?" Landis asked Denise.

"It was her first day."

That dropped the new volunteer down the priority list.

"Were you here other days that week, Denise?"

"Yes. Thursday."

"What were you doing?"

"Working on family profiles, putting them in order, filling in blanks."

"Left by Bethany," Kimby inserted.

Landis glanced at her, then back to Denise. "These profiles, they're applications to the foundation for help?"

"We don't call them applications—"

"Makes it sound too much like asking for a handout," Kimby said.

"—because profile is more accurate. They are a profile of a family's situation."

"So you didn't have any specific cause to talk to Jamison Chancellor either Friday or Thursday? An issue to go over with her pertaining to what you were reviewing?"

"No."

"But you did go into her office and talk to her?"

"Yes."

"Which day?"

"Thursday."

"What did you talk about?"

"My daughter's applications to colleges, the weather, the best way to prepare outdoor flower beds for winter, the Major League baseball standings, and professional football."

"Quite a wide-ranging array of topics."

"We were eating lunch together at her desk. We did that sometimes. Mostly another member of staff joined us. That day it was only the two of us."

"Anything else?"

"Yes. I told her she was working too hard and looked tired." The corners of her eyes lifted with faint amusement. "I have reason to believe Celeste Renfro overheard that portion of the conversation. She might have overheard all of it, but I can only say it was likely she heard that part."

"What do you base that on?"

"She called in through the open door that Jamie looked like—" *Death.* She broke off and paled, not completing the idiom. "That she agreed Jamie was tired and needed a break."

"Did others express concern about her?"

"Not in my hearing."

"Was writing the book supposed to be a break?"

Denise didn't answer.

Kimby did. "Being away from everyone here had to be a break for her. It can get to be like a nursery with every baby crying out, *Mama, Mama, Mama.* Except it's *Jamie, Jamie, Jamie.* And each trying to be louder than the other."

Denise's lips pressed together, but Belichek thought it was to prevent a smile, not in disapproval. She said, "Having one focus, even if it's a demanding one, can be a break after being divided among many tasks for a long time."

A measured, careful agreement.

"Is Bethany Usher among those who called out for Jamie's attention?" Belichek asked.

Kimby's mouth opened, then closed.

Denise looked thoughtful an extra moment. "Not as much. I mean, she certainly talked with Jamie, spent time with her, asked her questions, but it wasn't the same. It was—"

"She's not a fan of Jamie, the way others are. The way most of us are," Kimby said. "Jamie never got annoyed or irritated with people. She has a way of drawing you in, making you feel special that bowls over most people. Not Bethany. Bit of a cold fish if you ask me."

Something like a wince from Denise. An assessment of Bethany's nature or her reaction to Kimby?

Landis pursued with a direct question, "What do you think, Denise?"

"I haven't worked with her enough to have a true gauge of her personality."

"Are you kidding?" Kimby asked. "The way she went on and on about herself while we were working together. Nobody else could get a word in edgewise."

"What did she tell you about herself?" Landis asked.

"Oh, she knew this senator and she'd dated that staff member—which I knew was absolute hooey, because his husband is my neighbor's cousin, and he does not bat both ways. Much less cheat. So don't believe it for a second."

"She did drop a lot of names, with little to no supporting details," Denise said.

"What she did before she came to the Sunshine Foundation? Any background? Previous jobs? Schools? Where she grew up?"

"Also sparse on details."

"She did say Delaware beaches couldn't hold a candle to the Jersey Shore." Which apparently rankled, judging from Kimby's tone.

"She did." Denise looked from Landis to Belichek. "It's not a fact, but she gave the impression she grew up going to the Jersey Shore. She always said shore, never beach. And there was a trace of an accent at times."

"More than a trace," Kimby said.

Landis focused on Denise.

"Was there anything of particular significance in the profiles you worked on that week?"

Surprise lifted her eyebrows. "Not that I remember. Other than typos and missing information, things like that from Bethany, nothing has stood out with any of the profiles, not that week or any other time."

CHAPTER SIXTEEN

LANDIS WAS UNCHARACTERISTICALLY quiet on the return to his car. Belichek waited.

Only when he was pulling out of the parking area did Landis say what he'd been chewing on.

"Client family angle doesn't seem real promising. We'll try more promising angles first." He left a gap, then added, "That stuff from York about Jamison Chancellor being like her aunt, what did you think?"

"Judging from pictures, he's right that Ally looks the most like her."

Landis grimaced as he checked cross traffic. "Yeah. Like you think that's what I'm talking about. The stuff about strengths and weaknesses."

"He said drawbacks."

"Fine. Drawbacks."

"From the journals—" He underscored the word. "—Hendrickson York has some points. Wouldn't describe them the same way. But, yeah, I can see a tendency to see sunshine when most would carry an umbrella. When she probably needed an umbrella."

Landis nodded. He wasn't done, though.

Belichek waited.

"What he said about not seeing below a glossy surface... Thought sour grapes at first, but..."

"Mentor no longer being listened to? Resenting the outside management?"

"Maybe." Even as he said the word, Landis jerked his head. "No. More like a jealous guy. The one who got turned down."

Belichek felt the hairs on the back of his neck rise. That happened when he and Landis landed on the same and not very obvious page. Underneath all those words, there'd been strong emotion from York.

"He's had to share her with more people at the foundation lately and the management company coming in would be another layer, after years of, essentially, being her only advisor, of having her to himself."

"Yeah. Then there's the way Celeste Renfro reacted. She sure boomeranged away from York."

Belichek grunted agreement.

"I know that grunt. What?"

"When she jumped from York to Delattre, it was pretty damn obvious. So, we took her back to York. Wonder in retrospect if that was the intention."

"Get us away from Delattre? Interesting thought. We'll keep that in mind. Good grunt."

Belichek got halfway to a grin. "Something else. When she said she was worried about Jamie, you asked about other people at the foundation. Could have been taken as were they worried about Jamie? Or was she worried about other people at the foundation? She jumped on that first interpretation."

"Eager," Landis agreed. "Didn't want to talk about someone else she was worried about? Does that bring us back to Delattre?"

"Could. Or could be overthinking it and shouldn't miss the obvious."

"The former boyfriend. Yeah. He also could explain the car being left in the garage."

"Because she asked him to drive her to the cabin? Why, when she was trying to make it clear it was over?"

"Maybe it wasn't over and that's why she asked him for a ride. To get back together."

"Or she thought it was clear it was over between them, so she felt comfortable asking him for a ride when somebody needed her car," Belichek proposed. "But he thought it was to get back together, gets to her house, and discovers how wrong he was. He shoots her in rage."

"Having brought a shotgun along?"

"It's a weak point," Belichek agreed. "Lending it to her for her time in the mountains?"

Landis' turn to grunt. "But then why's the car still there?"

"The car might not tie into the killing. The person Jamie lent it to picked it up after she was supposed to leave, then returned it sometime before yesterday, not going in the house either time."

"We'll see what forensics says. Then make another pass at the Sunshine Foundation asking specifically about the car. But first, the neighbors."

"Did you notice York's only one-word answer?"

"About if he knew where Jamison Chancellor was going. And that might be helpful if she'd been killed at a secret destination instead of inside her front door. Or if there was some reason York or anybody else desperately needed to stop her from going wherever she was supposed to go. Anything from Mags?"

"No."

✧   ✧   ✧   ✧

THE HOUSE THAT backed up to Jamison Chancellor's across the alley was only as wide as a front door and a tall, narrow window, with enough brick work to keep them from blending together. The two floors above each sported a solitary window.

The woman who answered their bell-ringing was middle-height, gray-haired, and dressed in oversized shorts and t-shirt, topped by a beige vest like photographers used to wear, back when they needed lots of pockets to carry film canisters.

Each of the pockets in her vest bulged, whether it was with film or other items, giving her an overall lumpy appearance, not helped by her hair bun sliding to one side.

Her eyes were a sharp and warm caramel brown.

"Ah, the detectives are at my door. Did you come to see me as a palate cleanser after Phil's marble monument to bad taste? No, from your looks of confusion you haven't been to Phil Xavier's house yet, or you would have understood the allusion immediately. Thought you'd start with Jamie's next-door neighbor. My mistake."

They had tried the home of Phil Xavier—the neighbor Schmidt talked to last night, according to his report—but when there'd been no answer, they came around the block to start on the alley neighbors.

"Come in, come in," she invited. "I'm Imogen Wooton. I'll do whatever I can to help you catch the bastard who killed Jamie Chancellor. No, no, don't bother to say it. I know you're not officially ID'ing her."

Her house seemed like a half-sized model. Although it had enough smell for full-sized. Not a bad smell, but unexpected. Was the woman manufacturing corn chips?

"You'll have to follow me out back," she said as she led them through a front room with a couch on one side and a fireplace on the other, leaving barely enough room to walk single-file, with Belichek at the rear.

Past that, a narrow stairway led up on the left. They went to the right, down the center of a kitchen area with shallow counters on the right and appliances tucked in under the stairs. The next compartment in what felt like a railroad car of a house held a mini table against the left wall and three chairs.

Imogen kept on going, heading for a door leading out the back to a miniaturized enclosed patio.

"We'd prefer to talk to you inside," Landis said from right behind her.

"I'm sure you would, since voices can carry outside, not to mention offering fewer natural methods of overhearing. But I need to retrieve my dogs."

Without pause, she went out the door.

Landis gave a brief eye-roll over his shoulder, then followed her, not letting her out of his sight once contact was made.

Some might consider that overkill with Imogen Wooton, but you never knew. That's why you followed procedure.

In other circumstances, Belichek might have stayed inside, scoping out the interior. But, without going upstairs, they'd seen it all. And he wanted to hear what Imogen Wooton had to say.

He got one answer.

The source of the corn chip smell was a trio of medium-sized, mixed breed dogs, currently lying in a patch of sun atop a pile of damp towels next to an oval tub filled with water sporting dingy suds. At the moment, the dogs smelled like wet corn chips. Splatter marks on the brick patio inside a border of flower beds, indicated the dogs had expended their energy by shaking off excess water.

All three animals looked at the two newcomers, thumped their tails, then put their heads back down.

"Guard dogs," she said bitterly, though she didn't mean it. A fact proven when she dug treats out of the most convenient right-hand pocket of her vest and distributed them evenly. "Every last one of them. If someone broke in, they couldn't be bothered to even pretend they're a deterrent."

In that tiny house, Belichek thought, the three dogs would clog the passageways so much, they would be a deterrent.

The woman grabbed the side of the tub, clearly intending to tip it sideways into a flower bed limping toward the end of the season.

Belichek stepped in and edged her aside. "Where do you want it, ma'am."

"On the marigolds. The orange flowers. Thank you. I could do it myself—if I couldn't I shouldn't be on my own in this house, much less have these three mongrels." Three tail thumps indicated they were accustomed to being addressed that way and viewed it as affection. "But it is nice to have it done for me now and then. Thank you."

"It's an interesting house," Landis said.

"A spite house."

"A what?"

Belichek righted the tub with only minimal dampness transferred to him and turned in time to see Imogen Wooton's disapproving expression.

"How long have you lived in Fairlington, Virginia, young man, and you don't know what a spite house is? No, don't tell me—" She held out a commanding arm. "—because it doesn't matter how long you've been here. Shouldn't be allowed to walk through Fairlington, especially Old Town, much less police it without knowing its history. Shame on them. What are they teaching you young folks these days?"

She took the tub from Belichek and stood it on end in a shed that might have started life as an old-fashioned phonebooth.

"A spite house is a time-honored tool of getting even or—more accurately—going one up on somebody you're having a feud with. Blocking a view or building so the other party can't make full use of their property, that kind of thing. Some of the finest examples are right here in our region. Why, Old Town Alexandria has the narrowest house in the country. Though it's not truly a spite house. The owner of the two houses on either side of it built that house to keep traffic from cutting through the alley between them. He enclosed the alley and declared it a house.

"But a real spite house needs a story of revenge or a feud and this one does. Did you come along the side of my house that's on Porchester Street?" Getting their nods, she continued. "Figured. Other way you'd come the long way around the block. Now, the next house to my right, which you'd have seen if you had come the long way around, was built by a couple who had one daughter. When she married, they built a house next door to them, to the left, situated where it would now have Porchester Street running through it. Gave it to the young couple as a wedding gift. A nearly exact replica of the family home, which still stands next door.

"Everything went fine—least from what we can tell from this distance in time—until the daughter died in childbirth, along with the baby. Her parents were devastated. And from letters that still exist, they never felt the son-in-law grieved deeply enough. When he not only remarried in less than a year, but brought the new bride to the house they'd built for their daughter, they were furious. But they'd deeded the house and land, and it belonged to the son-in-law.

"The mother, not in the best of health and still mourning, took a turn for the worse with her daughter's replacement swanning around the place.

"So, the father had his workers build this place in the gap between the two houses. You notice how it's closer to the sidewalk than any of the other buildings on the block?"

Belichek had guessed it was to make up for its narrowness. He should have known better. More things have an emotional cause than practical.

He'd always liked the story that Andrew Jackson set the site for the Treasury building to block the White House view of the Capitol because he and the legislature didn't get along. A spite federal building.

"Sticks out more in the back, too. That's so the people in the original house—" She gestured in that direction. "—couldn't see the people in the other house. Wouldn't ever happen these days with zoning and setback ordinances and such, but it worked for them."

"What happened to the son-in-law and his new bride?"

She sent Landis a look of approval. "Turns out she was a free-spending shrew who made his life miserable, and he had to sell the house not long before he died, which might have been satisfying to the first wife's parents if they hadn't died long before. That's what happens with spite houses. Nobody in the feud truly comes out on top. Only the people who get to live in the spite house later, assuming it's a good one and mine is."

One side of her mouth lifted in a dry grin.

"The spite got better with the next generation. Fairlington bought the son-in-law's house and tore it down. Wiped his house right out of the town plan and put a street there. That's why my little spite house has windows on one side now. Jamie's house, too. And Phil's doesn't. Won't ever. Even if he got what he wanted—which he won't—he'd get windows in his garage and his wife's closet, but not in the living space where he'd be."

At the moment, she resided in a Gloat House.

"You should talk to Garrison Enderbe next door about Phil. That's the house that belonged to that poor couple whose daughter died. Wants to gut that house and make the first floor all kitchen. If he has his way, he'd blow out the alley, too, and have the entire part of the block. The man belongs out in some McMansion with fake grass."

"And Jamie's?"

"Garage. Not as wide as he wants, but he's got plans for a car elevator, if you can believe it."

"Phil Xavier has made an offer on your house?" Landis asked.

"*An* offer? He's made almost as many as he's made on Jamie's."

"Even though it's diagonal from his house and with the alley in between?"

"Idiot's sure he can persuade the county and—and this is where he's totally off his rocker—the Old Town Committee—to let him connect across the alley. He's got designs that look like a Rube Goldberg invention. Course he's planning to fill in the patios—Jamie's and mine."

She raised her voice. "Not that he'll ever get his way. Did you hear that, Phil Xavier? I'll never give in to you. And I know you're probably listening to me. Every word."

A sound resembling a window closing came to them. Possibly a coincidence.

Landis, no believer in coincidence, said, "Let's go inside to continue this. Unless you'd like to come to the department…?"

Nothing of threat was in his tone, but he was ready to get on with it.

"The police department?" Good thing Landis hadn't been using it as a threat, because Imogen set her head at an angle and looked up at them like a mischievous bird. "The interrogation room? Two-way mirror? Smell of despair and psychopathy?"

"We call it an interview room. No mirrors needed, because we video and can see the live feed. You're right about the smell, but it's more from old socks."

She grinned, clearly delighted with Landis' response. "Way to break an old woman's heart and shatter her cherished illusions. C'mon inside. I suppose you're right after all. No sense giving Phil Xavier what he wants, even when it comes to eavesdropping. Besides, sun's gone in and it would be just like this pack to get pneumonia on me." Her grumbling did a poor job of masking her concern for the animals, who lumbered ahead of her to be first in the door, a desire she accommodated. "Go on with you, get inside."

Waiting for the dog-jam to ease, Belichek looked around at the buildings connected by this alley.

Jamie's was significantly wider than this one, so Xavier's master plan would require complicated angles and offsets.

It made him wonder how much could be seen of comings and goings in Jamie's back patio and garage from her neighbors' second stories.

As she shooed the dogs inside, Landis turned his head to his left.

Belichek followed the direction of that look and saw wooden pegs on the wall inside the door, holding an array of keys, each neatly labeled. Below a label reading "Jamie," a peg stood empty.

CHAPTER SEVENTEEN

QUICKLY GAUGING VIEWING angles, Belichek reckoned the keys would be visible to anyone looking through the back door's glass panes.

Once they were all inside, Imogen gestured to the hard chairs around the small table near the back door.

Landis looked toward the sofa in the front room with a bit of longing, until the still-damp dogs jumped up on it with obvious familiarity. He arranged his long legs the best he could in the small space.

"My home is earning its *spite* stripes for this century as it denies Phil Xavier what he thinks he most wants."

"Thinks?" Belichek repeated.

"He's one of those who'll never be satisfied. If he got control of these three houses and made the mess of this half of the block that's his vision, he'd have yet another bigger, more grandiose, and uglier vision. It's the kind of man he is."

"What was Jamison's reaction to his plans?"

"Turned him down, of course. Nicely. Time after time, still nice. Not like me. Jamie's wasn't built as a spite house, but I sure hope it keeps on spiting Phil Xavier. As long as Jamie was there, I never gave a thought to him getting his way." She peered at them. "I suppose it's those two cousins of hers who have inherited it. Or her nice parents? Hope it's not her brothers—nothing against them, but with them living so far away, they won't be as familiar with the campaign waged by Phil Xavier."

"Do you have the key to Jamison Chancellor's house, now?" Landis said.

"No. Had it. That's how I got in. That policeman took it last night. Actually, one of those tech people. I was still holding it from when I opened the door... Odd, how your mind works at a time like that. Holding onto that key."

"Have you ever lost or misplaced it?"

Whether he'd meant it to or not, Landis' question irked her.

Before her lips formed words, Belichek could practically taste the tartness of her intended response.

Then the snap in her eyes shifted.

"You know, there was a time, about a week before she left, when I couldn't find that key to save my soul. Just when I thought I'd have to confess to her that I'd lost it, there it was, in one of my rain boots by the back door, like I'd gone to hang it on its hook and it dropped down into the boot instead."

Both men turned and saw how easily that could happen with boots and shoes on a mat directly below the key collection.

Belichek also saw she'd left the door unlocked. Was the gate to the alley locked?

"You hadn't gone into Jamison Chancellor's house in the weeks before last night?" Landis asked.

"Just how absentminded would an old lady have to be to fail to notice a corpse in the front hallway?"

"I didn't, uh, mean—"

Belichek bit back a grin at his smooth partner stumbling over his words. "Did you go into Jamison Chancellor's house by any door any time between seeing her on the Friday before Labor Day and last night?"

"Now, that's the way to ask a question." Looking pointedly at Landis, she simultaneously reproved and teased him. Turning back to Belichek, she rewarded him with a succinct, "No."

Landis asked, "Why'd you go in the front door?"

She nodded that he'd redeemed himself. "Same key opens the front and back doors. Did you know that? Well, it does. And sometimes I do go in the back. Mostly when I don't care if Mr. Nosy Xavier knows what I'm doing. Anyway, yesterday, I went out and walked around a few blocks, to get some exercise because it had been so hot all day and it wasn't until that hour that you could even breathe outside. And that brought me by the front of Jamie's on the way back to my house, so I thought I'd go in and get the next book in the mystery series I'm reading."

"When was the previous time you were in the house?"

"Let's see … that would have been the Tuesday night before Jamie left. For book club."

"Who else is in this book club?"

"No one."

"Just the two of you?"

"Yes. And we have withstood every effort to change that. Jamie and I share—shared—a penchant for particular kinds of books. Our favorites are strong mysteries with smart-ass humor. Don't look so appalled young man. I can say assed, just as I can still spot stupid asses." She paused for a thoughtful beat. "And appreciate good ones."

Red showed under Landis' collar, as if she had commented directly on his butt.

Possibly she'd eyed that part of his anatomy longer than necessary, but it had been subtle. Apparently, Landis had not missed it.

Belichek coughed, enjoying the woman and—especially—her effect on Landis. No wonder she and Jamie connected. The reference to appreciating smart-assed humor clicked with an element he'd picked up in the journals that had surprised him. It wasn't part of her public profile, yet it came through in those pages. Dry, understated, but definitely an appreciation for humor.

Had she also shared Imogen's puckish notice of a man's appeal?

Her journal writings about the men in her life gave no indication of their physical facets. Caution? Fearing the journals might someday be read? Though she opened up in other areas, including her cousins.

He jerked his head up, aware of both Imogen and Landis watching him.

"The book club—that's why you went to Jamie's house that Tuesday night?" he asked abruptly.

"*Jamie?*" she repeated, and Belichek wondered if the space on the back of *his* neck above his collar had turned red.

But she didn't pursue it.

Instead, she said, "In a way. She'd introduced me to a writer new to me on Tuesday and I've begun reading the series in order. After finishing the first book, I went into town and bought what Andersons had of the series, then ordered the rest. But I was ready to start the fourth book and that's one they didn't have in stock. I was down to the last chapter of Book Three. Didn't want to finish it until I knew I had the next one in hand. I knew Jamie had the entire series. I stopped by to get it."

"Did you notice anything odd, out of place, or that puzzled you?"

"That's your best question yet."

Landis tried not to look pleased.

Her gaze slid up to the crown molding at the juncture of wall and ceiling.

She blinked and focused back on them.

"Her clothes were ... odd."

Frowning, Landis asked evenly, "Last night, you told the responding officers that the clothes were Jamison Chancellor's. Are you changing your statement?"

"They were Jamie's clothes, like I said to that young officer at the scene, Officer Schmidt. I recognized them. But actually, what I said was I didn't know how it *couldn't* be Jamie, especially since those were her shoes. No doubt about that. There was a red stripe across the bottom of them from when Jamie stepped in some paint.

"But she never wore that black and off-white windowpane blouse with jeans. Always with a pair of slacks. Cream-colored."

Belichek asked, "Did you see any activity at Jamison Chancellor's property after the time you thought she'd left for the mountains?"

She raised both brows. "No. Would've told you, would've told the guys last night."

"Can we see the view of the back of Jamie's house from your upper floors?"

It was a cumbersome process, with the three dogs winding around their legs as they tried to negotiate the narrow stairs and even narrower paths between furniture upstairs.

The single back window on each floor showed a slice of the back of Jamie's house, including the glass-enclosed porch and a patch of patio in front of it. The garage structure blocked the view of the back door.

It also showed that at least four windows in Phil Xavier's house would look down into Jamie's patio and possibly into her house, depending how hard someone wanted to work at it.

✧ ✧ ✧ ✧

OUTSIDE IMOGEN'S FRONT door, Belichek asked, "Remember the guy at the scene when we walked Mags out? Medium height, well-dressed, lousy skin, receding hairline, compensating beard? That's Phil Xavier."

"Yeah. We'll check on the guy who lives here—the fourth corner of this quartet—then swing back by the Xavier house. The guy couldn't use an agent if he wants to buy these houses?"

"Jamie asked the same question in a journal entry about his, uh, persistence. Said it would make neighborliness much easier, and she wouldn't feel she was in danger of being pounced on every time."

"Pounced on, huh? And what Imogen Wooton said. He wants the house that much?"

"Seems to. Something happened soon after Xavier moved in that Jamie was vague about in the journal. Indicated she told him no— several times—and she suspected he's not used to that. At the scene, he emphasized she lived there alone and was real interested in who'd inherit."

"So he'd go over there, blast her in the face up close?"

"If he thought it would get him what he wanted and wouldn't get himself caught?" Knowing that was unanswerable and they'd both seen weirder, Belichek switched topics. "Interesting Imogen said Jamie never wore that blouse with jeans."

"First name basis with the victim and witness, huh, Belichek? Imogen Wooton caught that, too."

"We often refer to murder victims by their first names, treating them more familiarly in death than we probably would if we encountered them, unknown and a stranger, in life."

Landis breathed out through his nose, recognizing the diversion.

Belichek kept going. "But I think it's good. *Jamie*. It makes her a girl I could have known. Makes her more Individual. More vulnerable." His voice dropped on the last word, contemplating her absolute vulnerability in death. "And that makes us more human. Connected to her—to them—as people, not detective and victim."

"Makes perfect sense." Landis dropped his mock solemnity. "Or it could be a detective getting whacko about a victim."

"Investigating is putting together the right—"

"Pebbles to build a mountain. Don't start on that with me again."

"A witness' account that the victim was wearing a combination she'd never seen before is an interesting pebble."

"Fluke. An old lady—"

"Don't dismiss a witness because of age, Landis."

"I know, I know. Your grandparents were the sharpest folks around right up to the end. And, actually, I wasn't going to say that, which you'd know if you hadn't jumped to a conclusion—meaning you flunk Detecting 101."

"What were you going to say?"

"That an old lady as sharp as she is would still not see what a neighbor wore every time. And the shoe information trumps any doubt about the blouse. But if you want to ask Mags about the outfit, knock yourself out. Now, what I thought was interesting was that anybody coming in that back door—hell, anybody on the patio and probably anybody standing outside the alley gate when it was open—could see those keys hanging there, including the one to Jamie's—"

"*Jamie's?*"

Landis didn't pause, but Belichek was satisfied he'd made his point. "—and knowing it was there, it wouldn't have been hard to find an opportunity when Imogen left the back door open and unattended—"

"As she did to answer the door for us."

"Exactly. Lots of opportunities to come in the back. God knows those dogs wouldn't raise a fuss."

Landis punctuated that statement by ringing the bell on the house next to Imogen's.

The house's central door, flanked by symmetrical windows and topped by an arched fanlight, indicated the house had once stood alone. The houses built against their neighbors mostly had doors on one side or the other.

He should have used that bit of knowledge to win Imogen Wooton's approval, Belichek thought as the door opened.

CHAPTER EIGHTEEN

GARRISON ENDERBE BROUGHT them past impressive rooms still true to their eighteenth-century roots to a small room that shared a recent addition with a kitchen, well-outfitted but not flashy.

"This is about Jamie—Jamison Chancellor—I suppose. I knew her, liked her. But I'm afraid I don't know anything that will help you."

The hair thinning on top and shadows around his eyes should have gone with an older man—or a younger one pulling all-nighters.

"Did you see Jamison Chancellor the Friday night before Labor Day?"

"No."

"Or after that?"

"No. Last time I saw her was the weekend before, when I had a glass of wine with her and Imogen on Jamie's patio." He paused. His head cocked, his mouth still open. "Unless… One night that weekend, Labor Day weekend. Late night. Hardly anybody around, I was crossing my street, and here came a car barreling toward me. I thought at the time—It could have been Jamie's. Or similar."

"Color? Make?"

"Dark red like hers. One of those compacts that look similar." He shook his head, negating hope for more details.

"Which night?"

He grimaced. "I went to a party Sunday night that went late, so it could have been then. But I also was up late Friday and Saturday playing an online game with my nephew who's on the West Coast. One of those nights I went out and moved my car, there was a rare spot open across from the house and I had to load it with things I was taking to the Sunday party. But which night? I don't remember. I honestly don't remember. I could ask my nephew."

"I'm not sure—"

"He's not a kid. He works for a tech startup out there. He can be vague, but if he says he remembers, you can bank on it."

"If you could give us his contact information…"

"Sure. I understand. Anything I can do to help. Nice person, Jamie Chancellor. I hope you get the bastard who did this."

Belichek wondered if he was aware that as he spoke the last sentence, his gaze slide toward Phil Xavier's house, a slice of it visible above the privacy fence that showed in the back window.

"How long have you lived here?"

"My whole family lived here for a while when I was growing up. Then when I came back and started working on the Hill… It's not my house. It's my dad's. He's a great businessman. I'm not. But I'm lucky he believes in supporting civic-mindedness, so he lets me live here. I might have let Phil think my name was on the deed for a while."

He grinned, dissipating the shadows and looking more the age of his round face.

"Drove him nuts when he found out he'd spent time being his version of nice to me when I wasn't *useful* to him."

"What's his version of nice?"

"Glad-hand. Trying to find out if I had wine, women, or song weaknesses by dangling out temptations. Or, better yet from his perspective, gambling, drugs, or Internet porn addictions. He's not very subtle. I'd say *Poor Phil*, but he's too much of a jerk to feel sorry for him."

"What happened when he found out you didn't own the house."

Another grin. "First he let fly with the kind of insults you'd expect. Not imaginative after you've worked in the Capitol for a while. And then, when he realized Dad was the owner, he tried a cringe-worthy reconciliation—ha, ha, ha, it was all a joke. We're still buddies and you'll put in a good word for me, won't you?"

"Did you?"

"Reconcile? Or put in a good word for him?"

"Either."

"Definitely not put in a good word for him. Warned Dad. As for reconciling, we don't do the neighborly dance anymore, but I say hello if we pass in the street. Which is more than he deserves.

"You know why he wants to buy this house? Not to possess it and its history, but to obliterate it. To make the main floor a kitchen. The whole thing. Wipe out three-hundred-year-old hand-hewn floors and trim, rip out the grace and proportions, and toss in the fanciest, hot trend appliances. A wine cellar in the basement, TV room on the second floor, closets on the third."

He sneered his disdain. He and Imogen Wooton were on the same wavelength.

"What about Jamie's house?"

"Oh, yeah, he's been after her to sell. Quite the campaign. After his uncharming charm offensive didn't work, she was the first to get his dirty tricks treatment. And she's—she was such a nice person. She never gave him shit back. Even though she's worked so hard to fix up that house after her great-aunt wasn't able to do much in her last years. And Phil wants to turn it into a garage. Turn a historic building into a two-story *garage*. And tear the top floor off for a roof deck."

Tear out Jamie's office. Belichek shifted to absorb an unexpected discomfort at that.

"How do you know all this?" he asked.

Garrison Enderbe did some shifting of his own. Belichek felt more than saw Landis' increased attention.

"Victorina mentioned it."

"Victorina Xavier, Phil's wife?" After Garrison nodded confirmation, Landis asked casually, "You talk to her a lot?"

"Not a lot. Some. We're neighbors. She's not a bad person. He does crappy things to people, then leaves her to take the blowback— not that neighbors *do* anything to her. Most of them are cold, though, give her a wide berth. Because of him."

Belichek bet Garrison didn't give her a wide berth, and didn't treat her coldly.

"What sort of crappy things has he done to people?"

"The things that can get under your skin with an annoying neighbor. You know."

"Give me examples."

"It's nothing I know for sure. It's just… Okay, I'll tell you a few things. After my father told him there was no way in hell he'd sell to him, I'd come home and there'd be garbage in my back garden. Like somebody took a bag of trash out of the can and threw it over the back gate. Six days in a row—never Xavier's garbage, always somebody else's. Until I added cameras back there, along with a big sign saying I had cameras. My car got keyed, too. Twice.

"Before that, other neighbors swore he was the one who smashed potted plants they had on their front steps, had dog feces dropped in front of their houses—always right after some sort of run-in with Phil. No proof on those, but there is with what he did up in Delaware, I think. He owned a retail building in this little historic town and he wanted to expand it, *modernize* it, and the town denied permission because it was clearly against the code. So, he searched through the code, finds a loophole and opens an adult bookstore, right there in the middle of town. Finally, some of the people got together and bought the building off him, but he made an obscene profit."

"How'd you hear about that?"

"My dad tracked it down when he was doing background on Phil." He grinned again, this one not as pleasant. "As soon as Xavier bought that house, Dad researched him. Then he warned Jamie and Imogen and me, of course. He also warned the Old Town Committee what to expect. Even if Imogen, Jamie, and I gave in, they'd never let him do what he's talking about."

"But now Jamie's gone. That might change the situation," Landis reminded him.

The shadows returned that made him look older than his age.

"You don't think he… He couldn't have."

CHAPTER NINETEEN

THEY TOOK THE long way around the block to Xavier's house, with a pause where they crossed the far end of the alley while Belichek called back his most recent caller. "Mags."

He held the phone so they could both hear.

She answered with, "Nothing."

That was Mags, cutting to the chase with her first word so they knew where they stood.

"No sign of Jamie." She allowed no sorrow into the word. "No sign of anyone being here. But—I take it back. There is something from the sheriff who came out. The owner of the cabin is Hendrickson York."

"We just talked to him. Never said a word." Landis was pissed.

Approving his pissed state, Maggie said, "Wish I could be a fly on the wall of your next conversation."

NO ONE RESPONDED to their second round of knocking and doorbell-ringing at Phil Xavier's house.

They picked up takeout at a hole-in-the wall Landis knew.

Driving back to the department, Landis said, "Enderbe sure doesn't like Phil Xavier. His horror at the end, think that was genuine?"

"Politician," Belichek reminded him. "What about the car business?"

"Politician or not, I say he's probably telling the truth someone nearly ran him over. We'll check. Doesn't mean it was Jamison Chancellor's car."

"No. But if it was…"

"Look at the possibilities. At least the possibilities that would tie into our case. It's her car and she's driving and she's trying to get away? Then why go back and get killed in her house later? She *was* killed there. That much the scientists agree on. It's the killer in the car? Again, trying to get away? Then why go back and park it in the garage and leave it?"

"Second thoughts. Killed her, took the car to get away, then—when it's not reported right away—calms down and figures the safest thing is to go on with outwardly normal life. Puts the car back when nobody's around and quietly glides away."

Landis stopped sharply at a newly turned red light. "I'll get to forensics. Make sure they collect the car and process it, get what DNA they can. Should have done it in the first place."

"Looked like it had been sitting there peacefully. But the thing with DNA, just about anyone we've talked to so far could have ridden in that car under ordinary circumstances."

"Yeah. That's why they'll check the driver's seat extra carefully. Especially for that ex-boyfriend's DNA."

"He's top of the charts?"

"Aren't the nearest and dearest always? Besides, he'd be the most likely to give her a ride. Maybe she wasn't going to be alone at this cabin—wherever it is—for the whole time."

"Everyone says she'd ended it."

"Maybe their relationship was exes with benefits. You coming in?" He'd pulled into a spot in the underground parking garage.

"Thought I'd do some other digging."

"Another night at the Chancellor house?"

"We'll see."

"I've got a shitload of reports to go through." He looked significantly at Belichek.

"Hey. Why don't I come in, help go through them?"

"Great idea."

WHEN THEY FINALLY left the otherwise deserted detective bullpen, Landis went home for his first sleep in a bed since getting the call. Belichek returned to Jamie's house.

He parked a block and a half away and took a circuitous route, leading him into the alley from the opposite end of the block. No sense having someone notice his car.

The gates of the four dark houses—Jamie's, Imogene's, Phil Xavier, and Garrison's/his father's—were all locked.

DAY TWO

CHAPTER TWENTY

FORD BELICHEK SAT in his childhood room alone.

His own room. Neat and private. Windows that opened to trees and clear sky. A closet with clean clothes.

He didn't take any of that for granted, even though he'd lived with his grandparents six years now.

He could hear his grandparents' voices from downstairs.

Gran's concerned in a way he'd never heard before.

Grandpa's dug in deep, not giving an inch.

His grandmother said something about an old movie, which made no sense. Not at the time.

What could a movie have to do with Grandpa being away so much and, when he was here, not being like himself. Instead, looking gray and hard, but with something deep in his eyes that unsettled Ford, because he'd never seen it in the older man's eyes.

The man he most respected in this world. The man who'd arrived when he most needed him…

Or was that bit about the old movie something planted far more recently in his brain by Landis? Did he really remember that?

Did he really connect it with his grandmother saying his grandfather was taking some case far, far too much to heart?

✧ ✧ ✧ ✧

BELICHEK WOKE FROM a head-nodding drowse when Jamie's journal hit the floor.

He'd started by reading her journal, which ended in August. Either she hadn't kept one after that or it was gone. Taken? Despite nothing else up here in the office appearing touched.

If she'd stopped, that would be worth knowing. He'd ask Mags, but doubted she and Jamie exchanged journaling anecdotes. Maybe her cousin Ally knew.

After the most recent volume, he'd picked up the next oldest one, which had the two previous years in it. He started at its beginning and read through, then went to the volume older than that and started at its beginning, then the next volume older … and on.

It was a little disjointed, seeing Jamison Chancellor's life through her own eyes by jumping backward in a chunk, then moving forward incrementally.

The most recent volume he'd completed had started with the earliest days of the foundation. Within this one should be the death of her aunt and what preceded it. But the beginning of this volume showed her as a carefree kid, which must have let him relax enough to fall asleep.

He picked it up, debating going. The sky still had enough dark in it to give him a couple hours sleep.

Then he saw a phrase about the end of school the next day and the start of summer vacation, including staying at her Aunt Vivian's with Maggie and Ally.

He poured himself coffee from a thermos.

He needed to be alert to read this.

THE LISTENS FOR Death, Murder, Violence spiked yesterday. But if he had nothing new, they'd drop even faster.

Oliver Zeedyk stared at the graph on the screen. He couldn't wait until the next regularly scheduled episode. He needed to pick it up now to keep this growing.

The damned cops weren't doing anything.

He needed that to change.

Fast, before DMV lost momentum.

He needed more. Something fresh.

Let's see what he could stir up.

Kickstart this baby.

LANDIS PLANTED HIS hands on the desktop and leaned forward. He was tall enough to cover the depth of the desk and still loom above Hendrickson York.

"I asked you if you knew anything we should know and you lied to us. Outright lied."

"I didn't. I don't know—"

"You know Jamison Chancellor was supposed to go to your cabin in Pennsylvania."

Belichek could have told York it was no use. Landis was testy about the roadblocks to the investigation and itching to chew on somebody's ass.

He'd seen all that the minute Landis picked him up at the Chancellor house first thing this morning. Also, that he was better rested now, so he'd have more energy for that chewing.

"But she didn't. Go there, I mean. So, how could that possibly have any bearing on her death here, in her own house?"

"We decide what could or couldn't have a bearing on her death. You tell us everything you know. That's how this works. And if you don't tell us everything, how else it works is we get you down to the department for formal questioning because we're wondering what the heck you're trying to hide."

The man lost color so fast and so completely, that *heart attack* flashed into Belichek's mind.

"Hide? I'm not trying to hide anything. If you'd asked me—"

"We went through that before. You tell without us asking. No excuses. You knew she planned to leave town and go stay at your cabin and you didn't mention it."

"I didn't—I simply never thought of it. She has had a key to the cabin for quite some years. She could go there at will. She knew that. But it didn't matter. She never left Fairlington."

Landis went cool and calm. "I decide what matters."

He stared until the older man nodded.

Landis went over the questions again, digging into the details, getting the same answers.

Belichek wouldn't swear York didn't have more he could tell them, but he was sure the man wouldn't tell them now.

CHAPTER TWENTY-ONE

BELICHEK'S STRIDE SLOWED as he neared the detectives' bullpen and heard Terrington's voice.

"—can say what you like. He should be here no matter how many cases he's solved. You know where he's spending all his time? At the murder scene. Roy Isaacson heard it from patrol. What is he doing getting totally weird and spending the night at that dead woman's house?"

"Hey, Belichek," Felicia Ewer, one of the burglary detail, said.

She probably thought she'd done him a favor by shutting up Terrington, but he'd been fine with the guy running his mouth.

"Morning."

"Landis is in the break room."

"Thanks." He could have waited for his partner to return to the desk near his, but out of a sense of obligation for the would-be favor, he went into the break room.

Belichek had made a detour to call Maggie away from the nosiness of his fellow detectives, ostensibly updating her on the visit to York, but also assessing how she was. Not great about summed that up.

She didn't mention and he didn't ask if J.D. Carson was around. Maybe the guy had gone back to Bedhurst, where he was half of a two-person law firm.

The break room's institutional lighting bounced off bright white tables with a force reminiscent of the movies' versions of old interrogation techniques. On the upside, the fridge, microwave—and most important—coffeemaker all worked.

"What's this?" Belichek asked of takeout cartons spread across one table.

These didn't usually sprout until lunchtime. Full bloom came at dinner. Only the hardiest made a showing late-night.

"Civic-minded citizens showing their appreciation with a little breakfast buffet." Landis selected a breakfast sandwich and put it in the microwave.

"Huh."

Landis frowned, looking him up and down. "What's with you, Belichek? You're looking woebegone."

"You were the one griping yesterday about no ID."

"But that's me. You don't usually get this morose unless it looks like we're going to come up empty. You know something I don't?"

"Know a whole hell of a lot you don't."

Landis stayed on the scent. "About this case. Something from Maggie—?"

"No."

"Or something else that—" The microwave beeped. Landis punched the button to stop its noise, but didn't open it. "It's like you think we've already failed."

"She's dead, isn't she?"

Landis rocked back. "If that's your criterium, we're screwed from the get-go. They're all dead when we start."

"Have you ever thought about how much we know about the victims, about dead people? Except even with all we know, it's like encountering Frankenstein's Monster. Bits and pieces of a human being without the heart and soul."

"You're getting poetic on me, Belichek?" Landis opened the microwave, swaddling the breakfast sandwich with napkins with one hand while he looked at the screen of his phone held in the other.

Responding to Landis' frown, Belichek asked, "Something important?"

"Not to the case."

He groaned. He should have recognized that frown. "Which one?"

"The psychologist."

"Isn't she connected to the department? Not to mention married. Landis—"

"Consultant. Not department staff. As for married, that's her decision. Besides," Landis continued, "her husband's probably some soft bureaucrat who wears a three-piece suit to walk his dog. She lacked excitement in her life."

He used to steer well clear of women with any association with the department. This psychologist was bad, but there was another one that worried Belichek more.

A judge.

Not a judge they appeared before, but… Christ. A judge.

He'd seen Landis talking with her in a courthouse hallway, and knew immediately.

Landis and Isaacson, neither one could keep it in their pants.

The difference was Landis didn't mess close to home. Though he'd be uncomfortably close with this judge. In the building. That wasn't something he'd done before.

Roy, though, had gone after and caught Mags—temporarily. Until the dumb shit cheated on her with a fellow officer. By the time he tried to get her back, this guy Carson was in the scene.

He'd done right by Mags at the scene. Beyond that, they'd see. And judge.

Which brought him back to his partner and females.

"I don't give a damn if she's panting at your zipper, Landis. She's got that chunk of gold around her finger, stay the hell away, for once."

"I went to her talks on how to know if you're burned out because I was worried about my partner. You got what you want in here? I've got a mile-high stack back at my desk."

Landis was dishing bull, but Belichek wasn't going to fight this old battle right now.

"Only came in here to get you."

But Landis came back to the topic, at least the part he wanted to talk about. His voice lowered as they neared the door. "The glass offices are worried about you burning out, too, Bel. Having you working this case catches them by the short hairs. They know what HR and the medical people said about forcing you to take time off. But they want you on the case. And there's Terrington bleating about being told he'd be second, then getting booted down when the great and powerful Belichek rematerialized. Plus, some whack-a-doodle podcaster's shooting off his mouth. Then throw in Isaacson stirring the pot and I wouldn't be surprised if they sent out the guys with nets for you any moment."

"But not before I do more grunt work on this case."

"Exactly."

"Maybe I do need a vacation."

"More like a lobotomy."

Their departure was perfectly timed, with Terrington reaching the break room door as they exited, and Roy Isaacson heading for it from the far entry to the detectives' bullpen.

✧ ✧ ✧ ✧

DID YOU HEAR what that asshole podcaster said today?" Roy Isaacson asked loudly enough to be meant for general consumption.

Only Terrington responded. "Oz, the asshole podcaster from Death, Murder, Violence? What did he say?"

Terrington sounded like one of those guys making late-night TV ads for their own company. Not just wooden, but concrete.

That brought a few heads up—not from interest, judging by the smirks, but as commentary on the performance.

Isaacson was passably normal, though unnecessarily loud. "He was down on law enforcement. Some other media described it as ridicule. Especially over the investigation of the Old Town murder."

"Wow."

Terrington's response drew several low-voice chuckles.

His face reddened as he followed Isaacson into the break room.

"Left in the nick of time," Landis muttered.

✧ ✧ ✧ ✧

THEY WORKED STEADILY through the reports, with more coming in and Landis corralling detectives to pick up several of the threads.

Danolin followed up with the management company by phone, ambling over to share before he wrote up what he'd learned.

"Only took three, four transfers to get the guy dealing with the Sunshine Foundation. Very circumspect, of course, but his take is pretty much what Celeste Renfro told you guys. Financials are solid. If Jamison Chancellor could have cloned herself, she wouldn't have needed them. She could handle each job, but couldn't be everywhere at once.

"She'd considered hiring more people, but decided—wisely, from their biased point of view—that she'd still be a bottleneck. So this outside management company, which specializes in helping nonprofits navigate growth spurts, considered Sunshine a good prospect— financials solid—and was preparing to come in. Hendrickson York called them first thing after her body was found—they hadn't even heard the news—and said the Sunshine Foundation had to wait to make a final decision."

"Don't know it's her body," Landis said.

"Yeah, yeah." Danolin dismissed the fly the size of a dinosaur in Landis' ointment. "Thing is, a final decision *was* made. Jamison Chancellor signed the papers before she left for Labor Day. The management company has them. All valid."

"How'd Hendrickson take that?" Landis asked.

"They didn't mention it to him. Being sensitive in this difficult time. But don't think they're not aware they have a signed contract. Implementation was supposed to start two weeks after her scheduled return."

IT WAS JUST over an hour after lunch—ordered in and shared by most in the break room—that Landis called Terrington over to his desk.

"Look into Bethany Usher who hasn't returned to the Sunshine Foundation."

"She left without bothering to give notice," Terrington said.

The guy had pouted over checking what they'd been told about ownership of the houses around Jamie's, so you'd expect him to appreciate being singled out for this, but he rocked from foot to foot like a kid dying to be let out of school for summer.

"Find out. Check where she lives, neighbors, a landlord if she's got one. See if you can get a line on friends. If you can track her down, great. Otherwise, start working backward on her work history. Has anyone reported her missing?"

Terrington looked at his watch.

Belichek's peripheral vision picked up movement. Without looking toward it, he recognized Isaacson taking an unobtrusive route to the break room.

Twice in one day. How did they get so lucky?

"Check with the people in the restaurant that's on the first floor of the Sunshine Foundation building. See what they say about the foundation dynamics. Go back to all the people at the Sunshine Foundation. Push them harder for more people she might be close to. There'll be different volunteers there today. Talk to them."

Terrington's eyes lit up, presumably at the prospect of getting a toe over the threshold into the main areas of investigation. But all he said was, "I'll get right on this, Landis."

He belied that pledge by heading for the break room.

"Boy, that was rough, seeing how he ignored you," Landis said. "Hurt your feelings, Bel?"

"A display of studied ignorance," Jenkins said.

That drew hoots.

"Good one," Danolin agreed. He looked at Landis and Belichek with anticipation, "You going to pry him out of there and tell him to get his ass in gear?"

"No need." Belichek didn't look up. "Glass offices."

Half the detective section sneaked peeks at the Chief of Detective's office and saw Wilson Palery staring at the break room door.

LANDIS ENDED A short phone call.

"Come on. According to the uniforms patrolling the neighborhood, that next door neighbor, Phil Xavier, just returned home."

CHAPTER TWENTY-TWO

THE HOUSE WAS twice as wide as the others on the block, though it matched in style and brick. But as soon as the door opened—which happened only after a male voice demanded who they were through a speaker, then demanded they hold their IDs up to a tiny camera—they stepped into a different world.

The décor, like the young woman who led them to the living room, sported angles and spangles capable of triggering a migraine. A blue and white rug of swirls that seemed to move erratically could qualify as psychotropic.

"My husband's coming," the young woman said, voice and expression bored.

Landis turned on his auto-charm. "Thank you. Must be unsettling for you with what happened next door."

She was immune to the Landis charm. Belichek would have indulged a moment of satisfaction at that if he wasn't seeing the garish dining room through open doors at the end of the room.

"Nah. Not like somebody knocked on our door."

"Victorina means she's had no dealings with events next door." Phil Xavier spoke as he entered, adding a hand gesture to his wife to *scat*.

Landis subtly countermanded the order. "Before you go, ma'am. Did you see Jamison Chancellor at any time on the Friday before Labor Day or after that?"

"No."

"You, sir?"

"No. And—"

"Did you see her car?"

A flash of intelligence showed behind the indifference in Victorina's eyes. "Her car without—"

"Yes, her car without seeing her."

"That doesn't make any sense," Phil said.

Landis concentrated on the wife.

"No," she said after a moment. "Not her car or any car I noticed around."

"Like I said, she doesn't know anything," Xavier said. His voice bounced off the hard surfaces, amplifying it. On the other hand, Belichek realized, they'd heard nothing from outside since the front door closed behind them. The place was well sound-proofed. "Go on, get out of here, Victorina."

She did, her boredom restored.

"No Jamie Chancellor, no cars, no nothing. That, too, is all I can contribute." Xavier sprawled untidily on a modern daybed upholstered in silver material so reflective it looked like tin foil.

He didn't invite them to sit.

Landis did anyway, a sharp contrast to the other man despite occupying a purple and green pseudo-leopard-print chair.

"Were you aware Jamison Chancellor was going away for a month to finish her new book?"

"I'd heard something about her being away a while. Didn't know how long or anything about a book."

"How did you hear about her plans?"

"No idea. Pick things up. Don't remember where."

"How long have you and your wife lived here?" Landis already knew, since it was part of the material Terrington confirmed. But it was a soft entry to the discussion.

"Since March."

"Would you say you have good relationships with your neighbors?"

"They're okay."

Belichek would bet that what he knew of Jamie's movement came from his wife. Why not admit it? Protecting her or minimizing the entire topic to fortify the notion of his indifference? Or he truly didn't remember because it wasn't important to … and did that reflect his view of his wife or of Jamie?

"You consider the relationships good even though your efforts to buy their homes have grown … contentious?"

"They're whining to the police because I want to *pay* them for their sheds? Contentious? I'll give you contentious. That rat's ass real estate agent told us there'd be no difficulty expanding and then has the gall to say there was no guarantee. Didn't know his head from his asshole. Told me the guy behind us would be eager to sell and then it turns out the guy living there doesn't even own the place."

Belichek, still standing, found himself focusing on the baseboards, which appeared original and weren't headache inducing.

"Total obstructionist jerk wouldn't even tell me who owned the house. Made me get somebody to look it up. And it's the guy's *father*, the shit. So now the old man's not selling to me because his snot-nosed kid went running to him. Should've sued him."

"Which one?" Landis asked, deadpan.

"Both of 'em. Might still."

"When did you first approach Ms. Chancellor with an offer to buy her house?"

"There's nothing wrong with trying to buy something from someone."

"When did you first approach her?"

"March."

"She said no?"

"She didn't say yes. So, I sweetened the offer."

"Did you have any other interaction with her?"

"Sure. Said hello. More than once. She said hello back," he said with sarcastic accuracy.

"Did she say hello first or did you?"

Xavier exploded at Landis' deadpan. "Jesus H. Christ. I don't know. She did probably. Is that what you want to hear? Lock me up because I didn't say hello first to a neighbor?"

"You were the one to initiate conversations about trying to purchase her property, though."

"So what? So, the fuck what? Until then, unless she read my mind, she didn't know I wanted the property. So I asked her."

"How many times?"

"I don't remember."

"Too many to remember." Landis appeared to write something in his notebook. "That must have been frustrating."

"I would have kept at it until I got what I wanted. That's how I operate. No law against that."

"What were you doing Labor Day weekend, Mr. Xavier?"

✦　✦　✦　✦

"BOATING AND GOLF. Shit," Landis muttered when they were back on the sidewalk.

Knowing how his partner's mind worked, Belichek said, "You couldn't have gotten more out of him if you'd gone with conciliatory charm."

"Couldn't have gotten less, either."

"I don't know. We got a good view of him and a decent view of the lay of the land."

Landis shook his head in pseudo-disbelief. "A trophy wife who decorated the place to look like a trophy."

"Pink dining room," Belichek agreed.

"Salmon, not pink. Wasn't even the worst of it. That rug. People with too much money and no taste. You'd think they'd have more respect for someplace built in 1800."

"Jamie's was built then. Not his. About 1870."

"So that's his excuse? Not even good modern stuff. Looks like he bought it off some shopping channel. Jamie's is the real deal. It would be a crime if she'd sold to him. Hope Mags and the other cousin don't."

It figured a crime against aesthetics got under his partner's skin.

✧ ✧ ✧ ✧

DANOLIN INTERCEPTED THEM before they sat at their desks.

"Got the nephew of that neighbor, Enderbe. After bitching about what time I woke him up out there in California—after eleven for shit's sake—it was as smooth as a baby's bottom.

"Confirms he was playing an online game with Garrison Enderbe, a k a Uncle Garrison until after midnight his time, which makes it after three our time. Better, he says it was Saturday night—Sunday morning here—his uncle went out to move the car. Remembers because he was about to win and he thought his uncle was trying to postpone the inevitable. Came back and was flustered about someone nearly running him over. Uncle was gone seven to ten minutes. Uncle Garrison would be hard-pressed to run out his front door, around the block—with a shotgun—blast the victim and get back to his game in that time. Even going out the back door, he'd either have to go around the rest of the block to get to the victim's front door or—if he went in through the back, he had to maneuver the victim into place in order to shoot her in the hall like that. No way he could fool forensics about that positioning."

"Thanks, Danny." Landis meant it, but he wasn't cheerful about it.

He and Wilson Palery had been called to the chief's office to give an update.

Eliminating avenues of investigation didn't always translate well to the glass offices as progress.

CHAPTER TWENTY-THREE

THE WOMAN WHO walked up to Belichek's desk and took a chair uninvited also didn't wait for him to look around from the computer screen.

"You didn't call me from the scene." Not a question, an indictment.

"Why would I—? No."

The last word came far too late to cover his mistake of starting the question. Never give Nancy Quinn that kind of opening.

By job title, she was Maggie's assistant in the Commonwealth Attorney's office.

In reality she was a forceful woman, multiplied by a network of regional connections unrivaled for depth, spread, and utility.

"*Why?* Because I would have been there. Instead of—him. You didn't think of the talk *that* would start?"

"I thought about what she needed."

"Hmpf." That held unexpected approval. "About time one of you did, all she's done for you and Landis."

Not giving him a chance to say they'd done right by Mags, too, which is what made them a good team, she had more.

"What's the status of the investigation?"

He eyed her across his desk. The woman was really rattled to ask. She knew where they'd be this far into it and that he wouldn't tell her anything.

Hell. Nancy Quinn rattled.

Did that mean Mags was falling apart more than he'd picked up on?

He spoke none of that.

"Landis is primary."

"I know that." She packed a lot of disdain into three words. "That's why I'm not bothering him. Keep all his attention on getting the bastard. But you're not even officially the second."

In other words, fair to bother him.

"Early days."

"You still don't have an ID."

"Not official. Not yet."

"Not yet? Medical's a no-go. They'll have to use her mother or siblings for DNA, since her father's dead. Dental's out." How did the woman know so much? He answered his own question. Because she was Nancy Quinn. "Then what?"

He didn't answer.

She snorted her opinion of his non-answer. "So it's making the mother go through DNA and the wait."

He wasn't going to say the next part, until he remembered she already knew it or soon would. "The forensic anthropologist confirms white female, most likely late twenties-early thirties."

"Most likely? What good—?"

"You know age is toughest to pin down."

"So, you're going with the neighbor who found the body saying those were her clothes?"

"How do you—?"

Again, he didn't bite it off fast enough. Maybe he did need a vacation. Especially since *fast enough* with Nancy meant not having the thought.

"Give me a break," she snapped. "No firm ID, yet you ran to the family and broke their hearts—"

"Nancy, I don't want it to be Mags' cousin, either. But look at it. White female, right age range, in her house, wearing clothes a witness says were hers. Best thing you can do is support Mags in accepting this and let us do our jobs."

He met her flinty gaze. It took more than half a minute before she stood.

"Then do your damned jobs."

"We are." Before she responded—it wasn't going to be complimentary—he added, "What can you tell me about Jamison Chancellor?"

She sat. "First half-intelligent things you've said. Probably the first half-intelligent thing you've done on this investigation."

"Thank you."

And damned if the corners of her mouth didn't twitch.

"Maggie said she talked to Jamie, but they weren't real close. How do you see her and Maggie? What was their relationship?"

"You're going to make Maggie out as a suspect?" Disdain, not outrage.

"Insight to the victim as a person."

"Jamie wanted to draw Maggie into the Sunshine Foundation fold, have closer connections to the family, and be a happier and more sociable human being. You know she and Ally—the other cousin—planted bulbs at Maggie's townhouse?"

He grunted. He hadn't. But he had noticed the remarkable appearance of daffodils in a vase on Maggie's desk when she returned from Bedhurst in the spring.

"Thing is, Maggie liked them. Never would occur to her to plant them for herself, but with them growing there and blooming, she liked them. Jamie realized that and planted summer flowers, too—the kind that will come up year after year and Maggie doesn't have to do anything. Maggie kept saying no, but Jamie did it anyway. That's how she and Ally met Carson. They showed up at Maggie's to plant unannounced and there he was."

They exchanged looks across the desk. Each trying to give nothing away while reading the other, neither succeeding and both of them knowing it.

"Mistake a lot of people made was thinking Jamie was a marshmallow. Maggie knew better, even though she couldn't see that it made the two of them more alike than different," Nancy said. "You know what happened with her aunt—their aunt?"

Figured Nancy first assigned Vivian Frye solely to Maggie. After Nancy's kids, Maggie was her top priority. Might say something about Jamie that Nancy gave her any part of the aunt. Not the time to parse that, though, because this was tricky territory.

How much should he know?

"Her aunt being murdered, you mean?"

"Yeah. There was a guy—asshole pervert—who courted Vivian, but was really after Jamie. She's the youngest of the three cousins, was maybe eleven, twelve at the time. Maggie knew something was wrong, but nobody listened to her. Not until the pervert set up an alibi, then tried to snatch Jamie.

"Maggie saved her before the pervert could get her in a van. He got away but was arrested shortly after. There were other witnesses, but only Maggie was close enough to identify him."

Jamie was.

He didn't break into her flow to point that out.

"So the trial rested all on Maggie," Nancy said.

"She couldn't have been very old."

"Fifteen, sixteen."

Fifteen.

"He was found not guilty. She's always believed it was her fault, that she didn't hold up under cross-examination. She's never forgiven herself." She tipped her head sharply. "Or maybe she has started to. Lately."

Ah. He'd wondered… The doing of J.D. Carson? Or, at least, whatever happened up in Bedhurst.

"That was bad enough. Then, as if there'd been any doubt about it, the pervert proved he was complete evil—went to the aunt's house and murdered her. The three girls weren't there, but Maggie arrived as the police—called by neighbors—shot him."

She was wrong. Jamie and Ally had been there, too. Not as close to the scene as Maggie, but they were there.

"See this isn't a surprise to you," Nancy said. "Heard you were reading her journals. Jamie's."

He didn't even bother to wonder how she knew that.

Then something else struck him.

"You approved." That part he knew for certain. "Of Jamie Chancellor herself? Or of her plans for Maggie?"

"Both. She wasn't ever going to let Maggie be lonely. No matter how hard she tried. Jamie knew how to be loyal."

High praise from this woman.

She stood again. "Get to work."

"Nancy."

She stopped and looked back at him.

"What do you think of Carson?"

She studied him, then said. "Same as you. He'll do. But I'm not taking my eyes off him."

═══════════

Fairlington County Police Department News Conference

Fairlington County Police Department Public Information Officer Elliott Kepler: In response to your requests, Dr. Yale Huang Porter of the Office of the Chief Medical Examiner is here to make a brief statement. No questions will be taken. Dr. Porter.

Dr. Yale Huang Porter: Thank you. Good day, ladies and gentlemen. My office will not be releasing an identity of the victim at this time. This—

Unidentified Media: (Shouting.)

PIO Kepler: Please. We can stop this right now if you'd prefer not to hear what Dr. Porter has to say. Okay, Dr. Porter, go ahead.

Dr. Porter: Thank you, Officer Kepler. As I said, my office will not be releasing an identity for the victim at this time. That is why we are addressing this issue scientifically and responsibly. The Fairlington PD wants the identity of the deceased established even more than you do. However, we have encountered a number of difficulties—a perfect storm of difficulties, as it were. Rather than risk misidentifying—

Death, Murder, Violence Podcast: Everybody knows who it is.

PIO Kepler: Zeedyk, no questions or comments—

Dr. Porter: No, they don't. And those disseminating any supposed identification are doing the investigation, as well as family members and friends, a grave disservice. We deal with medical facts, not guesswork or supposition.

When we have overcome the difficulties in this case, which we will do, we will share with the media both the outcome of our efforts and—for those interested in the truth—the measures we have taken to ensure the accuracy of our results.

PIO Kepler: Thank you, Dr. Porter. No, no questions. I have one last statement.

If any citizens noticed unusual activity in the 700 block of Red Hill Street between the Friday before Labor Day weekend until two nights ago, please contact the Fairlington County Police Department. The methods of contact are on the handout you'll receive as you leave here.

I'll let you all know when we have further developments to report to you.

~~ End news conference transcript.~~

❖ ❖ ❖ ❖

DANOLIN APPEARED IN the aisle between Belichek's and Landis' pods.

"Got something for you. Talked to a contact at the power company. First, power didn't go out during that period. But he did some real interesting calculations. They don't only see how much power you use in a month. They can pin it down closer than that."

Landis' head came up.

"Won't keep you in suspense. Can't say precisely, but figure a twelve-hour window. Looks like the power usage in that house dropped like a rock starting at some point that Sunday, say between noon and midnight, more likely the earlier part of that period than the later.

"Not the precise time the app would have given you, but that sure looks like the window for when the AC was turned off."

CHAPTER TWENTY-FOUR

"YOU WANTED TO see me?"

In an official photo the department put out, Chief of Detectives Wilson Palery sat behind a clean expanse of polished desktop.

They must have taken that photo in his first two minutes on the job. Because every time Belichek had seen it since, whatever wasn't covered with papers, folders, books, and notebooks, held coffee mugs, plus the ghostly rings of coffee mugs past.

Never from the break room. Palery said he hated that coffee, but Belichek suspected it was from a kind of tact, leaving the detectives a place to talk without the boss.

Rumor was that when the coffee shop next door ran low on mugs, they dispatched someone to this office to retrieve their errant stock.

"Come in. Close the door. Sit down. Talk to me." Palery issued orders so fast Belichek hadn't filled the first before the last was out. That was normal. It was what followed that made the hard-seated office chair more uncomfortable than usual. "How's it going, Belichek?"

"Fine."

The Chief of Detectives glared at him from under twisted eyebrows. "Like hell."

Belichek said nothing to that.

Palery's gaze darted to the left and the glass wall of his office. Everybody in the bullpen swore that sitting at their desks, they'd feel a tingle in the hairs at the back of their neck. They'd look up, and the Chief of Detectives would be looking at them.

"You look like hell, too. You know, Landis said something a while back—"

Thanks, partner.

"—and I checked. You haven't been taking vacation."

Belichek had heard this before from HR. Only good thing about that was he hadn't had to have this conversation with Palery.

"There's a reason for vacations. Keep people fresh. Keep people from falling over dead of heart attacks. Keep people from going off the deep end. And you got a hell of a lot of time piled up."

He was fresh. Heart did fine in every physical. Wasn't crazy. If that's all Palery was worried about…

His boss's expression said reassurances weren't going cut it.

"I'm saving up. Thought I'd go around the world someday, you know, in one of those solo sailboats. Takes a long time. Need a load of vacation time."

"Yeah? That's real interesting. I guess you got the idea after Jenkins's wedding reception on that yacht last year, after you got done barfing up the hors d'oeuvres."

"It was something I ate."

"Cut the crap, Ford." Not a good sign. Palery used first names when things got serious. "You hate boats and you'd get seasick on the Tidal Basin. You haven't taken vacation like you're supposed to for years. The records say you're on vacation now. Yet you're here."

"I'll reschedule. The Chancellor case—"

"Word's come down, Ford. You are off the Chancellor case. You weren't supposed to be on it in the first place and now you're off it. As of this moment."

"You can't—"

"I damn sure can. And you will. Is that understood?"

"This case—"

"Okay, Belichek, you wanna talk about this case? Let's talk about this case. Where are you and Landis on it?" He didn't wait for an answer, but supplied his own. "You've interviewed the neighbors. You've interviewed the co-workers. You've interviewed the family. You've examined the scene. You're waiting for medical reports to confirm the ID and lab reports to see if there's anything else the body can tell you. In the meantime, you have no witnesses, no motives, no leads.

"Now let me tell you what I've got. I've got an understaffed department. I've got more crime in a month than we used to have in a year, and I've got about the same number of people to deal with it. I've got two of my best detectives tied up and they've got most of the rest of the section chasing inquiries for them. I've also got one who's taken to damn near living at a crime scene. I don't like it. I don't like it one damn bit.

"What *you've* got, Ford, is a week of vacation to get your head straight. I don't care what you do or where you go, but when you come back in here in a week, I want you to be ready to move on to other cases. Is that understood?"

"Yes, sir."

"Good. Now, have a nice vacation."

Landis looked up as Belichek returned to his desk, but said nothing.

The question came from Jenkins. "What'd you get?"

Belichek took out his phone and checked his messages. Nothing on Jamison Chancellor's medical records. He shoved the phone in his pocket. "A week."

"Suspension?"

"Vacation."

Tanner Landis leaned back in his chair, locked fingers forming a pillow for his head. "You don't think Belichek would look this pissed about a suspension, do you?"

Jenkins muttered a disgusted expletive and headed for the coffee pot in the break room.

Belichek glared at his partner. "Screw you, Landis."

"Wasn't me this time. You think I'm crazy? Terrington as my second, remember? It was Terrington whispering in the right ears— maybe Isaacson, too."

Belichek jerked his head around to him. "Terrington? But Palery said word came down, how would Terrington have the juice?"

"If you paid more attention, you'd know young Terrington started following Isaacson around a month ago."

Belichek groaned. He tried to open the desk's lap drawer. It stuck. He opened the top left drawer instead and used his forearm to scrape three pens, a dusty message pad, half a granola bar, forty-three cents in change, and two breath mints whose outer wrapper was gone into the drawer.

"Exactly," Landis continued smoothly. "And Isaacson, being the kind to suck up all the adoration a lap dog will give, might have given said lap dog a much-desired treat by cashing in some favors." He looked thoughtful. "Or dirt. Either way, I'm the one suffering here. I get Terrington. All you get is time off, poor baby."

"Screw you."

"You said that before. And it's just what I've been hoping for you, Belichek—that somebody'll screw you. Preferably a woman. And maybe even one who doesn't do it for a living. I strongly suggest you start your vacation by setting your hard ass on a bar stool in one of the establishments in our jurisdiction commonly known as a meet market. Try Duchess Street. Don't be fooled by the business suits, some of those bureaucrat-types can be hot. Especially the ones who're looking for adventure to mix with their routine and think a roll in the hay with a homicide dick will do it—that's where you come in, Belichek, in case you've forgotten how it works."

"Go to hell, Landis." He patted his breast pocket for his current notepad and found it there.

"More'n likely," he agreed easily. "Just so long as you don't go back to your own personal hell."

He didn't look at Landis. "Don't know what you mean."

"Don't go back there, Ford." Landis leaned forward, his voice low. "You can say it's only a couple days, but I can see it. That place is getting to you. That woman's getting to you. She's dead and you can't bring her back. Maybe it's the connection to Mags or—"

Belichek slammed the drawer closed and took out his key ring. "You think I've started believing in ghosts?"

"No, I think you've started hoping to believe in ghosts."

"You're full of shit."

"Am I?"

Belichek looked Landis full in the face. "Yes."

"Okay. Good. Then a week off should put you back on the road to normal." Landis leaned back. "Have a good trip."

Felicia Ewer walked past. "You going somewhere, Belichek? Where you going?"

"Vacation." He started walking out.

"You gonna send us a postcard from one of those exotic islands like Landis always does?"

"No." He kept walking.

He was on vacation. His time was his own. And he'd spend it how and where he damned well pleased.

OZ ZEEDYK READ the comments on the short bonus podcast he'd released today.

Things were heating up nicely.

Holding the police up to ridicule?

Hell, yeah.

It was the least they deserved—to be seen for the clowns they were.

Only reason they were putting people and money into this was the victim was a rich bitch—fitting that those rhymed—with a high profile and living in the right area. Only kind of people they cared about. And they get so lazy pretending to investigate the cases of real people that when it came to one they actually gave a shit about, they didn't know what they were doing.

He sipped the prime single malt he'd put on his credit card. Pushed it up to the limit, but he'd be rolling in money soon.

Sponsors were contacting him already.

Not the big ones yet, the ones he deserved. They'd come. For now, he'd swat away these small-time jerks.

...so lazy pretending to investigate the cases of real people that when it came to one they actually gave a shit about, they didn't know what they were doing.

That was good.

He'd use it.

That should stir things up.

DAY THREE

CHAPTER TWENTY-FIVE

BELICHEK WAS LEANING against the side of his car when Landis arrived at a Washington, D.C., address that real estate ads might try to sell as Foggy Bottom, but was mostly bottom. Especially in a building like this, with renters packed in.

Landis didn't even break stride.

Still, it was satisfying knowing his partner had to park a block away, while he'd found a spot nearly in front of the building.

"Shook off Terrington, huh?" he said by way of greeting.

"You think I'm an idiot? Of course, I did. Left him with a list a mile long to do from the office. What are you doing here?"

"You can use another pair of eyes and ears when you meet Delattre's ex-roommates—three of them, aren't there? Someone else to help watch reactions could be useful.

"Fine. If you do something for me. I don't have the manpower, but it needs to be done."

"What?"

"Talk to the other cousin. Mags said she's coming this afternoon. Talk to her somewhere away from the building. Less grim. Maybe at Mags'. I'll send you her contact info."

"You don't want to interview her officially?"

"Alibi checked out and she's far enough out of the circle to not put her through that. Lots of other things to do."

Belichek was good with the trade, mostly because he intended to get more out of it than this visit to the ex-roommates.

"I'll contact her after this interview. And see her after we go see the old boyfriend."

"Jesus, Belichek—do you want to get me fired? Wouldn't that be just the way? You get sent on vacation and I get fired."

"If you're going to get fired, it'll be over a woman." He knew and Landis knew he knew, that Landis had kept this assignment for himself, while others talked to neighbors and friends of the other Sunshine Foundation employees and volunteers, because it was nearest to where he'd met with the psychologist instead of getting some sleep. "Let's go. You're going to be late."

"Yeah, I got it. You hacked into the calendar."

"It's not hacking when you gave me the password."

"Semantics. Okay. But you are along for the ride. Not official anything, understood? Keep your mouth shut."

✧　✧　✧　✧

THE FOUR ROOMMATES tried hard to not be impressed at being interviewed by the police.

They knew each other from classes. Their apartment had a small additional room—a long-ago enclosed porch—and they decided to split the rent into smaller pieces by adding another roommate. Adam Delattre responded to a free listing.

He'd lived there for almost a year and left in February.

The most talkative said, "Pretty weird, but harmless. Never went out with us—"

The second-most talkative said, "We didn't want him to feel like the odd man out, you know? So we'd ask him."

"—never went out at all. Just stayed on his computer."

Landis slid in, "That is his job, right? Computers."

"Sure, but he wasn't normal. Like when he left, not a word. He was regular with his rent. Miss that."

The most talkative returned to his point. "And he wasn't always doing stuff for his job. He'd do all these weird searches."

"What kind of searches?" Landis asked less to hear their responses than to see their reactions. The department had Adam Delattre's computers, so the techs would know details of his searches soon.

The roommates pinged four-way looks. The one who talked the least shrugged. The one who talked the most took that as a go-ahead.

"We thought… You know, porn and stuff. We were kinda curious what he'd be into, considering he didn't show any interest in, well, anything. So, we set up a key-logger. Pretty slick, he never realized it was there."

The second-most talkative supplied, "But all he searched for were sob stories about families that lost their home or went broke because a kid was sick. Stuff like that."

"The sort of people the Sunshine Foundation helps?"

Belichek looked down to avoid grinning at the *you idiots* subtext to Landis' question.

Clearly, they did not speak subtext.

"Yeah, I guess. He was obsessed with that place. Not just a job, but like his total life."

"And then he up and left."

Landis covered some of the ground again, then wrapped up. But at the door, he looked back and said, "You sure he didn't know about the key-logger? Maybe that's why he left."

Belichek had an image of four open mouths before the door closed.

CARL ARBENDROTH'S MORTGAGE broker office was in a sandy-colored two-story building in a bland swath of Fairlington.

The assistant absorbed their identities with wide eyes, then hopped up and headed to a door.

"The police are here to see you. Two detectives."

"Police? Me? I don't want—"

But they followed the assistant in, ending the man's recitation of wants.

"Hello, Mr. Arbendroth. Thank you for seeing us. I'm Detective Tanner Landis. I'd like to ask you a few questions about your relationship with Jamison Chancellor."

While Landis moved forward to take a chair and cement occupation of the office, Belichek held the door open for the assistant with a compelling look. After she obeyed it, he shut the door firmly after her.

As he took the other chair on this side of the desk, he saw Arbendroth had regained command of himself.

He looked suitably solemn.

"I heard about that. Horrible, absolutely horrible." He looked from Landis to Belichek, then clearly decided Landis was the better bet. A lot of people made that mistake. "But you've been misinformed if you have the impression Jamie and I were seriously involved."

"Oh?"

"That's right," he said earnestly to Landis. "We dated for a while—a short while—but it never took off, if you know what I mean, Nice girl—don't get me wrong—but... Well, you know how these things are."

"How long did you date for?"

"Let's see, maybe four months? It's hard to pin down because it started gradually—we were more friends, you know what I mean, and then it kind of faded at the end. The sort of thing where you suddenly realize you haven't seen or been in touch with someone for quite a while and then it feels awkward to try to pick it up again, not to mention that when it slips away like that, it's a sign, isn't it?"

"When the other person is murdered, that usually sharpens the memories. When was the last time you went out with Jamison Chancellor?"

"Oh, wow. I couldn't say. I wish I could help you, but—"

"You don't have it on your calendar? In your phone?"

Arbendroth reached out to it on the desk, as if to take that device more securely in his possession, but drew his hand back.

"No, no. I don't keep personal information there."

"Oh? Where do you keep it?"

"In my head."

"You wouldn't mind us getting a copy of the data on your phone to help us get a window into Jamison Chancellor's life in the months before her death, then."

Landis' statement presented a substantial obstacle Carl Arbendroth needed to climb over to be credible.

"Really, it wouldn't be of any use to you."

He smiled at Landis, who looked back at him levelly. Arbendroth looked at Belichek, quickly returning to Landis.

"There's nothing there about Jamie. Nothing that would help you. I can't give you access to it because there's a great deal of proprietary information on it. Business, I'm afraid."

Landis didn't respond to the condescending tone, other than a tick at the side of his jaw, under his ear, that Carl Arbendroth wouldn't see.

Though he might feel the repercussions from that tick, Belichek thought.

"When was the last time you saw Jamison Chancellor?"

Arbendroth looked relieved Landis wasn't pursuing the phone records.

"As I think about it, I suppose it must have been a couple weeks before she was leaving town. We happened to run into each other at a restaurant we both like." He tried a wry smile. "Said hello to her, and some kid from the group got excited and created a scene. So I left."

"Did you make any effort to see her again after that?"

"No. It was a coincidence I'd run into her that day. Didn't cross paths again." He lifted one shoulder.

Landis let a silence grow. Until, when he finally spoke, Arbendroth started.

"So you knew the date she was leaving town to go work on her book?"

"I don't—I didn't say that. I didn't know."

"You said you ran into her at that restaurant a couple weeks before she was leaving town. To say that, you had to know when she was supposed to leave."

"I must have heard it on the news. The story's all over the news and—"

"When she was supposed to leave town hasn't been on the news."

"I, uh…"

"I suppose she talked about it when you were dating."

The fly not only stepped into the spider's web, it wrapped itself up in the tangles, thinking it was getting free.

"She told everybody," Arbendroth said eagerly. "Everybody. She talked about it all summer, going away to a cabin to write. You can ask anybody. She talked about it all the time."

Landis nodded. "So, you *did* know when Jamison was supposed to leave town."

"I, uh…"

His stutters continued until Landis' next question. "Where were you Labor Day weekend? Start with Friday."

Arbendroth answered meekly.

After work Friday, he'd gone to a bar where he was a regular. Saturday, he'd worked several hours here in the office, catching up on work and meeting with a prospective client. He volunteered the name. He'd watched baseball on TV at home that night—alone. Sunday, there'd been a brunch with college friends, then he'd stayed on to watch the early NFL game at the restaurant's bar. Then he went home and watched the late afternoon game and the night game. Monday, he went to a cousin's house in Maryland for a cookout, returning by nine for work the next day.

A few more details and Landis rose.

Belichek opened the door, started to follow Landis out. At the last moment, he turned back to look at Carl Arbendroth, knowing he might never have the answer to this mystery.

Why had Jamison Chancellor dated this guy?

CHAPTER TWENTY-SIX

"**He wanted to** make you his best buddy, didn't he?" Belichek said when they stopped by his car.

Again, he'd gotten the better spot. That had given him time to text Ally Northcutt while he'd waited for his partner before the interview.

"Him and me," Landis agreed, "men of the world, with enough women hanging around us that when one's murdered, we can say tut-tut and move onto the next. What did you get from her journals on him?"

"Needy. Demanding. Wanting more of her than she wanted to give. None of that said overtly. From the start, she was trying to slow things down, he was trying to warp speed them. He talked about marriage on the third date. Freaked her out enough to be emphatic with him."

Landis gave him a quick look. "But still dated him for months?"

"Trying to disentangle herself gradually."

"Yeah, like that would work with his kind."

"Not everybody uses a guillotine to end relationships."

"Quick, clean, decisive. Never leave any uncertainties."

"Clean?" Belichek muttered.

"For me."

"Someday you're going to forget to stand back from the blood splatter and get soaked."

"Nah. Too nimble. Anyway, this guy. She had to know what he was like. Or was she that naïve?"

"Wouldn't say naïve. Optimistic. Hoped for the best."

"Got the worst." He looked down the street toward his car. Probably mentally listing his to-dos. "Sounds like from the foundation people she still hadn't untangled herself when she died, not completely."

Belichek grunted agreement. "Maybe hoping the time away would do the trick. Not sure we could pull his phone records with what we've got."

"I'm betting we'll get more. Eventually. Keep the option open to get them if it's trending that way. It'll be a pleasure to turn those records upside down."

"Looking for proprietary information?"

"Hell, no. Dating tips." He straightened. "This is where we part. No more showing up places. I mean it, Bel."

"Okay."

"And do me a favor so I don't get dragged down with you, either sleep at your own house or get permission to be in that place now that it's been turned back to the family."

Not a bad point.

"Last two things," Landis said, "go get yourself laid, but do it after you write up—for my eyes only—what you heard this morning and anything you get from the cousin."

BELICHEK OCCUPIED THE hour before Ally Northcutt's scheduled arrival by picking up lunch in Jamie's neighborhood, watching people, then calling Maggie.

She answered with, "I heard that asshole took you off the case. He can't do that. He can't take you—"

"He can. But I'm not—"

"—off the case."

"—going to quit the case," he agreed, just behind her.

"You're off the case, but you're not quitting. You're going to keep investigating. Landis knows?"

"Not officially."

"Works for me."

"Good, because I need family permission to be in the house."

"Why? Not the permission—the house. No, never mind. Don't tell me why. I swore to—I told myself I wouldn't interfere. At least not if you and Landis get something soon. I know I'm too close to this to see straight. You've got the permission. I'll email you something to make it official and cover your ass."

"Good. Thanks."

"Why'd you call."

"Quick question. Maggie, from the scene, can you confirm that the clothes the victim was wearing were your cousin's? I can send an image of the blouse, if that would help."

He'd cropped a copy of one from the lab to best show the pattern and least show the destruction.

The pause didn't surprise him. Maggie would be sure of her answer before committing.

"No. I can't confirm. Image wouldn't help. I remember the scene—"

He closed his eyes at her voice on those words.

"—but I didn't see her often enough and when I did, I didn't pay close enough attention to what she was wearing to tell you now."

"Maggie—"

"What's this about? Trying for the official identification through *clothes*? That's weak. Even if you could prove she'd bought those specific items, a defense attorney would tear into that."

It figured Maggie thought of it in terms of a trial that would find the killer guilty. Belichek just wanted to catch the sonuvabitch.

She went on, "I know what you've run into with medical and dental, but the DNA shouldn't be *that* long."

"You know how backed up the lab gets, but we'll get it eventually. In the meantime, we wouldn't rely on the clothes for the official ID, but unofficially... Hearing it from you would help confirm our witness who found her."

"The neighbor lady."

"Right. Imogen Wooton." When—not if—Maggie found out he

hadn't mentioned the wrinkle in Imogen Wooton's statement about the two pieces of clothing not being worn together, she would have his head on a platter.

"Don't waste time on me, Bel. Call Ally. My cousin Allison Northcutt. You said there was an image? Civilian level image?"

"Yeah."

"Give me three minutes to call her, tell her to expect to hear—"

"Maggie."

"—from you. Send her the image, then call her. Here's her number." She rattled it off.

"Maggie. I have her number. I texted with her. I'm going to see her in half an hour. At the house."

Silence.

"Why?"

"Landis asked me to talk to her. He's swamp—"

"Why the house?"

"She asked to see it. The cleaners have been in. It should be okay—"

"What time? I'll be there."

ALLISON NORTHCUTT WAS taller than Maggie. She wore black jeans with a plain t-shirt under a denim jacket. She had an air of athleticism about her.

Yet, as the introductions were introduced, Belichek found himself thinking of her as more fragile. Not surprising, he supposed, with her husband comatose for a couple years now.

"Let me go in first. Make sure." He said it to Mags, but looked at Ally.

Mags followed the direction of his look and said, "Okay."

The cleaners had done a good job. Some things never disturbed by the intruder were not back where they'd been, but the smell was gone and the overall impression was of order.

He took that in as he double-timed his way to the third floor.

Didn't take long to remove evidence he'd slept in the office chair and to scope out the bathroom, but the run up to and down from the third floor meant he paused another moment to be sure his breathing was normal before he let them in.

Maggie's gaze went immediately to the area where the rug was missing. Ally's attention didn't snag on anything until they reached the archway to the living room and she stared at the painting over the fireplace.

Maggie joined her, pressing her arm against her cousin's.

After a beat or two, she said, "Okay, let's get to this. I have the list of what I told you was missing. Now that things are back in order and Ally's here, we should be able to tell you more."

Ally did add nearly a dozen items to the list, including distinctive silver pieces Jamie had kept in the second-floor guest bedroom and Jamie's cash stash that was gone from her bedroom.

They saw nothing missing from the third floor.

With little space to maneuver, Maggie sat at the desk, Ally had the upholstered chair, and he sat on the landing, with his legs down the stairs.

"They took her purse," he told them.

"Phone?" Mags asked.

"Her keys?" Ally asked.

"Both."

Ally looked toward Mags, who didn't return the look because, he knew, she was thinking about the investigative value of the phone and what it meant to not have it. "With her keys out there somewhere, shouldn't we see about changing the locks?"

"Don't," Belichek said. "Please."

Mags squinted at him, knowing immediately why not. "Are you sure?"

"Yeah. It's covered for now."

Ally looked from Maggie to him and back.

"Let us know when we should change them," Maggie said.

Her cousin's brows rose, but she didn't argue. He suspected that with the things Ally Northcutt was dealing with, a set of keys didn't rank very high. Nor did the security of this house. Now that Jamie was dead.

"What do you know about Jamie keeping journals."

"She still does that?" Maggie asked.

"Yeah." Ally looked guarded.

He said it straight. "I'm reading them. Did she stop this summer?"

Ally pulled her head back slightly. "No. At least not that I know of. I know she bought a journal—the kind she likes—when we were together this spring. But whether she stopped writing in them…"

He hadn't found a blank journal. Missing was looking more and more likely.

Did that make it less likely someone might try to come back?

"What happens with the Sunshine Foundation? Is there a succession plan?"

Both looked up, startled.

"No idea," Mags said. "The way she looked after the Sunshine Foundation, she must have made some provision…"

"I think it's us." Ally clearly knew she was delivering bad news, but didn't back down from it.

"Oh, Christ. Why would she do that?"

"Vivian."

"But—" A single syllable that conveyed Maggie's distance from the foundation's cause, compounded by her demanding job. And Ally's consuming care for her comatose husband.

"Yeah. And she knew that—she never expected that she wouldn't be able to keep running it until one or the other of us wanted—or could—step in… But she had to put down something."

"Why not one of her merry little band of faithful followers?"

"Vivian," Ally said again.

"Does the foundation hold substantial assets?" Belichek asked.

Maggie snorted. "Are you kidding? She flowed every cent through to their projects and more. If you're trying to follow the money to find a suspect, you're a lot better off with her personal assets, especially this house, and some modest trust from her father that her mother shifted all to Jamie when Dana remarried. And, since Ally and I are beneficiaries in her will, you should look at us. Go ahead, ask us for alibis. I don't have one, but I bet Ally was with her cop husband who's in a coma."

"Maggie."

"It's okay, Ally. I know Maggie. And she knows me." He switched to Maggie, holding her gaze as he added. "She knows we already checked your alibis."

Silence held for two, then three beats. Then Maggie burst out laughing. It had an edge to it that made Ally frown. "Fat lot of good that does you, since you don't know when she was killed."

"We have some idea—between when she was last seen by the Sunshine Foundation people and when the AC was turned off."

He saw Maggie's brain take in the information, smoothing the wash of emotions. "Hell of a lot more likely it was just before the AC was turned off."

"Yeah. For that most likely period, you were in Bedhurst with J.D. Carson—you two aren't as discreet as you might think you are—and Ally was at the long-term nursing facility in Maryland with her husband, seen by staff and others. Throw in commute times and..."

"We have alibis. Should make us even more suspicious."

"It doesn't." He said that with his gaze on Ally, who'd gone pale, whether from concern about her own status or—more likely— discomfort with looking at her cousin's death through a law enforce- ment lens. "There's something else. I'd like you both to take another look at your cousin's closet."

The first time had been looking for what valuables might be miss- ing.

"This is on you, Ally," Maggie said. "He wants to know about what she wore."

Down a flight, Ally looked over the clothes with a care Belichek appreciated.

She touched a few things, including a bulky red sweater, slid past the hangers of others with a faint frown.

At the end, she sighed.

"I recognize some as things she's worn a lot, but I couldn't tell you about a number of these. They could be newer, or things for work, or I don't remember them."

"Understood. I have a photo of some fabric that I'd like to know if you recognize in connection with your cousin."

Hesitantly, Ally took the photograph, then her attention focused on the task. She looked at it a long time.

"I'm sorry, Detective Belichek, I can't tell you for sure about this, either. Jamie has a blouse very similar to that, but I couldn't swear this photograph shows hers. That's what you want to know, isn't it?"

"That's part of it. Did she wear her black and white blouse with anything in particular?"

He thought he heard a smile in her voice—a sad smile, but a smile—when she said, "Not black and white. It's black and cream. She wore it with a pair of cream slacks."

The same description as Imogen Wooton.

She pushed aside several hangers, displaying light-colored slacks.

"She was thrilled when she found these and they precisely matched the blouse's cream. But the fact that I didn't see it, doesn't mean she didn't ever wear the blouse with something else."

And that piece of common sense also applied to Imogen Wooton.

He could hear what Landis would say when he reported the conversations.

Put that pebble on the discard pile.

CHAPTER TWENTY-SEVEN

Fairlington County Police Department News Conference
In progress:

Public Information Officer Elliott Kepler: …continue to pursue the investigation strongly, exploring all aspects of—

Death, Murder, Violence Podcast: Are you going to call on the FBI or other federal resources who'd have a lot more experience with a case like this?"

PIO Kepler: "We're fortunate to have good working relationships with federal agencies, including the FBI. A good mutual relationship. We cooperate with each other as needed on—

Death, Murder, Violence Podcast: You sure need. No progress made at—

PIO Kepler:—a case-by-case basis. It's far too early in this investigation to predict what resources beyond our own lab and investigative abilities might, possibly be called on. But if we define the need for such, we will certainly be calling on them.

Death, Murder, Violence Podcast: With a high-profile case you haven't—

PIO Kepler: Ted, *Fairlington Leader?*

Fairlington Leader: Officer Kepler, do you—?"

Death, Murder, Violence Podcast: You can't ignore the facts. The general view is the federal agencies lure the top talent from local jurisdictions—what with offering better pay and benefits. That leaves the dregs working on cases like this. Fairlington Police Department needs the help of those larger, more talented agencies.

PIO Kepler: This is not a forum for making speeches. This is for journalists to ask questions.

Death, Murder, Violence Podcast: What about an ID on the victim?

PIO Kepler: Asked and answered.

~~ End news conference transcript ~~

———

"Great side-eye at the turd, Kep."

"Hell, that was full-blown stink-eye."

Landis entered the break room with an announcement. "If you have enough time to listen to that, I've got work for all of you."

✧   ✧   ✧   ✧

FORD WATCHED HIS grandfather.

The strongest man he ever knew. Sitting with his head in his hands, rubbing at the short, stubby hair left in a horseshoe around his head.

He'd seen his grandfather worried before, but this … this was new the past week and horrifying.

His grandmother's hand on his shoulder. "Come away, Ford. We can't help him with this. It's his work. The only thing we can do for him right now is let him be."

She was right. It was the only thing he could do for his grandfather in that moment.

But that was not an end to it.

That day he realized Gran had been disposing of newspapers before his grandfather—or he—could read them.

He skipped baseball practice and rode his bicycle to the library.

It wasn't hard to find his grandfather's name in the paper and the reports on the trial from a case he'd led.

The not guilty verdict a week ago coincided with the day his grandfather's despair began.

He read the coverage backward. Looking for references to his grandfather. There were many. Including one with a photo of Vivian Frye walking into the courthouse.

She was a compelling woman without being beautiful. He'd seen her in town. Now he looked up her address in the phone book and, yes, he knew exactly which house. He could picture her on the swing on the deep front porch.

Had he seen that or only imagined it?

He'd gone all the way to the start of the story in the newspaper and read the articles through again, this time in chronological order.

There was something in them—not stated directly, but hinted at.

There'd been an attempted abduction of a young girl in town. It had been broken up by the girl's cousin.

His grandfather arrested a man for the attempted abduction.

The arrested man had dated the aunt of both the intended victim and the girl who'd broken up the abduction.

The man was found not guilty.

What the articles hinted at still hadn't been clear to him then, telling him pieces without letting him see the whole.

Now—now he saw it all.

Now that he understood police and courts from the inside, and could translate the coverage into what had happened beyond it.

Now that he knew the cousins.

Now that he knew the whole story.

A sexual predator, wooing the adult aunt to try to get at the girl.

The attempted abduction.

The older cousin breaking it up.

Everything relying on her testimony because the intended victim was traumatized.

The defense poking holes in the testimony of the teenage girl.

His grandfather trying to shore up the testimony, but it not being enough.

The man going free.

The guilt, the frustration, the concern. He knew his grandfather's feelings, because he'd taken them on as his own.

But that day in the library, barely a teenager himself, he'd struggled to make sense of what happened.

He'd left the library and went to find his grandfather. As he neared the station, he saw two cars speeding away, his grandfather in the lead car.

He put his head down and pedaled as hard as he could. His first tail job.

He'd lost his grandfather's trail—not surprising, since he was on a bike and his grandfather in a squad car.

But he had a hunch…

He went to the aunt's address.

That's when he'd first seen the girls—the older cousin, trying to get to the house, but held back by neighbors. The younger two in the shadows, frozen in shock as whispers of their aunt's murder reached them.

He'd also seen his grandfather, emerging from the house, crossing that deep porch, and coming into the light on the steps to the walk as a different man from the one he'd known all his life.

His grandfather looking at the oldest cousin, meeting her gaze, then giving a quick shake of his head.

As young as Ford had been, in that single moment, he had seen what his grandfather bore. His pain. His failure. His … defeat.

He'd promised then.

To take that away from his grandfather.

CHAPTER TWENTY-EIGHT

TANNER LANDIS PAUSED at the top of the third-floor stairs of Jamie's house, arms spread across the opening, hands wrapped around the railing at either side, and dropped his head in a pantomime of despair or disgust, or both.

"Now, how did I know I'd find you here, Bel?"

Belichek didn't answer. He'd heard Landis enter the front door and, recognizing the gait, followed his progress through the house and up the three flights. He didn't move from the overstuffed chair. He didn't lift his eyes from the pages of snapshots.

"Department would have a fit you being here," Landis added.

"Department can't tell me how to spend my vacation time. And I have permission. Written, if you want to see it."

"Maggie?"

"The parents."

"Because Maggie got it from them."

Belichek grunted.

"What did the other cousin have to say this afternoon?"

"Not much. Said Jamie had a blouse of similar material as the photo. Couldn't swear to it being the same blouse. But, same as Imogen Wooton about the clothes possibly being a different pairing from usual. She spotted more missing valuables, details on some we already knew about. I sent it to Felicia, since she's following that. Copied you."

"You brought Ally *here*? Why on earth—"

He looked up at his vehemence. To most people, Tanner Landis skated through stress. Belichek knew differently. "She wanted to.

Maggie, too. Don't suppose it was easy for either one, but easier with each other. I sent details to Felicia. The glass offices can think the information came before my forced vacation. Your ass is covered."

"Yeah. Good." He breathed out audibly. "Break the case yet?"

"All wrapped up."

Landis strode across the room and pulled out the desk chair, taking time to hitch his pants legs slightly to preserve the crease, and ignoring the lie. "You're obsessed, Belichek. That's one of the symptoms of burnout."

"Are we back to those talks by the department shrink again?"

"Consultant. Not staff. The talks are interesting."

"And she's got legs, but she's married and he's in one of those alphabet-soup agencies who could probably have you taken out with a snap of his fingers and nobody'd ever figure it out. Or worse, he could get you audited."

Landis twisted a grin. "If I get taken out, you sure as hell better figure out who did it, Belichek, or I'll come back and haunt you. Although I suppose I'd have to wait in line behind Jamison Chancellor. What with all this." He jerked his head toward the pile of journals.

"I'm not haunted, I'm not obsessed, and I'm not burned out. Not giving a shit about any case, that's how you know you're burned out."

"That's the end stage. But before you get there," his partner said in a disgustingly cheerful tone for discussing the hypothetical finish of a career, "you go through a lot of other stuff. Getting obsessed with a single, hopeless case is one of the earlier stages."

"This isn't hopeless."

"You're right," Landis conceded. Too easily.

"You don't start labeling a case that way that's only a few days old." No matter what the Chief of Detectives said.

"No. But you've practically moved in here. I wouldn't be surprised if you start sleeping in her—No, don't tell me. I don't want to know."

"I'm not sleeping in her bed, for Christ's sake."

"Is that because you're not sleeping at all?" Clearly not expecting an answer, Landis looked toward the photo albums and journals spread at Belichek's feet. "You're starting to scare me, Belichek. Maybe you're not obsessed with the case. Maybe you're obsessed with the victim."

"If doing a job's being obsessed, then I'm obsessed."

"We're doing the job. Interviewing family, neighbors, acquaintances—"

"Background on Carl Arbendroth done yet?"

"In process. Jenkins. As I was saying before I was so rudely interrupted, we're interviewing everyone."

"I want to go back to the Sunshine Foundation. Hendrickson York wasn't telling us everything. Probably not Celeste Renfro, either."

"Putting aside the fact that you're off the case and supposed to be on vacation, you'd get a second time. Yeah, neither of us took a shine to Hendrickson York and he was a bit pissy about Chancellor, but we go back again now, without something more to rattle him and we'd get that they all loved her. Worshiped her. She was a saint. Blah, blah, blah. Whether they did or not."

"Most of them probably did love her. Finding any who didn't is what matters."

Landis glanced at the glass-domed clock on the shelf by the window.

Jamie's aunt gave her the antique clock for her twelfth birthday. Belichek had seen photos of her opening it, and read the neat labels underneath. They weren't in Jamie's handwriting. Maybe her mother's.

It was Jamie's handwriting, though, in a later album that wrote under a picture of her aunt, "Last photo of Aunt Vivian." The articles on Vivian Frye's murder were not labeled, were not even attached to the pages of the album. They'd been slid in between blank pages of the album loose, as if they didn't belong to the same life.

"This doesn't smell right, Tanner."

His partner looked up sharply. "What do you mean?"

Ah. Landis felt it, too. Wasn't admitting it, but he wouldn't have responded so quickly otherwise.

"It's off. Something's not right."

"Great. That's what I'll tell Palery when he has me to his office tomorrow. The investigation? It's going great. We don't have the official ID yet, no suspects in sight, but we definitely know something doesn't smell right—and we're not talking about the decomp in the house. Hell, with insight like that, they'll have me lead the next news conference, too."

Undeflected by the sarcasm, Belichek said, satisfied, "You feel it, too."

"Are you back on the purse?"

"That and more. She's supposed to be leaving. Why isn't everything packed? Clothes hanging in the closet, cosmetics in the bathroom, and where were her suitcases?"

"The ones in the attic—"

"With a gap. Some are missing."

"Perp took them to carry the valuables," Landis said.

"The killer takes suitcases from the attic, but not the electronics up here? Takes the purse like he's in a big hurry, but tosses the first two levels like he's got all the time in the world. It doesn't add up."

Landis shrugged with impatience. "Who can figure these guys?"

"You've been around Terrington too much with a line like that." The back of Landis' neck reddened. "Why hasn't any of her stuff shown up? The electronics, maybe, since they've got a wide market. But that silver is a specialized market. Not one piece has shown up. You know Felicia would have found them."

"He dealt it at face value three weeks ago. He's an out-of-towner, so we should be looking in Dubuque or Peoria. He doesn't know what he has and isn't bothering with a specialized market. Or all three." Landis had his lines down.

They just didn't convince Belichek.

Landis continued, "I'm going to work this as hard and long as they'll let me. Maggie." The name stood in as a dissertation on motivation. "But you need to give it a rest, Belichek. Give yourself a rest."

He couldn't.

That was the hell of it.

Did that make Landis right? Did it make the Palery right? Was he getting burned out?

It didn't matter. If he burned out to a pile of ashes, he was working this case until it was solved. And then past that, until there was justice.

He owed it to Jamie Chancellor.

And to ... others.

"You've gotta go on that vacation, Bel. Look at you—you sure as hell need the rest."

Landis worried about him? Well, he worried right back. Him and that psychologist. Not to mention the judge.

"After. You get a break in a case by working it, not by resting."

"It's not your case, Bel."

"If you're going to pull primary on me—"

"Fuck you," Landis said evenly. "You don't think I'd rather have you than Terrington as second to make me look good and let me gather in all the glory?" He was rubbing it in that Belichek had stepped over the line with the primary crack. "Besides, it's not the case, it's the victim that's got your balls in a knot."

Landis took the closed photo album out of his hands. Belichek consciously eased his hold to keep from hanging on.

"Jamison Chancellor is a pile of bones in a box or, actually, in a drawer. This—" Landis hefted the album on one palm. "—is not Jamison Chancellor. And getting hung up on what's left of her is dangerous."

Belichek looked at his partner, unflinching. "I don't care if you are sharing a bed with that shrink, don't give me that psycho-babble."

"Actually, I'm trying to get out of bed with her. But you didn't think it was psycho-babble when you told me about your grandfather, and how he got about one case until he was like that guy in the movie who got obsessed with a victim. If you look in the mirror, that's what'll stare back at you."

"I'm not my grandfather."

"Can you honestly tell me you're not hung up on this victim?"

"I can tell you I'm hung up on doing my job and that's all that counts."

Landis stared back for another beat. Then he tossed the album about two inches above his palm and pulled his hand out, letting it fall to the floor with a thud. Belichek didn't blink.

"Okay." His partner stood, shifting his hips and slightly flexing his knees so his pants fell into place. "But you can't do the job this time, because you're on vacation. So, go get yourself laid."

CHAPTER TWENTY-NINE

BELICHEK PICKED UP a particular journal, feeling an odd reluctance to open it. Knowing it would take him deep into Jamison Chancellor's childhood and the innocence she'd carried into adulthood.

In the later journals it was clear to him that her work for the foundation served as a shield against the trauma of her aunt's murder. In that way, she seemed luckier than Mags or Ally.

Although meeting Ally today it was hard to tell what came from childhood trauma and what from living with what happened to her husband.

He opened the journal. Why re-read it now? It wouldn't tell him who killed Jamie. He flipped to the back, as if he needed to confirm that it brought him to the end of the school year before that fateful summer—that fatal summer for Vivian Frye.

She'd thought she'd met the love of her life.

He'd certainly been the last love of her life.

Impatient, he flipped the bulk of the pages to the right, taking him to the beginning.

He'd read his way through more than a month, his hand poised to flip to the next page.

A sound.

It came from below. Not an old house settling. Too deliberate ... *connected* ... for that.

This was why he'd told Mags to put off changing the locks. On the chance the person with the keys came back.

He'd hoped...

But there was something off about this.

Quiet. Yet not stealthy. Too relaxed. Not Landis.

Someone coming up the back stairs. At the second floor already.

Still holding the journal open, he got his gun out. Ready, but out of sight. And checked the time. Two minutes before two a.m.

Maybe Landis and Palery were right about his needing a vacation if he'd missed hearing someone coming in and starting up these old stairs.

Then, the person had left the second floor and was ascending the last flight to this level.

Partway up the flight of stairs, the top of a woman's head came into view. More. A face. Not looking up, like she would if she suspected or expected someone up here.

Then, visible from the waist up, a tote in one hand, heavy enough to require her hand on the railing to balance, she looked up, a frown rippling her forehead.

With him sitting and her on the stairs, they were nearly eye-to-eye across the open space of the landing.

The world tipped and narrowed. It felt like somebody pumped anesthetic into his bloodstream, like when he had that bullet taken out.

He'd fought it then, not knowing if he'd come back.

He fought it now, not knowing if she'd come back.

"Jamie."

Her eyes widened, then she heaved the tote toward him, turned, and ran down the stairs.

WITH HER HEAD start and needing to detour around the tote, he had to make up ground.

He almost caught her at the archway to the small room with the antique desk, but he skidded wide and lost time getting his feet back under him.

She had a phone out.

She had her phone?

She punched numbers, shouting, "Police! Police!"

"I am the police. Jamie! I'm a cop."

Manipulating the phone slowed her enough that he caught her left arm, trying to pull her around. She threw a purse at him. *Her purse.* He ducked and it glanced off the side of his neck, but he didn't release his hold on her. They spun around in the small space.

"Stop. I'm the police!"

With his free hand he dug for his badge.

She kneed him. Right on target. And hard. Real hard.

The world didn't tip this time, it slid, straight into hell. Fire and brimstone rose through his gut into his throat.

Through the haze he held on, but she dragged him along with her, his hand crashed against the doorframe as she ran into the glassed-in porch, and she used the doorframe edge to peel his fingers away, then locked the door. She'd taken her only exit, but they'd padlocked the porch's exterior door to the patio and he was between her and access to either the back or front doors. She had no escape.

Fighting the haze, he saw her rattling the door, expecting it to open, taken aback by the padlock.

She picked up a wrought iron plant stand, obviously intending to break one of the glass panels.

The motion sensor light on the patio came on.

Anyone looking out from the second story of the three neighboring houses could see something was going on. Not a clear view. But even an obstructed view might be enough to recognize Jamison Chancellor.

He wasn't working out every step in his head, but he damned well knew he wanted to avoid that.

"Jamie, I'm a cop! I won't hurt you!"

Still partly bent, he dug out his badge and held it up to the glass that separated them.

She didn't swing the plant stand, but she didn't put it down, either. From the far side of the glassed-in porch—which didn't offer her much protection if he'd broken the glass between them—she looked at the badge.

"How do I know it's not a fake?"

"Call police headquarters. The number's—"

"No, I'll get the number myself."

She not only took that precaution, she used the speaker-phone. That left her hands free. She put down the plant stand, but from the top of its twin, she picked up a ceramic pot holding an orange mum.

It wasn't a .45, but it wouldn't do his skull any good if he broke the glass and she used it.

She called information, and then she had the call put through to the number they gave. He could hear her fine because she was raising her voice for the speaker phone. He did the same so she'd hear him through the glass.

"Ask for homicide."

Her eyes flashed to his, big and startled, but she didn't argue. "Homicide, please."

"Ask for Detective Landis. Ask him if Ford Belichek is a homicide detective."

She followed both steps.

"Yeah," his partner said. "As of right now he is."

Landis' voice came through a little tinny, but clear enough for Belichek to hear the undercurrent of irritation. He wondered if she heard it. Or if she'd noticed Landis' wording. Chances were, she wasn't paying much attention to nuances.

"Can you give me a description, please?"

"A description? Listen, lady, I don't—" The rush of impatient words ended abruptly. There was no click that Belichek could hear.

"Hello? Mr. Land—"

"By God, he finally listened to me."

"Pardon?"

"So, you met Belichek and he told you he's a homicide detective and you decided to check it out, huh?" The voice over the phone line had turned teasing and friendly. "Wouldn't you know Belichek would pick a suspicious one. So, what do you want to know? A description? Let's see…"

She showed no reaction to Landis' assumption of how she'd encountered Belichek. She listened intently to the APB-type description Landis gave, her eyes checking the six-foot height, hundred and ninety-five pounds, brown hair, gray eyes.

He stood still, as straight as he could, and looked back.

She looked like her pictures, and nothing like them. Not even the videos had captured her, not all of her. It missed her presence, the full reality of her flesh and bone. The curve of her hip in worn jeans, the jut of her elbow pushing at a pale yellow sleeve.

Or maybe it had been his own mind that had subtracted something from those images, knowing the person they represented was dead.

Only she wasn't.

She was alive. She was here.

Jamie.

"…and when my mother's describing him to her friends," Landis wrapped up, "she always mentions he's got dimples when he's teasing somebody."

"There's been no occasion to observe that," Jamie Chancellor said.

She must be relaxing to say that. Good.

"As for scars and distinguishing marks," the telephone voice went on, "he's got a beaut on his right hip—that's not something my mother tells her friends, but I thought you might want to be on the lookout."

"I doubt that situation will arise, either."

"Oh, I wouldn't worry about things arising, I think that'll take care of itself."

The last sound Belichek heard before the line went dead was Landis' wicked chuckle. Nice to know his partner thought so highly of him.

Jamison Chancellor let her arms straighten, lowering the pot.

"You're really a cop."

"I'm really a cop."

"You're a homicide detective."

"I'm a homicide detective."

She drew in a deep breath. "Okay, so you are who you say you are. What are you doing in my house?"

"First things first. Let's get on the same side of the door." He pulled a key ring from his pocket and selected the right one on the first try.

She didn't move forward but she did put down the pot, if only to put her hands on her hips. "If you had the key, why didn't you open the door?"

"Because you would have broken the glass and kept running. One of the things a good cop learns is when not to chase."

"So what is a good cop—or any cop—doing *here?* In my house?"

"Investigating a homicide."

"Someone was murdered? *Here?*"

"Yes."

"Who?"

"You."

She stared at him. Not because she didn't understand, but because she was looking it over, considering the possibilities. He liked that.

"You might be a good cop, but you've made a huge mistake—"

He shook his head. "No mistake. I'm investigating your murder. The murder of Jamison Chancellor."

CHAPTER THIRTY

H_E _{DELIBERATELY} _{HELD} off on the questions pounding in his head.

There was a more important factor.

She shivered, and he handed her the quilted throw from where it was folded on the back of the upholstered chair in the corner of the first-floor office.

He'd settled her there when he moved her away from the glass porch, in case someone entered the back gate. No one could see her from the front window, either.

They kept the curtains closed, but he wasn't risking that someone could see—or photograph—through a crack.

He finished telling her the bare outlines of the case, an extremely condensed version, in the mode of the driest report he'd ever written. Just enough to get her to cooperate.

His mind was working hard now, taking him down a path he'd never have believed a day ago.

Then again, he'd never have believed he'd be looking at a very much alive Jamison Chancellor, either.

"It goes on the arm," she said.

"What?"

"The throw. It belongs over the arm, not the back."

"Sorry. Things get put back after collecting evidence, but doesn't all get back to the right place."

"It's okay. You had no way of knowing." She tucked the throw around herself. She'd drawn her legs up on the overstuffed chair, so all that showed of her was from the shoulders up.

Cold. Delayed reaction, Belichek decided.

She'd done no crying, showed no sign of hysterics, but he could tell the surge of adrenaline that had carried her flight through the house to the porch had ebbed, leaving numbed shock in its wake.

He had to ask a few questions to avoid potential landmines.

"Where were you, Jamie?"

Her eyelids flickered, maybe at his using her name. Maybe not. "A cabin in North Carolina, writing a book."

"North Carolina?" Not Pennsylvania. Where she'd gone the other times. Where Maggie, the people at the Sunshine Foundation, and her parents all said they thought she was.

"Mmm-hmm. A friend let me use a family cabin."

A friend who hadn't come forward. Or hadn't mentioned the loan of the cabin when they were questioned.

Who? But that wasn't one of the urgent questions yet.

"How'd you get back here?"

"My friend's truck. I drove straight through. Once I started, I wanted to sleep in my own bed."

"Did anybody see you when you arrived?"

"Here? Tonight? I don't think so. People are in bed by this time. What difference does that make?"

It could make all the difference. "You didn't talk to anybody, didn't see anybody you knew?"

"No. I got my stuff out of the truck, let myself in and… You."

She had faded blue shadows under her eyes. Her shoulders sagged. Her mouth drooped.

She was beautiful.

"You have a phone."

She brought her hand out from under the throw and looked at the device, as if she'd forgotten she held it. "Yes."

"But there's no SIM card in it."

"Sure there is or I couldn't use it."

"We've been trying to track your phone."

Her eyes flared a second with realization. "You mean my regular phone? I left that here. This is my cabin phone."

"Explain that."

"I leave my regular phone here and take this one with for emergencies."

"Why—?" No, he knew why she left her regular phone at home. To avoid interruptions. He also knew this meant her phone had probably been taken along with the other electronics and silver. That could all wait. "You didn't contact anybody while you were out of town? Using that phone or any other?"

"No, I never do on these trips."

"No call to family, no text to a friend? Nothing on social media?"

"No. The whole idea is to cut myself off from all that, from the world, and get work done. If I could do that around my family and friends, I'd stay here. But I don't have the discipline. This seems the only way to do it."

"You've done this before?"

She nodded, the motion slightly jerking. "Three times."

"Those other times—same place?" He knew the answer. He wanted to hear it from her.

"A different cabin the other times. In Pennsylvania."

Her eyes went to the built-in bookcase that had once held her TV and more. He stayed silent, waiting for her reaction to the losses, but she was looking at the photo back in its rightful spot.

"The person who was killed..."

"A woman."

"Oh. But that means... Somebody was in my house? Living here?" She sounded out the words as if trying to make sense of them. "How did they get in?"

A damned good question. "We don't know. To be clear about this, did you give permission to anyone to stay in your house while you were gone?"

"No." Her gaze came around to his face. "I would have told you right away if I had, if I thought I knew who..."

The clothes in the closet, the ones Ally hadn't recognized, but thought they could be new or Jamie's work clothes. But if they weren't...?

That had to wait, too.

"Who has your key?"

"Imogen, my parents, my cousins—Maggie and Ally. That's—" The recognition of why he asked the question intersected with her own thought process of who might have been in her house. Her mouth gaped with horror. "*Ally*. My cousin Ally—"

"It wasn't her." He used the tone his grandfather had taught him. Authoritative, no sliver of doubt, yet quiet. "I've seen her. Maggie and I have seen her, talked to her. Wasn't any of the others you mentioned, either. Why would you think it was your cousin Ally?"

She breathed hard for maybe twenty seconds.

"Her husband, Chad..."

"The cop who was shot, in a coma."

"Yes. Sometimes ... she needs a break. A rest." Her eyes flickered. "But ... but then who was it? Who was killed?"

"We don't know. Not anymore. We'll have to start from zero. Dental records, medical records. Same things we'd tried to get a positive ID it was you."

"Oh." She was grasping details around the edge of the lack of identification, but not the issue at its core. "Oh, dear. How—? But, you can't."

"Your medical records? We know. No hope of a dental match, either." He slid past that. "We were hoping for the medical records, but there was a fire at your doctor's and that's delayed things. DNA's in progress."

"His office called after the fire. My medical records are all gone. I was telling my friends at work about that this summer."

She was latching onto things that were part of her previous life. Ordinary things. Things she understood. She didn't realize the significance of what she'd said, but he did.

She'd told people about her missing records. Somebody could have remembered.

Was it only people at work she'd told? Other friends? Neighbors? She'd been dating Carl Arbendroth at the time of the fire. It wasn't unreasonable to think she told him, too.

How that fit in with an unknown woman being killed in this house? That required a lot more pieces to figure out.

"We'll have to start over with identification. It won't be any easier."

He wished he hadn't added that, because he could see a layer of numbness peeling away from her. He saw her recognition that the first try at identification had been when they'd thought the victim was Jamison Chancellor—not as an abstract concept, but as reality.

He saw the impact, the implosion of realization shudder through her. No screaming, no shouting, she took the force of this first layer inside.

"Oh, my God. Oh, my God. They think I'm dead. They all think I'm *dead*. I have to call—"

"No." His hold on her hand stopped hers from moving, but he would have used more force if he had to. "You're not calling anyone. Not until we know who tried to kill you."

She got it almost immediately, and it shook her in a new way.

"You suspect one of my friends?" Her hands loosened. He slipped the phone away. "No." She shook her head. "You've got that wrong. You can't suspect my friends. You don't know them. Not one of them is capable—"

"I suspect all of your friends. Anybody's capable."

"But—"

"Look, the one advantage we have going now is you. The biggest clue to most murders is the victim. We spend hours, days, weeks digging into the victim's life. But this time we don't just have bank accounts and phone records and friends and families—we've got the real thing."

"But I have no idea who could have done this. I don't even know who was killed."

"Maybe not, but you're our best clue. There's a chance you'll tell us who did it without knowing it. And we'll recognize it, because that's what we do. But we need time. Time away from all the shit that's going to hit the fan when it comes out you're alive. You have no idea what it will be like."

"I can't stay hidden forever, Detective Belichek. I won't."

He ignored that. "We'll go someplace where we won't stumble across anybody you know for a few days."

He knew he was taking advantage of her shock. He knew it and he didn't care. He'd do more than that to keep her alive.

"A few days?"

He had to get her out of here. They could deal with the rest of it later. "I've got a lot of questions."

She looked at him, at his eyes, at his hands, at his mouth, then back to his eyes. "I have to let my parents know I'm alive."

"No," he said automatically. "No one can—"

"I won't give you seconds, much less days unless—"

"It's for your safety—"

"—I see my parents and—Oh. They're asleep. I don't want to disturb them."

"That's right. Not your parents. But there is one person. Maggie. Your cousin."

"Maggie." Her eyes widened, seeing him, perhaps for the first time. "You—You said your name before. Your name's..."

"Belichek," he prompted after she faded to silence.

"Belichek. You're Bel. You're Maggie's Bel, the detective."

"Yeah. I am."

"She's talked about you—as much as she'll talk about anything."

He knew he had it then, even though knowing his connection to her cousin didn't make even a small dent in Jamie's mountain of concerns.

What he had going for him was she was still in shock.

He'd use every advantage he had.

CHAPTER THIRTY-ONE

AFTER A QUICK run upstairs for her to swap out clean clothes in her tote and for him to grab the journal he hadn't finished, keeping it out of her sight, he hustled her out the back, holding onto her with one hand, and using the other to sling the tote over his shoulder.

They passed a battered pickup he hadn't seen before. He mentally noted the Virginia license plate, the description.

But mostly, he concentrated on getting her out of there before any neighbors saw her. Or, for that matter, a patrol car. Especially one who'd share the news with Roy Isaacson.

At the same time, his mind was working.

Only when she was in his car and they were moving did he breathe a bit easier.

This time of night, the traffic was relatively light. They made good time.

She stared straight ahead without seeming to focus.

He didn't hit her with the questions piling up in his head. He didn't want her thinking right now. Not until he had her squared away.

She roused as he brought his car to a stop. "This is Maggie's place."

"Yeah." He hit the speed dial on his phone. He had a feeling…

A bad feeling.

After six, long rings she answered. But no light went on in the building in front of them.

Could be answering in the dark.

"What?" Alert, to-the-point. Not unlike J.D. Carson had been.

Maggie, too, was accustomed to calls in the night.

"It's me. Belichek. I'm at your place, out front."

"I'm not there." *Damn.* He hated when his bad feelings were right. Which was almost always. "I'm in Bedhurst."

With J.D. Carson, in the mountains.

He started another internal swear word, but didn't finish it.

This might be good.

"I'm coming there."

"Now?"

"Yes."

"What's going on?" She knew it was something big. She feared it was something bad.

Leaving her thinking about the possible bads for the hours it would take him to drive up there might seem cruel. But he couldn't afford the time to hash it out now. The eastern sky would be peeling back layers of darkness before they got there as it was.

Besides, how could what Maggie imagine now be worse than what she'd already accepted as fact?

"I'll tell you when I get there."

"You know who murdered her."

"No." Hell, now they didn't even know who'd been murdered. "We're working on it. You know that. But there's been a … development that's changed things. We're going to have to look at the case from the start again."

He heard an uneasy stirring beside him.

"Bel—" Maggie started.

"I'll tell you when I get there." He hung up.

He put the car in gear and drove toward I-66, past the turn that would have taken them to the station.

"You're… We're not going to the police station?"

"No."

She was silent for a moment. "Is Maggie with J.D.?"

"Yes."

"We're going there?"

"Yes."

"Why?"

"I'll tell you both at the same time, when we get there."

CELESTE RENFRO WASN'T sleeping much these past nights.

She sat in an upholstered chair by a bedroom window that looked out on the star-glinted leaves of an evergreen magnolia. She'd bought this house mostly for that tree's promise of solace all year round.

She hardly saw it.

She'd always thought of herself as one who faced facts and dealt with them. Not one who got bogged down in navel-gazing and second-guessing.

But now…

Should she have called the police when Bethany Usher didn't return to work? Would that have looked better?

Those two police detectives hadn't seemed to accept it as a natural consequence of the young woman's utter unreliability. But then they hadn't put up with Bethany for several months.

The tartness of that last thought gave her a spurt of her usual energy.

It faded.

Especially as she remembered the arrival today of another detective. This one wore his suspicion of everyone and everything like a badge of honor.

He'd disrupted everybody. Especially with extra volunteers clogging up the offices—odd how so many found time to show up and help with the possibility of sensationalism and gossip as a lure.

Even before he arrived, that Detective Terrington had the restaurant staff in an uproar of paranoia and drama that wafted upstairs to the Sunshine Foundation with the takeout lunch two volunteers collected for them all. Along with lunch, those two volunteers spread the uneasiness to the other volunteers, Adam, her, and—most of all—Hendrickson.

Even though the detective wasn't as sharp as Landis or his nearly silent sidekick Belichek, Hendrickson hadn't seen that. Of course, he hadn't. It had taken the rest of the afternoon to soothe Hendrickson's nerves enough to send him home to a peaceful evening.

Unlike hers.

Celeste rubbed at her forehead.

She missed Jamie.

THE GLAZE OF city lights faded to pin-pricks against the country dark. They drove on in silence.

Jamison Chancellor curled partially onto her left side in the passenger seat, and watched Detective Ford Belichek of the Fairlington Police Department between slitted eyelids, numbly amazed.

Unable to absorb what he'd told her, she focused on the one surprising element she could take in.

She didn't think she would ever meet this man.

Detective Belichek. Maggie's Bel.

At first, she and Ally joked Maggie made him up to prove that she did have a friend, that she did talk to someone.

They'd debated whether the details Maggie presented, including his woman-trap partner, meant he could be real or that Maggie knew how to be as incredibly persuasive with this story as they'd seen her be in a courtroom.

Except then Jamie looked him up and found him mentioned in media accounts of investigations. No photos. Only the name. Ford Belichek.

But that time she and Ally went to the court when Maggie was trying one of her early big cases. Maggie never even knew they were there, with her tunnel vision zeroed in on the case, ignoring—no, simply not seeing—the gallery.

This man had seen them, though.

A glance from him as they entered … she'd never felt more seen.

He hadn't turned again to where they sat. Neither had the taller, well-dressed man with him. Had to be the other one. His partner,

Landis.

Jamie had been sure she'd never forget him when he'd turned and looked at her. How had she not recognized him immediately?

She could arouse no passion for the answer.

She could arouse no passion for anything.

It was as if she didn't exist.

She glanced down at herself, surprised. She still wore the jeans and yellow shirt she'd had on when she left North Carolina today—no, now it was yesterday.

It always disconcerted her to move into or out of her self-imposed isolations, a sort of personal culture shock. But she'd been eager yesterday to return to what she called her regular life.

Now she had no regular life.

To the world, she had no life at all. She was dead. Mourned.

Except to this man sitting beside her.

"You're the only person on earth who knows I'm alive."

She felt awe at the words, yet they came out flat.

"You know it." He said it with a fierceness that surprised her, like he was willing her to life.

She hadn't been dead, not to herself. Yet it was as if this man had brought her back to life.

His voice came again.

"The big question is if the murderer knows it."

CHAPTER THIRTY-TWO

THE SILENCE AFTER that was long. He didn't want to invite a question he didn't want to answer by looking at her.

But the silence finally broke him down enough to shoot a glance her way.

She was asleep.

He reached one-handed over the seat back and snagged his raincoat.

She didn't stir as he awkwardly spread it over her.

The next time he looked, she'd hooked her hands over the collar and pulled it up to her chin.

She was out.

He glanced at her again. Not long, the twisting, dark roads didn't allow that.

He knew her.

The way he came to know all the victims.

But now everything he'd thought he knew of the victim, of her home, her heart, her soul. All gone.

Because she was alive.

And the actual victim?

She didn't belong to the house, the setting—the entire life—he'd come to know.

He drove.

There was probably another way to get to Carson's place, but it would take longer than going through town.

Isolated as Bedhurst was, he still wasn't taking chances. He tugged the raincoat higher over Jamie. He put on a ball cap and a pair of sunglasses.

Eyes followed them as they went through. Thankfully, not a lot of eyes since it was still less light than dark.

Thanks to the ground work he'd done last spring when Maggie was up here, he found the obscure route to Carson's isolated home readily.

He parked under a tree that would obscure the car from view, including from above.

He called. Maggie answered before the first ring ended.

"We're here. Open the door."

Jamie sat up at his first words.

"We—?" Maggie asked.

He hung up. Stepped out into the sharp chill of the mountain night, went around the car, and helped Jamie out with a hand under her arm. She moved stiffly, groggy. Emotional exhaustion and extended shock, he suspected.

"I can—"

Maybe she could have, but he wrapped an arm around her and the raincoat, pushed back to close the car door, and hustled her forward, across the opening, up the steps, onto the porch, past the door J.D. Carson held open—he wasn't the least surprised Carson opened the door, had Maggie well back from it, and the inside dim. Or that the guy surveyed the surroundings with sharp eyes.

Maggie kept her sharp gaze for him.

"What the hell is going on, Belichek? Since when did you go cloak and dagger?"

Respect dulled the edge of Maggie's irritation but didn't sheath it completely.

He didn't answer. He looked around at Carson.

"Shut the door."

He did.

Belichek felt Jamie beside him, letting the raincoat slide away.

She took a step forward, still in his hold, but revealed now.

Not making a sound, Maggie swayed.

Belichek reached toward her, but wasn't releasing Jamie.

"Get Maggie," he ordered.

Carson had done that before the words were out.

Maggie steadied herself almost immediately.

"Jamie? *Jamie?*"

"It wasn't me, Maggie. I'm alive. I'm sorry—"

"*Sorry?*"

"I should have made him break this to you before you saw me—The shock—"

"Screw the shock."

Belichek moved back as Jamie Chancellor and her cousin embraced, giving each other balance.

"Oh, God. You're alive. You're really alive," he heard Maggie murmur.

"I'm alive."

Maggie made a sound, like what Belichek had heard when somebody who'd been choking took their first clear breath.

He retreated.

But only a step. Privacy was great, but he wasn't letting Jamie out of his sight. Not even to leave her with Maggie.

"It's all right, Maggie," Jamie said. "Everything's all right."

Maggie straightened.

"Everything is *not* all right." She faced Belichek. "What the hell is going on?"

DAY FOUR

CHAPTER THIRTY-THREE

"LET'S SIT DOWN," Carson said.

He gestured them toward a soaring stone fireplace.

Belichek seated Jamie in the solitary upholstered chair and moved its matching ottoman to the side, sitting sideways on it. Maggie took the edge of a rocking chair. Carson remained standing, leaning against the fireplace.

"Where were you? Where the hell were you?" Maggie's hands fisted.

"I went to write my book in a cabin—"

"No. you didn't. You weren't there. We looked."

"What are you talking about, Maggie? I was—Oh, you mean Hendrickson's cabin? The one I'd used before?"

"Of course. that's what I mean. Where you'd gone to write your other books. Where—"

"To finish them. Not to write the whole thing on any of them, because—"

"I don't give a damn about the books. Or how much you wrote there or didn't write there. You were *not* in that cabin. You hadn't been in that cabin any time lately. You don't think when Ally came to your folks' house that first day, with everybody falling apart, and Ally took me aside and said maybe—*maybe*—there was the smallest chance you were actually at the cabin and it was all some kind of tragic mistake, you don't think I drove right up there to Pennsylvania? Walked out the door and drove straight there—"

"She didn't drive, Belichek." Carson said. "I see the horror in your eyes. I drove."

"Good to hear."

Maggie ignored them both. She was homed in on Jamie and only Jamie. That didn't mean they wouldn't pay for that exchange later.

"—and looked. Looked all over. Looked for any sign someone was staying there. Had been there lately. Checked with the neighbors. Law enforcement. Nothing. *Nothing.* Nobody had been in that cabin for months. You sure as hell hadn't been there. So don't tell us—"

"I didn't go there this time. Last time—I was offered a different cabin and I went there. The cabin in North Carolina was ideal."

"And you didn't tell anyone? Didn't contact anyone—?"

"That's the whole idea, Maggie. To not be in contact, to not be reachable. To pare away all the distractions and work on the book."

"You could do that at home, without—"

"No, *you* could do it at home. You're good at blocking out the rest of the world. Blocking out people. You're the champion at it. I'm not."

Jamison Chancellor had a stronger bite behind her bark than you'd expect. She'd hit a bull's-eye with Maggie and shut her up. No small feat.

But now she rubbed her eyes, trying to remove the regret.

"I'm not as good at concentration as you," Jamie said to her cousin. That wasn't what she meant, but it clothed her already-spoken words in softer fabric. "I don't have the discipline. So, I use crutches. Like going away to a cabin."

"Hendrickson York's," Maggie said with disdain.

Jamie went right past that. "Like not letting people know where I am. Like not connecting while I'm there—not having the *ability* to connect, so I don't give into any temptation."

Belichek asked, "The temptation to let people contact you? Or the temptation to contact them?"

Her gaze shifted to him. "Both."

A lie. The temptation was to let people contact her. She wasn't tempted to do the contacting herself.

But did she know it was a lie?

Belichek repeated to the others what she'd said about leaving her regular phone at home.

"You're wandering around in the mountains without a cell phone?"

"There's not good reception there, anyway, but no. I take my pay-by-the-minute cabin phone."

"You didn't have your main phone with you?" When Jamie shook her head, Maggie jumped on it, turning to him. "So it *was* stolen. The SIM card's out of it or we'd have it by now, but tracking the phone's IMEI should get us to who has it, then we can backtrack to the thief."

"They were already on it, Mags."

Carson pushed off from the stone fireplace. "Coffee."

It wasn't an invitation, but a statement of intention.

Leaving a silence behind, he went into the light-colored kitchen under a loft area, poured mugs of previously made coffee and returned.

"Caffeine delivered. We're all short on sleep."

Jamie wrapped both hands around the mug like a kid with hot chocolate. "This is good."

✧ ✧ ✧ ✧

JAMIE DRANK THE coffee gratefully.

Also grateful for the lowered emotional temperature in the room.

More light slid into the large room, the morning advancing toward day. It gilded the wood floor, the stairway rising to a loft over the back half, and bookcases across the front wall.

It was beautiful in its spareness.

"You look tired, Jamie," Maggie said.

She almost smiled at Maggie's trademark lack of tact. "I *am* tired. I started traveling… I don't know how many hours ago and I'm too tired to figure it out now. You look tired, too."

"I look like I'm half dead," Maggie corrected. "I've been investigating your murder since—Oh, shit. *Now* I cry." With impatient fingertips, she pushed at tears daring to escape onto her cheeks. "Your parents are going to—"

"No."

They both swung around to face Belichek at the single word. He directed his next words to Maggie.

"We're not telling her parents. Or anybody outside this room. Somebody out there thinks they've killed your cousin. They have to keep thinking that. They have to keep thinking they got the job done so they're not thinking about how to finish it."

Jamie protested, "Detective Belichek, you didn't have to be so harsh—"

"Yes, yes he did." Maggie straightened. "I was thinking like a family member. He's thinking like an investigator."

"Of course, you were thinking like a family member. That's what you are. And the rest of the family and everyone at Sunshine will—"

"No," Belichek said again.

"—feel the same … What?"

"No one else will know you're alive. Not yet. Maybe not—"

"That's impossible. Of course, they have to be told. My parents, my brothers and their families, Ally." She saw no give in Belichek's face, and turned to Maggie. "I let him bring me to you first, but we can't let them go on thinking—"

Maggie wasn't looking at her, didn't seem to hear her.

"How long?" Maggie asked Belichek.

"As long as it takes," he said.

"That might be—" Maggie started.

"I know."

Jamie looked from one to the other.

She knew her brain was foggy from lack of sleep and shock, but this was more. They seemed to speak shorthand with no need to complete thoughts or spell out implications, while she mentally scrambled to keep up with even the spoken words.

"And the logistics," Maggie said.

"An issue. But it can be done. Has to be done."

"Are you saying off the books? No support. No approval."

"Entirely off the books. No support. No approval."

"God, Bel. Does Landis—?"

"No."

"Because you're being an ass who's going to protect his partner while you jump onto the railroad tracks with the train speeding directly at you."

"It's the only way. You know it, with the leaks at the department—especially around homicide."

"The leaks. God. You're right. But if anybody finds out—" Repercussions Jamie could only guess at echoed in the silence between them. "What if we come up empty?"

"We can't be much emptier than we are now with no idea who the victim was. And Jamie—your cousin—is still alive. She could start a new life in our own private would-be-victim protection program."

"You're serious?" Maggie drove her hands through her hair. "My God, you are. I can't even begin to think how many regulations this breaks. Not to mention—"

"I know. If you say pull the plug, I'd go along with you."

Maggie grimaced scornfully. "No, you wouldn't."

"I wouldn't want to," Belichek said immediately. "I'd grab her up and put her so deep under wraps nobody'd ever find her. Including you."

"Wait a minute." It sounded more like a plea than an order, so Jamie tried again. "Just wait a minute. What if I don't want to be put under wraps? What if I—?"

"Doesn't matter," Belichek said.

"I have a right to—"

"Not to get yourself killed," he interrupted. "Again."

Maggie's eyes took on that calculating cast Jamie thought of as her lawyer look. "You *are* officially dead, Jamie. No, maybe not officially, because of the delay in identification. Still, you're dead as far as the world's concerned. That puts a big dent in your rights. And in the regulations they could get us on for breaking."

"Maggie, this is crazy. You have to tell him it is."

"He's made good points."

"My parents—"

Belichek said, "Would rather have you alive. You tell them now and then get killed, how much better do you think that'll make them feel?"

"Geeze, Bel. You can't talk to her like you do to me."

Jamie slid her cousin a look.

Belichek caught it. J.D. saw it, too, but Maggie didn't.

"This is ridiculous," Jamie said more strongly. "You're not even considering that whoever was killed in my house might have been the real target, when that's far more likely. No one would want to kill me. I—"

"That's not a bad point that the victim might have been the real target," Maggie said. "It is possible."

"Possible. But operating on that assumption would be criminally optimistic. Stupidly, criminally optimistic."

Belichek's blunt words had the force of a slap to the face. Jamie couldn't stop herself from meeting Maggie's gaze. She saw a glimmer of sympathy, along with a hint of I've-always-told-you-that. But mostly she saw resolution. The same resolution she'd heard in Ford Belichek's voice.

Ford.... Why did that ring a bell somewhere deep in her mind. Sure, his connection to Maggie, but something else…

Maggie unlocked her phone one-handed.

"What are you doing?" Belichek demanded.

"Logistics. We need a place to hide her. Some place where few people go. Some place safe. With somebody we can trust."

"Maggie," J.D. said.

She stopped punching numbers and turned to him.

"Here?" Maggie asked. "You're okay with that? Early in your law career to start breaking rules."

He didn't say anything or make a move, but apparently he answered her questions.

Maggie turned back to the detective. "It has upsides."

"Are you sure?" So Belichek knew what they were talking about—another example of their shorthand.

"Yeah. And he does know how to keep his own counsel."

J.D. said, dryly, "Lawyer jokes?"

Maggie's mouth twitched. But it quickly went solemn. "It's a big favor to ask."

"You're good for it. Besides, I think you'll find Belichek was planning this all along."

Jamie's gaze jerked to Belichek. He accepted the statement with equanimity. "Not moving her again is a big plus. No visitors expected?"

"No."

"Hoped for that. Security?"

"Yeah."

"Expected that."

"Okay. Settled," Maggie declared. "But not unlimited time. We can finesse this a day or two, but beyond that…"

Before Belichek could argue, J.D. asked, "How're you going to use the time?"

Jamie knew Belichek wasn't accepting the time limit, but he went along with the topic shift. For now.

He said, "Since it wasn't Jamie who died, there are two possibilities. She was the intended victim or she was the killer."

Jamie sucked in one breath, then a second one when she saw Maggie and J.D. were not rocked. And she couldn't honestly say which of those possibilities rocked her more.

"Not accepting the latter," Belichek continued without a pause, "that leaves us with two choices. The killer knew it wasn't Jamie or the killer didn't. Either way, she's the best lead. Either way, she's in danger."

"Why is she in danger if the killer knew it wasn't Jamie?" J.D. asked.

"Meant to kill her but recognized his mistake after he'd killed. Had to get out fast to avoid being caught at the scene," Maggie said.

Belichek nodded once. "Or intends to pin the murder on her."

Jamie shuddered.

His mouth went flat.

She could *hear* his thoughts. *No time to console her. What she needed most from him—from them was clear-headed logic.*

She looked down at her hands. She was overtired, in shock. She was *not* hearing a stranger's thoughts.

Besides, it was common sense.

"Either way," he was saying, "we have an opportunity here where we might know more than the killer. This is a gift. Which we badly need."

"It's also a more important gift." Maggie reached out and grasped her cousin's hand.

At Maggie's uncharacteristic emotional expression, Jamie's head came up and she returned the grasp.

"So, we start with questions," Belichek said. "The big one first. Who was killed? Was she the target? Or was Jamie?"

"And Jamie's our best source. Right." Maggie leaned back. "So let's start with—"

"I'm not starting anything else until I have a shower," Jamie declared. "I've been in cars most of the past twenty-four hours. I need a shower. I *really* need a shower. And a change of clothes."

Also a few minutes to think.

CHAPTER THIRTY-FOUR

WITH EXHAUSTION AND shock vying to overload her, Jamie's mind latched onto a different topic as she took toiletries and clean clothes from her tote.

J.D. Carson looked much as he had when she'd met him.

Not when he and Maggie became involved—first in a murder investigation and then with each other, but later, when he'd been at Maggie's place.

That was mid-May, when she and Ally arrived unannounced. It was always hit or miss whether she'd be there, but drop-ins were the only way they'd found to have any chance of seeing her.

Although, come to think of it, Maggie had agreed to—and kept—three meetings with them over the summer, on the one day each month Ally took off from her years'-long vigil at the bedside of her husband.

J.D. Carson's influence on Maggie?

Jamie considered the man as she brushed her hair.

Being cleared of suspicion of murder had not noticeably lightened the hard lines of his face.

Yet there was clearly a connection between him and Maggie.

A sexual connection and more.

Jamie hadn't wanted to like J.D. Carson. She'd always thought Maggie and her detective Belichek would get together. The way Maggie talked about the man…

But back in May, when she'd seen the way J.D. looked at Maggie and the way she returned the look, she'd wondered…

And now, seeing Maggie with the two men, Jamie let go of the fantasy pairing in favor of the obvious one in front of her, even as her heart twisted for Maggie's Bel.

She pushed aside thoughts of Detective Ford Belichek's romantic loss.

She had bigger things to try to absorb.

She stepped into J.D.'s oversized shower and stuck her head under the flow of water.

MAGGIE AND J.D. went outside after Jamie went upstairs for a shower.

Belichek scrubbed his face with water from the half-bath sink and dried off with a towel.

This wouldn't be any ordinary interrogation, but the questions that needed answering weren't that different.

He stared out the window to the right of the front door, ordering the questions in his mind, mapping approaches depending on responses.

Clattering on the stairs spun him around.

Jamie Chancellor stopped the second she saw him. Her hair was wet. She wore a shirt that reached mid-thigh with longer tails front and back. Her legs were bare.

She showed no sign of awareness of that.

He forced himself to look up to her face, and was rewarded by seeing she didn't look as drained. More of the shock was peeling away. He'd have to work fast.

Words jerked out of her.

"There were clothes in my closet that weren't mine. I don't know how I didn't see that. I mean, I did see it, but it didn't register."

"Shock."

She waved one hand. "Maybe, maybe. But it means someone was staying in my house for—I don't know how long. I don't know when the person was killed."

"Likely over the Labor Day weekend. Probably Sunday."

"Oh. Then the person was there overnight? Was it the woman who was killed? But why didn't everybody know right away that the dead woman in my house wasn't *me*?"

THEY WALKED FAST, Maggie appreciating the stretch in her legs, the air sweeping past her face to a rhythm of *Jamie's alive. Alive…*

She knew J.D. had her outside for exactly that reason … and to keep her from pouncing on Jamie with questions.

The leaf-littered trail through the woods in the rapidly brightening light took them to an old cemetery. She'd had no idea it was this close to J.D.'s place.

The trail must follow a crow's flight, while the road she knew circled wide.

They hadn't talked getting here and now they separated, walking softly between the markers.

At the far side, near a tree breaking into its autumn glory, she stopped at a headstone that read *Pandora Addington Wade.*

This is what she'd thought awaited Jamie. Not just the grave, but the emotions of those who visited it.

She'd been spared that. And that made her feel an intruder, though she would be no less of one if she left now.

Especially when J.D. came toward her.

She wouldn't rush away, but she did wish she could find something to say. Something that didn't have to do with the woman buried in front of them. Or the one come back to life at his cabin.

She asked, "Do you come here a lot?"

"Not a lot. Sometimes." His voice had a lazy edge, but only on the outside, where he kept most people. She heard deeper now.

"You should feel like you're at a family reunion. I came through a thicket of Carsons back there."

He looked in the direction she'd tipped her head.

"Not surprising. One way or another, the Carsons have pretty much killed themselves off."

"How did you end up different from the rest?"

He looked at the headstone. "Anya. The Judge. Pan. All of them together."

Anya Nouga had been an older woman living in the woods who'd taught him to survive and thrive in nature, left him the property he'd turned into a home, and gave him acceptance.

Judge Kimble Blankenship had given him justice—rules of right and wrong, with appropriate consequences for each.

And Pan...

He grinned unexpectedly. "Once had an Army instructor say they should sign up whoever'd taught me to give lessons on surviving in the woods. Got a laugh out of that. Anya teaching in the Army. Not sure which would have survived, Anya or the Army, but it was a sure thing they both wouldn't have."

"How'd you come to know her?"

"I'd run off from the trailer, and stumbled onto her cabin. She took me back, but I remembered the path, and went back. She used to say she decided she better teach me how to survive before I killed myself and she got blamed."

"But..." She remembered townspeople saying kids left J.D. alone when he started school because of his connection to the "Witch of the Woods." "How old were you when you met her?"

"Five or so."

"You ran off when you were five? Your mother must have been..."

Frantic. She didn't say it, because everything she'd heard said his mother wouldn't have been.

"Nola didn't know. Didn't know when Anya brought me back, either."

"Was Anya from Bedhurst?"

He shook his head. "If she'd been from here she'd've been just another in our bumper crop of eccentrics. It was being from elsewhere that got her called a witch."

"Along with speaking incantations over her potions and poisons," she said with a dry smile.

"Incantations? That's—" He cursed under his breath. "She had a Polish grandmother and an Indian father who taught her about herbs and plants. She'd repeat the recipes to herself in whichever language she'd been taught them to help remember. That's all."

"Why'd she come here?"

"Her father had told stories about the Cherokee living around here generations ago. She came here to die."

"But—"

"Yeah, she lived here more than twenty years. She said it was the medicines she made. Doctors had given up on her." He shook his head before Maggie could ask. "I never knew what she had. It was her story to tell if she chose. She never chose. She never explained, never complained. She said a person was the sum of what they did."

"Actions speak louder than words," she quoted. "Judge Blankenship's mantra."

He looked up. "That's right."

"Why didn't you hate the judge for saying that about your mother?"

He held her eyes a beat, then surprised her by smiling.

"You don't beat around the bush, Ms. Assistant Commonwealth's Attorney Frye." He continued, "It … settled things in my mind. I'd been between two worlds. At home, where my mother had all the *darlings* and *I love yous*, but not the actions, and at Anya's cabin, where she grumbled and spoke sharp, then fed me and taught me and looked out for me. I knew which one worked for me. But the kids at school, and people in town, and my mama, were saying Anya was a witch. So if I liked being around her, I had to have something wrong with me, too."

Actions speak louder than words.

"What Judge Blankenship said validated you."

"If you want to call it that. The judge and the law got my respect because Nola couldn't wave them off. She had to deal with them."

Maggie felt for Nola Carson's little boy. She saw the pain of his young life. She understood it.

She thought of Jamie. And Ally. Even of herself.

They'd known pain. They'd made good and valuable lives.

And someone had tried to kill Jamie.

Or had they?

"You would have liked her. You wouldn't have understood her, but you would have liked her."

At J.D.'s low words, Maggie's conscious mind took in what she'd been looking at

Pan Addington Wade

Beloved daughter, wife, friend

"You love her. Pan," she said to him.

He twisted his head to look at her for an instant, then returned to the headstone. "I do."

She nodded. Not surprised by his words. How she felt about them, though...

"She would have liked you, Maggie. She wouldn't have understood you, but she would have liked you. She would have loved you."

She looked up, met his gaze.

"She would have loved you," he said, "because she'd have seen that I love you."

✧   ✧   ✧   ✧

AS JAMIE STOOD on the stairs looking down to his serious, intelligent face, Detective Ford Belichek succinctly explained how three weeks in a house with the air-conditioning off during a heat wave could make a body unrecognizable and difficult to identify.

One track in her brain wondered how she hadn't asked the question earlier. At least asking it now meant she'd started emerging from the haze ... didn't it?

Belichek didn't fill in details.

He didn't need to. Her imagination did.

He didn't sugar-coat what he did say, but he also didn't say more than necessary.

She felt both grateful and oddly irked by his consideration.

Strange. She seldom felt irked with people.

She was still thinking about that when he stopped.

"Any more questions?" he asked.

"About that? No." What a strange, polite conversation to be having about an unknown person who died and decomposed in her house.

"Then you better get back upstairs and put pants on."

She stared at him for two blank beats.

Then she spun around, holding the bottom of her shirt tight against her derriere, suddenly—and much too belatedly—aware of the view his angle below her position on the open stairway gave him.

She ran.

CHAPTER THIRTY-FIVE

JAMIE STAYED UPSTAIRS until Maggie and J.D. returned a few minutes later.

When she came down, she wore the thick red sweater he'd watched Ally touch with such sorrowful affection in Jamie's closet.

She didn't meet his gaze.

He'd have to factor that in as he assessed her answers.

Before he could ask any questions, though, J.D. said something to Maggie, who looked up and said for them all to hear, "J.D.'s right. We should eat before we get started."

Belichek resisted grinding his teeth—barely.

But he couldn't complain too much—Carson quickly had scrambled eggs placed in front of them, along with toast and fruit.

With the dishes stowed in the dishwasher, they took their previous positions in front of the fireplace. Except Carson brought over a chair from the computer setup opposite the kitchen.

"Start from the top, Jamie," Maggie said.

"I finished the book last night—night before last—at the cabin. In the morning, I started packing. I'd thought I'd pack, get a good night's sleep, and leave early the next morning—this morning I guess." Her forehead wrinkled. The rest of them nodded, confirming that timeline. "But when I had things packed, I decided to drive on home. I thought I could—" She sighed. "—get things done around the house, kick back for a while, sleep in my own bed. Like I told—" She tipped her head toward him without making eye contact. "—I drove straight through."

"How long?" Carson asked.

"About eight hours. That includes a pit stop, gas, and fast food."

"Did you notice anything when you came in the house?" Maggie asked.

"I … I don't know. Not until—" Her gaze cut toward him, but again didn't reach him. "Everything happened so fast."

"Go back and start at the beginning," he said.

"I did—"

"Before you left Fairlington. When was your last day at work before you left?"

"Oh. That was the Friday before Labor Day."

"Everybody at the foundation knew you were leaving?"

"Of course."

"And knew where you were going?"

"In general, that I was going to a cabin to finish the book, yes. I guess only Bethany Usher knew precisely, but I asked her not to tell anyone and she wasn't going to be in the office much while I was gone."

He was aware of Maggie and J.D. connecting that name with the foundation employee who hadn't returned from vacation.

Before either—probably Maggie—could say anything, he asked, "Bethany Usher is the name of the person whose cabin you stayed at?"

"At her family's cabin. It was a different last name—Young."

"Why wasn't she going to be in the office much while you were gone?"

"Vacation time."

"Who is Bethany Usher?"

"She works at the Sunshine Foundation, helping Celeste—Celeste Renfro who runs day-to-day operations as well as coordinating client services."

"How long has she been with the foundation?"

"Celeste? More than ten years. She's the backbone of the operation."

"Bethany Usher."

"She started in early June."

He left a gap for her to add more. She didn't. "Who did you talk to at the foundation the last day you worked?"

"Everyone."

"Names? And what they do."

"Hendrickson York, he deals with donors. Celeste, I told you. She keeps the ship running and deals with the clients. Adam Delattre, who keeps us connected, runs the computers, and crunches the numbers." Those came quickly. She thought a beat, then said, "Denise Gutierrez, one of our volunteers. One of our best. I talked to her, too."

"Anything unusual happen that Friday?"

She shook her head. "Not at all. It was a good day. I wrapped up what I needed to for my time away."

"How about earlier in the week?"

"Unusual things happen of course—no two days are alike. But something that could explain this? Nothing."

"Unusual like what?"

"I… I can't think of anything right now. Celeste could tell you. She remembers everything."

"That Friday before Labor Day, did you go out after work?"

"No. Adam—Adam Delattre, the tech guru—suggested it, but I wanted to get home, read over my notes for the rest of the book so it was in my head during the drive."

"What did you do after leaving work Friday?"

"I went straight home. Fixed some dinner. I took a couple things over to my neighbor who lives behind me, Imogen Wooton, things from the fridge that would go bad being left for a month. Then I came home, packed, read the notes, watched a little TV, and went to bed."

"When did you leave for North Carolina?"

"Saturday, late morning. I had everything packed and I left."

"Was that your original schedule?"

"I didn't have a hard and fast plan. It depended how quickly I pulled things together at home. As it happened, it all came together great."

They'd said at the foundation she'd planned to leave Sunday. And she was hedging.

"Did you tell anyone you were leaving Saturday?"

"No."

"Did anyone see you leave?"

"I have no idea." She hadn't considered the matter until this moment. "I wasn't aware of anyone noticing me leave—didn't wave at anyone or talk to anyone or anything like that."

"Then what?"

"I drove to North Carolina."

"Where?"

"It's a little place along the New River, south of the New River State Park, in Ashe County."

"That rusty pickup we passed when we left your place, that was the one you drove to North Carolina and back?"

She looked at him blankly for an instant. "We saw—? Oh, yes. I parked it in back."

"Why not in the garage?"

"It would never fit. My little car barely fits."

So, she probably hadn't checked the garage. Hadn't seen her car there. Or she'd have added that her car was in the garage.

"Whose truck is it?"

"Bethany's. The woman whose family owns the cabin. She's been using my car while I was gone. It's a lot easier to street park than her truck and the truck made more sense for the mountains, so we swapped."

"Nice swap. Beat up old truck for a new car."

Jamie didn't respond, but Maggie's indignation rippled through the silence clearly.

"Did you spill potting soil in your garage?" Belichek asked Jamie.

"Potting soil? No. Why—? Oh. The bag leaning against the wall?"

He grunted confirmation.

"Bethany might have done that."

"You gave her a key to the garage?"

"Sure, so she could get the car."

"To the house?"

"No. The garage and the car."

She said it very firmly. She was telling him—and herself—the body couldn't be Bethany Usher. She expected argument.

He shifted gears.

CHAPTER THIRTY-SIX

"WHY ARE YOU bringing in a management company at the Sunshine Foundation?"

Her brows flicked up at the change of topic, but she followed willingly. "To take the foundation to—"

"The next level. Right."

Before he could form his next question, Jamie—looking at her cousin—said, "I'm not going to stop developing the Sunshine Foundation because you don't like it, Maggie. But, as it happens, I am going to do less of the day-to-day running of it. This management company specializes in supporting nonprofits. That's why this book had to get done. To fund organizational support for the foundation, letting the staff concentrate on what's most important."

"Your payment for this book is all going to pay for management?"

"It will benefit me, too. I won't have as much administrative work." She sounded a bit defensive.

Belichek pulled it back on track. "What made you think the non-profit management company would get the foundation up a level?"

Her face drooped an instant, then snapped back. "I took a hard look at myself, my running of the foundation, and ... other factors."

"You didn't think you could take it to the next level?"

"No."

"Why?" He thought he knew from reading her journals, but did she know? She hadn't said it right out.

"I... I realized I haven't been good at anticipating issues. Of seeing the signs of possible trouble ahead of time. We've come through those issues, but could we be a lot farther ahead if we'd avoided them in the first place?"

So, she did know, at least at some level, that her optimism could get her—or her foundation—in trouble. At the moment, he was more interested in the implications for her personal life.

"The same thing with your relationship with Carl Arbendroth?"

Unprepared for that question, Jamie looked up and met his gaze. "What?"

"Not seeing the potential for trouble ahead of time."

"How do you—?" Color rushed into Jamie's face. "That's what you were doing, when I came up the stairs and saw you. You were reading my journals."

"Yes."

"All of them? You read all—?"

"Yes." Not quite true yet, but it would be.

"Those are *private* and *personal.* You had no ri—"

"Nothing's private or personal in a murder investigation," Maggie said. "Especially not for the victim."

Belichek had heard her say that before—hell, he'd said it himself. Often in a tag-team with Mags or Landis or both. This was different— except it wasn't. It couldn't be.

He picked up the familiar thread and kept it going. "Knowing about the victim is usually the most important step in finding out the killer. That's my job and that's what this is about—along with making sure you stay alive."

Her color fled as fast as it had arrived.

She wasn't over this. She would neither forgive nor forget that he had breached her privacy.

He'd live with that. As long as she continued living.

Belichek returned to his question. "Why Arbendroth? Why date him?"

"It wasn't until we broke up and he had trouble letting go that…"

"Didn't ask about the breakup. Before that. Why'd you date him in the first place? Why keep dating him?"

"He's attractive," she said defensively.

"You base romantic decisions solely on looks?"

"No."

"You get asked out regularly and—" Her cheeks darkened again at the reminder of what he knew of her personal life and how he knew it. "—some must be at least as attractive as Arbendroth. They sure have to be smarter. Why him?"

Maggie stirred, then stilled.

Jamie cut her a look, a different kind of color coming into her cheeks.

Belichek tried again. "Why Arbendroth when he made you uncomfortable?"

"Uncomfortable? I wouldn't say that. He needed a little bolstering. A boost."

"And you had to provide it," Maggie concluded.

"If it gave him more confidence… It wasn't a sacrifice. We had fun."

"Until you broke up and he wouldn't let go," Belichek said. "What about the other guy you're uncomfortable with?"

"Other—? I'm not."

He studied her. She meant it. Did he read it into her journal writings? Or was she blind to it?

"Go back to Arbendroth. Why did you break up?"

Her glance toward him didn't reach all the way. "He was getting very serious very fast. I didn't want to lead him on when I knew…"

She didn't finish the thought as she pulled her bottom lip between her teeth.

"Did that figure into your decision to go to North Carolina?"

"Yes." Except she said it a little too fast. "The time away would help him with the break. And my being someplace he couldn't possibly—he didn't know about took away any temptation."

He didn't doubt that she viewed that as a bonus. He did doubt that it covered all her reasons. There was something else.

But she was tense, guarded against that topic. He shifted back to an earlier one.

"Tell me about Bethany Usher."

Her eyes blinked open. "What about her?"

"How did she come to work for the foundation?"

"Celeste hired her."

"How did she know about the job? Was it posted? Did she answer an ad?"

"No. We were thinking about adding someone. She was recommended."

"Who recommended her?"

"Oh, gosh, we get so many recommendations, I don't know how I could ever sort out who exactly..."

"How did she accrue vacation time for a week off?"

"She needed some personal time. That doesn't always happen according to the calendar or how long you've been employed."

"How well do you know Bethany Usher?"

"She's a nice person. She's been working for the foundation for months and she's enthusiastic."

Maggie raised a finger.

Belichek nodded, giving her the floor. "That translates to Jamie doesn't know a thing about the woman, who could be a saint or a sinner or anything and everything in between."

"That's not true. Just because I give people the benefit of the doubt—"

"It is true." Maggie, having prevailed in a stare-off between cousins, continued, "I bet she barely knows Bethany Usher."

Without a change in expression or position, he asked Jamie, "What do you know about her family?"

"They've had the cabin for years and she went there as a kid a lot."

"Where do they live?"

Her mouth twitched into a grimace. "I don't know."

"Is Bethany Usher married?"

"No."

"Based on?"

"Her job application." She added with a hint of triumph, "No ring."

"Ever married?"

"I don't know."

"Boyfriend?"

"I don't know."

"Where does she live?"

"In D.C."

"Roommates?"

"I… I think so."

"Previous work experiences?"

"I don't remember, but there's no reason I would. Celeste checks the work history and references of applicants. Hendrickson York and I meet them at the end of the process—though it's usually volunteers, since we don't have other employees." Her mouth almost lifted into a smile. "Celeste has already made the decision."

Not how Celeste Renfro presented it. Or Hendrickson York, either. Possible they'd undersold Celeste's authority, while Jamie hyped it.

But if Jamie's description was correct, it raised a real interesting question of why Celeste hired someone like Bethany, whom she had not exactly praised to the skies. Or did her opinion change after the hiring process?

"Did you work with Bethany?"

"No. She was hired to help Celeste."

"Yet she offered you the use of her family's cabin. How did that happen?"

"Very naturally. She came in my office and said she'd heard others talking about my going off to a cabin to write and her family has this great cabin in North Carolina and, please, would I use it."

Belichek kept his gaze on Jamie for several beats, then flicked it toward Maggie.

She was waiting. "It is natural in her world. At least she'd think it was natural for people just to do nice things for her." Almost reluctantly, she added, "And sometimes people *do* just do nice things for her."

"It's not for me. It's for the foundation or spreading the word or—"

He interrupted. "Who else knew you were going to that specific cabin?"

"No one."

"No one else at the foundation?"

"No."

"How can you be sure Bethany Usher didn't tell anyone?"

"I asked her not to."

Maggie sighed. Clearly saying, *Like that would stop anybody.*

Jamie shot her a look that didn't fit anyone's idea of a saint. Clearly saying, *Yes, it would.*

CHAPTER THIRTY-SEVEN

"…I'M TELLING YOU, I don't have enemies," Jamie said.

They'd covered co-workers, friends, and exes, so far. All peach and joy according to her.

"What about that next-door neighbor?" Maggie challenged her.

Belichek's focus tightened. She knew? Taking the stance that he didn't know might pull more details than if they thought he did know. "Neighbor?"

"Oh. Phil Xavier. He's not an enemy. He just wants something I have. His style is a little … abrasive."

Belichek asked, "What do you have that he wants?"

"My house. He wants to expand his house."

Maggie's dryness cut across. "Right after he moved in, the arrogant prick wheedled the key off the other neighbor—what's her name?"

"Imogen Wooten. A wonderful—"

"Easy mark."

"—woman. But she didn't give up the key. It was her granddaughter."

"Fine. Her granddaughter. Phil Xavier gets the key, has an architect in there, crawling all over, and does complete drawings, like Jamie doesn't have a choice in the matter. Had a rude awakening when she ripped him a new one."

"I simply told him no." One corner of her mouth twitched down, then up. "Forcefully."

Maggie and J.D. grinned.

Belichek didn't. "How'd he react?"

"He's persisted. I've persisted back."

"Any actions or events associated with his persistence?"

She eyed him. "Nothing I can ascribe to him with certainty."

"What happened?" Maggie demanded.

"Nothing major. It was—"

"Garbage thrown in the patio, dog feces, broken flower pots. Did your car get keyed, too?"

"Yes, it did," Maggie said. "You told me you had no idea who did it."

"I *don't* know."

"He's a bully. You should have gone after him criminally, then gone to that lawyer whose name I gave you and sued the jerk, make him hurt in the one area where he has feeling."

Belichek asked, "Has he been in your house since then?"

"No. I changed the locks after that happened—in case he had a copy of the key made. See, Maggie, I do think of those things. And when I gave Imogen the new key—"

Maggie groaned.

"—I impressed on her not to share it with anyone. She was so upset about him doing what he did, I know she won't."

Belichek looked around at Carson, then Maggie. Yeah, they saw the issue, too. Imogen Wooton might not give it to Xavier, but would he take it?

For now, though, better not to get bogged down on one possibility. This was the time to gather as many possibilities as they could.

LANDIS' COLLECTION OF non-leads grew.

The alibi-checking of the Sunshine Foundation staffers produced great Swiss cheese, but no leads. Phil Xavier and his wife had been boating on Chesapeake Bay on Saturday, but his planned golf outing Sunday was rained out.

They were down to two of Jamison Chancellor's boyfriends before Carl going back to high school without alibis, and neither looked good.

The family all checked out.

Beyond the three he and Belichek talked to, the neighbors came up as big, fat nothings.

Ignoring the Sunshine Foundation's sentiments that families who hadn't made the cut for their help remained big fans, they'd talked to half a dozen of them with nothing close to a complaint coming up.

And now here was Terrington, sitting beside his desk, adding to the non-leads.

"Everybody in that restaurant liked her. They liked taking takeout up there or waiting on the group. Apparently, she was a good tipper.

"They talked about a guy who came in and tried to manhandle her. Before they could react, the young guy from the Sunshine Foundation—Delayne—"

"Delattre."

"—stepped in. No other incidents. Only break in the ranks was one girl. She liked Chancellor all right, but not the Henderson guy. Said—"

"Hendrickson York."

"—he was nice on the surface, but underneath he could be—and I quote—*a real shit.*

"Then I went up and talked to the foundation people. Close-mouthed. Wouldn't say anything bad about the Chancellor woman."

"You were there to ask them about Bethany Usher."

"Yeah, sure, but hard to avoid the topic, with her dead body and all."

"What did they say about Bethany Usher?"

"Not much. Didn't seem to know her. The volunteers said they didn't work with her much. No idea where she could be."

"Her apartment? Vehicle? Landlord?"

"Getting to that after I write the report on the restaurant and foundation."

"Get to it fast. And get the names right on the report," Landis said as Terrington walked away.

CHAPTER THIRTY-EIGHT

"**What happened the** last time you were at the Pennsylvania cabin—the one you usually go to, Jamie?"

"What?"

It was partly legit confusion at the abrupt change in direction. It was also partly avoidance.

She folded her bottom lip in between her teeth again.

"What happened last time you were at Hendrickson York's cabin that made you go to North Carolina instead this time?"

"It wasn't *instead*. I had the offer—the generous offer—and it seemed churlish to decline when Bethany was so enthusiastic about me using her family's cabin and she had it all figured out how I could get supplies ordered in her family's name and delivered, plus more delivered while I was there if I needed them, so I never had to leave and there'd be no chance—" She stopped abruptly. Clamped her top teeth over her bottom lip for an instant.

He suddenly understood the mannerism didn't indicate regret over what she'd said. It was determination not to go any farther down that path.

And that made her a more complicated witness. Stewing in regret and a complete lack of determination made a subject a heck of a lot easier to question.

With that kind of witness, he'd press his question again. *What happened last time you were at Hendrickson York's cabin?*

But Jamie would slide away again, more determined not to reveal anything additional.

He felt impatience rising off Maggie like steam. She wanted to take her cousin by the shoulders and force the answer out of her.

No, not *the* answer. *All* the answers.

But Maggie was too much the professional to do that. Maybe it also was a compliment to him that she didn't try to take over the questioning.

Carson, on the other hand, sat back and watched. Seemingly relaxed. Yet coiled. Not only taking in everything going on in the room, especially with Maggie, but outside, too.

That left Belichek to concentrate on Jamison Chancellor.

And why she was avoiding answering this.

She pretended to be comfortable with the lengthening silence, but she wasn't.

She unclamped that hold on her lip. Her tongue came out and moistened her generous bottom lip. She shifted sideways in her chair.

As she fidgeted, Maggie calmed, experience telling her he'd hit on something.

Something Jamie wasn't ready to give up. If she even knew it herself.

"A new place means there's no chance of getting stale," she picked up. Too late. Far, far too late. They all knew it, including her. She kept going. "It's easy to get stale in that final push on a book. You go to the same place, do the same things, and there's the danger of producing the same thing. Going to North Carolina turned out to be the right decision—"

Ah. She'd wondered about it before she went. Worried about it?

Yet she'd gone.

"—for so many reasons, including it was gorgeous and I got good work done. More work and faster than I'd counted on. I finished ahead of schedule. That's why I came back early. That's why I drove straight through to get home last night."

"Finished early?"

She nodded.

"Seems like you'd take it easy coming back then. Why push yourself to get home?"

She looked straight at him. Eyes unblinking. "To have more time at home. Catch up on cleanup around the house. Routine."

He watched as the image—the *imagination*—of what the non-routine cleanup around her house had entailed shattered her lying wall.

A ragged breath came out. She stood.

"I need a break."

LITTLE MISS SUNSHINE lied her pants off.

Her pants off . . .

Get that image the hell out of your head, Belichek.

Jamie and Maggie were in the bathrooms, he and J.D. in the kitchen. J.D. handed him a coffee mug. "Good news is, she's a lousy liar."

It was as if he'd heard Belichek's train of thought—half of his train of thought.

He accepted the mug. "Good news for now."

While he was questioning her. But what about when—if—it was time for her to lie to other people. Not so good, then.

J.D. nodded, apparently keeping up with that line of thought, too.

But did the other man also follow up with wondering if Jamison Chancellor knew she was lying?

CHAPTER THIRTY-NINE

"**Let's lay this** out, Jamie. After you left, someone came into your house, with no sign of forced entry and that person was shot, also with no sign of forced entry. The most likely explanation would be that at least one, possibly both, of those people gained entry with a key. And that the killer turned off the AC before leaving. It's unlikely anyone would want to have been in the house for any period without the AC on. Who has a key to your house?"

"My parents, my cousin Ally. Maggie."

"I've never used it."

"Of course not. That would be too much like family or—"

Belichek broke in. "Anyone else, Jamie?"

"Hendrickson York, Adam Delattre, Celeste. And, of course, Imogen Wooton, who lives across the alley."

"What about Carl Arbendroth?"

"He had one—briefly—but he returned it."

"How briefly?"

"Two weeks."

"Plenty of time to make a copy."

"He wouldn't—"

"Okay, let's narrow this down. Who has stayed in your house in the past year?"

"They all did. That's why they had a key."

A beat of silence turned Jamie's head to her cousin.

"Don't look at me like I'm crazy. It's normal to have people stay at your house. Just because you never let anyone in the front door, much less stay overnight—" Her gaze slid toward J.D. and something like amusement crept into her voice. "—hardly ever."

Belichek pulled her attention back to the answers he needed. "Why? Why did all those people stay at your house?"

"My parents," she said pointedly, "because they had an early flight out of Reagan National to—"

"Skip your parents. Ally, too." At least for now. If they needed to widen the possibilities…

"Hendrickson York's building lost power and they said it was going to take at least two days to restore—it was actually almost a week.

"Adam Delattre's roommates kicked him out with basically no warning. He tried to hide it, sleeping at the office two nights, until we realized what was happening, and I insisted he stay with me.

"Celeste Renfro sold her house and had to be out of it, with a ten-day gap before she could get in her new townhouse.

"A college roommate stayed with me for about a week. She was here on business and I was working, so she needed a key."

"Any contact with her since?"

"Of course. We talk or text every few weeks."

"Any conflict? Any issues or disputes—?"

"No. We're *friends.*" As if nothing else were possible.

He took down the former roommate's name and contact information.

"What about Imogen Wooton?"

Jamie's mouth lifted. "She already had a key, but she stayed with me because a gaggle of her grandkids came to visit her and with them wall-to-wall in her tiny place, she needed a refuge to get some sleep. They had a ball and she was over the moon to have them around. There's talk about them doing it again next spring."

He found himself caught for a moment in the vision drawn by her happy memories once-removed. Sitting upright, he stretched his back from being in the same position too long.

"Those people stayed with you, you told them how to operate things in the house? The shower, the dishwasher—?"

All happiness fled. "You mean the air-conditioner."

"Or heat."

"It's only natural—so they know how to make themselves more comfortable if I'm not there."

Without commenting on her essentially offering open house to nearly everyone she knew, he said, "Go back to your parents and cousin. Did they ever stay there when you weren't there?"

"No."

"So they had no reason to know how to operate the air-conditioning?"

"No," she said more strongly. "They didn't. We never talked about it. None of them ever touched it, because I was there with them."

Belatedly, she realized that by celebrating that her relatives knew nothing about the system and had no experience with it, she'd spotlighted that the others had known about it.

"I always emphasized that leaving it alone was the best course of action."

"Do you know for a fact that they did leave it alone?"

"No." Reluctant honesty. But she couldn't let that view of the people in her life rest. "Even if they do know how to adjust the HVAC system, how can you possibly think that means one of them shot some unknown woman in my house and turned off the AC to… to… destroy evidence?"

"I don't."

She didn't look as happy about his admission as he might have expected. More wary.

Good.

Wary was a hell of a lot more utilitarian attitude in this situation than happy.

"You don't?"

"It's one point. Need a lot more than that. Building an investigation is creating a mountain, one pebble at a time. Finding the right pebbles and putting the other ones aside. The keys and knowledge of your HVAC system give us places to look for pebbles."

"My friends? You're going to investigate my friends? They wouldn't have done this. It's impossible."

"Someone did," Maggie said.

"No forced entry," Belichek reminded her.

"Imogen? You don't know her, but—"

"Met her," he said.

"—there is no way—Then you know. You can't possibly think she was involved."

"You gave her the new key you said?"

"Yes, but—"

"Do you know where that key has been since you gave it to her? If she had it copied? Gave it to someone else to use? Lost it? Had it stolen from her, including by someone who knew what it was for? Does she have it labeled? Somewhere visible?" Her expression said that bull's-eye hit home. "Visible to anyone who came to her back door?"

"But that means you can't suspect her," she said, "because anyone could have seen it, even taken it."

Including her neighbor Phil Xavier?

He'd get to that, but he had another destination first.

"Doesn't eliminate her. But it's true it's not only who you gave the key to, it's the spread of possibilities beyond that, including making a copy. It's like tracking a disease. Who the patient's been in contact with. Because any of those people are possibilities, too."

"But to look at every person as a possible murderer… It's horrible."

Belichek looked back at her as he'd learned to do. It wasn't the first time someone had looked at him that way. Wouldn't be the last. It sure as hell couldn't come between him and finding out what happened.

Until he did, she was in danger—of being killed or of being accused of murder.

The community was in danger—the one he'd sworn to protect and serve.

And another oath he'd sworn—only to himself, but no less binding—was in danger.

"Every person is a possible murderer." He said it without affect, driving home the horror, trying to pop the bubble of optimism she operated in. And then he drove it home. "Start with Carl Arbendroth. He had a key? Why'd you break up? Was he jealous? Abusive? Controlling?"

"No, no. It wasn't like that."

"What was it like?"

"He wanted more than I could give him."

"How serious was it with this guy?" Maggie asked.

"It wasn't like that, either. But... He wanted to explore if it could be. To do that, he wanted more of my time, my attention. He... he wanted me to back away from the foundation."

"So the guy had at least one good idea," Maggie muttered.

Jamie gave her cousin a less than sunshine-filled look.

She and Maggie did tie each other in knots. Belichek wondered how Ally, the third cousin, fit in.

"You broke up or he did?" He kept it neutral.

She dragged her metaphorical feet through two extra beats before saying, "I did."

"How did he react?"

"He understood."

"Right away?"

"It's hard for people to accept change. And it makes sense, with him being in a position in his life when he was ready to settle down, that he'd be disappointed."

"That would be a no—he did not understand," Maggie said. "Especially not right away."

Silence.

"Is that assessment correct, Jamie?" Belichek asked.

"I suppose. But just because it took him a while—"

"How long?"

She waved one hand, possibly intending it to be airy. *Irked* was the word that came to mind. "I didn't keep track."

"But you must have noticed behavior that let you recognize that he did not understand—or accept—your breaking up with him for a *while*. What were those behaviors, Jamie?"

Her eyes sharpened. "You talked to Hendrickson and the others at the foundation, didn't you?"

"Say I did talk to them, what would I have heard?"

CHAPTER FORTY

"**You have to** put them in context. Hendrickson is old-fashioned. And he still sees me as a girl, so he's naturally protective. So is Celeste, but that's because of her cautious nature. Which has served the foundation wonderfully, because she watches out for every possible problem, heads off most of them and is prepared for the ones that get through. And Adam Delattre is completely loyal to the foundation."

"Okay, you've given the context. Now, what would they say about Carl Arbendroth?"

"Whatever they said doesn't mean—"

Carson leaned forward. "You do know you're making it worse by putting off answering. What would they say?"

She looked only at him. "They'd say he called fifty times a day, texted more, showed up at the office, and came to the restaurant where we were having a staff lunch."

Belichek and Maggie glanced at each other, but Carson and Jamie didn't break eye contact. "How many times did he show up at your office."

"Four... No, five times."

"Did he ever put hands on you?"

"Not like—"

"Did he ever put hands on you?"

"It wasn't—He had my elbow. Wanted me to go with him to talk. Adam pushed him, he lost his balance. The restaurant—the foundation staff goes there regularly—asked him to leave."

Carson straightened from his lean, nodding at her.

Belichek slid in, "When did this happen?"

Jamie shifted her gaze to him, gave a little shift of her shoulders as if shaking off something—like the inclination to avoid answering him again.

"The week before I left."

"Heard from him since?"

She brightened. "No. No calls, no texts, no sightings."

Belichek waited.

Right on time, Maggie huffed.

Jamie shifted her focus to her cousin. "What?"

"Sudden backing off. I see you thinking it's a good sign. It's often not. Can be a signal of planning something … bigger."

"**THAT WAS GOOD.** You're good with witnesses," Maggie told J.D. as she took makings for a marinade out of his fridge.

He already had the steaks out for tonight's dinner. Once again, Jamie had gone upstairs and Belichek out on the front porch. Like boxers retiring to their corners.

"Maybe. Belichek laid the foundation."

"She resisted him."

"What're you thinking, Maggie."

"Hmm? It was … interesting watching Bel in action." She went silent for a moment. "God, I always knew he was methodical and that's how he produces such good police work, but to listen to him questioning her…" She dragged one hand through her hair.

"Because of how he questions? Or because it's Jamie answering?"

She opened her mouth. Closed it. Contemplated for a moment. "Both."

He kissed her hard.

His mouth nearly touching hers, he said, "You know he's getting a lot more out of her than you would."

She put a hand on his chest as if to push him away, but didn't. "Hey."

"You'd attack and she'd retreat. He's more neutral." He pushed back a sweep of hair from the side of her face. "It's giving her the room to see her bias."

"*Giving her the room?*" She snorted. "He's forcing her to see it."

"That makes you uncomfortable? When, if you were doing the questioning, you'd hit her with it straight between the eyes."

"Don't start asking me questions meant to make me see things and not just get information. Bel does that all the time. Fine. Yes. She's used to blocking out when I point out that her *Everything Is Sunshine and Lollipops* mode can expose her to dangerous people and situations. And—in this case—Bel's approach is more effective in getting in under her defenses. Is that what you wanted to hear from me?"

"Only because I love it when you talk dirty."

"Don't start what we can't finish, Carson."

"We can finish—"

"No, we can't because Belichek won't give us time. I know the man."

✧   ✧   ✧   ✧

ON THE PORCH, Belichek scrolled through his calls and messages.

A couple things on other cases that could wait. One email from a prosecutor about a case coming up in December. He answered that. The rest from Landis.

Mostly asking where he was.

But one was interesting.

Confirmed PX's Delaware efforts. Nastier than reported.

He looked out to the treetops.

They couldn't hold out here much longer.

He'd meant what he'd said about snatching Jamie. But the intervening hours persuaded him it wouldn't work. She wouldn't let it work.

And before they left here, he had something he needed to do.

He wasn't looking forward to it.

CHAPTER FORTY-ONE

BEFORE BELICHEK COULD restart his questions, Maggie had one. "Bel, you said someone entered her house with no sign of forced entry. Could whoever was shot have come with the killer?"

"Could have, yes. It's a little neater that way, too, because the alternative is one person got into the house with no sign of forced entry, then let someone else in. And that second arrival could be someone who knew or didn't know the first arrival was there."

"Or knew-slash-didn't know Jamie had left and this other person in the house wasn't her."

"That's it. A lot more variables than if the victim and the killer arrived together."

"But why in *my* house?"

"That's a real interesting question," Carson said.

"Not until we have an answer to it," Maggie said. "And to get to that answer, we need answers to the ones leading up to that, which are the questions Belichek's been asking."

✧　✧　✧　✧

LANDIS ORDERED TERRINGTON to revise his report on his trip to the foundation to include more detail. That was on top of his background checks on the foundation employees and the two volunteers who'd been there on Jamison Chancellor's last day.

Now, here Terrington was back, sitting on the chair beside Landis' desk, without the rewritten report, with a theory.

"Celeste Renfro has a financial motive. She's got major debt. She's carrying a big mortgage on that new house she bought," Terrington said.

"Who doesn't have a big mortgage around here?"

Ignoring that aside from Jenkins, Landis asked, "Is it in default?"

"No."

"Underwater?"

"I don't know."

"Does she have other debts—loans, credit cards—anything repossessed?"

"I don't know."

"Find out."

God, he missed Belichek.

He stopped short of wishing he was back here this instant.

Said a lot for his generosity of spirit and their friendship that, even to avoid being saddled with Terrington, Landis wasn't wishing away Belichek getting laid.

Sure, wishing wouldn't get him Belichek back and get rid of Terrington, but it was the thought that counted.

As Terrington stood, his expression sulky, Landis added, "How would Celeste Renfro benefit financially from Jamison Chancellor's death?"

It caught the younger man by surprise. The other questions he knew—at least at some level—he should have had answers to before approaching Landis, but he'd rushed it in his desperation to have an impact.

But this aspect had not occurred to him.

"Uh, maybe she could have moved up in the foundation. Better pay. Maybe more prestige."

Landis examined it, turning it over, mentally visualizing the facets. "It's something to look into. Now, go get those facts."

CHAPTER FORTY-TWO

BELICHEK HAD COVERED additional ground looking for what Jamie insisted didn't exist—an enemy.

They covered the foundation's financials. Top-rated.

Hers. Solid.

Previous boyfriends with a grudge. None.

Rivals for Arbendroth's affections. Nonexistent.

Disenchanted donors. Few ever stopped donating.

Disappointed applicants for help. Those rejected were helped to find better suited resources, never cut loose.

When Jamie's yawns made her responses jagged, Carson said it was time for dinner.

None of them talked much during the excellent grilled steaks and salad, but as they finished ice cream-topped brownies, Jamie said to Belichek, "I presume your goading me today stemmed from wanting to make me mad enough to fight. But I don't do that."

He looked back at her without saying anything as he took another bite of ice cream and brownie.

"You have to trust people," she said.

Maggie grimaced, but Belichek was the one who answered.

"You can't trust people. People lie all the time."

"That doesn't mean they're murderers. People have ... secrets. Wounds they don't want revealed to the air."

"It's my job to expose all those secrets. Because for one of them the secret could have led to murder."

"You focus entirely on the bad things. That must be so hard on you."

One side of his mouth lifted. "That's pretty much the job description of a homicide detective. Find a bad situation, sort through the bad things surrounding it, and find the bad guy."

Maggie's gaze followed Jamie as she rinsed her dish and put it in the dishwasher.

"I'm going to bed now. I'm very tired."

"I'll be up soon," Maggie said.

They'd decided earlier the two cousins would take the only bed in the place, the large one in the loft. J.D. had said he could sort out something for him and Belichek down here.

"Jamie."

At his single word, she stopped at the bottom of the stairs and turned back to him.

"I wasn't trying to get you mad enough to fight. I was trying to get answers to my questions."

✧　✧　✧　✧

JAMIE WAS IN bed, but not asleep when Maggie came up.

Shortly, her cousin came out of the bathroom in one of J.D.'s t-shirts.

Jamie almost grinned at her suspicion that Maggie didn't pack a nightgown when she visited here.

As Maggie put away her clothes, Jamie asked, "Why do you call him Belichek instead of Ford?"

She hitched one shoulder. "Just what I call him. Like Landis instead of Tanner. And they mostly call me Frye or Mags. Besides, his real first name is Rutherford. How's that for a mouthful?"

Jamie managed a smile, but something tugged at her. "Maggie?"

Maggie got into the other side of the large bed. "Go to sleep, Jamie. Goodnight."

She turned her back and pulled the covers up over her shoulder.

Before Jamie could move, she rolled back.

"We're going to figure this out," she said fiercely. "Nothing's going to happen to you. Understood?"

Tears came into Jamie's eyes, but her voice was firm. "Understood."

"Okay." Maggie turned away again.

Jamie slid down into the bed.

Something still tugged at her, but she couldn't identify it.

It didn't tug long. She fell asleep, fast, but not deep.

BELICHEK ASKED HIS host, with every expectation of a positive response, "You got anything that will mask where a text is coming from?"

"Which phone number it came from or where the phone was located when the text was sent?"

"The latter."

"Yeah. Write it as an email—" He tipped his head toward the computer. "—give me the recipient's number and I'll send it."

Bel thought a moment before he wrote to Landis:

Interesting on PX. If whereabouts of BU from Sunshine Foundation not pinned down, follow up. Hard.

He thought about the truck, the description, the plate number he'd memorized. But if he gave that to Landis, they'd be on the truck fast. Once they found it near Jamie's house and realized he'd been the source of the push, they'd track him down like the fox in a hunt, demanding to know what he knew, how he knew it, and a lot more.

He could handle that and its consequences, but that would end his time to question Jamie and to keep her safe.

DAY FIVE

CHAPTER FORTY-THREE

"AREN'T YOU HUNGRY, Detective Belichek?"

"No. Let's talk about Hendrickson York."

"He couldn't possibly have anything to do with this. And I *am* hungry. How about breakfast? It looks like J.D. left everything out— Where are he and Maggie?"

"Walk. Let you sleep in. Food after we finish this. How is Hendrickson to work with for the others at Sunshine Foundation?"

"Endearingly frustrating."

"Frustrating?"

"He is so absorbed in the foundation sometimes he forgets the practicalities, like sleeping or *eating*." She cast a significant look toward the kitchen.

"Anybody find him more frustrating and less endearing than you do?"

She tilted her head and her gaze sharpened. "I suppose some."

"Would you say he and Adam Delattre are in sync?"

She blinked twice. "They're very different people, from different generations, with different interests."

"Yes or no."

"Not especially."

"Hendrickson and Celeste Renfro?"

"Not especially. But what you're missing is each of them cares deeply about the foundation and—"

"It would be safe to say nobody cares more about him than you."

"I can't presume to delve into anyone else's heart and compare the results that answering that would require, Detective."

"No. You accept them at face value. Do you always look at the bright side?"

"I try to." She sighed. "Go ahead. Call me a Pollyanna. It's not the least bit original, but go ahead and get it off your chest." That was a little too tart to be nice.

He seemed to bring that out in her.

Or the circumstances did.

"You don't think you deserve the title?"

"I recognize my good fortune, not only my misfortunes."

"Your father died when you were a kid."

"That hurt, I wouldn't ever say different, but my mother found a wonderful man. A man who loves her and has been as good a stepfather as anyone could wish for. How can I not see how lucky I am?"

"Lucky? Is that what you call having an aunt you adored murdered?"

The skin over her cheekbones tightened until he thought it looked translucent. He refused to be sorry. If this is what it took to wake her up, that's the way it went.

"Even … even from that, some good has come. The Sunshine Foundation has helped people, many people."

"I wouldn't consider that a good trade-off for my aunt's life."

"It's *not* a trade-off for Vivian's life. It wasn't a choice I made, I had no choice. I was given a fact—Vivian was dead—and I could do nothing about that. All I could do was deal with how I reacted. So I tried to make sure something good came out of it."

"That's enough for you?" Under his crust of control, he felt the bubbling heat. He let a little spurt loose. "Don't you ever want to beat your fists into something? Don't you ever want to tear the world apart with your bare hands? Don't you ever want to scream until the banshees beg for mercy?"

As soon as he said that phrase, her face changed.

He'd gotten what he wanted—she was angry. Mad, furious. But he'd gotten more, and he didn't want this, this look of violation, of intrusion, of being stripped bare.

He'd occupied a world where a man could cut open his mother, where a woman could drown her babies, where a teenager could shoot a stranger for the color of his jacket. But this sliced right through a decade's worth of thick skin.

"Reading the journals—that phrase—it's my job, Jamie."

"You've said that before."

"Knowing the victim's a major part of my job." He closed his mouth. What was he doing? Explaining? Apologizing? Begging?

"Did your partner read it, too?" He said nothing, but apparently she didn't need words. "No, I see he didn't. Only you. I suppose I should be grateful for that, but you'll excuse me if I don't thank you."

"Jamie, right now, your optimism, your believing the best of everyone could get you killed. People have ulterior motives. You have to look for them."

"What's your ulterior motive?"

"To catch a killer."

"No matter what the cost to you or others?"

"No matter what the cost."

She stared at him a long moment. It was hard to stand still under that stare.

She jumped when footsteps sounded outside, moving to a window with her back to him.

✧   ✧   ✧   ✧

OZ SMILED AS he spoke into the microphone. It did not come through in his voice.

"Is the lead investigator distracted by his romantic life? Specifically with a shrink? One with great legs, according to talk among the FCPD detective squad.

"No one knows if the Old Town murder victim had good legs, because the Fairlington County Police Department still hasn't managed to identify her.

"Or is this lead investigator, Detective Landis, missing his partner so much that he's spinning his wheels while the real brains of the partnership is on vacation? And why did Chief of Detectives Palery send Detective Belichek on vacation and replace him with a less experienced detective?

"Because this investigation is not going anywhere. I'd say it's *not going anywhere fast*, but it's not even doing that fast.

"Or could it be because they view the women of their cases as Frankenstein Monsters? Pieces in an investigation, but not people.

"Well, wake up big-shot detectives, you're supposed to be solving crimes against people. *People*. All people. Real people. Not Frankenstein Monsters.

"Maybe if you recognized that, maybe you would start getting somewhere with this murder in Old Town. And not just getting it on with the shrink with great legs."

CHAPTER FORTY-FOUR

"**No one had**—has—a reason to kill me. I don't know how many times and how many ways I can tell you that. Following up what Maggie said about thieves taking my phone makes more sense."

"We are."

"Good. Because the most reasonable explanation is that the victim was one of the thieves. And not anyone connected to me."

Her defenses were repairing. A night's sleep could do that. Though he wouldn't call it a good night's sleep, considering the shadows around her eyes.

"Do you have any suspicions about who the victim was?"

"I told you, I can't imagine. I did not give anyone permission to stay at my house. I had no knowledge of anyone coming to visit. The only people I could imagine coming to stay without any warning and who'd have a key, you've already accounted for. Thank heavens."

"Not all the people who've had keys."

A wash of color crossed Jamie's cheeks. "You said the victim is definitely a woman."

"Your thoughts—suspicions—got to a man?"

"I didn't—"

Without emotion, Belichek said, "For starters, we've interviewed Arbendroth, so he definitely wasn't the victim. As for the murderer—"

"Of course, it's not Carl—the victim *or* the murderer."

Maggie stepped in. Not to keep peace, but to keep them on track. "The victim was female. Early information says about your age. Definitely about your size. I half hoped it would be someone shorter or taller, but when I saw the remains—"

"Oh, my God. Maggie, you saw—? You went there?"

"Of course I did. I do it for my job, for the victim I'm going to get justice for. I sure as hell was going to do it for you. And… I had to know."

Jamie's eyes filled with tears. Maggie's did not. But when Jamie reached across and covered her hand, Maggie turned hers up and it became a mutual grasp.

Belichek could feel time running out. He forced his impatience to hold off until their hands separated.

"What made you leave for North Carolina on Saturday, instead of Sunday?" he asked.

"Don't you ever just change your mind?"

Deflecting the question. Interesting.

"No."

Jamie glared at him. Maggie coughed. Carson remained silent. Belichek waited her out.

"Well, I do. I was ready to go, so I went."

"Telling no one?"

"No." It was impatient. Then her face changed. "Oh. Wait. I called Bethany before I left, to be sure I could get into the cabin that day. She said it was fine, any time I wanted to go."

For a beat, Belichek enjoyed the satisfaction of adding one potential pebble to the build-the-mountain pile. Then got back to it. "You had no logical reason? You just went?"

She responded to that tiny needle. "I thought I could get more work done at the cabin."

"Because?"

"It's quieter."

"Something at your house wasn't quiet?"

She stared back for a moment. "You've been talking to my neighbors?"

"Yes."

"Then why are you asking?"

"To hear your answer."

She streamed a breath out through her teeth.

Kimby was wrong—Jamie Chancellor could get annoyed. By him.

"You talked about it yesterday. A neighbor who has been persistent in wanting to buy my house."

"Persistent in what way?" he asked.

"I said I have no interest in selling, yet Phil continues to make offers."

"How much?"

She named a figure.

Belichek was used to masking surprise and accustomed to Fairlington real estate prices. It still knocked him back. "For a garage?"

Maggie's head snapped up. "A garage?"

Jamie raised one open, dismissive hand. "That's a rumor. That he thinks he'd use it as a garage."

"Has he done anything other than make offers?"

She smiled. "That's enough for me to dodge him."

Call her on it? Or keep moving ahead?

He regarded her steadily. She looked away. Tried Maggie, bounced away toward Carson, then down.

He waited.

She wasn't used to looking down. She was used to looking up.

She didn't last long.

Back to him, she met his gaze. He held it.

"Did you talk to him Friday night or Saturday morning before you left?"

"No." Relenting, she released a breath. "I did hear him over the back fence Friday when I came home from work."

"Directed at you?"

"No. Victorina, his wife. They were walking out as I was crossing the patio to my back door and he was commenting—complaining—about being in the heat. He said he needed an air-conditioned garage, and he wasn't waiting any longer. He was going to make me an offer Sunday afternoon after he played golf and pin me down, once and for all."

An offer at the end of a shotgun? Shot before he identified the person who opened the door? Never realized his mistake?

"So, you packed and left."

"I was mostly packed already." She shrugged. "Better to start early on the book and avoid unpleasantness."

And he would have had plenty of time for unpleasantness. It rained hard that Sunday. No golf for Xavier.

"You left Saturday morning, before noon, but you're not sure exactly when. Say before eleven. Did you leave the air-conditioning on?"

"Yes." After their conversation while she stood on the stairs, she knew the significance of the air-conditioning.

"Leaving for that long, it would be natural to adjust the temperature," he said.

"I rarely touch it since I bought a new HVAC system last year. It's programmed and it switches on its own when the weather changes. But it's complicated. I tried to adjust it one time, messed up the whole thing, and had to have the company back out. I don't touch it."

"Someone did," Belichek said. "Because the AC was turned off Sunday afternoon."

Maggie raised one eyebrow.

He answered, "Power usage."

"I did not touch the thermostat. I don't keep the house that cool anyway and I didn't want the plants to wither."

"Anybody see you arrive in North Carolina?"

"Not that I know of."

"Did anything happen while you were in North Carolina? Anything suspicious?"

"Suspicious?" she repeated as if she had no idea what it meant.

"Someone hanging around." She'd think they were friendly. "Unexpected noises." She'd think they were innocent sounds from the woods. "Anything."

"Nothing."

CHAPTER FORTY-FIVE

"OKAY. WHERE'S THE painting from?"

She blinked. Whether at his *okay* or the switch in topic, he didn't know. "Painting?"

"Over your living room fireplace."

Her gaze flicked to Maggie. Communication and connection sprang up, strong enough to offset any differences.

Then both looked away.

"That's Ally's. Our cousin. She…" The trailing off referenced the tragic murder of the three cousins' aunt and their ongoing connection.

"I know about Ally Northcutt. Why do you have her painting over your fireplace?"

"Why wouldn't I? It's a wonderful painting and…" More referencing. This time to the fact that it meant something to her, to them all. She pulled away from it, strengthening her voice. "I like having something Ally painted."

That's Ally's… She hadn't meant possession, but creation. "Artist's signature is TL-something."

"Theodora Allison Lindell before she married Chad Northcutt," Maggie said. "But she's always gone by Allison—Ally. Her husband didn't approve of her painting, so she didn't use his name on them."

"And the photograph from the same place?"

Another flash of connection between the cousins.

Maggie drew in a breath. He moved only his eyes to her. But she caught it, and said nothing, though it cost her.

"We all went back there for the dedication of a park in our aunt's name." Jamie's voice washed warm memories over pain. "She loved that place and her estate bought the property and gave it to the town."

"Would that photo mean anything to anybody else?"

Her brows drew together. "Other members of the family, probably."

He let it go. For now.

"JAMIE NEEDS A break," J.D. said.

Maggie and Bel turned nearly identical expressions to him. Partially blank at the concept of a break, partially fiercely determined to wring every last ounce of information from a source.

"I'm taking her for a walk," he added.

"You can't," Belichek said. "If anyone sees her—"

"They won't. Not the route we're taking and wearing Maggie's jacket, with the hood up. Even if someone saw us, they'd think it was Maggie."

He ignored their disapproval, got Jamie up, and held the jacket for her.

At the door, he turned back. "You two could use a break, too."

MAGGIE WATCHED THEM go. "He's right. Jamie needed a break. She's not used to this the way we are. She's not as tough."

Not as used to it, true. Not as tough? He wasn't so sure.

He got up and headed for the coffeemaker. After a minute Maggie followed him, and took one of the stools on the far side of the island.

"What about your other cousins?" he asked her.

"What about them?"

"You talk about Jamie and Ally." Mostly in connection with eluding Jamie's efforts to involve her in the Sunshine Foundation and concern about Ally. "But you've got other cousins, too, right. Jamie has siblings. What about Ally? Others?"

"Yeah, I've got other cousins."

Not exactly a wide-open door. He went on anyway. "Don't have much to do with them?"

"Don't know them as well."

"Because?"

She side-eyed him in irritation. "Just the way families shake out. I crossed paths with Jamie and Ally more when we were kids."

"Ah."

"Ah what?"

"Shared experiences."

That closed her down.

He wasn't sure he wanted to go there, either. He'd have to at some point. Soon.

If it came too late, whatever trust existed would…

Real soon.

Instead, he asked, "That happen a lot?"

"What?"

"Carson being right. And you admitting it." He placed a fresh mug in front of her.

Her mouth twitched. More than that, her eyes softened. "A fair amount."

"This thing with you two is serious." He didn't make it a question.

She said nothing while he returned to the coffeemaker, poured himself a mug, then faced her, his hips propped against the edge of the counter.

"I'm scared." She lifted her head. Her gaze met his then ricocheted away. "And happy."

"Guess the happy's obvious. What's the scared about?"

"That I'll stop being happy."

He *huh'd* comprehension. "Stop wanting to be with him? Him stop wanting to be with you? You screwing up? Him screwing up."

"All of the above. And more." Her voice went small, totally unlike her lawyer voice. "Something happening to him. He never backs down. Came back here *because* there were people who thought he'd committed murder."

Including her. No need to remind her of that.

"Sounds like a match for you."

She grinned, but so fleetingly it could have been a grimace. "You're saying he might be scared, too?"

"No might about it. That man's shaking in his boots that something'll hurt you. Ready to slay dragons."

She tipped her head, skepticism rising.

Slowly, deliberately, Belichek added, "And he'll do his damnedest to slay that dragon—even if it's inside you."

CHAPTER FORTY-SIX

BACK IN THEIR positions, Belichek didn't begin with questions. "There's something I need to tell you."

Maggie's brows popped up.

He'd gotten this far. Now he stalled.

There should be a way to say this that would make it easier on them. A way that got in the implications and side history all neat, so they got the whole picture...

Oh, hell. There wasn't.

"My grandfather was the chief of police who investigated the attempted kidnapping of Jamie and your aunt's murder. I lived with him and Gran then."

Silence fell like a wall.

What else there was for him to say depended on them.

"The chief of police. I remember him." Maggie's eyes narrowed, her lawyer face on. "I *said* you looked familiar. First time we met—or *was* it the first time? You said we'd never met before, but you lied—"

"I didn't tell you this, but I never lied to you, Mags. We didn't meet until I was a detective and you were an ACA. Back when your aunt... I saw you, saw all three of you a couple times. I would've just been a face in the crowd to you."

Into the silence—the silence of Maggie's suspicion, the silence of his patience—Jamie's voice came in hesitant steps.

"Rutherford. His name was Rutherford. Your grandfather's."

He looked at her, surprised she remembered. "Rutherford Webster."

But she wasn't seeing him, only looking into the past. "He… he was kind to us. He cared about Aunt Vivian. He's a good man."

Gratitude opened almost painfully in Belichek's chest. "He was… He was a good man. He died a number of years back."

"And then your grandmother a few years ago," Maggie murmured. Neutral.

"She put up a good front, but she wasn't the same after he died. They'd been together a long time."

"You were named after him," Jamie said. "It sounded … familiar when Maggie said it. That's where Ford came from, right?"

"Yeah." He cleared his throat. "I wanted to get this out there. It doesn't affect this situation, but if it came up another way…"

He left another pause, but they didn't appear to have any questions for him.

Thank heavens, because he felt as if he were walking a tightrope over their raw memories.

"So, we'll get back to work. Jamie, what happened last time you went to the cabin you usually go to?"

"What? What do you mean?"

Delaying tactic? Or truly caught off guard by the switch.

"What I said. What happened the last time you were at the Pennsylvania cabin you used to go to? Hendrickson's cabin."

"Nothing." She pushed at the air with the back of her hand as if that would make something disappear. "Really nothing."

"Not nothing. Because it made you more willing to accept the offer of the North Carolina cabin."

"Even if it did, that has nothing to do with what happened."

"You can't know that. We'll only know after you tell me and we can look into it."

"You don't think I want to know what happened, who was killed in my house, and why? You don't think I want this to be over? But I can't possibly tell you every tiny, unrelated thing that's happened in my life."

"You might have to. If we can't get answers from the big, related things."

Her eyes widened slightly. He let that sink into her new vision of reality before continuing.

"But this *is* related, Jamie. Anything that changed, anything unusual, we need to know about. You'd gone to that cabin previously. You didn't this time. Why?"

"I told you, Bethany offered and—"

"You wanted to make her happy."

His deadpan delivery irked her, but he'd bled out any sarcasm she could grab onto.

She did that with Maggie. Made it about what Maggie's tone said about Maggie, instead of what the words said about Jamie. Grabbed onto Maggie's tone and her sharp slant on the world to deflect the reality Maggie spoke.

So he couldn't give her that easy route to avoidance.

"There's nothing wrong with wanting to make someone happy—to have them feel valued, to acknowledge a generous offer by accepting it. Changing my routine was a small thing to do to accomplish that."

She sounded defensive. Good. Less certainty from her might serve them well.

He chose an angle to keep her unbalanced.

"What about the owner of the cabin where you usually went? Wouldn't that person feel less accepted and valued when their generous offer was declined in favor of the newcomer's?"

She quickly said. "Hendrickson knows how I feel about him. That would be no issue."

"He offered the cabin as usual and you refused?"

"He was fine with—"

"Let's take this one step at a time. He offered the use of his cabin while you finished the book?"

"Yes."

"You refused?"

"I declined. Not the same thing."

"Why did you decline?"

"I told you before—"

"No, you didn't. You talked about how nice the scenery was in

North Carolina, how convenient it turned out to be—things you couldn't know when you made the change. But you did know what happened the last time you were at the Pennsylvania cabin."

She met his gaze.

Longer and straighter than anyone else he'd ever questioned.

In the end, she looked away. But she answered, "I need to get over being so finicky about how I finish these projects. But when time's tight I go back to the way I've always done it. That's why I thought the North Carolina cabin was a good idea after Bethany offered and I thought it through."

"How did Hendrickson York take it when you told him?"

"He totally understood. He said he'd hate for me to feel I was getting stale and if a change of scenery could prevent that he was all for it."

Did she not hear the undermining sting in those words?

Belichek could. The older man's intimation that *stale* was already upon her and changing scenery was a pitiable attempt at self-delusion.

"I meant how did he take it when you told him to leave the previous time?"

Her eyes didn't just widen this time, they went a bit wild.

Caught.

Not like a wild animal. But like a human forced to open a door she preferred closed, locked, barred, and hidden from anyone else's sight.

"Not well, huh?"

"I never told him to—I wouldn't. He had entirely generous intentions. He wanted to help, to make things easier, to take care of the mundane details that distracted me from the work. What he didn't understand—not at first—was that the mundane distractions are part of my routine. They give me a chance to do something while I think through the next part."

"He showed up uninvited."

"It's his cabin."

"Even though he knew you wanted to be alone. Even though he knew you had worked alone the other times."

"The foundation had grown tremendously since my previous book.

But—"

"Because of the previous book you wrote."

She ignored that. "—there'd been a longer gap between books. I hadn't kept the same rhythm."

"You were worried about writing that book?"

"Not really, but Hendrickson worries about me and can be overprotective, so it would be natural for him to think I might be worried."

"So, he disrupts your routine by showing up uninvited and unannounced, trying to elbow his way into your solitude."

Not denying was as good as a confirmation.

She stood. "This is crazy. You're asking the same questions—"

"Get a bit more with each round—"

"Don't talk over me, Belichek."

He dropped his head slightly, looking at the pattern of the wood floor. *That's* what got her ticked? Not worrying about somebody out there probably wanting to kill her, but whether he interrupted?

"You're asking the same questions and I'm giving the same answers. This is going nowhere. And in the meantime, my parents, my family, my friends all think I'm dead. They must be getting ready to bury me in Richmond next to Aunt Vivian."

"Not with an ongoing murder investigation," Maggie said. "And not without a positive ID."

A shiver moved Jamie's shoulders, but she didn't relent. "I'm going home. Now."

CHAPTER FORTY-SEVEN

BELICHEK KEPT HIS head down.

It gave the impression he wasn't listening. That he'd tuned out. Maybe that he didn't care.

It even could be interpreted as vulnerable, with his eyes not on the job, not watching for a potential attack.

But Jamie knew better.

It wasn't vulnerable. And he was entirely on the job.

Didn't she know that first-hand?

The layers of shock, of numbness were long gone. But he kept peeling, until she felt raw. Fighting to hold onto what covered her raw nerve-endings, consigned only to the safety of her journals.

Which he had read.

Her friends, her neighbors, her relationships, each exposed and examined.

Her, exposed and examined.

And then even her excruciating memories of Aunt Vivian and of what came before… Even those weren't safe inside the protections she and Maggie and Ally had implicitly built. Because *he* shared them, too. He had been there.

Detective Rutherford Belichek with his questions and his probing and his unblinking relentlessness.

Even in this moment, with his head down, it was more like he needed to disconnect his eyes from what was in front of him to let his other senses and intellect apply fully to the matter under consideration.

Her.

The bug under the microscope.

The bug had to escape. Now.

She expected to hear about how she was their only clue, how she held the secret, how she could die.

What he said was, "You don't have a way back to Fairlington."

Her jaw dropped. "You won't drive me back when you—you practically kidnapped me the night before last to bring me up here?"

"Didn't kidnap you then, even tougher argument to make that I'm kidnapping you now when all I'm doing is refusing to drive you someplace. Particularly to a place explicitly dangerous for you."

She jerked her head around to her cousin. "Maggie? You know— I've got to see to my parents. I can't let them go on thinking…"

"That's not why," Belichek said quietly.

"Maggie," she repeated.

Maggie hissed out a breath. "He's right. It's not why. You're tired of the tough questions because you don't like the possible answers. Even though they're necessary." She turned toward Belichek, though he still looked at the floor. "But she's right that this can't go on, Bel. And I can't be part of it going on and not telling her parents, Ally, and the rest of the family."

For a beat it seemed that no one breathed.

"Yeah," Maggie said, "I'll take you to Fredericksburg, to your parents."

"I drive," J.D. said.

JAMIE SET HER tote by the front door, then went to where Ford Belichek sat alone at the kitchen counter with an empty glass in front of him.

She poured water from the nearby pitcher into his glass, stopping when it was a little over half full.

Still holding the pitcher, she said, "I recognize that my answers haven't let you solve what happened at my house while I was gone. But I can only give you the answers I know. And I have—multiple times.

I'm going to Fredericksburg to see my parents. You're going to have to accept that your glass is half-full, Detective Belichek."

"This is a serious business, Jamie—deadly serious. And you're in a dangerous business, trying to change people."

"I'm not trying to change people."

"Foundation. Books." As if those two words proved his point.

"They're not trying to change people. They're offering people opportunities to change themselves. Sometimes people can't change because of circumstances. But if you show them how they might change their circumstances or when you have the opportunity to directly change their circumstances, then people can change themselves."

"Do you believe your aunt's murderer would have been a different person if his circumstances had changed? Do you think she'd still be alive?"

"We'll never know, will we?"

"What we do know is if he'd been put away or killed before he entered your aunt's world, she'd still be alive. And you do try to change people. You just tried to change my view of this glass."

He picked up the glass, tipping it as if preparing to taste fine wine.

"This glass is not only half empty, it could be poisoned and it's for damned sure polluted."

He righted the glass, then drained it in two long gulps.

He stood and placed the empty glass directly in from of her without releasing it.

"It's your glass, Jamison Chancellor. The one where the best-case scenario will probably be that you're suspected of murder and the most likely scenario is someone finishes what they started Labor Day weekend."

He let go of the glass, turned, and headed out, joining Maggie and J.D., standing at the bottom of the stairs.

He shook hands with J.D., thanking him, and hugged Maggie. Without looking back, he left.

CHAPTER FORTY-EIGHT

J.D. Carson driving was some consolation. Certainly safer than Maggie behind the wheel, the poster girl for hard-driving in more ways than one. And his training would have him on the alert for any threats.

Not likely, maybe, that a killer would be hanging around the Chancellor home in Fredericksburg on the off-chance Jamie showed up—assuming the killer meant to kill her and knew he hadn't.

But Belichek didn't fool himself that Jamie would stay at her parents' place.

Now that she was out of the cocoon of shock and J.D. Carson's cabin, she'd get herself back to the Sunshine Foundation pronto.

Maggie might be able to delay her a day, maybe two, but then…

Jamie also would want to be back in her own home again. Probably trying like hell to do that alone.

Only way to keep her safe was to figure this thing out fast.

He had pieces from their time in Bedhurst. Important pieces. But not enough to know which ones fit where.

He called his partner as he neared the metro area.

"Landis. We need to talk."

"We need to talk? That's how you say hello. First you have a woman call for an ID on you, which I thought was a real hopeful sign. Until you disappear—yes, I checked Jamison Chancellor's house so I know you weren't there. And then you send me a cryptic text about deep-diving on that Usher woman, don't answer any of my replies, and now you say—"

"What did you find out about her?"

"Why should I tell you? You're still on vacation. Speaking of which, I don't have time to hear about your exploits, buddy—even if she was as hot as she sounded. I've got this little investigation going, in case you don't remember."

But Belichek heard it in Landis' voice. "What did you find out about Bethany Usher?"

"Possibilities. Not definite, but possibilities."

Belichek grunted. "You're not telling me on the phone. Not with the leaks."

"Right. Been more, by the way."

"Okay. The place we'd get food during the Dorset stakeout." Belichek's mental map of the county was based on cases. Landis' on food. "You bring your possibilities and I'll bring my ... news."

"When?"

"An hour."

"Give me two."

MAGGIE TURNED FROM the front passenger seat. "You know that stuff with Bel with the glass wasn't about water, don't you?"

Jamie breathed in, then out through her nose. Maggie wasn't asking if her younger cousin was bright enough to see what was obvious. She'd made it a statement as an opening to something else she wanted to say.

The chances of stopping Maggie from saying whatever was coming were slim and none—no, they were none and none.

Jamie took in another slow breath. "He was trying to scare me to do what he wanted."

"That's not how Bel operates. He tells you the truth as he sees it." A beat passed. "Including about you being a possible suspect. That's a stronger possibility with you not going to the authorities."

"But he said—you both said there's a leak in the department that—"

"There is and it does make it more dangerous for you to go to the police. That doesn't change how you will be viewed for *not* going to them, especially by the police department. Bel knows that. It's why he was driving so hard to get answers."

"Then I'll have to prove I had nothing to do with this. After I see Mom and Dad."

THE FOOD CAME first with Landis.

They ordered kafta sandwiches from the Lebanese restaurant and deli, added knafeh for dessert. They ate in Belichek's car before talking.

"You don't look like you've been to a spa for your vacation, Belichek." His partner's mildness was dangerous.

"What have you found out about Bethany Usher? I've got to know that first."

"What you've got to do is talk to me, that's what you've got to do. What the fuck is going on, Belichek?"

"Tell me about Usher and—"

"I've left you a hundred frigging messages. I thought the first day maybe ol' Ford got real lucky with the female he met. But then I got to thinking maybe it wasn't so lucky, some females are crazy, and where the hell is he? So, then I leave messages. Nothing. If that leak hadn't made me jumpy, I'd've sent you a message saying we got a break in the Chancellor case, knowing—"

"Did you?" Belichek's gut tightened.

"No, but I figured that was the one way you'd call back. But you didn't, so I go to that house, because I wouldn't put it past you to blow off your chance to get laid in order to go back and re-read those diaries—*journals*. But guess what?"

"What?"

"You weren't there."

"Guess you don't know me as well as you think you do, Landis."

"That's what's got me worried. Because you know what I did find out at her house? Some of her clothes are now missing."

"Did you tell anybody?"

"No."

Something in his tone arrested Belichek's attention. "What are you—? You can't—" He fought against laughter. "God, Landis, you've been around that shrink way too much."

"Something's going on," Landis said doggedly.

Belichek drew in a long breath and wiped the corner of his left eye. "Yeah, something is going on. I swear, I will spill all. I got you here to do that. But if you've found out anything vital about Bethany Usher, it could change things."

Landis stared at him an extra beat. "Don't have a lot. Terrington went to Bethany Usher's apartment—looked like she'd cleared out. He reports nobody knows where she is. Vague impression she was going to the beach—maybe Delaware, maybe Jersey. She was supposed to be back to work a week after Labor Day. They all agree on that, including additional volunteers we've talked to.

"What's your interest? Her being away at the same time is interesting, but if there's a motive for her to go to her boss's house and unload a shotgun in her face, I haven't heard a whisper of it. And nobody at the Sunshine Foundation liked Usher near enough to be quiet about a motive for her. I wondered if she had something on Chancellor to get that unearned vacation time, but then, the shotgun should have been aimed the other direction." He turned his head. "Have you picked up a motive involving her?"

"No." He shoveled out a sigh, then just said it. "I have reason to believe she's likely the victim."

Landis didn't object or deny or argue. He stared at him, cogs in his brain shifting and adjusting to the theory—because for him it was still theory.

"What makes you think that?" he asked.

"Process of elimination. Because Jamison Chancellor is alive."

CHAPTER FORTY-NINE

"**S**HE SHOWED UP night before last at her house. About two in the morning."

"What the *hell*, Belichek? What the *fucking hell*? Where is she?"

He ignored that, because his partner needed to expel steam. "She couldn't stay there. Neighbors might see in. People going by—it would have been impossible to keep it a secret."

"A secret." More curses followed that mutter.

"Started to take her to Mags', but she wasn't at her place. She was up in the mountains with J.D. Carson. I drove Jamie there."

"Jesus, Belichek, you've lost your mind. This *is* about reading those journals and—"

"No. It's about keeping her alive and solving a murder."

His partner wasn't with him on this. Not yet. Maybe never.

He'd deal with that as he had to.

Landis continued, "We've got to go get her. Right now. Bring her in. Hope to God nobody notices the gap and—"

"She's not at Carson's anymore. She's at her parents' in Fredericksburg. Carson and Mags drove her."

"We've got to get her. Now. My car. And—"

"You can still stay out of this, Tanner. I'll take—"

"The hell I can. I'm lead. And I know now. We need to figure out how to handle this with the glass offices—fast."

"We can't assure her or her family that we can keep her alive if we do that. Not with that leak."

Like taking a pot off a burner, that simmered down Landis' boil immediately. This string of curses was thoughtful.

"We've got to get her," he said. "Maybe she was the target. But maybe not. Either way, you're going to tell me every word she's said to you on the way."

CHAPTER FIFTY

LANDIS HAD BELICHEK drive so he could keep up with texts and phone calls, which regularly interrupted Belichek's report of his questioning of Jamie.

"I can't believe Frye went along with this. Hard-assed Margaret Frye, who—"

"Wants to keep her cousin alive, now that she's back from the dead."

Landis grunted. "Weak alibi, being alone at a cabin, nobody saw her, no communication the whole time. And the idea that she hadn't heard anything about this… Definitely weak."

Belichek didn't respond to that. Landis wasn't wrong. But he was goading him, trying to get a rise out of him, which would prove he wasn't being reasonable.

Because Landis wasn't anywhere near ready to sign on to this.

Belichek wasn't going to wait around if his partner didn't get on board. "What about Bethany Usher?"

Landis swore again. "If I'd known how she fit in, instead of some vague text from the oracle, I'd never have given the assignment to Terrington."

"As long as he doesn't know the context—"

"Which he doesn't because I didn't, damn you. She's a fairly recent hire at Sunshine Foundation. Last spring, I think. Not part of the inner circle. Said she wanted this time off and Jamison Chancellor said she could have it—paid—even though she didn't have anywhere near that much vacation time in the bank."

Landis used his phone like a big finger to point at him.

"And that raises a question that didn't matter so much when Jamison Chancellor was dead, but sure as hell does now. Why would she? Give this new hire time off. But if she wanted Bethany Usher to take her place for some reason, if she knew that shotgun was out to get her, or—"

"No way. You don't know Jamie."

"And you do? Since when? Since reading her journals or since seeing her in the flesh." He emphasized that last word.

"Ask Maggie."

"Right. Like even Mags could be cut and dried about her own cousin. God, I'm the only sane one left."

"What else on Bethany Usher?"

"We weren't exactly blitzing her. Tried calling. Phone's not working. Like the SIM card's out."

"Does she match physically with the victim?"

Landis' mouth jerked. "Close enough. Terrington's not imaginative, but he did get the driver's license info. Same height, close to the same weight. Hair color similar."

"DNA?"

"Not yet. We'll push that, along with medical—assuming her records weren't burned, too. That would fit the rest of this damned case. Dental's still a long shot because of the damage, but we'll try that, too."

"We do have more answers than we did, including the purse issue."

Landis evil-eyed him. "Great. We've got Jamison Chancellor's purse, but not Bethany Usher's now. That's a draw at best."

Navigation announced their arrival.

"Take a breath, Landis. Remember her parents didn't know anything about this. They've had their daughter returned from the dead. And taking her to the mountains ... that was all me."

"Fuck you," Landis muttered. But he did take a breath.

✧　✧　✧　✧

BELICHEK WATCHED LANDIS' handling of the Chancellor family, particularly Jamie's parents, with appreciation.

Jamie did not seem as impressed. She sat between her parents on the long couch, her father's arm around her shoulders, her mother holding both Jamie's hands in her lap.

Maggie was mostly silent, Carson completely so. Belichek matched Carson.

With reluctance, but recognition of the wisdom of it, the senior Chancellors agreed to keep Jamie's survival a secret, even from her siblings.

For now.

With full dark, they'd pull Belichek's vehicle into the garage and put Jamie in it then. Belichek was relieved, but not surprised, that Carson had used a similar maneuver to get her from his truck into the house.

The one danger point came when her mother said—with tears in her voice—that they'd only had a couple hours together and Jamie objected to returning immediately to Fairlington.

"I can arrest you as a material witness," Landis said.

Jamie's gaze went to Belichek. Then, as if she realized what she'd done, she shifted it to Maggie.

"He can," her cousin confirmed. "But he won't."

"Unless I have to." Landis relented enough to add, directing it to her parents, "For her own safety and to find out who shot a woman, most likely thinking it was your daughter."

Dana Chancellor sucked in a breath.

Wes Chancellor extended the arm he had around his daughter to touch his wife's shoulder.

She nodded. "We have to be realistic." She looked at Jamie. "You need to be realistic."

"It's okay, Mom. Don't worry about anything. This is all a mistake."

✧　✧　✧　✧

A HURRIED CONFERENCE while Jamie said good-bye to her parents determined that she would ride with him and Landis, but Carson and Mags would follow in Carson's truck. They also decided on a specific destination.

Landis wasn't happy, but he'd live with it. For now.

There was a lot of that *for now* going around.

CHAPTER FIFTY-ONE

"YOU MISSED THE turn to my house."

Jaimie's first words since long hugs with her parents.

Landis had taken back the driver's wheel, though he had Belichek check messages and a few dictated responses, both screened for what they let Jamie hear.

Now, his glance put the job of responding on Belichek.

Without turning around from the passenger seat, he said, "You can't go there. Don't want to risk it."

"People don't even know I'm alive."

Before Belichek could respond to her pointed tone that preserving that state was his goal, Landis said coolly, "Not your life, our careers."

She digested that in silence for a moment. "I should have realized… You didn't tell your superiors about going to the cabin with me?"

Not only not pointed, but she made it sound like a Sunday picnic that had been her idea.

"No."

"You didn't tell them I'm alive?"

"No."

"Why?"

"There's a leak. Not risking your safety."

"And he was taken off the case," Landis said.

"Off … But … You *lied*? When Maggie said that I thought it was harsh but—"

"I didn't lie. I told you I was investigating your case. I was. I am."

"Will they put you back on the case because you have me as your star witness?"

He cut a look at her via the rearview mirror in the illumination from another vehicle's headlights, but she was looking out the side window. "Probably."

"Shit," Landis said.

Belichek caught the motion of Jamie's jump in the rearview mirror. He couldn't swear he didn't jump, too. "What?"

"My car's still back at the restaurant." He stopped at a yellow light and pounded numbers into his phone. "Schmidt? It's Detective Landis. Yeah. Remember you saying if there was any way you could help on the case? It's not what you're hoping for, but I need my car brought to me… Yeah. Get somebody to drive you out, then bring it to me. I'll text where it is and where to bring it. There's a key fob in my desk, second drawer, right side, under the napkins."

He ended the call.

"You're going to take advantage of that kid that way?"

"Hell, yes. It's all in service of the case."

JAMIE SHOOK OFF her lethargy as they turned into a warren of winding streets with individual homes, apartment buildings, town homes, all in red brick. They shared a certain pared-down colonial feel of a college campus or Army post where everything was built at the same time.

Jamie knew of this area. The times she'd been here, she always got lost.

She hoped the same happened to Landis now. Maybe that would give her a chance to restore those protective layers Belichek stripped away. Seeing her parents had helped.

But not enough. Not nearly enough.

Without needing directions, Landis made four turns, then pulled into an empty parking spot in the middle of three town homes.

J.D. pulled in next to them. Maggie had the passenger window down and gestured to Landis to lower his driver's window.

"Bel, even I don't have that black a thumb."

Jamie turned, seeing her cousin focused on the left end of the building. In a brick-enclosed planter at the door, a single blighted evergreen survived amid late season die-back.

"You still win that prize, Mags," he said easily. Almost everything between him and Maggie was easy. Comfortable. Secure. Familiar.

"Stay here," he ordered. "I want to check first."

He went up the sidewalk to the right end of the building, unlocked the door, checked inside before emerging and nodding to them.

"*This* is where you live?" Maggie asked, when they entered.

"It's nice," Jamie said. Warm light showed a long couch, a couple upholstered chairs. Behind them, a table and chair for dining. To the right of that a kitchen at the back.

"It is," Maggie said.

"They're surprised, in case you can't tell, Belichek," Landis said. "They expected a rundown bachelor pad."

"Go on downstairs," Belichek said. "I'll bring food down—"

J.D. interrupted. "Thought I'd go get takeout. The chicken place by the entry to here any good?"

"Great," Belichek said.

"Passable," Landis said.

Jamie felt a smile tug her mouth.

Landis added, "But none for me. I'm going to the office, since one of us is still working."

"Before you go, Detective Landis," Jamie said, "in the car, you said doing this was risking your careers."

"That's not—"

Looking at Jamie, not Belichek, Landis said, "It's true. And don't let him tell you otherwise. So you better be worth it, because it's his career."

"Landis—" Belichek started.

Maggie protested, "Your career, too."

"Not if I can help it," Landis said.

Maggie scoffed, "Like you'd throw him under the bus, Landis. Give it up."

He shrugged and left, ending the subject. Though Jamie didn't think any of them forgot it. She certainly didn't, as they settled in the basement.

It was furnished as a family room with an impressive TV, wrap-around couches against two walls and a computer area.

By the time Belichek showed them around, explained how to operate everything, and they'd each had a bathroom break, J.D. returned with food.

Done eating, Jamie cleaned her hands on extra napkins from the takeout place, then yawned hugely.

After discussion about J.D. leaving the next day—at least long enough to check in with his job and his house in Bedhurst—Belichek said, "As for Jamie tomorrow—"

"Tomorrow, I'm going to the foundation," she said.

"No." It came from three of them—Maggie, J.D., and Belichek.

"I can't hide out for—"

"The hell you can't," Maggie said. "Jamie, this is not something you can wish away by being optimistic. This—"

"I know that, Maggie. But if the person who was killed was Bethany Usher, then it's my responsibility, because she worked at the foundation."

"It's our job, not yours," Belichek said.

"It's my responsibility," she repeated.

"You two can argue about that later," Maggie said. "The priority is figuring this out. And tomorrow morning, Landis is going to interview you. Tonight, get some rest."

Because you're going to need it hung in the air.

Belichek's calm voice broke the somber mood.

"Jamie sleeps down here. Less chance of being spotted from outside. I'll be on the stairs." Unspoken was that no one would get through him.

Maggie said, "Not you, Bel. You need to sleep—Landis, too—to work this. I'll stay down here with Jamie. And J.D.—"

"Will keep an eye on both of them."

Mild words. An unmild promise.

CHAPTER FIFTY-TWO

MAGGIE AND J.D. went out to his truck, they said for something Maggie forgot.

In the silence between him and Jamie, Belichek looked toward the stairs.

The others had already been gone long enough to retrieve multiple items.

Jamie also glanced toward the stairs, the look in her eyes saying she realized they'd been gone longer than necessary.

Abruptly, she said, "You told me focusing on the bad is your job description, but Tanner isn't like that."

Was she talking to distract herself or him from contemplation of what else they might be doing out there alone in the dark?

He said none of that.

"Don't let him fool you."

Her eyebrows requested more information. He wasn't sharing the gloomier aspects of his partner's personality.

She gave a soft huff of acquiescence. "Then you both focus on bad things and that has to wear on you."

"Not when we catch the bad things."

She looked at him, her head at an angle, as if trying for a different perspective.

"Like another man whose job was to catch bad things," she said softly. "That must have been so hard for your grandfather. For your family."

"Not like it was hard on you and your families. But ... hard."

"He's the reason you went into law enforcement."

Silence.

"There's more?"

More silence.

"You don't need to tell me. But you need to tell somebody."

He cut her a look.

"Is it working for you not to tell anyone?"

Finally, he said, "He carried it. Carried it to his grave."

"Carried what?"

"Failing. Failing your aunt. Failing the three of you. Especially you. The little one, he called you."

"Failing? Me? Oh… No. No."

Before she could assemble more words, Belichek said, "You were there when the police caught your aunt's murderer."

"How do you—? From reading my journals." A frown crossed her eyes.

Because she didn't remember writing that? She hadn't.

But she'd moved on.

"Maggie doesn't know. Doesn't know Ally and I were there that day." She stood, paced to the bottom of the stairs and back. "Ally and I agreed she shouldn't ever know. You can't tell her. She was so concentrated on protecting us from… from everything that happened. Even now. There's no sense in letting her know that we saw … what we saw."

A sound came from the front door.

Jamie sucked in a breath and instinctively stepped back. Into him because he was already behind her.

Then she pulled in another breath, he felt it on hairs at the back of his neck.

He stepped to the side, then forward, blocking her body with his.

Pressed against him, she didn't back up.

The front door opened slightly. He'd given Maggie a key, still…

A voice came low, relaxed. "It's J.D. and Maggie."

Jamie's hand touched his side. He held for a moment, then stepped forward.

Away.

✧ ✧ ✧ ✧

BELICHEK WAS ON the stairs leading to his bedroom the next time the sound came at the front door.

He'd spent the past two hours accessing what information he could from home.

All had been quiet from downstairs, indicating Jamie and Maggie might be getting much-needed sleep.

As he passed the stairwell to the basement on his way to the front door, he saw only the gleam of Carson's eyes—and that for an instant.

He stood on the hinge side of the door. "Who is it?"

"Landis."

After Belichek opened the door, he looked around. "Early to bed group, huh?"

"Not much sleep the past few nights."

"Tell me about it. I'm using your couch tonight."

Belichek nodded, heading into the living room. Other detectives might steer clear of the contagion of potential career suicide. Landis' need to know the truth wouldn't let him. It's why they were good partners.

"You know where the stuff is. Anything new?"

"Some of the DNA's in."

"Anything?"

Landis opened the ottoman that held a pillow, a sheet, and a blanket. He dropped the pile on the couch, slid off his shoes, and sat beside it.

"Yeah. The victim. The foundation folks." His grunt could have been amused, except it wasn't. Not the least amused. "Before you jump, let me tell you I'm the only one who knows. They found the victim's not related to the Chancellors."

"Good to know." Belichek took the chair that went with the otto-man, closing its lid with his foot.

"Would've been, if we didn't already know it. And if it didn't risk alerting our colleagues, not to mention our bosses, to something hinky going on. Then, for an added bit of non-information, the DNA tells us nobody in this case is related to anybody else, except Jamison and her mother. That's it. Period. The Chancellor family story as told to us by Maggie Frye appears to be the truth. Hold the damned presses."

"That's not the complete DNA?"

"They're still running the evidence since they did the ID first, with us pushing for an official way to say Jamison Chancellor was dead."

"Good thing it didn't come through earlier then, huh."

"I hate it when you're the cheerful one." Landis stretched his legs out to prop his feet on the closer side of the ottoman.

"Here's another cheerful aspect. It clears up a lot that wasn't making sense. Jamie took her purse and the suitcases. The thief— theorizing for now it was Bethany Usher—took her time because she thought she had weeks to search for valuables. She'd only dealt with a couple rooms before she was killed."

"That means an accomplice to take the valuables … somewhere."

"Or Bethany Usher took it out herself. That could explain Enderbe seeing Jamie's car in the early morning hours. Could have been Bethany Usher taking a load somewhere."

"Possible. You know, if this didn't involve a nonprofit, I'd be following the money. All that stuff about taking the foundation to another level, that perked me right up until I remembered these folks aren't looking to cash in the way for-profits would."

"Nothing like having a good greed motive ruined by people trying to do good," Bel said dryly.

"Disgusting," Landis agreed. "Though there is what you said about those people being vulnerable to pressure to keep ill deeds quiet."

Belichek sidestepped that needling. "There were three takes on the management company coming in. That might be a crack to work."

Landis raised a finger at a time. "Hendrickson York said he wanted it so the foundation could grow, Adam Delattre said Jamie said they needed it so the foundation could grow, Celeste Renfro said Jamie had to be persuaded so she didn't have as much burden."

"Last two could both be true if you flip the order."

"York tried to kill her to keep the management company out? That seems extreme. He'd still be in charge of donors."

"Doubt that would be his motive."

Landis gave him a sharp look. "That stuff about the cabin … you know something?"

"No. Wonder about? Yeah."

A short exhalation through his nose expressed Landis' lack of enthusiasm. "Don't see any motives for Celeste or Adam, either. Despite Terrington's effort at a scoop."

He told Belichek about Terrington's theory of Celeste's financial motive.

"Looks even weaker after he dug into it. She has no other debts than the mortgage, is on time with that, and already has a chunk of equity in the new house. You could say her financial house is in order.

"Adam might be a true believer, but nothing fishy there, either. Taken together, I don't see much of a crack at the foundation, especially without a money motive. Hah. A crack in the foundation."

Belichek grunted. "Non-money motives? That takes out greed. There's still revenge, jealousy, self-protection…"

"You're forgetting one. Love. In all its potentially twisted glory. So, maybe Celeste protecting Adam Delattre? Young guy, mother complex?"

"Might be more specific than that. Remember, she deals with the families the Sunshine Foundation helps out. She shepherds them through the whole process. And his family was one of them. Her protectiveness might go back to his first dealings with the foundation. He said she helped his family."

"But why would he try to kill Jamie? No bad blood there at all that we've heard of. And would Celeste go along with it?"

"Good points."

"Gee, thanks." Landis moved on. "What about the neighbor, Phil Xavier?"

"Two possibilities there."

"I'm getting tired of countdowns."

Belichek ignored that complaint. "First possibility. He got fed up with hearing no, went to Jamie's front door, shot the person who answered in the face, and thought that would pave the way to his real estate vision."

"Or had someone do it. Wait a minute."

Landis got up, went into the kitchen to the fridge, poured himself a glass of orange juice and brought Belichek back an ice water.

While Landis drank the OJ, Belichek looked at his glass thoughtfully.

Landis put down his empty glass. "No. Xavier would do it himself. Wouldn't give anyone else the leverage over him."

"Yeah. Second possibility. He had nothing to do with the killing. When it happened, he did not mourn, again thinking that was the answer he wanted. Got his hopes up and could be more determined than ever to get Jamie out." He'd be on the watch for that, whether she liked it or not.

"Even odds. More questions." It was a demand, not a request.

"Yeah. Assuming from the lack of forced entry, one of the apparently dozens she gave keys to, should have walked up to the front door. Cameras?"

"Nothing so far. We've asked the neighbors and we've worked from Friday—caught Jamie coming home—through Sunday night. We do see Jamie's car leaving for a time late Saturday, or more accurately Sunday morning, that coincides with Garrison Enderbe's near-death experience. Can't see the driver, though they're trying experimental software beyond the usual that they're excited about."

"It won't be Jamie. She'd already left in the truck."

Landis cut him a look. "If you say so."

"I do."

"We'll have to go back and look for the truck."

They sat in silence for a minute.

Belichek broke it. "Remember that figure I mentioned from the video going up to Jamie's door and next door? Could that be someone checking if their key worked? Jamie changed locks after Xavier."

"Yeah. You said you couldn't identify anybody."

"Couldn't. But maybe Jamie could. If it's someone familiar."

"Worth a try. Send the clip." Belichek switched gears. "I've been thinking about this. Short of pumping Jamie over and over again—and that's if she'd cooperate—I'm going to be hamstrung on what I can do unless Palery knows she's alive. If he puts me back on the case, even low-key, I can contribute more."

"Leaving Jamie alone?"

"With Maggie. And I could do a lot from here, once I get the okay from Palery. Plus, as long as no one outside of us and Palery knows…"

"Better hope Palery isn't the leak."

"Or you."

"Right." Landis stood, grabbed a back cushion off the couch and tossed it onto the other upholstered chair, then repeated with two more. "Get out of here, Belichek. I need some sleep."

He spread the sheet, then started stripping his clothes.

Belichek headed for the stairs.

"One last thing," Landis said. "Bethany Usher. I got the ball rolling tonight on hitting her hard. She's our best clue. She's where the story ended, so she's where we start."

Belichek read before sleeping, finishing the remaining journal. Though that left the most recent one. He'd thought he felt the edge of it when he carried Jamie's tote.

To discover what that journal told about her life would take more than reading pages.

DAY SIX

CHAPTER FIFTY-THREE

"**You were uneasy** about a couple guys—"

At Landis' words, Jamie shifted her focus from him to Belichek with a distinct lack of appreciation.

Landis had been questioning her in the basement for two hours with one short break.

Maggie and J.D. had left for J.D. to drop her off at her own place before heading for the mountains. Maggie had returned forty minutes ago in fresh clothes and with her car.

Still, Landis asked questions.

He took her back over the material Belichek had shared with him, but with different slants and a different rhythm.

Jamie seemed more relaxed. She didn't object as much.

Would they have gotten more out of her at the cabin if they'd both been there, using their usual method? No point wondering now.

And Landis hadn't gotten anything new enough to send them in a different direction.

"Yeah, Belichek read it in your journals. He said you were uneasy about a couple guys. If it comes to that, he also said the Sunshine Foundation was a prime spot for evil-doing and chicanery, but—"

"Chicanery?" Belichek muttered.

"Specifically, he mentioned money laundering and drug running," Landis added in retribution.

"Money laundering and drug—Are you nuts?"

Landis grabbed back her attention. "But what I want to know is if Xavier is one of the guys who made you uneasy."

"I told you, I changed the locks after that episode with the architect early this year. Phil Xavier doesn't have access to the current key—"

"Yeah, I've seen the Fort Knox where Imogen Wooton keeps your key," Landis said dryly.

"That's the point," he said. "Who inherits your house if you die?"

Her eyebrows hiked, but she answered. "My parents. If they predecease me, then Maggie and Ally in equal shares. The same with everything else."

"Jesus, Jamie. I thought Ally was nuts. Why—?"

"Don't worry, Maggie, I intend to outlive you." A slight, strained silence followed her light words. "Despite any recent events to the contrary."

Maggie grimaced. "But it's a point. None of her beneficiaries seem likely to want to jump into living there. The most likely result is they put the house up for sale and there's Xavier ready to step in."

"Even in the D.C. area real estate market, can you see someone doing that?" Jamie asked. "I can't."

"You couldn't believe Peter Rabbit really ate Mr. McGregor's vegetables."

"I was four years old."

"You still believe—"

"Stop." Landis' tone, rather than the word did the trick. He looked at Belichek. "Jamie's the obstacle. He wants the house, that's the goal. Ring the doorbell. Shoot the person who answers—presumably Jamie. He overcomes the obstacle and achieves the goal."

"That's—That's—Horrible. He's not a monster. You can't suspect he'd—He's a bull in a china shop, that's all."

"They can do a lot of damage."

She opened her mouth. Shut it. Looking more thoughtful. "You're right. They can. Whether they intend to or not."

"How did he react when you said no to his offer to buy?" Landis asked.

"He wasn't happy. He seemed… unnecessarily harsh. More angry than disappointed. And confused."

"Confused?" Angry, disappointed, he'd expected. Not confused.

"He kept talking about how I needed to take this generous offer to anyone else involved in the ownership of the house. I kept telling him I own the house. Then he'd say, then sell it to me, then I'd say no thanks, then he'd say I had to take it to these mythical other people. It was like he couldn't believe I owned the house."

"Is there anything unusual in your ownership?"

"No. It's in my name and only my name. I own it outright… I suppose that could have surprised him because of my age."

"Or he was having a flashback." Landis explained about Garrison Enderbe and his father.

She smiled. "Mr. Enderbe is quite a character. I can see him yanking Phil's chain for the fun of it."

Belichek said, "Phil Xavier is a suspect. You said he could do damage whether he intended to or not."

"I said a bull in a china shop could."

He exhaled sharply through his nose, dismissing that qualification. "Phil Xavier would intend to. He's frustrated. He's angry. Not the mood you want a bull to be in if he's in your china shop."

"Well, I'm not going to sell my house to him to put the man in a better mood—not that I'm sure such a thing is possible. What? Why are you looking at me like that for?"

"Not finding any good in Phil Xavier?"

She cocked her chin up. Not pugnacious, but contemplating. "I suppose I'm not." Now a glitter came into her eyes. "You must be rubbing off on me."

Abruptly, Jamie looked toward Maggie. Doing the same, Belichek saw her and Landis exchange a speculative look. Retroactively, he realized both Maggie and Landis had shifted from participants in the conversation to audience.

The bad news was they appeared to enjoy the show.

With something close to a smirk, Landis stood. "I'm going to the office. Belichek's relieved of that duty. No sense waving a red flag—that would be him—under the glass office's noses."

"I'm going to have to at some point."

"Just let me be out of range of the shrapnel."

BELICHEK ANSWERED HIS phone while slicing apples to go with the peanut butter and jelly sandwiches he'd scraped together from his fridge. The lowering sky had broken open and the rain was coming down like it had no intention of ever quitting.

Landis started with, "We've tracked her phone down."

"Jamie's or Bethany's."

"Jamie's."

"Where are you?"

"Break room. Nobody around. No SIM, of course, but it's better than nothing. They've tracked it from the guy who had it when they caught up with it, back through a couple re-sellers to the guy who appears to be the original holder of the stolen property, whether he stole it or not. Though his record shows a certain propensity for that activity. He's being held north of Baltimore. Ewer and Knarr are going up there to talk to him. Think he might clear some of their cases. They're also checking out his associates."

"Falling out among fellow thieves? Though body position and blood splatter argue against that."

"Argues loudly. To have it *not* be a case of the victim being shot by whoever stepped inside through that door would take contortions."

Landis paused. "I know you want to keep Jamie safe, but thinking about what you said about coming in… That DNA…"

"Is a hot potato burning your hands."

"I could handle that, even if—when—Palery finds out Jamie's alive. But it's going to come out sooner rather than later, and the best protection she has is catching the shooter. You being fully involved…"

"I've been thinking along those lines, too."

"Good. Somebody's coming—damn their need for caffeine. We'll talk later."

CHAPTER FIFTY-FOUR

"I HAVE QUESTIONS," Belichek said after they finished lunch.

Jamie had been quiet during lunch, frequently looking toward the rain-coated basement window and not meeting his gaze. Now, all the equanimity she'd displayed with Landis' questions evaporated.

"I'm tired of these same damn questions over and over, and all they boil down to is, which one of the people you trust and work with and love do you think wanted to kill you? Why, for God's sake can't you ask something different?"

"Because these are the damn questions we have to answer." His own rare temper flared up. "What do you want, celebrity interview questions? Well, you're not going to get 'em, because I don't give a shit what you think the toughest part of doing your job is. I—"

She spun on him, quick enough to jam words in his throat.

"The toughest part of my job is dealing with people like you looking at me as if I didn't have a single cell or maybe a few screws loose because I've chosen to deal with the world a certain way. No— Chosen's not the right word. I deal with the world this way because it's the only way I can. And it's not easy. Sometimes I have to fight every single second."

"Like with Hendrickson York?" he slid in.

"Hendrickson?" Her voice rose with surprise. She lowered it, "I rely on him. He's been my mainstay. The rock of the foundation. He's been very good to me."

"To your face. But if you have cuts in your back, check him for a hidden shank."

They locked eyes. He didn't relent. She looked away.

"Don't be ridiculous," she said stiffly.

"He wasn't exactly broken up about your death."

"He's very fond of me, but the foundation comes first. Thinking I'm dead, I wouldn't expect him to react any other way. I'm sure he's devoting every moment to making sure the foundation endures and thrives in the aftermath of my supposed death. It can't be easy on him. The shock, compounded by a triple workload."

"He's holding up okay." He edged toward sarcasm. "He was in your office the day the news broke, practically measuring for curtains."

She didn't hesitate. "Of course. It's far easier to run things from that office. His own doesn't work for senior staff meetings, while mine accommodates them fine. I'm glad he reacted quickly for the welfare of the foundation."

He eyed her. Not a doubt. Not a crack.

On the surface.

"You gave it away, you know," he said.

"I have no idea what you're talking about."

"Math, is what I'm talking about."

"Math?" That was genuine confusion.

"For you to say he tripled his workload by taking over your job, you have to know—even if you won't say it to me—that you do twice the work he does. You work twice as hard as he does. Does that make you resent him?"

"No."

"Because it could contribute to how much he resents you."

"He doesn't—"

"He talked about it being remarkable for you to be smart, considering how young and pretty you are. Sometimes with the slant that your lack of maturity—"

"Lack of—?"

"—should be overlooked because what else could be expected of someone young and pretty."

"He has never—You misunderstood. Or put your own interpretation on innocent comments because all you see is the darkest—"

"Carl Arbendroth."

"Haven't we gone over Carl enough—"

"York told us about Carl Arbendroth. Raised him as further proof of your poor judgment."

That knocked her back. Not permanently. But definitely a timeout when her honesty bubbled up past her cloak of optimism.

"Hendrickson worries about me. Needlessly, but he does. Some men do take that attitude. You should understand that." Ah, some claws showing. "He never thought Carl was a good match for me. That's all."

He waited. So did she. She wasn't going to succumb to that ploy, using silence to press weight against the interview subject's nerves until breathing pressed and muscles jumped.

"He didn't like Arbendroth being with you, because Arbendroth occupied the edge of the spotlight Hendrickson York previously claimed."

"That's—"

"And he didn't like Arbendroth stalking you, because it distracted you, putting more work on him than he liked."

"Carl didn't stalk—"

"Want to read the legal definition? Why didn't you tell me—us when we asked if there was anyone we should look into?"

"Because you *shouldn't* look into him. He's a perfectly normal—"

"A woman who resembled you, wearing your clothes, is shot in your house and your ex—who had access to a key to your place—was stalking you. Doesn't get much more relevant. Are you trying to impede this investigation, Ms. Chancellor?"

"You're trying to bully me."

"This is a murder investigation. I'm treating you as a witness, as a potential intended victim, and as someone deeply involved with the crime."

"You make it sound like I'm a suspect."

"When you said you decided to go to the North Carolina cabin after you thought it through, did anybody help you think it through? Did you talk to anybody about it?"

"Well, Bethany, I guess, when she urged me to go. And Adam Delattre and Celeste a bit, though only in general terms. They didn't know who had offered the use of a different cabin or where it was, but they talked about a new environment."

"How about Hendrickson York?"

"No. Not… not until I decided not to accept his offer of his cabin." Clearly anticipating his next question, she quickly said, "He totally understood. Like I told you before."

She could do without understanding like that, if she only recognized it. Maybe she was starting to. Maybe.

But that was beside the point. What mattered was Hendrickson York could have heard it from the others well before Jamie told him. Could have put bits and pieces together, with information on Bethany Usher's background pointing toward North Carolina. Could even have gotten the information from Bethany Usher herself.

Could she have been killed to keep her from giving away Jamie's whereabouts?

No. He was more tired than he thought. That only made sense if something happened to Jamie while she was in North Carolina.

"Let's talk about Bethany Usher and your keys. You said garage and the car only."

"That's right. I don't know how she could have gotten in the house. She's never even had my keys in her ha—" She broke off.

"What did you remember, Jamie?"

"The week before I left. I was working late, trying to get ready to go. My car was in the shop for routine stuff. Bethany offered to go get it for me before the place closed. I hadn't given her the key to the car yet and I gave her all my keys—house, car, everything."

"Well, that answers that question," Maggie said. "But don't beat yourself up too much, Jamie. If she was a pro, she wouldn't have had trouble getting your key. Even an amateur could've walked into your office and taken it out of your bag a dozen times a day."

"Yeah, that makes me feel better."

❖ ❖ ❖ ❖

DANOLIN CAME INTO the break room, but did not head for the coffee.

"Landis. Forensics is coming up with some weird results."

"Weird?"

"They've got prints from the house that match prints from the victim's office once they eliminated the other people in and out of there. In other words, Jamison Chancellor's prints."

"What's weird about—?"

"Wait. They also have prints overlapping those prints. Around the house, especially where things were taken. Also in the car—driver's seat. Blurred on the inside of the front door knob, as if a gloved hand overlapped them. Like the killer leaving."

Landis held silent.

"I'd ordinarily run these new prints through IAFIS next."

What were the chances Bethany Usher wouldn't come up on the national fingerprint system as belonging to those prints?

If Usher were identified as the victim, that would be the end of keeping Jamison Chancellor being alive from being known around the department. How long after would it leak to that damned podcaster?

"Hold off on that, Danny."

"My Spidey sense is telling me the DNA report won't come back to Jamison Chancellor."

"Don't ask."

Danolin swore under his breath, wonder mixed with worry. "I can take retirement any time, but you..."

"I know. Just give me a little time."

CHAPTER FIFTY-FIVE

MAGGIE NUDGED BELICHEK. "Go to the department. I know you want to. Jamie and I will be fine here. I'll look after her."

Jamie jerked up to standing. "Look after me? I'm not a child. And I don't need people thinking they know what I need or trying to run interference or wrapping me in cotton wool." She gestured at the walls around them as she paced. "Or deciding what's best for me.

"Being optimistic doesn't mean I don't have a brain. Focusing on the good, doesn't mean I'm not competent," she glared at Belichek. "Choosing to emphasize the bright side, doesn't mean I can't function on my own."

"People think she's a marshmallow," Maggie said to Belichek. "She's not. But people do want to take care of her."

Jamie gaped at her cousin. "*People* think—? Like *other* people, not including you, because you might be the worst offender on the planet—"

"I know you have a brain, you're competent. I see—"

"Then why do you avoid my phone calls? You think I don't know? You think that as much as Nancy Quinn would go off a cliff for you, even she can't hide behind your flimsy excuses?"

"You call about the same thing, over and over. The foundation, the foundation, the foundation."

"If I don't keep asking you, there'd be no chance for you to change your mind about participating in the foundation."

"I'm not changing my mind about that, Jamie. Not ever."

The corners of Jamie's mouth drooped.

"You're not blackmailing me into it, either."

"I'm not—"

"You are. Trying to. You have all along. Ever since you started that thing."

Belichek leaned back, watching them under lowered lids.

"What?" Maggie demanded of him.

Jamie turned, following her cousin's gaze.

"Neither of you is going to do what the other one does. Neither of you is going to be what the other one is. You're different people."

"You think, Sherlock?" Maggie's impatience flared.

Belichek didn't flinch. "Accept it. So you can both admit you respect the other one. You waste a hell of a lot of time. Both of you."

"You mean waste time with your investigation."

Did she realize her delivery could sting more than Maggie's? Maggie's was a quick, clean strike. Jamie's planted barbs that sank deep.

"Can't afford to waste time with the investigation if we want to keep you alive. Assuming we manage that, then you two can't afford to waste your living by going on this way."

He stood.

"I'm going into the office for a short time. Both of you stay here. Out of sight. If anything—*anything*—happens, call me immediately. I can be back in ten minutes, have a squad car here in half of that."

He looked from one to the other of them, then walked out.

JAMIE DIDN'T KNOW how to start.

But into the silence of Belichek's departure and the echoing of their long past, Maggie said, "Look. I accept—trying to accept that the foundation gives you what you need. But you've got to accept that it isn't what I need and stop bugging me.

"I base my judgments on facts and evidence. Not on feelings or intuition or any of that other crap. Because I need to be right. The stakes are too high for me not to be right."

She wasn't talking only about her job. She was talking about Aunt

Vivian. About all of it.

"Only, then I found out that sometimes feelings are true." The slightest softening of her eyes spoke of J.D. Carson. "What you do with the foundation… It's not how I function, how I … cope."

Jamie's breath hitched. Maggie talking about coping.

She expelled the breath, long and slow.

"I know."

Maggie nodded.

They sat in silence.

"I… I couldn't do what you do, Maggie. I respect what you do, but I couldn't do it."

Another nod. Slower. "I couldn't do what you do, either. And I respect it."

Do you? The question came so fast she almost spoke it, holding onto the words by the tip of their tail as they tried to escape.

She didn't need Maggie to respect—to approve—what she did. If she had, she'd never have started the foundation, much less continued it through all the difficulties.

"I respect you."

Maggie's words came as if there'd been no gap, no deep thoughts by Jamie.

Maybe there hadn't been.

"Do you?"

"Yes, I do, Jamie."

"Because the foundation's become a success."

"No. Because you did—do—what you believe in. … Even if it does—did—drive me crazy. Maybe *because* it drove me crazy and you stuck with it."

Maggie really felt that way? Jamie couldn't find words, suddenly exhausted from the buffeting of emotions from the moment she'd walked up the back stairs of her house and saw Rutherford Belichek there in her office and one instinct said *run*, while another said *don't run*, which made her want to run even harder.

"You do know why you fight against Belichek so hard, don't you?" It was weird having Maggie follow her thoughts. "Why you're your usual positive self with Landis' questions but snap at Bel's?"

She did not want to hear this. Did not want to—

"Because you're falling—"

Maggie's phone rang.

They both jumped, but Maggie had it on the next ring.

Fairlington County Police Department News Conference
In progress:

Fairlington Leader: … to say about the information that Jamison Chancellor's medical records are not available because of a fire and that that's the holdup?

Public Information Officer Elliott Kepler: I hear your frustration that we don't yet have a positive identification to give you. I share it. Our detectives share it. But It's too important to rush the—

Unidentified Media: Rush?

PIO Kepler:—identification and get it wrong. Not only for the family and other loved ones of the victim, but for the investigation.

Making sure that identity is correct and solid is at the core of any investigation.

When we have that, we will release it to the public through you all. We're not withholding anything—

Death, Murder, Violence Podcast: Oh, but you are. You're withholding a lot.

PIO Kepler: For the integrity of the investigation, we will withhold some information. It's a necessity to find the perpetrator and to give our prosecuting team the best opportunity for a conviction.

Death, Murder, Violence Podcast: I don't mean that routine stuff. I'm talking about on the identification of the victim. You're withholding basic information.

PIO Kepler: I don't know what you think—

Death, Murder, Violence Podcast: Not think. Know. I'm saying you *are* withholding information from us. Or you were. Because I announced on my podcast that was released twenty minutes ago that the Fairlington County Police Department knows something vital about the victim's identity. You know who the victim *isn't*. Because—

———

Landis jolted upright, barely avoiding dislodging the earpiece giving him the live feed into the news conference.

Several heads came up at his abrupt movement.

"Jenkins, Terrington. Get down to the news conference."

"What? Why?"

Simultaneously, Landis was looking for a phone number. "Go. Get the guy from that Death and Murder podcast—"

"Death, Murder, Violence? That's the one I was telling you about. The guy with the leaks about—"

"Get that little shit—that Oz podcaster and bring him up here. Now. Grab some uniforms on your way. I want him in the interrogation room in two minutes. *Go.*"

———

PIO Kepler: Your information is not—

Death, Murder, Violence Podcast:—you know the victim is *not* Jamison Chancellor.

Unidentified Media: What do you mean, not Jamison Chancellor.

Unidentified Media: Kepler, is that true?

Unidentified Media: Has Jamison Chancellor been ruled out as the victim?

Unidentified Media: Are you withholding the identity of the victim, Kepler?

PIO Kepler: That's not—

Death, Murder, Violence Podcast: There's more. And it's even better. Because I'm telling my listeners at this very moment on my podcast that the Fairlington County Police Department knows the murder victim is not Jamison Chancellor, and the reason they know that is because they know she's alive and they have her in custody.

———

Landis clicked a listing on his phone. He swore at the offer to leave a message and searched for another one.

"Danolin, get everything we don't already have on Bethany Usher as fast as you can. Check criminal records. Got it?"

"Got it."

"Somebody get me Felicia. I want her before they come back from wherever they are north of Baltimore."

———

Unidentified Media: Shouting. (No words discernible.)

PIO Kepler: (On his cell phone. Inaudible) … right now.

Fairlington Leader: Is this true, Officer Kepler? Do you know Jamison Chancellor's alive?

Two unidentified plainclothes officers and three uniformed officers enter the room.

Death, Murder, Violence Podcast: Listen to my podcast—Death, Murder, Violence—if you want to know what's really happening. It's available on all major podcast outlets. Review and subscribe, so you'll get the real news, including what the Fairlington Police Department doesn't want you to know. Hey! Hey! Police state!

Officer: Sir, please come with us.

Death, Murder, Violence Podcast: No. I don't have to talk to you.

PIO Kepler: If you have information about the murder, your duty as a citizen—

Unidentified plainclothes officer: Bring him upstairs.

Death, Murder, Violence Podcast: Freedom of the press! First amendment! You can't force me to talk!

Unidentified plain clothes officer: We can ask you questions. And ask your cooperation as a citizen. Kep, you going to wrap this thing up?

PIO Kepler: That's all for today. We'll follow up—

Unidentified Media: When will you comment on Zeedyk's assertions? Is Jamison Chancellor alive? Does the department have her in custody?

Unidentified Media: Where are you taking him?

Unidentified Media: Hey, I've got his podcast on right now. He's definitely saying Jamison Chancellor is alive.

~~ End news conference transcript ~~

CHAPTER FIFTY-SIX

BELICHEK ENTERED THE police department by a door he rarely used.

Not precisely a backdoor, but one where he would not be looked for.

Low profile, but not low enough to be accused of skulking.

He headed up the stairs and down one hall past booking cells that smelled of urine, sweat, fear and stupidity, around a corner and up the back stairwell that led into the bullpen from the opposite direction of the main entry.

He walked into a firestorm. People were hustling, making calls, and getting instructions from Landis, standing at his desk, hands on hips.

"Belichek!" Landis' voice.

Dropping his voice Belichek said, "I'm going to talk to Palery. There's no reason—"

Landis shoved him into an empty glass office and slammed the door.

"Too late. That scum podcaster just busted up a news conference saying he knows Jamison Chancellor's alive and he's already had it on his podcast."

"Shit." Ramifications clicked into his brain. "Shit. Shit. Shit."

He grabbed his phone and hit speed dial.

"Maggie? I tried her—"

He cursed again when the call went to voicemail. "Maggie. Word's out Jamie's alive. Don't move. Either of you. I'll be back as soon as I can." He clicked off. "You might as well be there when I tell Palery."

"Damn right I'm going to be there."

Landis was on his heels when he knocked once, then walked into Palery's office and closed the door.

His boss was on the phone. He glared at him silently.

After what felt like a lot longer than it could have been, the Chief of Detectives spoke into the phone, "Yes, sir. I intend to do that right now."

Then he hung up.

Belichek didn't give him a chance to draw breath. "This isn't on Landis, sir."

"How do you know what—?"

"The news conference, as you probably just heard. I'm the one who decided not to let my superiors—or Landis—know Jamison Chancellor is alive."

"*You* did. What do you think gives you the right—"

"Because of exactly what happened with this podcaster putting out the word. We have a leak in the building." That phone call with Landis. Had to be, but how…? "A major leak, who's feeding information to this podcaster, who's putting it out all over. Small stuff at first, but that shouldn't be known outside the department. Stuff he couldn't have known without someone inside."

Palery's solitary blink was as good as a nod.

"With that leak active I determined it was not safe to bring Ms. Chancellor in, nor to reveal her location and what information she has. I would have continued that way if she hadn't insisted on returning to Fairlington. As this podcast shows, I was right. There was a leak. And now the information that she is alive is out to the world."

The chief and Belichek stared at each other, neither relenting.

Finally, Palery said, "You said she returned here—where was she?"

"Somewhere safe."

Still staring at Belichek, the Chief of Detectives said, "Sit. Both of you. You're about to tell me everything. And I do mean everything."

"Landis was not part of this, sir," he repeated. "Also, I'm reluctant to—"

"You are not going to say the leaks came from my office."

Belichek wasn't sold, but he relented. "No, sir."

"Good. Because, first, I've had this room routinely checked since that slime started blabbing things he shouldn't have known, most of them about this section. And, second, the leaks concern things that never reached this office—matters that should have. Now, you are going to tell me all the facts concerning Jamison Chancellor turning up alive. And why you don't look real rested for a man who's had days off."

Belichek ignored that. "I stopped by Jamison Chancellor's house this morning and—"

He felt Landis' eyes slice into him, but kept his attention on Palery, who boomed, "I *told* you, I *ordered* you—"

"—had a hell of a surprise." He kept on, upping his volume to top Palery. "Jamison Chancellor was there."

"—to stay away from—"

Palery didn't just stop shouting, he seemed to shut down—moving, breathing, blinking. Nothing. Absolutely still.

"*Shit,*" Landis breathed under his breath. "That's—"

Belichek cut off his partner.

"Screw off, Landis, I'm not nuts. This is no hallucination. This is the living, breathing Jamison Chancellor." Landis' glare said he wasn't thanking Belichek for cutting him free of this. Too bad. He wasn't taking his partner down with him. "We got the wrong ID on the corpse."

The tenor of Landis' *sotto voce* swearing shifted into a cross between wonder and irritation.

"Jamison Chancellor was in North Carolina, working on her book, not connected to the outside world. She does not know who the victim is. She did not give anyone permission to be in her house. However, multiple people have a key to her house."

"Including her. Where is she?" Palery demanded, still unnaturally still.

"Somewhere safe. I wanted to see how you wanted to play it before I brought her in. And—" He rested his palms on the desk and leaned forward. "—I wanted it to be damn straight that I'm back on this case."

Only Palery's eyes moved. They went to Landis.

Belichek looked over his shoulder at his partner.

Landis suppressed whatever emotions boiled beneath his stormy face, tense shoulders and tight mouth, and jerked out a nod.

Palery straightened. "First, we'll have to figure out a safe way to bring her in here. Especially with the media. Her family—"

"There is no way. It's not safe. As for family, she insisted on contacting her parents. I impressed on them the importance of not letting this out. Maggie Frye knows, too. They're together now."

"I see that."

Belichek spun around in the direction of the Chief of Detective's gaze.

Jamison Chancellor strode through the bullpen heading toward this office, with Maggie in her wake.

✧ ✧ ✧ ✧

THE COFFEE IN Hendrickson York's cup slopped to the brim.

He put it down on his desk, looking toward the door. The door was closed. No one could see him.

He stared at the screen again.

Alive.

Was that possible?

That's what the bulletin on his screen said.

Then it said the statement that the body found at her house was not Jamison Chancellor and Jamison Chancellor was alive, was from a report on some podcast.

He clicked on the link to read the entire article. It was only four paragraphs and everything new it said was attributed to a podcast called Death, Murder, Violence.

He clicked to that site.

His top lip curled. Self-aggrandizement at its most blatant.

Who could believe a source like this?

No. It had to be this podcaster fellow seeking attention.

He reached to close the screen.

A scream from beyond the door jolted his hand. It knocked the cup, spewing coffee.

CHAPTER FIFTY-SEVEN

Jenkins and others gaped at Maggie Frye being second—to anybody. Terrington, coming in from the back stairs, stared without awareness of the identity of the female he was ogling. Danolin recognized her. He choked on his coffee.

A perfunctory knock, then she was in the room.

"Hello. I'm Jamison Chancellor. I believe you've thought I was dead. I am not."

Belichek thought he had a glimpse of how she'd handled those businesses when she was a kid, and why they might have donated before they were fully aware they had.

"I was made aware of that a short time ago, Ms. Chancellor. My detectives—"

Belichek said, "It was me. It wasn't La—"

Jamie interrupted him. "This has nothing to do with Detectives Belichek or Landis."

Belichek stood and gestured Jamie to the chair. She shook her head.

"Let me get this straight, then. Your flight came in this morning—"

"No."

Palery nodded, as if he understood, agreed. "We've checked every flight in and out of National, Dulles, and BWI from the Friday before Labor Day. Jamison Chancellor wasn't on any of those flights."

It didn't fluster her. "I drove. To and from the cabin where I stayed in North Carolina. Arrived home last night."

Belichek kept his eyes on Jamie, sending her messages to shut up that she refused to receive, yet felt Palery's sharpened attention.

"You didn't call anybody when you got home?"

"It was late. Plus, I planned to decompress a couple days at home."

"You didn't notice anything in your house? Read a newspaper? Hear a news report? See an online story?"

"I was lying low. I thought… I thought I noticed some things gone last night, but I was not calling the police until I'd slept. And then I slept very late. Besides, from the layer of dust on everything, I knew whatever was taken, it happened weeks ago. So, what difference would it make if I didn't call the police right away? Even a couple more days."

She truly wasn't a good liar. Ardent, but not practiced. She shouldn't have gone into the detail of the dust.

Palery might not know when her place was cleaned, then again, he might. Not worth the gamble.

"You needed food, didn't you?" Palery asked her. Still with an air of mild curiosity.

"Made do with what was in the freezer and the pantry. But mostly I slept. Until I heard a report that made me realize the Fairlington Police Department had the mistaken impression that I'm dead. I came directly here to clear that up."

"And we're certainly glad that you are not dead, Ms. Chancellor. However, someone is. A violent death. In your house."

Jamie didn't waver. "I know. Now."

But Belichek knew his boss. He was loaded for bear, and aiming at Jamie.

"Sir, what she said isn't true. She didn't come in last night and sleep through until this morning. I've been questioning her and while this isn't—"

"Orthodox." His boss held his gaze, issuing clear commands to shut up. "Or according to the book. Or any of a hundred other things I've complained about you—and Landis—being. And after this is all over—"

Belichek shot a look at his partner to see if he was getting the same message. He was.

"—we will have a … conversation. A long, detailed conversation with consequences. But right now, what matters is solving this case. Finding the killer and getting a conviction."

"We'll get a conviction," Maggie said.

The Chief of Detectives shot her a look that did not include gratitude.

"Ms. Chancellor, I want you to consider what I say now very carefully. It's imperative that you tell us everything, whether we specifically ask you about it or not. The questioning will be long and tedious—"

She emitted a snort that said it already had been long and tedious.

"—but we will get to the answers. We'll put you in protective custody and—"

"No thank you. I have other arrangements."

"You don't understand the seriousness of this situation."

She said nothing.

The Chief of Detectives let the silence spread.

But silence could be as stubborn as any words and hers was.

"Ms. Chancellor, you could be charged with obstructing justice."

"Are you going to charge me?"

"Don't tempt me. Also, don't lie to me or other investigators. You're not good at it."

"I didn't—"

"You did and, as I said, you're not good at it. *This has nothing to do with Detectives Belichek or Landis.* According to your story, the longest you could know Ford was an hour and you've never been introduced to Tanner. Yet, you not only knew their names, the first thing you did was absolve them of involvement."

Jamie swallowed twice, but she did a decent job with her expression. And her posture straightened slightly.

"I will repeat that no fault should attach to Detectives Belichek and Landis. I will also tell you, I have protection."

"Who?" It clicked. "*Belichek?* He is not officially on the case. He is on *vacation.* He cannot—You cannot—"

"I can. I'm a private citizen. Unless you are about to charge me with something? Though I can't think that would be good publicity for the department after thinking I was the one dead. And especially not when I tell my story and am proven entirely innocent of any wrongdoing."

Muscles at the corners of Palery's eyes flinched.

"*Are* you charging me with something?" She sent her challenging look from Palery to Landis to him.

"We strongly advise—"

"Are you charging me with something?"

"No."

"Good. Then I'm leaving."

"We will need to talk to you—" Palery sent a cold look from Belichek to Landis. "—*again*. Officially. And soon."

"Fine." She turned without looking at anyone in the office, which took some doing with not much room left over from the people.

Maggie grimaced at Belichek, then went after her cousin.

He could swear he heard her saying, "I told you you're not a good liar."

✧ ✧ ✧ ✧

BELICHEK WAS OUT of his chair when Palery said, "You two have your asses in a sling. The only way you have a chance in hell of getting them out is to solve this thing fast. If you've—No. That's for later. Landis, I believe you were issuing orders earlier. Get back to that. As for you, Belichek, you better not let your witness get away. Or get dead. Or talk to the damned media."

"Am I back on—"

"Get the hell out of here while you're still in the department."

They sir'ed him, left the office. As they walked across the bullpen, Landis said, "She really is a lousy liar."

Belichek heard relief in that. His partner hadn't bought in a hundred percent that Jamie couldn't have killed Bethany Usher. He'd gone along on Belichek's assessment.

"Yeah."

They exchanged a short look, then split up.

Terrington followed Belichek toward the back stairs, out of sight of Palery's office. "Belichek, wait up."

"Landis is calling you."

"But why's Palery on your ass? Where have you been?"

He kept going. "On vacation."

HE CAUGHT UP with Jamie and Maggie by jogging down the steps, arriving as elevator doors opened in the parking garage, revealing them.

"What the hell, Maggie?"

"Nancy called and told me about the news conference. Jamie—"

Jamie said, "Don't ask her. And don't blame her. I—"

"—was halfway to the main road to—"

"—made the decision to come here. To get it all out."

"—flag down a taxi so your address wasn't connected to her. I tried to tell her—"

"And I didn't listen. Be quiet, Maggie. This is mine to tell. You and Landis are not falling on your swords for me, Belichek. I'm sorry I blew it by using your names. I'm not good at that sort of thing." She truly seemed to regret being a lousy liar. "I was surprised..."

"Surprised?" She'd taken a turn and he hadn't followed it.

"By your office. It looks so ... ordinary."

He didn't care about the office's ordinariness.

But she'd turned the conversation for a reason.

He'd been pushing and prodding at her and he wasn't going to stop if that was the best way to get this resolved with her safe. But interviews—even interrogations—were not one-way streets.

He'd follow—for now—to see where she wanted to go.

"You expected manacles attached to the walls? A display of whips and chains?" he asked.

"No. But I wasn't expecting just an office. It could be almost any office." She turned her head. "Though it has fewer plants."

"Yeah? Yours isn't exactly the Taj Mahal."

In the look she flicked at him, he knew she was taking in that he'd been in that part of her life as well as her home and her past.

"Don't want to waste any of the donors' money on décor."

"Same with us, except the donations aren't voluntary. They're taxpayers. Makes them crankier about money being spent on decorative details."

Her mouth twitched and the corners of her eyes lifted. "Because you all would love decorative details."

"Oh, a few pillows, maybe lampshades, and, uh, different artwork wouldn't go amiss."

"I'm sure they wouldn't."

She looked toward Maggie.

Belatedly, he realized how still and quiet she'd been. He looked at her, then immediately away.

Jamie turned to a diagram on the wall of where they were. "We should have gotten off at street level to catch a cab."

"You are not taking a cab back to my house," he ordered.

"No, I'm not."

He started to relax.

"I'm going to the Sunshine Foundation."

CHAPTER FIFTY-EIGHT

Danolin ambled over as if it were the boringest day in the boringest month of the boringest day. Instead of him being loaded down with assignments, including checking the string of guests Jamie had given keys to.

"Celeste Renfro did sell her house, and her possessions were in storage for less than a month before the movers took them to her new address. That's from the storage portion of what she paid the movers. For exactly how long, they'd have to go into the detailed records of the storage facility, which, it turns out, is on an older computer system that's being replaced now. Upshot is, they'd have to scroll through all the old records. Want me to get that?"

"Not yet. We'll see if we need it later. Danolin, I've got—"

He rumbled an acknowledgment. "Hendrickson York's condo building did have a water issue. Water was turned off for three days, while it was fixed. About half the residents toughed it out and stayed there. Of the other half, Hendrickson York was the last one back. They joked that he must have finally found a place where the service was up to his standards."

"Okay. Thanks. Put it in the report—"

"I always do. Adam Delattre has been in his current apartment since the end of May. Good tenant. No problems. His previous address, the lease was not in his name."

"We know. He had roommates. We talked to them."

"Nobody where he lives now—been there since February—seems to know anything about him. Lot of young kids. Want me to try more tomorrow?"

"You workaholic, you. How about now?"

"I'm going home for dinner."

Landis tried to not sigh. You took the bad with the good when it came to Danolin.

"February," he repeated. "Damn. Should have realized that before. Jamie changed the locks in March because of her neighbor. Never mind that follow up."

"Good with me. By the way, they're waiting for you to talk to that podcaster in Interview Two."

"NO WAY IN hell are you going to the Sunshine Foundation, Jamie," Maggie said.

"I have to. Right away. If they've heard—The shock—"

"They've survived the shock of your death, they can deal with you being alive."

Maggie's reasoning didn't sway Jamie.

Belichek tried a different tack. "Even putting aside that one of them might have tried to kill you, do you think it will be easier to have you just show up if they haven't heard?"

"You can go in first, but I have to go there. No more questions, no more answers until I've seen my people."

LANDIS QUESTIONED THE podcaster hard, but Palery pulled the plug.

Landis wasn't totally disappointed. With the news about Jamie out, he had a lot of catching up to do on checking her story and tracking Bethany Usher—alive or dead.

A terse statement was issued from the public information office of the Fairlington County Police Department that expressed support for Detective Tanner Landis' handling of the investigation into the homicide on Red Hill Street, along with "the entire investigative team."

A separate one-line release said Oliver Zeedyk had helped with inquiries.

"I GO UP first. Alone." Stopped in the Sunshine Foundation parking lot, Belichek directed the next order at Jamie. "Stay here until I come back for you."

"I want to—"

"Just spring it on them?" Belichek interrupted her. "Looking for heart attacks? I'm going up first."

"You just want to see their reactions," she accused him.

"You're saying I have an ulterior motive?"

"Yes."

He nodded slowly. "And you spotted it. I can live with that. And no more than half an hour."

He exited the car before she could respond, gesturing for Schmidt.

He'd secured the uniform with a quick phone call before they left the underground parking lot, with Jamie and Maggie with him in his car and Schmidt driving Maggie's.

After giving the young officer explicit instructions, Belichek went inside and up the stairs to the offices of the Sunshine Foundation.

CHAPTER FIFTY-NINE

AT **FIRST GLANCE,** the scene duplicated when he and Landis first came here, with Celeste at the desk, Adam on one side, Denise and Kimby on the other. Shock. Tears.

But a pale Hendrickson joined the group this time, standing out of the circle, past Adam.

"Detective Belichek," Kimby screamed. "Is it true?"

Everyone turned to him. "It is. Jamison Chancellor was not the victim of murder at her house. She's alive."

"Thank God," Denise murmured.

Adam hiccupped a breath.

Celeste declared, "I will not believe it until I see her. I will not. There could be a mistake. This could all be a trick."

"No trick."

"Maybe not you, but what about that horrible podcaster who's been trying to make a name for himself off Jamie's death." Celeste gripped the arms of her chair and breathed slowly, in and out, in and out.

"I would not put anything past that creature," Hendrickson York said.

"Do you know where she is? How she is?" Denise asked.

"Have you seen her? Talked to her? What happened? Where was she? Was she kidnapped? Hiding out?" Kimby's questions tumbled over the calmer ones of her fellow volunteer.

He held up a hand, stopping the words.

Then he turned and went down the stairs.

Jamie opened her car door as soon as she saw him. He mostly closed it before she could swing her legs out and blocked the gap with his body as he bent to speak into the car, feeling the rain on his back.

"We go up with me first, then you and Maggie, then Officer Schmidt."

"Is that really necessary?"

"It's the way it's going to happen."

He'd already had a good look around, but liked the way Schmidt did, too, as he came around the car.

They went up deliberately, but when they reached the third-floor landing, Jamie darted around them.

York and Delattre turned even paler. Celeste flushed scarlet. Kimby gaped. The only one who smiled was Denise.

The women swamped her, the volunteers first. Celeste, handicapped by being seated at the desk, made up for it when she got her arms around Jamie.

The tangled hug loosened only when demanded by the need for tissues to mop eyes, cheeks, and noses.

Jamie turned.

Hendrickson lurched forward and wrapped his arms around her. "My dear. My dear."

She hugged him back, smoothing out the awkwardness of his movements. "It's okay, Hendrickson. I'm so sorry you were frightened for me."

Frightened? Was he?

Releasing the older man, she turned to the younger one. He had hung back, pale enough that Belichek sent Schmidt a look, and the officer moved within catching range.

"Adam." Jamie tried to smile. Tears slid down her cheeks, matching his.

"It's you," he whispered. "It's really you."

And then she did smile.

"It's me."

He put his head on her shoulder and sobbed.

✧　✧　✧　✧

"WELL, NOW WE can put all this behind us," Hendrickson said.

Celeste expressed the reaction of the others. "Put it behind us? It's just starting."

"Nonsense. We can all get back to work now. Except Jamie. She needs time—"

"I'm coming back right awa—"

Celeste commanded, "Stop. You are not coming back right away." She aimed that at Jamie, then turned on Hendrickson. "As for you… Someone's still dead. We all say thank God it's not Jamie, but it's someone."

Now she zeroed in on Belichek.

He had to shake off reacting to her as if she were his grandmother by straightening and saying, *Yes, ma'am.*

"You think the person who was killed could be Bethany Usher," she accused.

The suck-in of air by the others could have started a vortex.

Jamie said, "They don't know yet if—"

"We are actively investigating the identity of the victim. The department will issue a statement when there is an official identity."

"Why Bethany? What would she be doing at your house, Jamie? Did you know she'd be there? Wasn't she on vacation? What—?"

"Kimby." Celeste stopped her with that Gran voice. "Detective Belichek can answer better than Jamie."

"I'm not here to answer questions. I'm here to ask them."

"We've already answered all the questions and done everything we can to help with this matter," Hendrickson protested.

"No, you haven't." Belichek held the older man with his gaze. "Even when you thought Jamie was the victim. You knew she wasn't going to your Pennsylvania cabin and you didn't tell us."

"I didn't know that."

"She told you—"

"Oh, yes, she told me she was considering going to a different cabin, but since I knew nothing about *where,* much less that she was certainly going there, I could contribute nothing to your investigation. And since she was killed—we thought she had been killed—in her home well before leaving for anywhere else, what possible difference could it make?"

Belichek felt a muscle under his jaw tick. His voice remained even. "It might make the difference of whether or not you are charged with obstruction."

Jamie drew a breath. He moved his hand, a short, brief shift. She didn't speak.

"You never asked me—"

"Detective Landis went over that with you before. On top of that, Margaret Frye of the Commonwealth Attorney's office went to that cabin, hoping against hope her cousin was there, alive. A painful trip you could have saved her."

Maggie looked so fierce that when Hendrickson glanced toward her, he seemed to shrink. Not from guilt or sorrow for causing her fear, but more likely trepidation.

Jamie's look toward her cousin was entirely different.

"York, you'd said you called Jamie on the Saturday morning before Labor Day? Did you also call her Sunday?"

He flashed a look at Jamie, wondering what she'd told the police.

She looked back, but Belichek couldn't see any message transmitted. Then she glanced toward Belichek, but didn't connect with him before she looked down.

Hendrickson licked his lips. "No. I thought she had left. She never took her phone—"

"Another fact none of you told us."

"—so what was the use?"

"You said you didn't know when she was leaving."

Kimby's mouth opened. Denise and Celeste flicked looks toward Hendrickson.

Hendrickson said nothing.

"Why did you think she had left Saturday when the others said her plan was to leave Sunday?" After a beat, he cracked out, "York."

"All right. I didn't know she left Saturday. I didn't want to talk to her. That's why I didn't call her Sunday. We had a disagreement when we talked Saturday. I thought a day to cool off—"

"Disagreement about what?"

"The management company," he snapped.

"It's a foundation matter that has no bearing—"

Indignant or eager to get his view out first, Hendrickson cut across her words. "Jamie refused to give me assurances that it would not encroach on my area of authority."

"Hendrickson, this isn't the time—"

"After all I've done, using my contacts to create a solid financial base for this organization."

"Fiefdom," Celeste muttered.

"The management company needs to have access—"

"I've built that donor list. I will not have oafs interfering."

"They'll work with you, Hendrickson. It's—"

"No. I shall not allow it. That is all there is to say."

He had an entirely new slant on Jamie snapping *Don't talk over me, Belichek* at Carson's cabin.

"As we've talked about, it needs to happen for continuity and it's going to happen." Hendrickson opened his mouth and before he could speak, she added, "*Soon.*"

Belichek supposed he should count himself lucky she hadn't closed him down that way. But did that mean she'd listened to him?

He looked around at the uncomfortable group.

"None of you has done everything you could to help solve this murder. Why did none of you tell us of the resemblance between Jamie and Bethany Usher?"

Adam's mouth dropped open. Celeste looked shocked.

"There was no resemblance to tell you of," Hendrickson started dismissively. He sure didn't give up.

"There was." Denise's disagreement drew a dark look from York. "But it was more in things like height and build and coloring than—"

"Oh, I suppose," York interrupted again. "Like a blurry reproduction of a brilliantly vivid photograph."

Belichek dropped his head to keep from staring at the man, to keep from revealing his processing of what York revealed.

The disdain in those words could be considered harsh. But there was more. Guilt? Like he blamed himself for . . . what? That Bethany Usher resembled, but didn't match Jamison Chancellor? That made no sense.

Or… Or was it something else entirely in the words?

Not dismissing Bethany Usher, but exalting Jamison Chancellor.

But how did that match with his belittling Jamie's abilities?

Did he see her as a blurry reproduction of her aunt and therefore not to be valued? Or was it overcompensation to mask other feelings? Or, simply, to prop up his own ego.

Belichek thought of that photograph turned askew on the shelf in Jamison Chancellor's living room, the same one on the wall in the conference room.

She could dazzle you with one look.

So much so that York couldn't look at the photo of her beloved nieces?

If so and if York was the murderer, the thefts and rummaging almost certainly happened before the murder.

Someone who couldn't bear to have the photo watching him wouldn't have searched for silver and taken electronics with Jamie's dead body there in the hallway.

"I never thought of there being a resemblance until you brought it up," Denise said. "And even now… It's the kind that shows more in photos than when you're with the real people."

They piled on that explanation with relieved agreement. Relieved to have a reason for failing to see the resemblance or something more?

✧　✧　✧　✧

Fairlington County Police Department News Conference

Good evening. I'm Fairlington County Police Public Information

Officer Elliott Kepler. That's E-L-L-I-O-T-T. K-E-P-L-E-R. I have a statement on the investigation into the homicide on Red Hill Street. There will be no questions taken at this time.

The Fairlington County Police Department now confirms that the residence on Red Hill Street where the victim was found is the home of Jamison Chancellor.

Death, Murder, Violence Podcast: We know that. What we want—

PIO Kepler: Further, the department confirms that Jamison Chancellor is not the victim. To repeat, Jamison Chancellor of the Sunshine Foundation is not the victim. Ms. Chancellor is cooperating with this inquiry. That is all for—

Unidentified Media: Where is she now?

Unidentified Media: Where was she?

Unidentified Media: Who is the victim?

Unidentified Media: Does Jamison Chancellor know who the victim is?

Unidentified Media: What's—?

PIO Kepler: No questions. We are not releasing any further information at this time. If the public has any information to aid in our investigation, we ask that they contact us through the means provided again in the handout at the door. We will notify you when we have a further statement.

Death, Murder, Violence Podcast: Is Jamison Chancellor a suspect?

~~ End news conference transcript ~~

CHAPTER SIXTY

BELICHEK ENFORCED HIS half-hour curfew and escorted Jamie down the stairs over the combined objections of everybody except Maggie and Schmidt.

Celeste Renfro caught up with the departing group at the bottom.

"Detective Belichek. After you were here last time, I looked up Bethany Usher's reference. I almost forgot in the excitement. It was Nancy Quinn, an assistant in the Commonwealth Attorney's office."

Not *an* assistant. *Maggie's* assistant.

"Nancy? I never knew she was the reference." Jamie looked past him to her cousin. "I would have called you—or her—right away if I'd known."

Hair on the back of Belichek's neck rose. The circumstances under which he could imagine Maggie's tough-minded assistant recommending Bethany Usher to the Sunshine Foundation were none, nada, zilch.

He thanked Celeste, who looked puzzled, but headed back up the stairs. Then met Maggie's gaze.

"You drive, I'll call Nancy," she said.

"Don't call Nancy directly. Call Landis. This needs to go through official channels."

He had a weird feeling.

He hoped his weird feelings were as accurate as his bad ones.

✧　✧　✧　✧

"NANCY QUINN."

"Nancy. It's Tanner Landis. Something's come up in the Jamison Chancellor investigation that connects to you."

"More like the Bethany Usher case now."

"How do you—?"

"What's your question?" She meant a real question, not a useless one like *How do you know that?* Also, none of the normal *Me? In connection with me? What are you talking about?* for Nancy.

"Did you recommend a woman for a job at the Sunshine Foundation?"

"No. What woman?"

"Let's take that one at a time."

"I have never recommended anyone for any job at the Sunshine Foundation. Covers all your bases. Who said I did?"

"We're looking into that. Have you ever met Bethany Usher?"

"No." She didn't ask if that was the person killed at Jamie's house. She'd consider it a waste of time because she knew it was.

✧ ✧ ✧ ✧

OLIVER ZEEDYK WAS flying high.

The cops had to let him go.

They'd seen he wasn't going to tell them anything.

Yeah, that lawyer he'd hired had come in and done some stuff, but it was his own determination that made them let go.

If the police idiots had realized how much coverage it would get from the mainstream media idiots, they never would have taken him out of the news conference, which would have been a shame, because it had drawn even more listeners to the podcast.

Too bad they backed down by release instead of at a news conference.

Walking into the news conference where the Fairlington Police Department had to own up and say Oz Zeedyk had been absolutely right, now that would have been sweet.

Even without that, the media guys were panting after him.

Best of all, Death, Murder, Violence's numbers had caught the eyes of top sponsors. Finally.

"Oz?" the voice of the remote temp he'd hired to work the comments, keep up with links, and keep the tech rolling while he was delivering the podcast, came through his headset as he'd prepared to do a short bit about his time with the Fairlington County Police Department today.

"What are you doing on here?" he snapped.

"You're not recording and I thought you should know there's a weird message in the comments."

This chick should know weird, because she was. With the sponsors knocking at his door, he'd be able to do a lot better than this temp from someplace where two roads came together that they called a town in Oklahoma or Arkansas or Arizona. Somewhere like that.

He had to slap her down on the previous episode when she'd fed him a comment questioning his sources and whether he should be putting information out on his podcast that might jeopardize the investigation.

Jeopardize the investigation, his ass. Like those clown cops knew what they were doing. If they did, they'd be a helluva lot closer than they were.

The commenter clearly was a stooge for the cops. And if this temp—Annie, Audrey, Ariel, something like that—couldn't tell that, she was either stupid or a stooge herself.

He'd have gotten rid of her right then, but the pickings were slim in the responses from the offer for a virtual assistant he'd put out. You'd think these guys thought they were the stars. Even when money started coming in from the sponsors, he wasn't wasting it on peons.

He huffed out an exaggeratedly patient sigh. "What kind of weird message?"

"This guy says the woman who was supposed to be dead, but isn't...?"

"Yeah, what about her?"

"Says she will be dead for real. And real soon."

CHAPTER SIXTY-ONE

LANDIS CALLED AND told Belichek what Nancy Quinn said. "No big surprise."

"No," he agreed. "What's bugging you, Landis?"

"This podcaster. I don't know if he's gotten under my skin or there's something there. And I have no one to check on him. Or to listen to all his podcasts. Not sure I could justify the time if I did."

"You think there's something there?"

"I don't know. Maybe grasping at straws. Those leaks bug me."

Belichek moved to the bottom of the stairs, but still with an angle to see Maggie, Schmidt, and Jamie—who'd had long calls with her family, Imogen Wooton, and other friends on a secure line—doling out dinner from the takeout Schmidt picked up.

"Leave it to me," he told Landis.

"You're not busy enough with the damnedest vacation I ever heard of?"

"Leave it to me," he repeated.

Landis clicked off.

"Schmidt."

He came into the stairwell with his mouth full.

"Interested in doing something on the case? Unofficially."

Schmidt's eyes lit up at the question and didn't dim at the statement. "Yes, sir."

"See what you can find out about that podcaster, Oz Zeedyk. Death, Murder, Violence podcast. General background. Any possible connections to this case. As fast as possible."

"The guy with the leaks?"

"Yeah. What's available publicly only, because you can't use department resources or time. And this is not an official assignment."

SCHMIDT LEFT IMMEDIATELY, eager to start.

J.D. Carson arrived before they finished dinner.

Maggie glowed, even as she demanded to know what he was doing in Fairlington.

"Heard when the news broke about Jamie being alive, thought you could use more eyes on the situation."

"Won't turn it down."

After cookies for dessert, Jamie released a satisfied breath. "Everyone knowing I'm alive is such a relief. And now that I'm an official person again, I can ask, what avenues are the police investigating?"

Maggie snorted. "You were more likely to find out when you were semi-officially dead. They're not going to tell you. And it's sure not a relief to Belichek or the rest of us that the whole world knows you're alive."

"You all can tell me what ground you've covered, though," Carson pointed out.

In catching up Carson, Jamie objected to Belichek's characterization of Hendrickson York's reaction at the Sunshine Foundation.

"He can sound a little… Hoity-toity." She wrinkled her nose with a faint, indulgent smile at the appropriateness of the word for Hendrickson's old-fashioned and finicky ways. "But he could have continued a lucrative career in public relations—there's always need for public relations professionals in the Washington area—and instead he's been the foundation's longest and most steadfast employee, earning a pittance."

"Living off the proceeds of the fortune he'd already made," Maggie muttered.

Before Jamie could respond, Belichek revisited one open question. "Did you tell Hendrickson you were leaving Saturday?"

"You heard what he said—"

"I want to hear what you say."

"No, I didn't tell him. When we ended our call, I didn't know myself when I was leaving."

"That's too bad. For Hendrickson."

"Oh. Because if he'd known I was leaving Saturday, he'd have had no reason—in your mind—to come to my house Sunday and shoot the person there, thinking it was me."

"Right. Unless he knew the person who was at your house and had a motive to kill that person. Did York support your creating the foundation?"

"Absolutely. He's worked with me with on it from the start. The donors love him. He's quite charismatic."

"He sure doesn't want to give that up."

She ceded that point. "No. But you did not need to be so rough on him—on any of them."

"I wasn't rough. Has there ever been more to the relationship than professional?"

"Of course. He's a dear friend. Practically a member of the family."

"Not my family," Maggie muttered.

Jamie ignored that. "The foundation wouldn't exist if it weren't for him."

Maggie said emphatically, "The hell it wouldn't. Don't sell yourself short."

Belichek stepped in. "Romantic relationship. Does he have romantic feelings—?"

Momentarily blank, Jamie then interrupted by repeating, "Romantic?" and jolting erect. "Oh, my God. Ally said that. Hendrickson and Vivian. Remember, Maggie? The summer before—Before. Hendrickson York came from his cabin, took us all out for dinner, and Ally said she was sure he liked Vivian. Like a boyfriend, she said. Remember?"

"No, I don't remember. She could have said it, but I didn't listen. Ally tried to pair off squirrels, toys, and total strangers for heaven's sake. I never saw anything romantic between Aunt Vivian and him. Not on her side."

"But you did see something on his part?"

"I suppose he loved Vivian in his way, but I heard him propose to her at the beginning of that summer, Jamie. And I heard her tell him no. Gently, but leaving no doubt. She wasn't interested in him or his money, which was how he tried to sell himself. He was rich and Aunt Viv could live a life of comfort and ease as his wife.

"The damned shame is she was interested only in Glenn."

"Poor Hendrickson." Jamie turned to Belichek. "That's what you were asking—if Hendrickson had unrequited romantic feelings for Vivian? I knew he *loved* her—but as a friend. It's so sad he watched her fall for someone else, and then that person turned out… After all that, to show his love the only way he could all these years with the foundation. It's—"

"Before you're in tears," Maggie said, "you should know you haven't sold Belichek, me, or J.D. on Hendrickson's life-long devotion to Viv."

Jamie looked at him. She clearly read that he agreed with Maggie. "But… Don't you see—?"

"Doesn't matter. Because I wasn't asking you about how he felt about Vivian. Was asking about York's romantic feelings for you."

CHAPTER SIXTY-TWO

BELICHEK WATCHED IT sink in. Her mouth formed a *No*, but no sound came out.

"Huh." The idea intrigued Maggie. "Interesting, Bel."

"Credit Landis. He spotted Hendrickson York sounding like a jealous guy. Especially when he talked about your romantic interests, including Arbendroth."

That focused Jamie's denial. "You can't seriously think Hendrickson—"

Without moving, Belichek's words cracked across her protest. "Yes. We think. Seriously think. Everything. And you do, too, starting right now. You aren't dismissing anything, you aren't cutting off possibilities. Somebody shot a woman dead in your house. A woman they most likely thought was you. Nothing is impossible. Including you being a suspect."

"Belichek, that's—"

"Quiet, Maggie." He didn't look away from Jamie. "No investigator would miss that angle. As suspect or intended victim, you are the best lead. No amount of optimism changes that."

She didn't look away, either. She had a reaction, but she reined it in, breathing hard at first, then steady and slow.

"I understand." Back to upbeat, possibly even humoring him. "But I can't believe—"

"Believe, don't believe. It doesn't matter. Just answer the questions."

But she wasn't relenting.

"I know these people. They couldn't—"

"You know who you want them to be." Maggie's interruption didn't break his connection with Jamie.

Even if he was tempted to agree with it, he saw it threatened his inroads against Jamie's armor.

"There's at least one of these people you don't know," he said.

The trouble with making inroads against her armor was it dimmed her shine. He hated that. But he needed it.

She tried to rally. "If Bethany Usher was the target—"

"Not as likely as you. If that was what happened, it meant you didn't know her as well as you believed." He gave that last word a little extra to drive it home. "Everybody knows you're alive. Including whoever shot Bethany Usher. We don't have time for you to believe. We don't have time."

Two beats. Four. Six.

She streamed a breath out. "I'll do my best."

"Hendrickson York."

"He never gave me any reason to think his feelings were remotely romantic. Ever."

He nodded recognition of her response, considering how best to check it. "Okay."

"Good." She nodded, her good humor partially restored.

"He didn't mean he accepted your rose-colored glasses view, Jamie, for God's sake. He was acknowledging you had spoken words in response to his question." Maggie plunked her cup down. "When are you going to start to see reality?"

"WHERE? WHERE'S THE guy saying she's going to be dead?" Oz demanded of the assistant as he scrolled.

"Uh, down toward the beginning."

"Where? It's not here."

"Not all the way. Look about an hour ago."

"Jesus, an hour ago? Why didn't you flag it earlier?"

"When you got back from, uh, the news conference, you said not to interrupt you."

"If you had a brain, you'd know the difference between regular crap and something important. And you wouldn't be wasting my time, leaving me scrolling around because you're an—"

Had it.

At least A-whatever-her-name-was got the gist of the message right.

Jamison Chancellor was the one who was supposed to die. She will. It has to happen. Soon.

The signature was "September."

Oz typed short and fast, hoping the poster was still watching the comments.

Contact me.

That part was easy.

He thought.

If this person wasn't a flake, he'd be wary of how he got in contact. Email could be tracked with enough time. If the person was smart, they'd be using a burner phone. But if Oz put his phone number in the comments, every one of the podcast fans would use it. He couldn't afford that. Not with sponsors contacting him.

He gave the assistant's phone number.

"Hey," she protested when his reply went live on the screen.

She didn't like it? He'd dump her ass.

But not until this commenter contacted her phone and Oz had a line to him.

✧　✧　✧　✧

THE COUSINS WERE getting on each other's nerves. Or the strain was and they let it out on each other.

Belichek offered a distraction. "Jamie, I want you to look at a short video clip."

He keyed up the video Landis had sent on his monitor.

She watched intently. "That's my house. But what…?"

When it was over, she looked a question at him.

"Did you recognize the person?"

"It's only a blur between the rain and whatever they're wearing puffing out in the wind."

"Watch it again. Don't try for details. Look at it overall." He hit play again. "Just watch."

She shook her head. "I get what you're trying for—the walk, the way of moving. To see if it's familiar. But with the wind and rain, the person's mostly staggering. I can't even tell if it's a man or a woman. Sorry."

"Don't apologize. Something else. Do you know anyone named Oz?"

"The Wizard of?"

From the couch, Maggie snapped, "Knock it off, Jamie. This is your life—"

"I know it is."

"Let up, Maggie," Carson said quietly.

"I won't. She wraps her refusal to see reality around her like some magical cloak a child would believe in. But it's dangerous. There's a price to be paid for not seeing reality. A price she pays and others pay."

Jamie paled.

She's thinking of her aunt's death.

Maggie wasn't. But Jamie was.

Belichek stepped in before either cousin could continue, asking again, "Do you know anyone named Oz?"

"No." After another beat, Jamie asked, "Who is Oz?"

"A podcaster. The DMV podcast—Death, Murder, Violence. His full name is Oliver Zeedyk."

She shook her head. "Never heard of the podcast or him."

"With Maggie and J.D. here, I'm going into the office to help Landis, but I want you to listen to Zeedyk's recent podcasts. See if anything strikes you. He's the guy who's aired the leaks."

"She'll listen," Maggie said. "And I'll listen with her, so if she tries to slide past something, I'll spot it."

"I wouldn't do that. You always think I take the easy way out."

Jamie started slowly, but each word came faster. "That only you are strong. And you are strong. You saved me. *Saved me.* I know that and I can never thank you enough—"

"Don't thank me—"

"I will. I do. I know you were there right after Aunt Vivian… And how awful, how devastating that was—" She swallowed. "—for you."

"If I'd been half an hour earlier. If I'd—"

"No. *No.*" Jamie's great eyes were trained on her cousin.

Belichek glanced at Jamie, but said to Maggie, "You'd've been killed, too."

"I was the one he wanted because I testified—"

"He would have killed you both."

"I…" Without moving, Maggie seemed to shrink away from them, as if pulled back to that horror. Then she shook her head and her eyes found J.D. After a breath, she turned to Belichek. "Your grandfather was the one who shot Glenn, I remember that. Remember him. Arriving on my bike to see him go in—he went in first, with one deputy behind him. Others held me back. Wouldn't let me go in. I remember the sound of the gunshot."

The fine muscles around Maggie's eyes flinched, as if hearing it again.

"Glenn came at my grandfather when he realized he was trapped."

She nodded slowly. "I've always been grateful the sheriff—your grandfather—killed him. That there wasn't a trial. Another trial."

"It wasn't enough for Grandpa. He went to his grave feeling he should have done more, better, sooner."

Jamie sucked in a gasping breath that had them all turning to her.

"It wasn't his fault. It wasn't Maggie's. It was mine. None of it would have happened if it hadn't been for me."

"Jamie, that's not true. You were a kid. You had nothing to do with that asshole—"

"But I did."

Maggie's face went dark. "You said he never—"

"He didn't—He didn't molest me. Not really. I know now he was grooming me and—"

"Then you know it wasn't your fault. You were a kid and he was a master manipulator."

"It *was* my fault. I never told Aunt Vivian or you or Ally—or anyone. I *knew* I should. I knew it. But it was … heady to have someone pay so much attention to me. At home, Mom and Dad were busy. At Aunt Vivian's, you and Ally could always do so much more than I could. It felt like you two and Vivian were equals, friends, and I was the little kid trailing along. And I missed Daddy—my biological father.

"And then there came Glenn, a grownup, saying I was special, saying I was beautiful … and other things I didn't understand. I never told, because I wanted that attention. Even though I *knew* I should tell Aunt Vivian. Even though it made me feel … bad.

"After he tried to grab me… That's why I cried all the time when they talked to me about being a witness, because I would have had to admit I knew and I hadn't told. Your grandfather… I think he knew. I always thought he knew. My parents wanted to have me talk to a counselor to see if I could. Aunt Vivian said absolutely not to my testifying.

"I could have told them everything. I told you to forgive yourself, Maggie. I told you that last spring, when it was all *my* fault. I was the only one who knew and I kept the secret. I let him get off. I let him murder Aunt Vivian. It's my fault she's dead. I let him—"

Maggie almost stumbled coming out of her chair, but held steady when she jerked Jamie up by the shoulders. "You did not. You did not. Do you hear me, Jamison Eleanor? You did *not*. Neither did I. Neither did Bel's grandfather. The only one responsible for Aunt Vivian being dead is Glenn. May he rot in hell."

She wrapped her arms around her cousin in a fierce hug.

✧ ✧ ✧ ✧

THE TWO COUSINS sat together, looking stunned and drained by the emotions. All the years of emotions.

"We'll all listen to those podcasts," Carson said quietly. "Tomorrow. Right now, Maggie, let's you and I go upstairs for a while."

"You think separating Jamie and me will—"

"Give you both a chance to take a breath? Yeah. C'mon."

To Belichek's surprise, she went.

"Okay if I take a shower upstairs?" Carson asked from the bottom of the stairs.

"Sure."

"We take a shower," Maggie amended.

"Leave the walls standing," Belichek ordered.

CHAPTER SIXTY-THREE

Jenkins had that look, like a dog who'd been sent to fetch a stick and brought back a chunk of gold.

"Tell me," Landis ordered. "We could use something good."

"Heard back from the North Carolina sheriff's department. They checked out the cabin. Said there are signs of it being occupied recently, though it was cleaned up well. A couple neighbors had seen signs of life there, too."

"That goes to confirm Jamie Chancellor's account." But didn't rise to the level of gold.

"They went one better. They checked with the Young family that owns the place. They'd never heard of a Bethany Usher. But I'd sent photos of all our folks, the sheriff's department showed them to the Youngs, and they recognized the one of Bethany Usher.

"It gets better. She worked for them—using a different name—as a nanny for three months about five years ago. They went on a vacation, all their valuables stolen, a couple bank accounts cleared out, their car taken, and—" He looked up from his notes. "—she wore some of the woman's clothes. Like our victim did with Jamison Chancellor's clothes. No sign of forced entry. The nanny was gone when they got back, the house was wiped clean by a pro. Not a trace of her since. They never thought at the time to look to see if a key to their cabin had been taken."

"Give that to the guys doing the records search and—"

"Wait. It gets even better. Seems the nanny used to put up the daughter's hair. Fancy dress, you know? And she'd hold bobby pins in her mouth and open them with her teeth."

"Spit DNA," Landis breathed. "Did they keep the pins?"

"Sure did." Jenkins grinned. "They took a couple and submitted them to one of the public access genetics companies. Trying to do some of their own sleuthing. No match. But it's out there."

"Don't do anything yet. I want to check with Mags—somebody in the CA's office on how we can use that. But—"

"Thought you might say that. How do you feel about old-fashioned fingerprints? One of the things she put in the kid's hair was a tiara—one of those crown things—and she missed it in her wipe down."

✧   ✧   ✧   ✧

"IT'S STILL RAINING."

At Jamie's tone, Belichek looked up from listing the podcasts he wanted them to listen to tomorrow. Not likely anything would come of it, but it would cover that base and keep Jamie occupied.

Maybe it was time to get them all more occupied. And for him to spend less time with Jamie.

He didn't examine that thought, but said, "You don't like the rain?"

"Not this kind. When it seems like it will never stop and the clouds will smother you."

She had her feet on the seat cushion, her arms wrapped around her knees, not watching the TV show she'd selected.

"There were a lot days like this in Seattle when Daddy was dying. He'd gotten a job and we moved there. Then he got sick. They wouldn't let me see him for a while, then they did. I thought it meant he was getting better. I didn't know what hospice meant."

He moved to beside her on the couch, never taking his eyes off her face.

"I'd sit with him on the bed and when I said I was tired of the rain, he said I had sunshine inside me no matter what the weather. That I was his sunshine. All the sunshine he'd ever need. And I needed to be

Mom's sunshine, too. Always."

She swallowed, tears tracking down her cheeks and into the corners of her mouth.

"After… after he died, I tried to be Mom's sunshine. I tried. I was so relieved when we moved back here and there were more people to help her and then she met Wes and I wasn't the only one.

"Except, then Vivian."

She pulled in a shuddering breath.

"I had to be the sunshine. Somehow. I had to create the sunshine and believe there was something on the other side of my guilt, of my absolute failure to Aunt Vivian, to Maggie, to Ally, to the whole family. And now I know to your grandfather, too.

"I had to make something good from it. Guilt… Guilt wasn't enough. I had to *do* something. Create something. I couldn't undo what I'd done—failed to do—and its evil, evil consequences—" Tears dropped off the ridge of her jaw "—but if I could help bring more good into the world, if I could help balance out what my actions caused…"

"They didn't cause them." He pushed the hair back from her face. "You didn't. You were a kid."

She looked up at him.

He tasted the salt of her tears before he realized he intended to kiss her.

The salt and the softness and the response.

He kissed the corners of her eye. As he kissed the tears down her cheek, she lifted her face.

Their mouths met, opened, parted, caught.

Her hands touched his face lightly, then offered the warmth of her palms, as he met her tongue. He pressed her back against the cushion.

Oxygen demanded a breath.

With it came reality, sense, regret.

His arms still around her, he righted her, then released her. Not yet able to back away. When she opened her eyes, tears still sheened them.

"Jamie, I'm on this case. It's unethical."

"We only kissed, Ford."

"It's not all I wanted."

She raised her eyelids to meet his gaze. "Me, either."

"You're a witness."

"Or a potential suspect?"

"Yes. Either one is unethical and for damned good reasons. To-gether…"

She straightened, still watching him.

"I'm sure you have good reasons, Detective Belichek. But none of those are the real reasons. But you don't owe me an explanation."

She stood.

"I'm very tired. Do you mind leaving now?"

DAY SEVEN

CHAPTER SIXTY-FOUR

BELICHEK SLEPT A few hours, stared at the ceiling a couple more, then gave it up.

He left the quiet, dark house, raising a hand in silent farewell in the direction of the stairwell. A suggestion of movement might have been a similar response.

He worked almost three hours at his desk going through reports before Landis emerged from the empty glass office, yawning and looking unlike his usual pulled-together self.

Belichek handed him the extra coffee he'd picked up on the way in.

After a couple gulps, Landis said, "See the report on Bethany Usher's activities?"

"Yup. It's starting to open doors to more, too. Still don't have the DNA confirming she's the victim, but in the meantime, we have quite a trail."

"Including theft. Our friend up in Maryland who seems to be the first one to have Jamie's phone? I'm betting he shows up connected to Bethany as we dig deeper. I messaged Felicia Ewer to go back up there and talk to him with that in mind. Also, to make sure jurisdictions up and down the I-95 corridor have the word on the silver, because—"

Belichek's desk phone rang.

"Homicide. Belichek.... Just a moment."

He put a hand over the mouthpiece as he held the receiver toward Landis. "It's for you. The lady shrink."

"Shit. I blocked her because she wouldn't quit calling." He waved away the receiver. "Tell her I'm not here."

"The hell you're not—"

Landis leaned over. "I'm not talking to her, Belichek."

"Why? Did the husband come after you?"

"I could handle that. They're getting a separation. Legal, filing for divorce."

"The lady being available has you in a sweat. You're a sick bastard, Landis."

"You're a great one to talk, falling for a woman you thought was dead. Now, tell her you don't know where I am or when I'll be back."

"I'm not lying for you."

"You don't have to. I'm going to the locker room for a shower, shave, and change of clothes." Landis turned smartly around and disappeared from the room.

Belichek mixed a heavy sigh with some curses before speaking into the mouthpiece again. "I thought he was here, but he must have stepped away from his desk. … Sorry, I don't know when he'll be back. … You could leave him a voicemail or—… Yeah, I'll be happy to tell him. Bye."

He wrote in crisp, legible letters the department psychologist's crude and final analysis of his partner's character and morals.

Then he placed a call to Nancy Quinn.

✧ ✧ ✧ ✧

"YOU HAVE A problem, Belichek."

He looked up to Terrington, standing beside his desk, straining for a serious, even concerned look.

Usually, Belichek would say nothing. This time he allowed himself a solemn, "We all have a problem until this murderer is caught," knowing the sentiment would irk the hell out of Terrington.

"Right. Yeah." He shifted his weight. "This might help with that. But you're not going to like it." That last part clearly cheered him.

"If it gets us closer to the answer, I'll like it."

Dissatisfied with a response he couldn't pick holes in, Terrington dropped papers on the desk, splaying messily.

Credit card records. Belichek prepared to return to his own work. "Thanks."

"Don't you want to know what they say?"

"Sure. Going to finish this first, though."

"I'll save you time. Jamison Chancellor wasn't at that cabin." Terrington tapped the records. "And these prove it."

"THAT'S IT, ZEEDYK said."

A-whatever-her-name-was grumbled, "It's about time." She'd been playing him the messages that clogged her phone.

What was she bitching about? He'd had to listen to them, too. Most of them totally useless.

Then he heard a voice he recognized.

He was good at that. One of the many skills he'd honed.

The guy from the night they found the dead body at the Chancellor house.

Mr. Right, Right.

Who'd been right on the scene.

No way was he taking this to the police.

He could try to track down this guy, figure out who he was. But that would take time and wouldn't do anything for the podcast.

On the other hand, releasing a special podcast could happen really fast. Hell, it would even serve as a warning for Jamison Chancellor.

And the sponsors would eat it up.

JAMISON CHANCELLOR WASN'T at that cabin.

Belichek's gut tightened, but didn't let it show. He turned toward Terrington.

"Other information said she was at the cabin. From the thorough job North Carolina did—"

"Not this time. The other cabin, writing the previous book. Still means she lied. She was at some inn near Berkeley Springs, West Virginia. Not at that cabin in Pennsylvania where she told you she went."

"Good work, Terrington. Send me a copy of the file."

Belichek neatened the stack of papers, then focused on his screen again.

He doubted anyone had ever been more disappointed to be told *Good work*.

Fairlington County Police Department News Conference

Good morning. I'm Fairlington County Police Public Affairs Officer Elliott Kepler. As I said last night, we are keeping you updated as we have information that can be released to you.

We know there is great interest in this situation. This is a fast-evolving investigation. We will attempt to keep you abreast of developments as we can.

This morning, Dr. Yale Huang Porter of the Office of the Chief Medical Examiner is here to make a brief statement. After his statement, I will take a few questions. Dr. Porter.

Dr. Yale Huang Porter: The Office of the Chief Medical Examiner's Northern District has issued a finding. The identity of the victim from the Red Hill Street homicide has been established as Bethany Marie Usher, age thirty-six.

This identification was based on medical records.

Cause of death is gunshot wound. Manner of death is homicide.

That is all the information the Office of the Medical Examiner will be releasing at this time. Good day.

PIO Kepler: Thank you, Dr. Porter.

Fairlington Leader: What about a time of death?

PIO Kepler: We are not releasing that information at this time.

WTOP Radio: Officer Kepler, where is Jamison Chancellor now?

PIO Kepler: We are not releasing that information at this time.

ABC: You said she was cooperating with the investigation. How? What information is she providing?

PIO Kepler: We are not releasing that information at this time.

NBC: We have reports that she was supposed to be off somewhere writing her new book. Can you confirm that?

PIO Kepler: We cannot confirm that at this time.

Fairlington Leader: Did Bethany Usher work for the Sunshine Foundation?

PIO Kepler: We are not releasing that information at this time.

Death, Murder, Violence podcast: We all know she did, even if they won't say so. Doesn't sound like you have any information, to release or not.

PIO Kepler: Any more questions?

Death, Murder, Violence podcast: When did the department know Jamison Chancellor was alive and you had a different corpse on your hands in her house?

PIO Kepler: The knowledge that Ms. Chancellor was alive was closely held within the department and strictly on a need-to-know basis for the safety of Ms. Chancellor, as well as the integrity of the investigation.

Death, Murder, Violence Podcast: Closely held? Couldn't get much more closely held than only Detective Ford Belichek knew.

~~ End news conference transcript ~~

CHAPTER SIXTY-FIVE

HE ENTERED HIS house to a different atmosphere.

Maggie sat on the couch with her laptop, Carson was on one side of the dining room table with his, and Nancy Quinn opposite him, on another.

Barely looking up, Maggie said, "Jamie's downstairs. Can't decide if she's happier about having a phone again or a laptop. She's sworn she won't log into any of her accounts or Sunshine accounts, in case someone could use that to locate her, but I said it was okay for her to look at public sites."

"Thanks, Nancy." He'd known she could arrange all this, including a phone for Jamie and a workload for Maggie, to ease the tension.

"Don't thank me. Glad to get some of this backlog off Maggie's list. It was slowing me down."

He almost smiled as he started down the stairs, but it was gone by the bottom.

Jamie was in the same spot where he'd held and kissed her last night, though she was far from crying now. She scrolled through her phone with one hand and checked a website on the laptop with the other.

"We're going to have a problem if you haven't been honest with me," he said.

"Honest with you? You know every detail of my life. Yes, I know, you thought I was dead. I understand. But I've answered all your questions. If you're going to accuse me of lying by omission when you've already—"

"Intruded on your privacy—got it. But it's no lie of omission. This is a lie of commission."

She didn't ask what lie of commission.

Did that mean there was only one?

Or that she didn't want to say anything to open a door to his suspecting multiple lies?

He stared at her.

She stared back.

He felt the muscles around his mouth twitching. It took a beat to realize they wanted to form something like a grin.

She wasn't backing down.

And why the hell he wanted to grin about that was beyond him.

"You weren't at York's cabin," he snapped.

She blinked. "I've said that all along."

"The previous time."

Her eyes stayed wide, blank.

"You lied about that because you didn't want me to know how uncomfortable you were with Hendrickson York even then."

"I wasn't. I just—"

"Bullshit. You are too smart for this. You're going to nice yourself right into being dead."

"That's not what I'm—"

His deeper voice rolled over hers. "Think, Jamie. Not about the strangers and near strangers whose feelings you're so careful about and think about the feelings of the people who truly love you. Your parents, your family, Maggie and Ally, and all the rest of them. What they went through already. You want to put them through that again? This time for good? Think about how you felt when your aunt was killed."

Something shifted in her eyes. He wouldn't go as far as thinking he'd persuaded her, but he'd driven in the start of a wedge.

"What happened the last time you used Hendrickson's cabin?"

"What you said before. He showed up. Unannounced. Unexpected. He tried, he really tried not to interrupt. But he'd tiptoe so ... so *loudly*. And make such a big deal of it, apologizing, and asking if this was a good time, then five minutes later all over again. And… And, yes, I was uncomfortable with him there. But *not* like what you're thinking. More like having someone looking over my shoulder all the time. Wanting the best for me, but not knowing when to back off. Until I felt like… I felt like I was suffocating."

She sucked in a breath, looking at him sideways, as if afraid he'd upbraid her for fighting suffocation.

"And?" he nudged.

"And I left. I went to a nearby inn and holed up in my room for the last week. He was hurt and it took a long time to soothe his feelings. When Bethany offered her cabin—I *thought* her cabin—it was a way out without risking another interruption. I couldn't afford the time on this book, not with the management company coming and needing the submission check from the publisher. And, truly, Hendrickson took it better than I expected. You can't possibly suspect he is capable of—"

"Anyone—*anyone*—is capable, so everyone is suspected."

"MY COUSIN JAMIE raising her voice. You *do* have a way with women, Belichek," Maggie said as he reached the front door.

"Afraid I'll take over your role as sparring partner?"

"Hah. But, don't worry. We'll listen to your podcasts. As soon as I go through this filing again—"

"One hour," Nancy Quinn called from the dining room table. "Then the podcasts. Then some decent food instead of all this takeout."

SCHMIDT REPORTED IN by telephone.

"Not much on him for general background, except he's lived here all his life, went to Fairlington schools. After high school he went to community college, then got a bachelor's online. Entry level job at the

Fairlington Leader—like a copy boy. Then he switched to podcasts, got in years ago.

"Lots of info about him podcasting. He used to be on another true crime podcast. A big one. He was one of four hosts and they'd rotate around, each with different guests. There were a couple incidents where commenters blasted Zeedyk, including for recording a conversation with a witness who didn't know he was being recorded and some about the editing. The other hosts backed him at first, but after a couple, they stopped.

"And then, he had a guest on who espoused really raw stuff. Anti pretty much everything—women, minorities, law enforcement, even speed limits. According to the other hosts, they'd told Zeedyk not to have this guy on. He did it anyway, springing it on them by pulling another episode and putting this one in live.

"They kicked him out. He tried suing them, saying it was First Amendment. They had a contract and good lawyers. He didn't have either. The podcast's gone on fine with the three remaining."

"Zeedyk disappeared for a couple years, then showed up a few months ago with his own podcast—Death, Murder, Violence— focusing on crimes around here. Bumping along at the bottom until this murder, which has coincided with him airing what he says is inside information from Fairlington PD. Nobody knows who's leaking to him, but it's pretty good stuff.

"I mean… I mean it's accurate."

Belichek digested it. "Any arrests? Charges?"

"No trouble with the law that I could find. I've got my shift tonight, but I could keep digging on my own time."

"Good. Thank you, Schmidt."

"SCUM," MAGGIE MUTTERED after another slam of law enforcement for not pursuing cases unless they involved the rich. "It's not even original. He repeats the same stuff."

Carson grunted agreement.

Jamie, sitting cross-legged on the couch, leaned forward. "Play that part again, will you, J.D.?"

He sent her a level look, but said nothing before sliding the timer bar back on the screen.

The voice of the podcaster came again, talking about law enforcement being lazy, not bothering to investigate crimes against real people, but only high-profile cases.

When it finished the repeat of what they'd already heard, he paused it.

"Something?" Maggie asked.

She flashed her cousin a look, checking what she'd heard. It was there in her eyes, too. Taking her seriously.

Too bad that wouldn't last, since what she had was not factual, concrete, or provable—Maggie's preferences.

She wasn't going to keep her quiet.

"It's personal for him. Angry, hurt, cynical," she said. "Definitely personal."

J.D. slid the bar back and played it again.

Then Maggie told him, "One more time."

After, they all stared at the screen for a moment. Were the other two also rehearing the emotion in the man's words? Or solely the words?

"If he's had a bad experience with law enforcement…" J.D. murmured.

"We can track it down," Maggie completed.

Jamie sat back as the discussion turned to *how* to track down the information.

They'd taken her seriously.

SCHMIDT CALLED BACK, trying to sound calm.

"Oz Zeedyk just had a special podcast episode on, made a big deal that he had an exclusive. I recorded the whole thing, but here's the part you need to know about."

A tinny voice came through the speaker.

…this source said Jamison Chancellor was the intended victim a month ago on Red Hill Street. Not Bethany Usher. And this source said, that error will be fixed—that Jamison Chancellor will be killed. And soon.

"Play that again, Schmidt. Wait. Give me a second. Landis." His partner turned from his desk as Belichek switched to speakerphone. "Go ahead."

The voice went across the bullpen this time, gathering an audience paying closer attention to Oz Zeedyk than he could have hoped for.

…this source said Jamison Chancellor was the intended victim a month ago on Red Hill Street. Not Bethany Usher. And this source said, that error will be fixed—that Jamison Chancellor will be killed. And soon.

Do we believe this source? Well, I have reason to believe the source has, let's say, an ongoing interest in the case.

On the other hand, this new threat might be a ploy to elicit more donations to the Sunshine Foundation. The funds that were pouring in after the assumed death of Jamison Chancellor are down to a trickle since she came back to life.

What do I think?

I think DMV—Death, Murder, Violence will be the first place you'll find out the truth.

CHAPTER SIXTY-SIX

"WE HAVE SOMETHING," Maggie as soon as he entered the basement.

"What?"

"Background on that podcaster. Jamie picked up on it being personal for our friend Oz when it comes to his attitude toward law enforcement. We started digging. J.D. had a friend in Bedhurst—"

Had to be the wily lawyer who'd gone against Maggie in court.

"—call in some favors with his connections all over the state. Turns out it circles back to here in Fairlington."

Maggie's voice gave him a heads-up, but he turned to Jamie for the finely gauged emotional temperature.

"It was long before you were on the force," Jamie said. "Long before."

How did she—?

He put that aside. "What was it?"

"His sister was murdered. Older sister. Raped, murdered, and dumped. Never solved. And he might have cause to complain. Murder book's thin. Definitely thin."

"That's rough," Belichek said. "But doesn't give him any right to interfere with this investigation—and that's if he's not more directly involved.

"A little while ago we picked him up for questioning. I'm going right back in case Landis wants a hand interviewing him. I came back to tell you he had something on his podcast today you need to know about."

✧   ✧   ✧   ✧

OLIVER "OZ" ZEEDYK was scared, but not scared enough.

Landis asked him, "What is your basis for the report you had on your podcast today that Jamison Chancellor was the original intended victim and someone is saying she's going to die soon?"

"I'm a journalist. You cannot infringe on my First Amendment rights, freedom of the press, by trying to force me to give up my sources or—"

"How did you find out Jamison Chancellor was not the murder victim at Red Hill Street?"

"I'm a journalist. Freedom of the press. You cannot infringe on my First Amendment rights. You cannot force me to give up sources—"

"You don't have sources. What you have are felonies. Felonies stacking up fast. If you want to help yourself—at all—you better talk. Now."

Zeedyk crossed his arms over his chest with smug dialed up.

"Here's what I think. I think you know this stuff because you're doing it."

It took three beats for that to penetrate the smug.

"I'm reporting—"

"How much easier to report big stories when you're creating them? Intend to shoot Jamison Chancellor, but screw up and shoot Bethany Usher. But you see a way to make it work for you. Wait until the body's found, then start coming up the 'scoops.' I've listened to you—"

"A DMV fan," Zeedyk sneered with bravado.

"Not your podcast. Your performances at police news conferences. You were questioning things nobody else knew about right along."

Uncertainty crept into Zeedyk's eyes.

"And how else could you know the victim wasn't Jamison Chancellor? How else could you know what you reported today, that the first murder was a screw up, but the murderer is going after Jamison Chancellor again."

"Sources."

"Uh-huh. These mythical sources you can't produce."

"Won't produce. First Amendment. Besides, why would I go after this Jamison Chancellor? I never met the woman."

"I'll tell you, I've been in this job long enough to know the better question is, why wouldn't you? You or any of the other murderers out there. Although in your case it's pretty obvious why from what's happened with your podcast. Ratings up, sponsors signing on. All sorts of good things happening for you since—you say—somebody tried to kill Jamison Chancellor and got Bethany Usher."

"That doesn't mean *I* did it."

The podcaster was going to talk. He just didn't know it yet.

"Let's start with your whereabouts on Labor Day weekend…"

DAY EIGHT

CHAPTER SIXTY-SEVEN

THE REST OF them were in their working spots already when Belichek came down from his bedroom, including Nancy.

"I've got an update for Jamie if you want to come down."

They did, including Nancy.

When he was finished describing last night's interview of Zeedyk, the podcaster, there was a moment of silence.

A frown tucked Jamie's brows. "Why would he have shot Bethany?"

"He thought it was you," Maggie said. "He was going for a big story and he got the wrong person—the first time."

"We're working on his motive," Belichek said, more cautiously. "He says he didn't kill anybody. It was a mysterious stranger in the dark."

Maggie's face sharpened. "You're not sure he's *not* telling the truth that it was this other guy. His so-called source."

"Not sure of anything. Yet."

"Sounds more like he made the guy up," Nancy said.

"I agree," Jamie said. "And with him in custody, that means I can resume living."

"Maybe."

✦ ✦ ✦ ✦

SITTING DOWN WITH the computer guys was never Landis' favorite thing. They insisted on telling him what they were doing and why.

Worse, they'd delve into how.

He wanted the result. Preferably without a visit to Geek World. But it never worked that way and, in the end, he paid the price of admission with as good a grace as he could manage.

This time it came after a "progress" report to the chief, so, by comparison, Geek World was a fine place to be.

"It pulled up what you'd expect since she—Bethany Usher—had that kind of background—police reports, court records, news accounts. Delattre did a real nice job with his searches. Amazing actually. Never took a wrong step. And thorough. He also went a step above and beyond."

"Meaning?"

"This guy got her texts. Cloned them over to his phone—this second phone. She probably never even knew it happened. For us, it's almost as good as having her phone." He grinned.

"What have you found?"

"Among other things, she apparently ran some website that posed as a legit testing site for paternity cases. But it was more like a shopping site for the test result of your choice. She pulled one herself in early June. Can't see any indication tests ever happened."

"Anything else?"

"We'll keep checking over Delattre's work in case he missed a trick. We're also going through her contacts, which he didn't delve into much, and we found something, uh, interesting. An unexpected connection." He gave Belichek a look from the corner of his eyes.

"What is it?"

"A police officer in her contacts list. And among the people she texted with. Including about getting the job at the Sunshine Foundation."

"Who?"

"Roy Isaacson."

✧　✧　✧　✧

FELICIA EWER CALLED in with an update while Belichek ate lunch at his desk, with Landis off at the bigger glass offices to deliver an update.

Not only had the guy she'd talk to in Maryland admitted doing business with Bethany—and having sex with her Saturday night, proving in his mind he'd had no reason to kill her Sunday afternoon—but he'd also cleared up the missing purse and keys.

Bethany made a habit of having another vehicle—a "clean" vehicle not attached to whatever name she currently used—parked away from her target. She left her purse, ID, and her keys secured there. That was the fourth key found on her body.

Belichek started Fairlington PD on the hunt for that vehicle as soon as he ended the call with Felicia.

Checking off questions was always good. He wished Oz Zeedyk would check off the big one with a confession.

Belichek's phone vibrated with a text as he studied the phone records for Phil Xavier and Carl Arbendroth.

Xavier had a gap in calls from twelve-thirty to five p.m. the Sunday before Labor Day, noticeable amid a stream of calls.

None of Arbendroth's scattered calls were during that period, but he had enough gaps to make it less remarkable, as well as raise questions about how his mortgage brokering business was doing.

His text came from Landis.

Parking lot. Now.

He closed up and left.

Landis waited in his car by the elevators.

"What did you get from the computer guys?" Belichek asked as he got in.

"A lot of nothing and two interesting things. Nothing on the computers. But they found a series of searches on Delattre's phone, along with a complete clone of Bethany's phone. They first took the searches to be checking out someone the foundation might help. Until they dug deeper. One of the things he'd dug up was a police record for a woman named Boda Uria from western Connecticut."

Belichek raised his brows. "The foundation helps ex-cons?"

"Don't know about that. But—"

He pulled out a paper and placed it in front of Belichek. It showed a grainy mug shot of a woman whose height, weight, race, and coloring description would match Jamie's.

Like a blurry reproduction of a brilliantly vivid photograph.

"—the Sunshine Foundation might have employed one."

"Bethany Usher was Boda Uria."

"Yup. And Adam Delattre knew she was an ex-con. Young Adam's been keeping things from us." He put the car in drive. "Which is why we're on our way to the Sunshine Foundation. And not questioning Roy Isaacson. Yet."

"Isaacson?"

Landis explained the other nugget the tech guys had found from Adam cloning Bethany's phone. Ending with, "You think?"

Belichek understood he meant the leak. "Possible, but..."

Even of Roy Isaacson that was hard to believe.

"We'll save that for dessert," Landis concluded with a wolfish smile.

❖ ❖ ❖ ❖

LANDIS AND BELICHEK swore in unison as they pulled into the parking area behind the Sunshine Foundation.

Jamie stood about a dozen feet from the door, clearly on her way in.

Carl Arbendroth held her by her arm, tight enough to whiten his knuckles while his lips drew back from his teeth.

❖ ❖ ❖ ❖

"...THIS ISN'T A good time. And, really, Carl, there's nothing to talk about. I appreciate your concern for me, but—Oh."

Belichek stepped into her line of vision.

"Let go of her, Arbendroth."

The man started, and turned toward the new voice without releasing Jamie, which caught her off balance and made her stumble forward. Belichek steadied her with one hand, never taking his eyes from Arbendroth.

"Let go of her now."

"This is none of your business."

"Now."

Jamie said, "I'm fine. I—"

Arbendroth changed his tactic. "I was just—"

From the vicinity of Landis, joining the group, emitted the distinctive ticking sound of someone adjusting the size of handcuffs. He must have had a pair in his car.

Arbendroth looked toward Landis, then back to Belichek.

He released Jamie's arm. He spoke to her, but looked at the two men. "You wouldn't answer my calls. I had to let you know how happy I am, how relieved I am that you're okay. To be sure you know I wouldn't hurt you."

"I do know. I don't have my phone anymore. I can—"

"That's enough. We're going in." Belichek didn't touch her but jerked his head toward the door.

Jamie clicked her tongue, but went inside.

While Landis lingered outside, Belichek followed her.

"That was entirely unnecessary."

"Had you asked him to let go? Or tried to move away and not been able to?"

He had her and they both knew it.

"You're a cynic."

"Realist. And you shouldn't be here."

"It's a choice to always see the worst possibilities," she said.

"Experience."

"Ford, if that's your experience—" She broke off as Landis joined them.

"Don't mind me," he murmured.

"It's perfectly reasonable for me to be here. And I'm not alone. J.D. went into the restaurant to order lunch for everyone, and Maggie just ran in to remind him one of the volunteers working today is a vegan. What are you two doing here?"

Which meant Carl Arbendroth had been watching for an opportunity when she was alone—watching her. He'd get to that later. "Pursuing our investigation."

She frowned.

CHAPTER SIXTY-EIGHT

JAMIE INSISTED ON accompanying them to Adam Delattre's office.

Landis took the lead. "Adam, our experts have been looking at your computers. They're impressed with your set-up. And how you've used it."

Jamie smiled. Adam did not appear gratified.

"They've also retraced the steps of your searches into the background of Bethany Usher."

Jamie's focus jumped from Landis to him to Adam. "Adam? You were searching into Bethany? Why?"

The skin across his cheeks seemed to stretch thin, while his shoulders hunched.

"I… I was just curious at first, you know? Couldn't figure out why she was here. She didn't do any work. Hendrickson was all weird about her, tried to avoid her, yet she'd smile at him like… I don't know like what. Celeste hated her, but she's the one who hired her. None of it made sense.

"I started doing searches, just, uh, to see if there was anything." He looked up under his brows toward Jamie. "There was."

"What did you find?" Landis asked.

"Bethany Usher's not her name. It's something else. And that person has a criminal record. Fraud and scams and break-ins."

Air streamed out between Jamie's lips. She looked to Belichek.

He lowered his head in a solitary nod of confirmation.

Adam rushed his next words, "I didn't know what to do. I was going to tell you, Jamie, but I didn't want to land that on you right before you left. I figured it could wait. The management company might pick it up if they did good background searches. Or I could drop it in their laps and you wouldn't ever have had to know. And then, with everything that happened… It just… I didn't know…"

"How did you do that search, Adam?" Landis asked.

"Oh, uh, I tried basic search terms that led to—"

Jamie intervened. "You mean what device? He must have used the foundation computer. That's what you took to check, isn't it?"

"We have his phone, too."

"Which phone?" she asked.

Landis snapped to Delattre. "You were asked for all communication devices."

The guy looked miserable, though whether that was from being caught or the anticipation of losing another device, Belichek couldn't tell. On the other hand, the cause of Jamie's misery was clear. She felt she'd inadvertently betrayed Delattre.

Landis collected the phone. "Anything else?"

"I just bought a new one. I didn't even have it until a week ago."

"Hand it over."

"I'm sorry, Adam," Jamie said. "Get yourself another one. Make it a foundation phone."

"But when am I going to get my stuff back? This set-up…"

Telling him to wait in his office, they left him in mid-techno lament.

LANDIS FROWNED DOWN at her. "If you can't keep quiet, we'll conduct this questioning without you, and if your people don't cooperate, we'll be questioning them at the police department."

Unintimidated, she said, "Or we could all talk here—all the foundation people—and get this cleared up quickly and completely."

Landis looked over her head to Belichek.

"Okay. Get everybody together."

✧   ✧   ✧   ✧

LANDIS AND BELICHEK stood at the door of the conference room, directing the foundation employees inside. Hendrickson York marched down the side of the table and took the chair at the far end. Delattre shied away from joining him. Celeste t'ched at him, maneuvered past and took the middle chair on that side. Kimby eased behind those two and sat in the chair closest to York.

On the opposite side, Belichek sat across from her. Jamie left a space between them.

"Yes, please come in," Landis instructed someone, who turned out to be Denise. She sat between Jamie and Belichek, sitting well back from the table as if to pretend she weren't here. Or to leave the people on either side of her a view of each other.

Landis, after closing the door, took the seat at the head of the table.

Celeste scowled at Landis, clearly thinking Jamie should be in that spot. Adam kept his head tipped forward in apparent contemplation of the table top. Jamie looked around at the foundation staffers, lingering on Hendrickson.

Belichek shifted his attention from Jamie on his left to the man on his right. His face was flushed, making the mustache stand out against the ruddy color.

As Landis recapped what the police techs found from Adam's cloning of Bethany Usher's phone, Maggie came in quietly and took a chair away from the table by the door. No doubt Carson was on the other side of the door.

When Landis synopsized Adam's reasons for his searches and what those searches raised, both Hendrickson and Celeste stiffened noticeably.

At the end, though, all eyes went to Hendrickson York.

"Yes, yes, all right. You've been nosing around and pushing and prying and now you should all be happy at my complete and utter humiliation. She came here because of *me*. A felon, introduced to the Sunshine Foundation because of *me*," he said with bitter self-pity. "At the perfect time to give you the excuse you were looking for to force me out."

Jamie was horrified. "Hendrickson, we'd never—"

Celeste was outraged. "That is entirely unfair to Jamie."

"Fair? Fair? Nothing was fair." He stabbed a finger toward Jamie. "*You* should have been my daughter. Mine and Vivian's. *That* would have been *fair*."

York's protectiveness and possessiveness took on an entirely different cast in Belichek's mind.

People have … secrets. Wounds they don't want to reveal to the air.

Had Jamie known how the man truly felt?

"You're just like Vivian. Spending all your time on grubby little people instead of seeing what was right in front of her—"

"You. Oh, Hendrickson, I am sorry. All these years, loving her so much, and she chose someone else."

"A child molester! A murderer! She said no to me and chose *him*. How could she do that? How could she? And then you with those boyfriends of yours and the families—all that grubby neediness. Pawing at you—"

Delattre's head jerked up. "We did not paw at her. *Grubby neediness.* Rude of us to want lives. Rude of us not to stay out of your way so you could play the generous philanthropist with all the donors without being bothered by the people you're *supposed* to be wanting to help."

"I don't mean you, Adam. You—and your family—have done admirably raising yourselves up. But it doesn't change that I received nothing. Pushed to the edges. Allowed the merest crumbs of attention when I gave up my business, my life, to run this foundation. And then you—" Pointing at Jamie. "—were going to bring in this company to push me out completely. I should have known. It's how it's always been. Look no further than there—"

Another finger stab, this time over Jamie's head. To the photo that was the twin for the one in Jamie's living room.

"The perfect template for how I've been treated. The dedication to the park honoring Vivian, that I worked so long and hard for. But do you see *me* in that photo? Oh, no. I am *taking* the photo. Not good enough—"

"Hendrickson, we never meant—You have to know how appreciated, how loved—"

He talked through Jamie's attempt. "—to be included in the commemoration of the culmination of my effort, but not only pushed aside, made to be of *service*. Because I was not appreciated. Not recognized for—"

Landis cut across the pity party. "Why did you bring the woman you knew as Bethany Usher into the foundation."

"Because I had no choice. My whole life lived to a standard and then, gone, all gone. My reputation, the foundation's reputation… I didn't believe it at first, but she had proof. The dates. The name. She was my daughter. My natural daughter. It was so wrong. So unfair. *Unfair! She* was my daughter."

"No, she wasn't."

CHAPTER SIXTY-NINE

THE HEADS THAT had been turned to York, swung to Landis at his declaration, then back to York for his reaction.

York looked down his nose at Landis. He hadn't lost all his assurance. "Don't treat me like a fool, young man. I insisted on a paternity test. She *was* my biological daughter."

"She must have rigged the paternity test because our lab found no family connections in the DNA in this case. That would include you and Bethany Usher."

Hendrickson repeated to Landis, "That is impossible."

"She owned a website producing bogus paternity test results. She definitely used them herself. More than once. She didn't miss a trick. Blackmail a guy *and* make a profit on the paternity test that gave her leverage to squeeze harder."

Hendrickson looked both outraged and hopeful.

"But Hendrickson, if she was your daughter or you thought she was, why didn't you tell me. We'd have hired her and—"

"I didn't want her *here*. The harpy was blackmailing me—she tried to blackmail me."

"*Blackmailing? You?* What in the world could she blackmail you over?" Kimby's voice rose with each question.

"Over her existence, of course."

"Which was it? Tried or was blackmailing?" Landis asked.

"She was blackmailing me for money. An allowance she called it. Making up for all the lost years." His voice was dry and bitter. "She also tried to blackmail me to get into the foundation."

"Tried? But—"

"Yes, but she *did* get into the foundation. Not through my auspice, however. This was the last place I wanted her to be."

"And yet, she started working here at the beginning of the summer," Landis pointed out. "How did that happen?"

"*She* hired her." Now his bitterness speared Jamie. "I told her no. I told her to look at the work record. But, oh, no, she had to give someone another chance. Be the one to hire the person nobody else would hire—for good reason."

Jamie opened her mouth and closed it. She was going to let Hendrickson blame her.

Belichek said, "You and Jamie approved the volunteers, right? And the employees…?"

He felt Jamie's frown directed at him.

This wasn't about good feelings among the foundation staffers. It was about getting to the truth.

"Yes. What does that—?" Hendrickson stared at the foundation's office manager. "*You.* Oh, yes, I can believe that. *Now* it makes sense. Celeste found her somehow or Bethany told her who she was and Celeste could not resist the opportunity to triumph over me as she has sought to for years. And now she has her complete and total victory."

"Shut up, Hendrickson," Celeste ordered.

"Oh, you'd like that, wouldn't you, so you could tell the tale, and thus enjoy your triumph to the fullest."

He faced Landis down the length of the table.

"Officer, I confess. Once Bethany was working here, she pressured me more and more for money. I told her I couldn't pay her more. She said she'd tell not only Jamie our true relationship, but the entire world, exposing the whole sordid past and harming the foundation any way she could in the process." He drew in a breath that hitched partway through. "And then she drew a check on foundation funds and wrote my name to it and said if I exposed her, she'd do as she'd threatened. I didn't know what to do. I was frozen. But Jamie was leaving to write her book and Bethany was leaving for a vacation and I thought it would give me the time to… give me the time to regain my footing. To figure things out."

"Optimism over action," Belichek muttered.

Jamie didn't look toward him, but he knew she heard, because color marked her cheekbones.

But at the same time, he was hearing again Jamie's words about wounds.

And then Celeste…

That man couldn't conspire over a surprise birthday party.

Belichek heard the click in his brain.

He looked diagonally across the table to the office manager. "You tried to lead us away from York. Carefully and strategically."

"I have no idea what—"

Without taking his gaze from Celeste, he said, "Adam, have there been any financial transactions such as Hendrickson described being flagged in the foundation's online account?"

"There… uh, there was one I mentioned to Celeste, but she said she'd take care of it. And the next day the balance was right. The check was canceled."

"Celeste? What did you do?"

She reached across the table toward Jamie, her fingers well short of the younger woman. "It's all right, Jamie. The foundation was covered. I canceled the check." She pulled in air. "Then I wrote a personal check to Bethany for the same amount. And told her not to come back from her vacation."

"But… But then she'd have kept coming to you," Hendrickson said.

"That's what I figured."

"Why? Why would you do such a thing."

"You stupid old goat. You think I'd let you do that? You think I'd let you betray Jamie, the foundation—*yourself?* You think I'd stand by and let you be hurt—hurt yourself that way? I wouldn't. I couldn't. I canceled the check, cut her off from foundation funds. If she'd come back in here and tried to make life a misery for you, I was prepared to do more."

Stunned silence greeted this declaration.

Hendrickson shook his head. "You...? No, no.... But..." The head-shaking slowed, then stopped. "Why?"

"Why do you think, you stupid old goat. Because I love you. Always have, despite your being a crotchety fool."

Hendrickson's mouth gaped open in shock.

Against all his personal rules, against the habits of a career, against the training of his grandfather, Ford Belichek looked away from the possible suspects to the likely intended victim.

People have ... secrets. Wounds they don't want to reveal to the air.

She'd known. She'd known all along how Celeste Renfro felt about Hendrickson York. And she hadn't given as much as a hint.

His attention snapped back. York hadn't moved or changed expression. Celeste's color had deepened, but her stubborn jaw remained set as if daring her eyes to let loose the tears standing in them.

✧　✧　✧　✧

"POOR HENDRICKSON."

"Do *not* feel sorry for him," Maggie ordered.

"I do. He carried such a weight. He was unraveling and I didn't even notice."

"He's got one heck of a motive," Landis said. "We'll start on how he'd get his hands on a shotgun."

"Celeste, too," Belichek said.

"Yeah—"

"You can't." Jamie directed it all at Belichek. "You cannot suspect either one of them—"

"We do. Out of their own mouths. And we're going to investigate them."

She threw up her hands, then spun away from them.

Then she turned back. "I am staying here to work the rest of this afternoon."

"Jamie—"

"No, Maggie, just no." She pulled in a breath. "I appreciate your concern for me. All of you. But you have a suspect in custody and I have a foundation that has been torn to its core. Starting this minute, I give it the attention it deserves."

This time when she turned away, it was measured. She didn't look back as she entered the door and went up the stairs.

"We'll stay here in the parking lot," Maggie started.

"She's a grown woman," Carson said to her.

"We do have a suspect in custody," Landis muttered.

He and Maggie looked at Belichek.

Staying here would tick her off. Worse, he wouldn't be pursuing the investigation that could make her truly safe. But to leave her on her own...

CELESTE WALKED INTO Jamie's office and went to the window.

"There's a young guy hanging around outside." She gestured to the arched window. When Jamie joined her beside it, she pointed down. "Tried to hang around in our lobby and I told him he had to get out."

"Oh." How could she be both angry and touched? "His name is Schmidt. Be nice to him. Tell him to come inside. It looks like it might rain again."

Celeste's eyebrows rose, but she didn't directly respond as she made for the door.

What she did say was, "Never heard you sharper with anyone than you are with that detective."

"You would be sharp with him, too, if you were in my shoes."

"I would be sharp with him in my own shoes. But you usually aren't. Except your cousin Maggie, though you're sharper with this detective."

She walked out.

Leaving Jamie to get back to work.

If she could stop thinking about why she would be sharpest with Ford Belichek... If she was.

CHAPTER SEVENTY

WITH SCHMIDT IN place, and leaving Jamie's car there for her, Belichek, Maggie, and Carson got in Landis' car and began running through what happened for Carson.

Landis said, "Delattre was suspicious because there was something hinky going on between Bethany and York."

"Yeah," Maggie said. "Celeste probably picked up on it first. Though I wouldn't be surprised if jealousy made her think it was something other than blackmail. At least at first. Probably worried she had a rival."

How much of this had Jamie known or guessed or intuited? Belichek was a lot clearer on how much she'd shared. Zero.

"He runs the search that turns up Bethany's background, right back to being born Boda. But keeps it to himself," Maggie continued. "Celeste starts to pick up on Bethany's true designs. Meanwhile, York's being squeezed. Not knowing Celeste stopped the check and covered his tracks, would he have tried to kill Jamie to keep her from knowing?"

"Could." Landis asked, "What's with them all keeping things from Jamie."

"It's what people do. They try to protect her. Not make her deal with the real world. It's always been like that."

"She deals with the real world." Belichek raised his gaze to the rearview mirror and saw Maggie staring at him, while Carson studied her.

"You don't," Maggie said abruptly.

"He doesn't deal with the real world? I've said that for years," Landis said, unaware of the interplay of looks beside and behind him.

"No. He doesn't try to protect her."

"Like hell. Taking her to you in the mountains, risking his career—"

Maggie cut across Landis, still staring into the rearview mirror at Belichek. "I mean he tells her the truth. He ... makes her tell the truth. To see things. Reality."

Before Maggie could say more—because she clearly had more to say—Belichek dropped his gaze. Better, Carson spoke up.

"So, Delattre runs the search. Celeste intervenes in York's attempt to commit a crime. But York doesn't know it. Means he still has motive to kill Bethany Usher ... or Jamie, if he was that unable to face disappointing her."

Carson's gambit worked, to Belichek's relief. Maggie followed the lure of exploring motives—and away from examining him.

"Kill her, but not disappoint her," she repeated in disgust. "Not out of the question, though his motive's stronger for killing Bethany. On the other hand—"

Landis broke in. "Yeah, this is fun and all, but some evidence would be nice. The Commonwealth Attorney's office won't stick their lily soft necks out and indict without a truckload of evidence."

Maggie growled, but her teeth weren't in it.

"Too bad you can't help us when we talk to Isaacson in an hour," Landis said.

"Not a good idea," Maggie said with great regret.

Landis nodded. "But you can take a closer look at the searching Adam Delattre did. Maybe you guys will see something I didn't. Come with now to the department and—"

"Send it to Maggie to look at from home," Carson said. "We're going to her place as soon as you drop us off at Belichek's for our vehicles."

"You're going to have to break this habit of making decisions for me," she said to Carson.

"As soon as this situation with Jamie's resolved."

And Maggie didn't argue.

✧   ✧   ✧   ✧

TELLING THE REST of the foundation staff and volunteers they would hit the ground running tomorrow, Jamie ordered them to leave early today, and they had. Even Adam, who said he needed to pick up some components before a favorite computer store closed. Celeste gave Schmidt a measuring look, *humphed*, but left, too.

The oppressive atmosphere immediately improved. In the hours since, Jamie made a respectable dent in the first level of getting back up to speed on foundation affairs. Momentum kept her going, without letting anything else slide into her thoughts.

Twice, she'd waved to Schmidt at his post by the entry when she left her office for the supply closet where Celeste also kept paper files on the families they helped, including handwritten thank you notes, which gave Jamie a lift on her worst days. But no time for those today.

Tonight, she corrected herself wryly. It was fully dark outside.

Her third trip was for the most mundane of reasons. She needed pens. She didn't see Schmidt. He must be down the hall or outside the office suite door. She'd heard him making rounds before.

As she turned to go into the closet, her angle gave her a different view.

Officer Schmidt's feet extending past Celeste's desk.

She swallowed a cry and ran to him, her heart squeezing painfully. He had a gash on his head, oozing blood, and he was unconscious.

Could he have fallen? Caught his head on the edge of the desk?

You aren't dismissing anything, you aren't cutting off possibilities.

She pulled her phone from her sweater pocket to call 911.

The lights went out.

She knew where the breaker box was on the first floor. She knew how long it took to climb those stairs. Not enough time for 911 to get here.

She couldn't leave Schmidt and run out the back way.

She couldn't leave Schmidt…

Sliding her phone back in her pocket, she grabbed his arm with both hands and pulled as hard as she could to drag him.

It was only a few feet to the door to the conference room, but she had never worked harder. She switched to his other arm. At the door, his unconscious body got caught on the frame and she'd have shouted her frustration if she had breath.

She yanked him to the side by the belt, then grabbed the bottoms of his pants up like they were doing that two-person gymnastics roll. When he cleared the doorframe, she dropped his legs forward, leaving him mostly bent double, crawled over him and closed and locked the door.

Leaning against the wall, trying to get her breath back.

She'd probably done all this for nothing. The power went out often enough. Nobody was out there.

You aren't dismissing anything, you aren't cutting off possibilities.

Then she heard the footsteps coming up the stairs.

The room had no windows. No other exit, even if she could have gotten Schmidt up.

They were trapped.

She had her phone in her hand again.

But how fast could 911 get here? And how close were those footsteps?

CHAPTER SEVENTY-ONE

"WHAT WAS YOUR relationship to Bethany Usher?"

"No relationship."

"You knew her." Belichek left no maneuvering room. It was the only way with Isaacson. "When did you meet?"

"You're making this sound like an interview—like I'm a suspect."

"It is. What comes out of this interview will determine your status."

"Wait a minute. That's—"

"When did you meet Bethany Usher?"

After that initial protest, Isaacson had himself back under control. He knew what was at stake, but he still produced an off-hand half-shrug, meant to convey he met so many women so many ways he couldn't be expected to keep track.

"When?"

"Must have been spring, because the tourist surge had started."

Isaacson had thought she was an out-of-towner. The easiest of no-strings one-night-stands.

"We got together a few times. Nothing serious. And then she asked me for a favor. To help her get a job."

Belichek sat back, looking at him, good-looking, smart in some ways ... and incredibly stupid in others. He also thought of Bethany Usher and how she'd operated.

Odds were good, she had something over him. Isaacson didn't help people for nothing and wasn't inclined to altruism.

"Why did you use Nancy Quinn's name?"

He smirked. "For exactly the way it turned out. With all her connections, it wouldn't surprise people she knew anyone, no matter how unlikely. People wouldn't think of questioning someone Nancy Quinn recommended. And, best of all, nobody would want to contact her and ask her about her rec in case it sounded like they were questioning her judgment."

"Had it all figured out, didn't you?"

"Pretty much."

"All except the part about Bethany Usher being shot in the face."

"I had nothing to do with that."

"You started the chain of events," Landis said.

"That's like blaming the butterfly in the rainforest for flapping its wings and causing—whatever."

"Did she ask you to get her a job at the Sunshine Foundation?"

"No. Said anywhere."

"Why did you send her to the Sunshine Foundation?"

"Must've heard something about an opening there."

"Why did you send her to the Sunshine Foundation?"

"It was months ago. Seemed like a good idea at the time. I—"

"Why did it seem like a good idea?"

"I thought it would be amusing."

Belichek came at him again in the same unemotional tone. "Why would it be amusing?"

"Because she looked like Maggie's cousin. Could've been her sister."

"What about that amused you?"

"Because Jamie's like Maggie, thinking she's better than everybody else and maybe if she saw this other woman who looked like her and was the farthest thing from Saint Jamie, she'd get over herself."

Belichek stood slowly. "You came onto her and she rejected you. And you wanted to play a mind game to punish her."

Isaacson's strong jaw worked hard.

"Jamie doesn't think she's better than everybody else. But she sure as hell knows she's better than you."

"I CAN'T TELL you what I don't know," Oz Zeedyk complained.

The miracle was he hadn't lawyered up. The consensus was he didn't want to share talking time with a lawyer.

Though Zeedyk seemed to respond better to Landis than Belichek's silent presence.

"You keep saying you have sources for your stories and that's proof you're not the perpetrator, but you're not giving us the proof, Oz."

"Anonymous sources."

"Oz, Oz, Oz, I thought we were past this. You can't help yourself if you don't tell us the truth."

"It is the truth. I only saw the guy once and I don't know who he is, except he's a listener to the podcast."

"When did you see him?"

"At the scene."

"What did he look like?"

"Too dark. He was a shadow. Probably a guy, but I couldn't swear to that."

"He was at the scene?"

"Yeah. That first night when they found a body in Jamison Chancellor's house and Red Hill Street had all the lights and TV trucks and forensic vans."

"Why were you at the scene, Oz?" Landis asked.

"It's expected of a crime podcaster. Pick up local color, get the feel of the crime, and let fans meet you one-on-one. This guy was a fan. We talked a bit, then he walked right by you—" He jerked his head toward Belichek. "—before you went in the house."

"WE CAN NARROW down the time, have the tech guys jump to then, and you know what path you took into the scene, so we narrow that down. We might get something on this guy."

Belichek had a bad feeling. "We have to try for it, but it was damned dark back there, Landis."

"If we come up empty on what the department shot and what we already have from neighbors and social media, we can ask the public for more."

"Another factor we can't lose sight of is somebody else at the scene, by his own admission. Our friend Oz. He could be making up the whole thing."

BELICHEK WAS RIGHT. It was damned dark beyond the police lights. Plus, neighbors and spectators focused their video across the street at Jamie's house, not on the dark sidewalk below their front steps.

All they got was a smudge of a shadow moving away from another smudge of a shadow, that might or might not have been Oz, and moving behind a third smudge of a shadow that resolved into Belichek in the next frames as he walked into the light.

"Well, whoever it is, is about your height, Belichek," said the tech on their fourth squint-eyed viewing of the video.

"Not an NBA player. That narrows it down," Landis grumbled. "Anything you can do with the quality?"

"I'll see, but don't count on it."

Landis and Belichek started back to the detective section.

"What are you thinking, Bel?"

"I'm thinking this adds some credence to Zeedyk's story. Which adds to the possibility he's not the killer and somebody's still after Jamie."

Landis grunted. "Good thing you got Schmidt to the foundation."

"VIOLENT CRIMES. TANNER Landis."

"Landis, it's Jamie Chancellor. Is Belichek there? If—"

"Yeah."

Hurriedly, she said, "Please don't tell him it's me. Please."

His gaze cut toward Belichek, concentrating on his screen.

"Okay. For now."

"I wasn't sure I should call you, but… I… uh, I was wondering if you could come help me."

"I got that, but where?"

A jumbled sound came through the phone. A cross of laughter and tears. "Thank you. I wasn't sure… Especially since this was my only phone call."

His hand stopped in the act of closing his notebook in preparation for jamming it in a pocket. "This was—? Where are you?"

"I'm in jail. For calling in a false bomb report."

CHAPTER SEVENTY-TWO

"FIRST, I THOUGHT I'd say it was a break-in, but I wondered if they'd send enough people, because if they sent just one officer, well, I already had Officer Schmidt injured and I didn't want anyone else picked off. How is he?" Jamie asked Landis. "They wouldn't tell me while I was waiting for you."

"He should be okay. Hell of a headache, some stitches, they're watching him for a concussion. Also, some rug burn, which is understandable from your account, and a few sore muscles in his back."

She did not answer the question implicit in that last part.

"Thank goodness. My second thought was to call in a fire," she explained, "but I thought all the uproar might give somebody the chance they wanted. Plus, I wanted police. I figured with a report of a bomb, they'd keep everybody else out and send in the police. I was right, too."

Landis resisted the temptation to drive his hands through his hair. "Yeah, you were right. Only now they think you're a wacko."

"I was convincing," she said with some pride. "I thought since you're all police… Can't you explain to them what's been happening? Can't you vouch for me? Or will they think you're a wacko, too?"

"Probably."

But he talked the guys downstairs into letting her go, even skating on the paperwork. Palery might not be happy he'd used his name liberally—like the security on a loan—but they let her leave with him.

"I want to go to my house."

"That's not a good idea—"

"You've said you think that podcaster is the killer. There's no reason for me not to go to home and I want to go there."

He did a quick calculation in his head. "We'll pick up takeout on the way."

After a minute of driving, he said, "You didn't do half-bad, all things considered. Were you scared?"

She nodded and swallowed. "Spitless."

"Spitless?" he grinned.

"Just because I don't use the language you're probably accustomed to doesn't mean I don't feel as strongly, so shut up."

"I didn't—"

"I said, shut up."

He complied, speaking only after picking up the takeout order.

On the way out of the parking lot, he said, in his most winning tone. "You know, saying you were scared spitless makes sense, because your throat goes dry. Tight, too. So you really are spitless."

She looked at him, really looked at him, her eyes wide and open. It was if he could see clear through to her backbone. He saw not only how she viewed him, but how she saw Belichek. It left him with a little regret, some disappointment, a trace of envy, a bit of pleasure, and a dose of worry.

She shook her head. "Aw, shut up, Landis." And then she was laughing. It made her damned sexy.

But it stirred nothing in him.

Nothing.

A self-protective mechanism? Or part of the partnership code.

Though in this case, the ball had never been in his court. She wasn't the least bit interested in him, because she was falling for his partner.

Or had fallen.

He hoped to hell this podcaster really was the killer, they could keep him in jail, and get a conviction.

Fairlington County Police Department News Conference

I'm Fairlington County Police Public Affairs Officer Elliott Kepler. I don't see any unfamiliar faces, but if you need my name spelled, let me know. As promised, I have more information on the background of the victim in the Red Hill Street murder. She has been identified as Boda Uria, who used the name Bethany Usher while she has been in the area for at least the past six months.

We have connected her forensically to other names. Under those names she has convictions or outstanding warrants in fourteen jurisdictions in nine states. We have listed those on the handout available for download or the printed version by the door.

Those convictions involved crimes in which she illegally took up residence in a house, most often by misrepresentation, stole property, especially collectibles, as well as cash, then left before the homeowners returned.

Our investigators are currently tracking her known associates, with potential leads to items taken from the house on Red Hill Street.

She was hired by the Sunshine Foundation in June. It has been determined her references were falsified. That, too, matches her methods in the crimes outlined in her convictions and warrants.

Her fingerprints at the apartment she'd rented, her place of work, her truck, and the house on Red Hill Street all matched fingerprints obtained in connection with a criminal record for Boda Uria, including Bethany Marie Usher, the name she used most recently.

Washington Post: What about the body's fingerprints? Is that how you identified her?

PIO Kepler: Identification was initially made through medical records and has been confirmed by DNA.

Washington Post: Are you saying the body has no fingerprints?

PIO Kepler: Identification was initially made through medical records and has been confirmed by DNA. The department will not be commenting further on that aspect.

Fairlington Leader: What kind of crimes, Kep? Can you get us a copy of her criminal record?

PIO Kepler: This information has just been received by the Fairlington County Police Department. We will not be releasing details at this time. However, I can tell you charges were filed in two cases involving obtaining illegal entry to a home.

WTOP Radio: Where were these cases?

PIO Kepler: One in Pennsylvania and one in Maryland.

Fairlington Leader: Were those the only charges associated with those cases?

PIO Kepler: No. As you can understand, since these were not our cases, the release of detailed information should come from those jurisdictions.

Washington Times: Did Bethany Usher have connections to Jamison Chancellor? Before she was hired? Or more of a relationship than working together after?

PIO Kepler: Our investigation has found nothing to indicate that. As you'll see from the convictions and warrants, she most often moved to an area, worked her way into positions of connection, even trust.

Jamison Chancellor's movements have been corroborated in leaving the Red Hill Street on the Saturday of Labor Day weekend and arriving at a cabin in North Carolina, where she remained, writing a new book in isolation. She did not learn of the murder at the Red Hill Street until her return to Fairlington.

Bethany Usher did not have permission to be in the house.

Washington Post: When was Bethany Usher killed?

PIO Kepler: We are not prepared to release that information at this time.

ABC: So far, the stories reported on the Death, Murder, Violence podcast have proven correct. Has the Fairlington Police Department given DMV exclusive information?

PIO Kepler: No.

CBS: Is the department investigating possible leaks?

PIO Kepler: We are always interested in unauthorized releases of information because of the harm they can do, first, to the investigation and, later, to the pursuit of a conviction by the Commonwealth's Attorney's office.

WTOP Radio: Do you have Oliver "Oz" Zeedyk, of the Death, Murder, Violence podcast, in custody again?

PIO Kepler: Mr. Zeedyk is cooperating with our investigation.

ABC: Are you demanding his sources for the stories he's released, including that Jamison Chancellor was not the victim at Red Hill Street and now he's saying she remains in danger of being killed?

PIO Kepler: We cannot release details of an active investigation.

Fairlington Leader: But you can't make him give up his sources. Aren't they protected?

PIO Kepler: We would hope any citizen—including a journalist or podcaster would share information that might save someone's life.

Washington Post: Have you charged Zeedyk with anything?

PIO Kepler: At this time, we have not.

CBS: Are you going to?

PIO Kepler: I cannot speculate on the future course of an investigation. If that's all…

Washington Post: Understand there was a suspicious package called in at the restaurant in the same building the Sunshine Foundation is in.

PIO Kepler: There was. The bomb squad cleared the building. It turned out to be a false alarm. No one was hurt. No device was found.

Washington Post: Was it connected to the Red Hill Street murder?

PIO Kepler: I know of no connection and I don't expect further developments there, but we'll let you know if there are.

~~ End news conference transcript ~~

CHAPTER SEVENTY-THREE

"WHAT ARE YOU doing here?" Jamie demanded when she opened her front door.

Fire surged through Belichek. What the hell was Landis doing letting her answer the door? It didn't help much that she'd opened it only about a foot.

"You weren't going to come to me after your bomb scare. Were you?" As he spoke, he made another scan of the area.

She held the door in front of her. Not much of a shield. He could still see the way she was backlit, just the view the killer would have had of Bethany Usher on that rainy Sunday of Labor Day weekend.

Something—

Jamie's strong, "No, I wasn't," broke across his not-yet-born thought.

Still, she stepped back a little, opening the door more. Not inviting him in, but close enough.

Except what had driven him here was backing off. Letting his brain engage. He hesitated.

"Aren't you coming in?" she asked.

"Why?"

"Well, you don't seem to have crossed the threshold, so I wondered—"

"Not why are you asking if I'm coming in, why should I come in?"

"I could use the company?" She sounded vulnerable.

He gritted his teeth. "It's not—"

"I'm not asking you to sleep with me for heaven's sake."

"I'm still investigating this case."

"I didn't know you were such a stickler for the rules, Detective Belichek, considering you kidna—spirited me away to J.D.'s place. But by all means, do come in—" She swung the door wide with a hard push and moved deeper into the hall. "—I promise not to force myself on you."

She didn't look around to see if he followed. Not even when he closed the door softly.

But she reacted when his shadow reached her peripheral vision by shying away. "There wasn't really a bomb," she said.

"I know."

"Somebody hit Officer Schmidt."

"I know. And turned out the lights."

"How did you find out?"

"I know Landis. When he left, I tried your phone with no answer, tried the foundation. Someone from the bomb squad answered. Wouldn't fill me in. I talked to some guys I know. That's when I heard you'd been taken in. Went back to the desk ... and you two had merrily skipped away."

Before either of them said more, Landis' voice interrupted.

"Actually, he was slower getting here than I expected. Dinner is almost cold." He leaned against the doorframe at the end of the hall. "C'mon, you two. Dinner is served."

He'd arranged a spread on the antique desk in the small room past the living room. With three chairs.

"Peruvian chicken, yucca fritta, and tomato onion salad."

"This is takeout?" Jamie asked.

"Just so you know, he also eats at McDonald's."

"Ah, a man of many parts," Jamie said with would-be lightness.

Over the meal, they took her back over what happened, step by step from when they left her at the foundation.

By the end, she was back in the upholstered chair, looking tired but not as pale.

"Okay, that should do it for now."

She lifted an eyebrow at him. "You mean you're not going to ask me the same questions four more times? I know how you work, Belichek."

Before he could answer, she shivered.

She stood, but he beat her to her red sweater on the back of the desk chair. He held it up for her. She glanced at him over her shoulder. He settled the sweater, then took his hands away immediately.

"Figured you could use a break from the questions tonight, Jamie. You did the right thing today, listening to your instincts."

"My darker instincts." What started as a chuckle came out as a gulp. "I hate that. When I don't see the good, when I don't cling to the bright side, then it's all dark."

"Those darker instincts can keep you alive. You can get over dark, you can't get over being dead."

"A couple of crazy kids from two different worlds." Landis' dry voice startled them both. He'd been so quiet, they'd forgotten he was here. "What you need is back story. I guess Belichek knows a fair amount of your history…"

Landis got the answer to that non-question when Jamie shot Belichek a look mixing questioning and accusation.

"…but do you know the story about how he ended up with his grandparents?"

"Shut up, Landis."

"He was a kid in a tough part of town, the toughest. Him and his mother—"

"For God's sake. The way you sound, there should be a violin playing."

Landis focused on Jamie. "Him and his mother, except she was involved with this guy who scared people, even in that tough part of town. And Bel was, what was it? Ten? Nine?"

"Shut up, Landis."

"Think it was nine. His mother was out somewhere—"

The object of his story walked out of the room, not looking back.

It didn't stop Landis.

And Jamie wanted to hear this story.

"—left Bel with this guy—great babysitter. Anyway, a woman

stopped by. Her story was she was being neighborly and he pounced on her the minute she's in the door. No provocation. Nobody believed that. One report was she owed him money and went there to try to get out of it, and he got mean.

"Either way, he was beating on her—she ended up in the hospital a couple days—and getting ready to—Well, he had her clothes mostly off. Belichek walks in cool as can be and says to stop and he'd called the police.

"Guy goes into a rage. He starts in on Bel and Bel was giving back enough that when the police showed up, they used that as an excuse to take him in, too."

"That's awful."

"Better than leaving him out in the neighborhood. The guy's people would have taken care of him as an example. Couldn't let a kid get away with turning him in."

A kid who'd turned a feared adult into the police and taken him on directly.

"His mother...?"

Landis' expression hardened.

"His mother, what? Stood up for him? No. Backed him up? No. Was proud of him? No. She was pissed he'd gone against her meal ticket. Didn't care he'd been beating another woman, wouldn't have surprised anybody by killing her. After the maggot was put in prison, she visited him. Currying favor. When he got out—not much of a sentence—she got her old position back, too. Briefly. Trouble was, nobody thought he was such a tough guy anymore. Rival who'd taken over welcomed him home with gunfire. She was killed in the cross-fire."

Trying to absorb the layers of horror, sorrow, loss, Jamie felt surprise come in. "He... Ford told you this?"

"No. Doesn't talk about it. I wouldn't know if his grandmother hadn't sat me down and told me the first time I met her. Remarkable woman."

✧ ✧ ✧ ✧

WHEN BELICHEK CAME back in with his kit from the trunk of his car, Jamie was gone, Landis was in the comfortable chair.

Landis leaned back, his fingers locked behind his head, his eyes on Belichek.

"She's upstairs. Since you're doing guard duty, I suppose I can go home, huh."

Belichek said nothing.

"Unless you want me to stay and chaperone."

More nothing.

"You're caught this time, my friend. And not even your career's going to save you. Take it from an expert. You let yourself fall for her when you thought she was dead, because that was the perfect woman for you, then—"

"Not what you said before. Wronger even than your lousy choices, was what you said."

"Yeah, well, I was wrong. Falling for her when you thought she was dead was perfect. You could give everything and not have any chance of getting anything—or getting any, for that matter. And now she's alive and you have to deal with it. This is going to be entertaining." He released his hands and sat up. "At least it would be entertaining if my career wasn't on the line, too."

CHAPTER SEVENTY-FOUR

When Landis left, Belichek climbed the stairs.

Jamie was in her third-floor office, listening to some audio something, curled into the chair, wearing a robe that covered all of her, yet had him thinking… or not thinking.

"I locked up. I'll be on the couch in the living room."

All people. Real people. Not Frankenstein Monsters.

"There's no need to be uncomfortable on a couch. The guest room is available."

He hesitated, caught by what she was listening to. "What is that?"

"The podcast—Death, Murder Violence. Re-listening, in case there's something I missed. Some reason he might…"

"No reason. Don't look for one. It's not your doing. But play that back."

"What?"

He reached past her, not willing to examine how much of it was impatience because the audio was running on, away from what he needed to hear, and how much was wanting to be closer to her, to smell the freshness from her shower, to feel her heat…

All people. Real people. Not Frankenstein Monsters.

That was it. He checked the date of the podcast. Then he played it back into his phone recorder. Maybe he took a little longer doing those tasks than necessary.

Finally, he stepped back from her.

"Is it important?"

"Maybe. I'll take you up on the guest room. Thanks." Sleep would clear his head. It had to. He'd nearly missed that. Had he missed more? "Good ni—"

"Belichek—Ford. What Tanner said about when you were a boy— how you ended up with your grandparents…"

"It wasn't complicated. A sorry excuse for a man beating a woman. I saw him. I turned him in."

"You were a kid. And even after you called the police on that man and went after him yourself, the police took you in?"

"Didn't hold me long. After things calmed down, they listened to the call again and knew I'd called it in."

They hadn't believed him. "How long were you in jail?"

"Not jail. Juvie. Two nights. Local cop called my grandfather. He came and got me. I went straight home with him. Lived with them until I was on my own."

"Yet, after that experience, you went into law enforcement."

"Better to be the arrester not the arrestee."

She stood. "Because of Sheriff Rutherford Webster."

"I have to go—"

"I haven't broken my promise not to throw myself at you."

"I'm staying here or wherever you are, tonight and every night until the last corner of this is resolved and we—I—know for damned sure nobody's after you. But—Look, there's some connection, chemistry. But in the real world, we both know we're about as far apart as people come. Let's leave it at that, Jamie."

LANDIS WALKED INTO the detective bullpen to hear Oz Zeedyk had asked to talk to him.

They'd been so sure Landis would be back, they'd kept Zeedyk at the ready.

"Nice to be wanted." He took a slug of coffee, paused outside the interview room and walked in to find Zeedyk with tears in his eyes.

Angrily, he wiped them away.

A hunch, intuition, experience, or the putting together of pieces,

Landis went with it.

"Thinking about your sister Sandy?"

"How… How do you know her name?"

"Came up in connection with you. Were you in police stations when she went missing?"

"No. I was too young. They kept me away."

Landis tried to put acceptance into his silence.

Almost two minutes went by. Then Zeedyk spoke.

"She put me to bed every night. Sometimes she read me a story. She was… she was pretty. And kind.

"Mom was a nurse. Dad worked for the railroad. A porter on the trains up to Boston, down to Florida. Grabbing all the overtime he could get. They were saving to send us both to college. That was the plan. Send Sandy, she'd get out, start working, then all three of them would work and save to send me. It was all planned out. I'd be a doctor. And then I'd take care of our folks in their old age. The old age neither of them lived to see."

He drifted a moment.

Then his mouth formed a sour, twisted smile. "How's that for a bedtime story for a kid barely in school. Already had college, med school, and profession planned out for him. Along with a lifelong repayment schedule."

"Sounds like a good family. Close."

The muscles holding that rictus grin twitched.

"Yeah. Close. After Sandy… Mom died first. Cancer. She fought. I was scared about losing her. She was scared about not being there for me. Dad was drinking hard by then. Had a couple suspensions already. But by the end, Mom and I were both ready for her to go. It was too hard. Dad… Dad was permanently anesthetized from the minute the news came about Sandy. Eventually the rest of his body gave out. Then it was just me."

Landis said nothing for several long moments.

"It sucks, Oz. There's no way around it. It's the reason I do this job. So it will suck for fewer people than if I didn't do it."

✦ ✦ ✦ ✦

BELICHEK TOOK A shower with more cold mixed in than he usually liked. He needed it.

Then he called Landis, winning the bet with himself that his partner would be at his desk.

"You're hopeless, Belichek," Landis said immediately. "Alone with Jamie, and you're calling *me*?"

"Got something for you to listen to."

"Before that, you want to hear what Oz had to say a little while ago?"

"Yeah."

Landis wrapped up his report by saying, "Nothing actionable, but Jamie nailed it. He still thinks he's not going to tell all. Letting him soften up now."

Belichek knew his role in this dialogue. "Why go after Jamie?"

"High profile. Crossed paths with her sometime. Fixated on her because she built something worthwhile after a relative's murder and he didn't. Feels he let his whole family down."

"Why now?"

"Could be anything. Long-term buildup hit critical mass."

"You could ask your department shrink."

"Very funny."

"Do you really think it's him, Tanner?"

Three beats passed. "No. But he's still not telling us everything."

"You'll get it from him. Now listen to this."

All people. Real people. Not Frankenstein Monsters.

"Sound familiar?" Belichek asked as soon as it was done.

"It's Zeedyk. On his podcast."

"Not the voice. The words. *Frankenstein Monsters*. I used that phrase talking about trying to know a victim when they're dead. I said that to one person. You."

"Are you accusing me of being the leak."

"For that phrase, yes. No. I take that back. *I'm* the leak."

"What the fuck—?"

"Shut up and listen, Landis. I said that to you early on—not the morning after you caught the case, the next one. Talking about knowing so much about a victim, but still only having bits and pieces, not seeing them as a living, breathing human. Only time I've said it. And you accused me of getting poetic. Remember?"

"Nobody else around. Breakfast sandwich."

"Right."

The squeak of his chair through the phone announced when Landis jerked upright. "Just before Isaacson and Terrington showed up in the break room. You think they—?"

"They couldn't have heard us. We didn't see them until we were leaving, when they were across the bullpen, and we'd talked about Frankenstein monsters earlier."

"But then how the hell—? Son of a bitch."

Nobody ever said Landis was slow.

"The son of a bitch is listening in to the break room. And I felt sorry for him. What's been on Oz's podcast, it's all been talked about in the break room. Terrington being pissed off about not being second. You supposed to be on vacation. The shrink with legs. Jamie being alive… Son of a *bitch*. That was me. On the phone with you. *Me*—"

A bug."

"How—? The food? It's gotta be. Delivery guy never comes up to the bullpen. But if it's in a box… We throw them out. Must cost the turd a fortune, which would warm my heart if I weren't so pissed."

"I was thinking that container of napkins. They keep sending wads of napkins, we drop the new ones into that basket and keep using it."

"Yeah. Yeah. Going to stomp that sucker to bits, right after—"

"We get forensics to confirm it without warning him we've figured it out and we're coming for him."

"I was going to say right after stomping that piece of shit podcaster, but your timeline works, too."

✧   ✧   ✧   ✧

JAMIE WOKE FROM a deep sleep to darkness where dawn was only an idea, knowing he wasn't in the other bedroom. He had been when she'd come down from the office and gone to bed. She heard his voice.

Too low for words, but it had been oddly reassuring, even in her own room with her door closed, too.

But now, he wasn't in the guest room and she was awake.

She opened her door and listened. Heard a faint creak. It sounded like… But the back door was louder.

Then she realized when she heard that creak she was usually beside the door, not at this distance.

She put her phone in the pocket of her robe, cinched it tightly around her waist and, barefoot, started down the old back stairs.

Wearing only a pair of running shorts, he stood in the open doorway to the patio, one forearm resting on the doorframe. The other hand held the t-shirt he'd been wiping his neck and chest with. Beyond him the light from the back hall fixture spread into a diffused rectangle, swallowed by threads and swirls of vapor rising from the ground.

Power. The shadow and light revealed the topography of his back's musculature, but that wasn't where the sensation of power came from. Ford Belichek's power came from heart and lung, and maybe from soul. It was packaged in sleek lines and tempting hollows. It frightened her a little.

But not enough.

CHAPTER SEVENTY-FIVE

SHE WAS A shadow in the hallway beside her bedroom door.

He turned his back to her, stopped in the doorway to the guest room.

"Go back to bed, Jamie."

He'd given up on sleep an hour ago. Retrieved running gear from the kit he'd brought in from his car. But he couldn't run fast enough and he wouldn't run far enough to make a difference. So he came back, with nothing changed.

He knew when she hesitated. He knew when she started toward him.

He waited until she stood behind him, until the heat of her body breathed against his back.

She laid her palms to his waist, slid them forward.

A cool touch against his heat, raising a fog that bent and diffused his reason.

"This isn't…"

But what it wasn't evaporated before the strength of what it was.

"I'm about to break my promise, Ford. I'm throwing myself at you, because I was wrong about you," she said. "You don't solely focus on the evil. You try to help people. Me. You've helped me."

He turned to her.

"I'm no do-gooder."

She slid her palms over the stubble of his jaw, then to his cheeks. She stretched up, her head tipped back to look at him.

He watched her.

"You do good, Ford."

"Don't fool yourself, Jamie. I'm not like you. My job's finding the bad guy. Get them off the street so they can't hurt anybody else. It's their victims I'd help if I could. But it's too late when I know them."

She slid her fingers into his hair, giving her purchase to draw his face down to hers, to draw his mouth down to hers.

"It's not too late. You know me. And you do good."

Then she kissed him.

He didn't let himself hold her, but he took her mouth, angling, gliding, delving, returning. Panting.

She put her palms on his chest, not pushing him away, but connecting.

"I want to know I'm alive, Ford."

If her voice hadn't cracked, just a thread of a shiver, he might have made it. But it did, and he didn't.

He covered her mouth and pressed against her body in a single, desperate move. A man diving into ice-cap water all at once before he lost his nerve—or regained his sense. Only it was heat he dove into. Heat and scent and sensation.

He'd make her know, at the most elemental level, that she was alive. He just couldn't let himself...

"Let me touch you, Ford."

"No."

But her robe was gone. In his hands, then released to fall wherever. She wore nothing under it.

His chest hurt as if he'd run beyond his endurance and kept going.

She had her hand inside his shorts, feather-touching the scar on his hip, bunching the material as she slid forward, finding him, sliding the material away, until she held him. Completely.

She was trying to guide him into her right there. He turned them both, going down to the bed, trying to regain control. Not all of it— that was gone—but enough to protect her. He achieved that at a cost of restraint.

He entered her.

She screamed.

He angled himself up to look at her. "Jamie. God, *Jamie*. Are you okay?"

"No."

"I hurt you." He should pull out. He couldn't move. He was that close.

"No. You didn't hurt me. That wasn't pain. You asked if I was okay. *Okay* is not the word."

He dropped his forehead to hers. "You scared the hell out of me."

"Belichek," she started in a low, fierce voice, "if you don't move—now—I'll do worse than that."

Then she moved her hips, tilting them back a fraction of an inch, taking a fraction of an inch more of him inside. Shattering his stillness, becoming their movement.

Still propped above her, he watched a tear slip from the corner of her eye. If it hadn't been for that tear and the scare she'd given him, he'd have gone with her, or maybe beaten her there. Instead he watched, awed, frightened, humbled. Feeling her body under him, around him…

She opened her eyes. No guile, no defense. Totally open. To him.

She accelerated the echoing pulses of her body, drawing on him.

He closed his eyes. Pumping, her arms and legs around him.

Coming…

He'd never before wanted so badly he couldn't say no.

Yet his wanting was nothing compared to the need to meet hers.

JAMIE DRIFTED.

Their legs entwined, her head on his shoulder, his arm around her, her hand on his heart, his face into the top of her head.

"You said you needed to be the sunshine for your folks, when you were little."

She blinked, feeling the drag of her lashes against his skin. "Mmm."

"Did you notice what your mom said when we were leaving Fredericksburg?"

It felt a million years ago. "Be careful?"

"She said they had to be realistic, you had to be realistic."

She heard her mother's voice. *We have to be realistic. You need to be realistic.*

"Mmm-hmm."

"You told her not to worry. It was all a mistake."

"Mmm-hmm."

"She didn't believe that. And she worried more because she thought you might." His voice was dragging. She could hear sleep sliding over him, could feel it in the beat of his heart under her hand. "You don't have to always be the sunshine, Jamie. You can let it rain."

A sound vibrated low in her throat. She couldn't have said if it was acknowledgment, resistance, or acceptance.

As he slept, she thought of all three.

And of the man who'd come to know her from the journals she'd never thought would be read by another human being.

Of Celeste saying Jamie was sharp with Ford.

She slowly, carefully disentangled her body from Ford's and slid out of the bed to climb up to her office and write in her journal to discover the truth of herself.

LANDIS LIGHTLY TAPPED his water bottle on the table.

"Oz, we know how you got most of your supposed scoops. But you did not hear about Jamison Chancellor being the target—still being a target as you said on your most recent podcast—through your snoop food. So—"

"I prefer the term Trojan pizza." Oz's smirk faded under Landis' stare.

Clearly the guy couldn't help it.

"I've told you everything. A guy recognized me at the Red Hill Street scene the night the body was found and asked about the podcast, a guy who said *right, right* a lot. You know, like a habit."

CHAPTER SEVENTY-SIX

HE WOKE UP reaching for her.

She wasn't there.

In the same instant he realized her robe wasn't in the room, either, he saw the light from the big office window above lighting the patio and the roof of the garage visible from this room's window.

She was upstairs. Reading her journals? Maybe writing in the new one. Either way, in private.

He stretched and put his hands under his head.

Landis' voice came into his head for no reason he could think of. Something about motive…

He sat up.

He pulled on the shorts and retrieved his phone.

Landis answered with his name.

"We've been looking at this the wrong way. We've been looking at it from my eyes—hate as a motive. We should have been looking at it from Jamie's eyes—love as a motive."

"The killer loves Jamie? Are you confessing, Belichek, because I'll want to record this."

He wasn't derailed by his partner. "For hate, I thought the two guys were Xavier—"

"Obvious."

"—and York. Despite not wanting to see it, she felt resentment from him—because she wasn't Vivian, because she headed the foundation, because she wasn't his daughter. But flip it. The guys who love her."

"Not our friend Oz, who definitely loves himself the most."

"Agreed, but what made us really dig into Zeedyk, Landis?"

"That podcast about a source telling him Jamie was going to die after all."

"Yeah. The guy you said Zeedyk calls *Mr. Right, Right.* Easy vocal tic to throw in. So obvious it can sound made up. What if the reason was to focus attention on Zeedyk?"

"You're thinking the real guy we're after is also Zeedyk's so-called source? In that case we're back to the love motive. Say, Arbendroth— though he, too, seems to love himself more."

Belichek's head came up. "Adam Delattre as the second. Though he loves the *foundation* more. Jamie said it, whether she knows it consciously or not. She said Hendrickson York and Celeste were protective of her, but Adam Delattre is protective of the foundation."

The sound of Landis slapping the desk came through. "The donations that jumped up with the news Jamie was murdered… But he's the only one who didn't have a current key. Because he stayed with Jamie before she changed the locks because of Phil Xavier."

Belichek swore with low-voiced vehemence. "Last night—I almost had it last night when Jamie let me in. The way she was back-lit so I couldn't see much detail and the way she backed up from the door when she saw it was me. Bethany Usher could have let the shooter in and then backed up. It didn't have to be the shooter getting in with a key and meeting her in the hall. I got too hung up on all those keys floating around. The killer never needed a key."

Landis took a beat. "And what are the chances Adam knew all about Usher before he supposedly checked into it because of weirdness between her and Hendrickson. Those computer searches on her, what did our guys say? They were almost miraculously on point. Because Delattre already knew what to look for? If he's stashed away even more equipment, he could have done those searches earlier, then recreated them on the foundation computer so we'd find them."

He was tapping at his department phone. "This is Landis, homicide. That search history on Bethany Usher you found—? Yeah, the Sunshine Foundation computer. You said the guy never took a step wrong. How common is that? ... Uh-huh. ... Uh-huh. ... Okay. Thanks."

He clicked off and came back to Belichek. "Not common. In fact, it pretty much doesn't happen that somebody doesn't hit a single dead end and have to back up. I'm pulling Adam Delattre in for questioning right away."

"I'll talk to Jamie. There might be more she can fill in."

"She's going to love that. Tightening the noose on one of her people."

"Yeah."

BELICHEK HAD HIS foot on the bottom stair to the third floor when he heard a tread above him that made him stop.

Then Jamie's voice.

"*Adam?* What are you—? How did you get in here?"

"I got your key. Your new key. Just the way you told Celeste that Bethany got your old key. Took it out of your purse, got it copied. But you must have heard me come back in and try to return it..."

Belichek eased back to the bedroom for his weapon and to call Landis in a whisper.

"He's in the house. Third floor office with Jamie."

"Armed?"

"Have to assume he is. I am. No lights, no sirens. With her up there, nobody spooks him. Understand? Sniper shot from Enderbe's best bet. I'll leave my line open but mute you. I'm going up."

"Bel—"

He muted his partner's warnings of caution.

"...barely got away before all those emergency vehicles showed up. And then had to wait outside here for hours and hours before I could get in here without you hearing me."

Adam's tone held reproach. That fell away with his next words.

"I had to do it, Jamie, I had to. For the Sunshine Foundation. To make it greater. You understand, Jamie. I know you do. You're the one who taught me how important the foundation is. More important than any of us, more important than anyone. Sacrifices have to be made. You said that. I heard you telling Hendrickson. Sacrifices had to be made for the foundation to reach the next level, to do all the good it can do. That's the most important thing."

"That was about a job title, not about killing someone."

Belichek heard such horror in her voice. Would she crack under the weight of it?

"It's about the foundation." That was rougher than he'd heard Adam before. He was on the edge. Jamie needed to bring him back, to keep him from unraveling completely.

Hold on, Jamie.

Belichek crept up, pressed against the side of the stairwell.

He saw a shadow of Adam, standing in the bathroom, mostly obscured from this angle by the half-open door. Adam pointed a shotgun toward the easy chair.

That must be where Jamie was, though Belichek couldn't see her.

"I don't want you to get hurt, Adam. Please—"

"I won't get hurt. I have the gun," he said simply. "Anyway, I don't matter. If I die, that's okay. Someone else can do what I do at the foundation. But nobody else can make everyone in the world aware of the Sunshine Foundation the way your tragic death will."

"I want to live, Adam."

Good. Remind him of the person you are, not an abstraction.

Belichek came up another stair.

"But you will live, don't you see? You'll live forever. It's the perfect story. The beautiful young woman who'd wanted to help other people. Then tragically dies. Twice, I guess." He gave a little giggle. "That's what I was trying for the first time. No one would ever forget you. No one would ever forget the Sunshine Foundation. It could do more and more and more good. Like you wanted.

"I'm sorry that didn't work. But now it will. Everybody will remember you, the good you did in your life and your tragic death. Before, I *thought* that's what would happen, but I didn't know for sure. But now I do. More donations to the foundation than ever. All the stories about you.

"Only when you came back, there weren't as many donations. We need them so we can do more good."

"Adam, what…? Open your eyes."

"No. No. I can't open my eyes. I couldn't before and I can't now."

"What are you talking about?"

Belichek came up two steps, still below the level of the floor, keeping his weapon out of sight, but with no protection from someone aiming down.

"He's talking about—"

Adam gasped and swung the gun toward him.

Still calm, but with greater urgency, Jamie said, "Ford, go downstairs. Adam—"

"—shooting Bethany in the face. But—"

"—and I are talking foundation business."

"Don't move," Adam shouted. "Don't move or I'll shoot."

Belichek kept talking. "—you didn't have your eyes closed, did you, Adam? You knew where to shoot. You knew where the face was. You thought you were looking at Jamie's face when you shot. The woman who helped your family, who gave you a job, who helped you so much."

The shotgun's barrel waggled with the shaking of the hands holding it.

Belichek took some of the pressure off by not addressing Adam directly.

"That's why he didn't know he'd shot Bethany Usher instead of you. She answered the door—the light backlights anyone standing there—and she probably stepped back, either to let him in or in surprise—"

"Surprise. *Oh. Oh. How did you know?*" Adams falsetto jarred every taut nerve. "She said that when she answered the door. I didn't remember until later. I remembered the words, but I couldn't remember the voice. It *could* have been Jamie's. I thought it was Jamie's. Asking how I knew she was home. That's what I thought for those weeks. But I wasn't sure. Not totally sure. And then when Jamie came back… I knew it was Bethany. Then I could remember it was her voice, not Jamie's. I don't know what she meant. But that's what she said before…"

"Before you stepped in after her, raised the gun and shot her. Thinking she was Jamie."

He had to make her see. To tear away all her optimism, all her seeing the good in people, and see the harsh truth that the young man she cared about had meant to kill her.

Would kill her now.

And he couldn't take his eyes off the guy to check if she understood.

"How did you know she was dead, Adam?" he asked.

"She had to be. I was sure she was. She made—There was a … sound… when I went past her to turn off the air conditioning. But I didn't look at her. Not directly at her. So I couldn't be entirely sure. I should have checked. I really, really should have. I realized that when I got home. Because then I couldn't be absolutely sure and I had to wait. You know, for the official confirmation… Waiting. That was hard.

"The only time I could stop thinking about that was at the foundation, working. And then it was all okay. They found her. You found her. Everything was clear again. And it was all worthwhile, because the donations were amazing. Truly amazing, Jamie." His face changed. The confusion gone, the zealotry vivid. "Then you came back. And that ruined everything. Have you seen the numbers? They're down. *Down*. How many people will that hurt? All so you can keep living?

"Maybe some of them believe Oz. Believe what he said about maybe it was all a publicity stunt by you, when it wasn't. But it's okay now, because they've arrested him. And donations rise again when the story goes back the way it was."

Belichek came up another stair. From his peripheral vision, he could see Jamie in the chair. Between the window and the door to the bathroom.

"Or they'll dry up completely," he said, "because people will know it's a publicity stunt. You doing this to try to get publicity for more donations."

"No. No. It's not like that." Adam stepped forward. Better, but not clear of the door. "You shut up or I'll shoot you first."

SWAT hadn't had near enough time to get here and set up a shot. And even when they did, Jamie would be between them and their target.

He needed to get Jamie out of here or Adam out of that bathroom.

"How would you explain that, Adam? Two dead bodies."

"I'd... I'd think of something."

"Better to let Jamie go and keep me. Detective as a hostage—you can't beat that."

He shifted the gun toward Belichek, but said, "You wouldn't help the foundation any. Jamie needs to be shot. But you shut up or I'm going to—"

"No. Please. Adam, talk to me." Jamie twisted more in the chair. The barrel swung back toward her.

"I have to do this, Jamie. I have to."

Tears tracked down his cheeks. Sorrow, loss, even a kind of remorse before committing the act—none of that changed that he would pull the trigger.

"I don't want to die, Adam. Not even for the foundation. I would never sacrifice you for the foundation."

"But you said—"

"I was telling Hendrickson he would not be running the foundation. Even though I was taking a step back, he wasn't going to step up, the way he thought he would—assumed he would. I was telling him there would be a new structure when the management company came in. That was the sacrifice—his ego and my ego, sacrificed to make room to help us grow. But never, never to sacrifice people, Adam. You know we want to help people. We don't sacrifice the families we help, even to help other people."

"You should," he said earnestly. "If it can make the foundation stronger, you should. You see that, don't you, Jamie? I have to. I have to."

He tightened his hold on the gun, his finger on the trigger.

Different light filled his eyes.

Belichek had seen that light before. But Jamie kept trying.

"If you thought I wanted this, you wouldn't have stolen my key and sneaked in. You know you shouldn't do this. You know it's wrong." Her eyes flicked to him, then back to Adam. "Just like reading someone else's journals is wrong."

Her journals...

"No, no, you're trying to confuse me. Stop that. Stop."

Belichek surged up the stairs as Jamie threw the journal at Adam. He flinched as the hard spine connected with his cheek, fired off one deafening barrel into the ceiling. Before he could do more, she threw another journal, then another.

But he was lowering the barrel to aim at her again when Belichek cleared the stairwell and shot him.

CHAPTER SEVENTY-SEVEN

ADAM DELATTRE WAS expected to survive his injuries, but he'd have no escape from a list of charges topped by murder and attempted murder.

The people around Maggie saw her brain spinning a narrative for the trial … along with a strategy to try to sell her boss, the Fairlington County Commonwealth's Attorney, that she should prosecute the case. Wasn't going to happen with her connection to Jamie, but she'd try her damnedest.

Oz Zeedyk admitted to setting up the bugs for his "leaks," paying delivery guys extra for including certain items, though they hadn't known about the bugs. In addition to the napkins, they found a bug in each of three new sets of salt shakers.

He was on the hook for charges. If Belichek and Maggie had any say there'd be major charges for exposing Jamie to danger. But at least he didn't face a murder charge.

The Sunshine Foundation faced major changes. But Jamie had already talked to the management company about proceeding. Celeste remained. Jamie asked Denise to transition from volunteer to paid staffer, especially focusing on donors. Hendrickson tried pretending nothing had changed, Jamie didn't. They had only gotten as far as agreeing to talk.

But today, they were all at the Fairlington County Police Department, having been individually debriefed in preparation for a wrap-up news conference tomorrow.

Nancy Quinn was also here, using spare moments with Maggie to catch up on work, or so she said. Some observers suspect it was more of a mother hen checking in on her chick and her chick's cousin.

Landis had arranged coffee and refreshments—provided in an empty glass office, since everyone was still shying away from the break room—while they waited for questioning of the foundation staff to end in case there were follow-up questions for them.

As they headed for the office, they encountered Landis escorting Oliver "Oz" Zeedyk out of an interview room. Hemmed in by the pods, there was no way to avoid each other.

Belichek angled to be between the guy and Jamie, but she put a hand on his arm and stepped forward to the podcaster.

In someone else, Belichek would say the guy was thrown by coming face to face with the woman whose danger he'd traded on for podcast ratings, and trying hard to hide it with defensive bravado.

"I'm so sorry about your sister, Mr. Zeedyk. Your sister and your family." Without diverting any focus from what his family had suffered, she'd connected into his experience because of her own.

No one could doubt Jamison Chancellor's sincerity. Not even Oliver Zeedyk.

The clenched muscles that had twisted his face relaxed a half turn. Not completely. But they eased. Some.

Before he said anything, another joined the clot. Detective Danolin said, "Would you come with me, Mr. Zeedyk, please?"

His facial muscles reclenched. Not quite as tightly, though. "What? More? I thought—"

"This is a separate matter. About your sister, sir. I wasn't on her case, but I remember it and something of interest's come up."

"My … sister?"

"Yes, sir. If you'd come this way."

The rest of them stayed where they were, watching Danolin guide Oz around the bullpen pods to the Chief of Detectives' office.

Belichek asked, "Did you find something, Landis?"

"Wasn't me. All Danolin." Landis gestured them toward the office as he explained. "When Sandy Zeedyk's case came up in connection with this, Danolin remembered a similar case over in D.C., a couple years after he made detective, about seven years after Sandy Zeedyk's murder. They got the guy on the more recent murder. Danolin dug through case files and contacted the retired lead from D.C., who said he'd always believed his guy wasn't a first-timer, that he'd killed before, but the communication wasn't like it is now. They went through the cases and several points matched. Danolin checked the evidence on Sandy Zeedyk's case and there was enough to run DNA with methods available now, but not back then. He got Palery to put in a request. It'll be a while, but we're working the case again—Danolin is working it."

"What I want to know," Maggie said, when they were all in the office, "is about *this* case. Did you two have any idea it was Adam Delattre before he showed up in Jamie's house? And how the hell did he get in? When did he get in?"

"Working backward on those question," Landis said, handing Nancy a coffee cup. "He got in while Belichek was running, using a key he'd copied when he swiped the new set from Jamie's purse in the foundation office."

"I shouldn't have left—"

Jamie talked over him. "I should have heard him *and* I shouldn't have left my keys out. I never thought…"

"Enough with the self-blame," Nancy ordered. "Did you two *suspect* him?"

Landis nodded to Belichek to answer. "Not soon enough. I should have picked it up early. Adam said he'd planned to drop Bethany Usher's background into the management company's lap and Jamie would never have to know. But if she'd come back like she was supposed to, she *would* have had to know, even with the management company running the office. Only if Jamie was dead would she not have ever needed to know Bethany Usher's background—because she'd be past caring."

"He was going to murder her, but spare her feelings over a con— in both senses of the word—in their midst," Landis added. "Mixed-up little shit. Just before the shit hit the fan, Bel called me, saying Adam Delattre was the guy."

"How did you arrive at that conclusion, Bel? That's what I want to know," Maggie said.

"Was thinking about … things, and I remembered Landis saying he was having a hard time getting a grasp on a motive because he kept coming up against the foundation employees being do-gooders."

Jamie's gaze slid to Landis. He shrugged unapologetically.

"And he said the foundation folks weren't trying to cash in. I agreed when he said it. But then I got thinking maybe they were trying to cash in, just not in the way we're used to seeing. Hendrickson York was. Only his currency was ego. Celeste's was unrequited love. Even Jamie's in a way was—"

"That's—"

Belichek cut across Maggie's protest. "Protection. Security. Hiding out."

Jamie's cheeks pinkened but she never looked away from him.

"And then I started thinking about Adam Delattre. What was his currency? What transaction was he after? Making the Sunshine Foundation a major player. A force to be reckoned with—how much from self-interest, how much from a twisted version of altruism—?" He lifted one shoulder. "But then it started to make sense. Without professional management coming in, the foundation couldn't keep running without Jamie. So it was never even a possibility, a consideration. But bringing them in changed Jamie's role. She didn't have to handle the day-to-day running—you said it and Celeste repeated it. You wanted the foundation to be able to survive without you. And it could. But that made Adam look at how you could become even more valuable to the foundation. The financial fuel that could keep the engine going for a long, long time.

"As long as you became a story that was big enough, tragic enough to supply that fuel, he considered you worth more to the foundation dead than alive."

"For God's sake, Belichek—"

"He's right, Maggie," Jamie interrupted.

"Not me. Adam."

"As much as you hope the mission's enough, a good story trumps all," Jamie said. "And what's a better story than the founder being murdered?"

"The young, attractive founder being tragically murdered leaving an unsolved mystery behind," Landis said. "Hell of a story."

Jamie nodded. "The donations after the discovery of my supposed corpse prove that." Her mouth twisted. "They'll drop hard after this. Not only a staff member arrested, but the end of the story."

"Not necessarily," Maggie said. "Feed the media monster right and you could draw this out. Lots of interest now, then resurgence for the trial. Of course, you'll need to be the one out there flogging the stories. Then the public will eat it up."

"Oh, Maggie. I don't know…"

"It'll help the foundation. You'll do it," her cousin said with certainty. "Now, get back to Adam, Bel."

"Not much to get back to. After that motive turned on the light to view his words and deeds from a different angle, it was obvious. He practically told us the first day. He said, *Since her death—since the news of it—donations are through the roof.* He was the only one to separate out those times. For the rest, it was like the news of Jamie's death was also the day she died. Not for Adam. Because he knew when the death happened. He'd been waiting and waiting for the body to be discovered."

"Poor Adam."

The rest of them groaned at Jamie's words.

"No, really. I know he's done horrible things, but also think what strain he was under from the time he shot Bethany until the body was found. That must have been so difficult."

"A difficulty he could have avoided by not shooting someone in the face, thinking it was you," Maggie reminded her.

"So, what about you two now?" Nancy waggled two fingers between Belichek and Jamie.

They didn't look at each other or speak.

"I wondered. J.D. said, but I thought he was crazy, but then…"

"Pretty obvious," Nancy said. "He read her deepest and darkest in her journals—"

"*Maggie,*" Jamie protested.

"I didn't tell her. Didn't tell anybody. J.D. already knew."

"—and accepts her clouds along with the rest. Woman would be a fool to pass that up. At some level Jamie knows it, too. Because she's been able to be cranky and irritated at him when she didn't trust anybody else with that part of herself except her cousins. And—"

"Okay, I did tell her that," Maggie confessed.

"—if Belichek doesn't grab Jamie, he's stupider than I ever thought."

"On that cheery note," Landis announced, "the rest of us are all wanted—somewhere. Including you, Nancy. Only Bel and Jamie get off from this round. Everybody out."

Maggie, J.D., and Nancy cooperated fully.

Just before Landis closed the door, he hung on the frame on one side and the edge of the door on the other and said to his partner, "Jesus, Belichek, I said you were like the detective in that *Carol Burnett* skit, preferring the portrait—or journals—to the real-life woman because it's simpler, but don't be an idiot."

Then he closed the door.

"Carol Burnett? A portrait? What's that about?" Jamie's voice didn't sound quite right.

"Ravings of Tanner Landis."

Belichek caught a faint reflection of himself and Jamie in the window of the office, now empty of everyone except them.

They stood with the corner of the desk between them. Her looking up. Him looking down.

"You don't have to say anything, Jamie. Now or—"

"Now," she said.

But he could hear her breathing. Fast, uncomfortable.

"Thank you, Ford." She rushed out the words.

"Doing my job."

"You were right about me. I needed to stop closing my eyes to what I didn't want to see because I was trying so hard for all sunshine."

"Like I said, doing my job."

In the reflection, her chin came down, so she was looking toward him. He didn't meet her gaze. "Was that all? I was a job to you?"

Say *yes,* and he'd know right where he was. Where he'd been for a long time.

"No."

Breath streamed from her. Still, he didn't look toward her.

"I needed your strength, your knowledge of the dark side, Ford. You made me face it, accept it. Those minutes with Adam, I don't think I could have accepted what could really happen. I wouldn't have acted. And now. I won't ever be without a piece of that, no matter how much I look on the bright side. But you need my strength, my vision of the bright side, too."

He breathed, feeling pain in his chest.

"Look at me Rutherford Belichek." He did. "You can't afford to be a pessimist all the time. You can't survive without ever looking on the bright side. I won't let you. Because you've been hiding out, too. Hiding out where it's dark and familiar."

As if she'd seen inside his thoughts.

"Jamie."

"We're going to do that for each other—so we see both sides. Together."

"You have no idea what being with a cop's like. Especially me."

"You have no idea what being with Little Mary Sunshine's like. Especially when I'm not."

"I wanted to watch out over you—all three of you. It was a boy's dream to help his grandfather. To carry on for him. I owed it to him. That's not a basis—"

She stepped up close to him, tipping her head back. "Quit hiding behind that. Because then you fell in love. With me. Not with Maggie. Not with Ally. *Me.* What was it Tanner said? It was safe for you to fall for me because I was dead?"

She leaned in, her body close enough to his that breathing made them brush.

"But I'm not dead, Ford."

"Jamie." Two syllables. Warning. Stern. In control. Then none of that, as he said the same two syllables again. *"Jamie."*

When they came up for air, she looked up at him. "We're very different. I do see we could have problems."

"That bothers you?"

"No."

"I would've said before that problems didn't bother you because you don't see them, but you brought them up, so you must see them."

She tipped her head, one eyebrow up. "Hazily. But I'm an optimist, you know."

He quirked a smile. "I do know that."

"And you're not."

"And I'm not," he confirmed. "On the other hand, problems aren't terminal. And I'm pretty good at solving them."

She smiled broadly. "You are, aren't you?"

"I am."

"Detective Ford Belichek, I finally get to see those dimples Landis' mother describes to her friends."

EPILOGUE

Weeks later

FORD AND JAMIE walked into Imogen Wooton's patio gate as she was escorting a young woman dressed in a wool jacket over jeans and conservatively casual boots out of her back door. The three dogs trickled out after them, greeting the newcomers with wagging tails and snuffling.

"Sorry, we didn't know you had a guest," Jamie said. "We wanted to drop off these cookies for you."

They'd come to the Red Hill Street house to check on the reconstruction of the third floor. Jamie wanted an overhaul up there to banish bad memories from the space. In the meantime they were living at Belichek's. After the reconstruction? They'd decide then.

"Come in, come in," Imogen ordered. "She was just leaving."

"Hello," the young woman said to each of them with a shy smile.

Belichek held the gate open for her with a sense of familiarity.

Imogen Wooton cackled as she drew them inside. "Didn't recognize her, huh. Not even the great detective."

That nudge clicked the familiarity for Belichek. "Victorina."

"*Victorina?*" Jamie's voice skidded up. "No way."

"Uh-huh. Phil's moved out, moved on. Rumor is, he's found someone new."

"She doesn't look very broken up about it."

"She gets the house. It's what she's always wanted."

"Decorated to her taste, huh?"

"Not at all. But she was quite adroit in having the workmen erect all that folderol of Phil's as free-standing walls. Cost the idiot a fortune and he didn't even know why." She cackled again. "Like a spite house inside of another house. It'll come out slick as a whistle. Then she can start restoring. She's been consulting me and Garrison next door. Turns out there might be a connection between those two houses after all."

She emitted a final cackle.

❖ ❖ ❖ ❖

Months later

OVER. IT WAS over.

The case finished. The news conference finished, the questions asked and answered.

Yes, a half dozen people with cameras—still and video—walked backward in front of them, snapping and videoing, as her family crossed the plaza, leaving the Fairlington County Courthouse. But this counted as barely a trickle compared to the height of the attention.

In a while even this interest would wane. It always did. No matter how notorious. No matter how intriguing. No matter how dramatic. Wasn't she the proof of that?

Ally Lindell Northcutt allowed herself a small smile. Something she never did in public.

It was all over.

She tightened her hold where she had her left arm hooked through Jamie's right, as Maggie did on the other side with J.D. Carson. Jamie's parents and their family lawyer were behind them.

By rights Ford Belichek should have been with Jamie.

But *by rights* wouldn't preserve his career. Jamie had been adamant about that.

Ally had watched her sweet cousin overrule the detective and make it stick. Though she suspected the dozen officers split to either side of them well out of camera range had been Bel's doing.

She and her two cousins paused, just an instant, getting their rhythm for the three steps down to sidewalk level so they wouldn't jostle each other in their locked-arm hold. Before that next step forward—

Sound.

A single sharp burst.

It swallowed the hearing in her right ear. Reverberated distantly in her left.

Before she could absorb that, she felt her hold on Jamie being torn away. She turned that way. Saw J.D. encompassing Maggie and Jamie in a flying tackle, his body between them and the street. From the corner of her eye, she saw Jamie's parents huddle together, dropping low, even as they reached toward the three cousins.

They'd be okay.

With that thought, she released her hold on Jamie.

On the same instant, felt herself being brought down. Half turned toward her cousins, she couldn't see by what.

"East. Shot came from the east."

Somehow, she knew that was roared near her right ear by whoever had taken her to the ground, yet it came muffled to her.

"Are you hit? Ally. Are you hit?"

"No. I'm fine. Everyone else—?"

"She's not hit. Anybody hit?" the same voice demanded.

From a great distance, she heard what sounded like Maggie, then Jamie's father.

"Everyone's okay. Stay down." She'd started to try to rise, but felt herself firmly shoved down.

Then the covering body lifted before a new one draped over her.

How did she know it was a different body? She hadn't seen—

"Stay there. All of you. Don't move. Got them, Bel?"

"Got them."

Jamie's Detective Belichek was here. He gave orders sounding from that same muffled distance.

The officers who'd been along the sides, now stood between them and the street. They hustled the family backward to the courthouse doors, and inside.

They hugged each other and surreptitiously—or not so surreptitiously—checked for injuries.

Jamie's dad said to the lawyer, "Thank you for protecting Ally. We couldn't reach her."

"It wasn't—." Ally bit off her correction.

Smell.

She *knew* that first protector.

But—

"That wasn't me." Behind her, the lawyer spoke at a speed powered by fear and adrenaline. "The guy came from the police line. Wasn't in uniform. He—There he is. That guy."

Ally turned, first glimpsing a pair of trousers marred by ground-in grit at the knee, a streak of something on the thigh. The streak continued up the front of a suit jacket to…

"Tanner."

That first protector's smell. She *did* know it.

Had known it.

But her brain rebelled at her senses. It wasn't possible…

"*Tanner Landis?*"

The End

To get briefed on upcoming books, as well as other titles and developments, join Patricia McLinn's Readers List and receive her twice-monthly free newsletter.

patriciamclinn.com/readers-list

You can buy this book and all my others, including print editions and audiobooks, from my online store. I've added direct-to-you buying options to better control how my books reach you, while giving you special bundles, early offers, and exclusive bonuses.

Patricia's Bookstore

shop.patriciamclinn.com

The last woman Detective Tanner Landis is prepared to face is the one he must save. Ally Northcutt, the third cousin of The Innocence Trilogy.

Jamie, Maggie, Bel and J.D. ask if you'll help spread the word about them and The Innocence Trilogy. You have the power to do that in two quick ways:

Recommend the book and the series to your friends and/or the whole wide world on social media. Shouting from rooftops is particularly appreciated.

Review the book. Take a few minutes to write an honest review and it can make a huge difference. As you likely know, it's the single best way for your fellow readers to find books they'll enjoy, too.

To me—as an author and a reader—the goal is always to find a good author-reader match. By sharing your reading experience through recommendations and reviews, you become a vital matchmaker. ☺

If you'd like to investigate Patricia McLinn's mysteries with humor and a hint of romance, try her **Caught Dead in Wyoming** series:

SIGN OFF

Divorce a husband, lose a career … grapple with a murder.

LEFT HANGING

Trampled by bulls—an accident? Elizabeth, Mike and friends must dig into the world of rodeo.

SHOOT FIRST

For Elizabeth, death hits close to home. She and friends must delve into old Wyoming treasures and secrets to save lives.

LAST DITCH

Elizabeth and Mike search after a man in a wheelchair goes missing.

LOOK LIVE

Elizabeth and friends take on misleading murder with help—and hindrance—from intriguing out-of-towners.

BACK STORY

Murder never dies, but comes back to threaten Elizabeth, her friends and KWMT team.

COLD OPEN

Elizabeth's looking for a place of her own becomes an open house for murder.

HOT ROLL

One of Elizabeth's team of investigators becomes a target.

REACTION SHOT

Homicide on the range, where clouds darken over Elizabeth.

BODY BRACE

Everything can change … except murder.

CROSS TALK

Prime suspect: The most annoying man in Sherman.

AIR READY

Love and death decisions.

HOLIDAY BULLETS

A Christmas wish with Elizabeth's name on it.

CUE UP

On the trail of murder.

"Colorful characters, intriguing, intelligent mystery, plus the state of Wyoming leaping off every page."

—*Emilie Richards, USA Today bestselling author*

And the **Secret Sleuth** series:

DEATH ON THE DIVERSION
Final resting place? Deck chair.

DEATH ON TORRID AVENUE
A new love (canine), an ex-cop and a dog park discovery.

DEATH ON BEGUILING WAY
No zen in sight as Sheila untangles a yoga instructor's murder.

DEATH ON COVERT CIRCLE
A supermarket CEO meets his expiration date.

DEATH ON SHADY BRIDGE
A cold case heats up.

DEATH ON CARRION LANE
A reunion for murder.

DEATH ON ZIGZAG TRAIL
A spooky legend twists grave matters.

DEATH ON PUZZLE PLACE
Season's greetings: Whodunit?

If you like Patricia's romantic suspense, you might also try:

Ride the River: Rodeo Knights

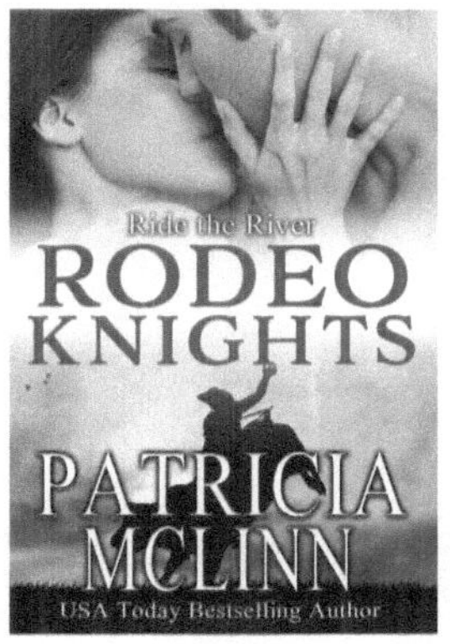

Her rodeo cowboy ex is back … as her prime suspect.

Explore a complete list of all Patricia's books
patriciamclinn.com/patricias-books

Or get a printable booklist
patriciamclinn.com/patricias-books/printable-booklist

Patricia's Bookstore (buy online directly from Patricia)
shop.patriciamclinn.compatricias-books/ebookstore

About the author

Patricia McLinn is the USA Today bestselling author of more than 60 published novels cited by readers and reviewers for their wit and vivid characterization. Her books include mysteries, romantic suspense, contemporary romance, historical romance and women's fiction. They have topped bestseller lists and won numerous awards.

She has spoken about writing from London to Melbourne, Australia, to Washington, D.C., including being a guest speaker at the Smithsonian Institution.

McLinn spent more than 20 years as an editor at The Washington Post after stints as a sports writer (Rockford, Ill.) and assistant sports editor (Charlotte, N.C.). She received BA and MSJ degrees from Northwestern University.

Now living in northern Kentucky, McLinn loves to hear from readers through her website and social media.

Visit with Patricia:

Website: patriciamclinn.com

Facebook: facebook.com/PatriciaMcLinn

Pinterest: pinterest.com/patriciamclinn

Instagram: instagram.com/patriciamclinnauthor